Joyce Carol Thomas

COLLECTED NOVELS FOR TEENS

BRIGHT SHADOW • WATER GIRL
THE GOLDEN PASTURE • JOURNEY

JUMP AT THE SUN
HYPERION PAPERBACKS FOR CHILDREN
NEW YORK
AN IMPRINT OF DISNEY BOOK GROUP

1 3 5 7 9 10 8 6 4 2
Printed in the United States of America
Library of Congress Cataloging-in-Publication Data on file
ISBN 978-1-4231-0154-3
Visit www.jumpatthesun.com

DEDICATION

I dedicate this collection to all my children and grandchildren, and to the memory of the women who provided early inspiration and support, mother Leona Haynes and Aunt Corine Coffey, now resting in their heavenly home.

ACKNOWLEDGMENTS

I am indebted to my ace editors, whose splendid comments always shimmer with light. I thank the Jump at the Sun/Hyperion Books for Children creative team for their affirmation and faith in publishing this collection.

My appreciation also to my ICM Talent literary agent, Christine Earle, for her brilliance. Her illuminating comments echoed and echo still in my dreams day and night.

I am indebted to you, my devoted audience. Many times I felt chilled as I sat in my pajamas at the computer before dawn, intent on getting the words to dance or cry across the pages. Soon enough I felt the warming glance of daylight on my shoulders as the sun's rays made their way across the sky.

As always, I am uplifted by the cheerful encouragement from family, friends, librarians, teachers, literary critics, bookstore owners, and you, my faithful readers. Your Jump at the Sun/Hyperion Books special parcel includes the entire series of Abyssinia books: *Bright Shadow*; *Water Girl*; *The Golden Pasture*; and *Journey*. What a joy it is to have these four novels embraced in one package!

Thank you all for reminding me of my devotion to waking up every morning to write yet another page.

DEDICATION

ACKNOWLEDGMENTS

CONTENTS

Bright Shadow 1

Water Girl 117

The Golden Pasture 237

Journey 375

Teacher and Teen Discussion Guide 518

Bright Shadow

1983

ONE

"Waiting for somebody?" The words boiled thick, like gravy just before burning. The scorched voice of Abyssinia's father leaped at her from the hot shadows of the porch.

"Who would I be waiting for?" asked Abby in a whisper faint as water. She knew perfectly well her father was speaking about Him. At the thought of Him a hot flare burst her heart orange. In the summer sunshine her long brown legs stretched down, but her feet still barely touched the planked wood beneath the porch swing as she stopped swaying.

"That young whippersnapper walking past here every day, that's who!" bellowed Strong.

Abby hunched her shoulders in a show of ignorance and innocence, and ducked her head down into her book. She didn't know that much about Him. She had never said much more than hello to Him. But she glowed with the sweet guilt of her waiting.

Her father studied this transformation of a brown daughter blushing so deeply. A frown wrinkled his forehead for a moment as he bit his bottom lip. Then he whammed a heavy fist into the broad palm of his hand.

Abby was looking at her opened book, but she stared blindly. She was thinking about how this mirage of a young man was the flesh and bone reality of her dream. Her cocoa eyes sparkled wet under the scrutiny of her father's stern gaze.

He turned abruptly away from her just as her mother called him. "Strong?"

Strong slammed the screen door behind him as he went into the house to talk to Patience, muttering under his breath about "wolves sneaking up on lambs."

Feeling marinated from the heat of the sun and the heat of her own blood rushing to her face, Abby began fanning herself with the paperback book.

Oh, how she wanted to know this young man. To know his voice. To taste it like night on her tongue. To know the current of his heart when his hands touched hers. To know the height, the dimensions of his mind, the smolder of his eyes just before he leaned over to give her a tall kiss.

A sensation like liquid lightning coursed through her when she had first spotted him months ago. She had fumbled with the book and pushed it aside. Her dusky-lashed eyes sparkled. The deep dimples in her pecan-colored face flashed with barely restrained excitement.

The focus of her attention had ambled down the road toward the Jackson house at an easy pace, a thin, tall rope of a young man she remembered seeing at Attucks High.

As he had come nearer, she sighed deeply, her face glowing with heat as if he had touched it with warm hands, her heart tripping lightly against her breast while trickles of delightful unease shivered down her spine.

She whispered, "Here he comes with his fine self," her full lips curving into an infectious grin.

"Good afternoon, boy," she had managed to stammer.

"I'm not a boy. The name is Carl Lee," he had answered, ending this with a deep laugh that spilled from the top of his six-foot-six frame down to his sneakers. But she had continued to call him boy, mischief in her voice.

"Boy, where're you going?"

"Just taking a walk."

"Yeah, boy?"

"Yeah."

His eyes reminded her of still water. They were black, shiny, liquid. Hair of blackberries. Skin of ripe plum. Laugh upsetting the air. She had thought she would surely drown if she looked into his eyes too long. After gazing at him from her station on the front porch, she had tucked her head down as he nodded his good-bye.

Every day, in the late afternoon, it was the same ritual.

Abby would stop sewing or cleaning house or preparing supper for the family. She would go to the mirror and rebrush her hair, anoint her arms with water pressed from roses, and smooth down the front of her dress. Then, taking whichever novel she was engrossed in, she would sit on the porch, reading as she waited.

Today it was by the plum tree just in front of her yard that he paused.

She took a deep breath. Feeling extra bold, she propped her book on the chair and walked to the gate. The fruit tree shaded his rich honey skin a blue-black like the color of ripened plums.

"How're you doing?" she asked, throwing modesty to the wind.

"Okay. Yourself?" he answered, laughing, his face glowing with animation.

"Fine."

"You sure are."

She smiled in spite of herself.

"How come you walk by here every day?" she ventured.

"For my evening exercise. It's healthy, you know."

Looking him up and down she quipped, "You look in good physical shape to me."

"Oh, it's not my legs or muscles or anything like that. For that I work out at the track. No, this is for my eyes," he drawled, a tomcat purr in his throat.

"Your eyes?"

"Yeah. My eyes need to gaze on a little beauty every day." When he made this response, she was sure that the light in his glance defied the glint of the sun.

On Sundays she had noticed him, all dressed up, walking to church in the opposite direction from Solid Rock Church of God in Christ. Though he was not a member of her church, he clearly attended service somewhere.

Now Abby asked, "Are you saved, boy?"

His eyes seemed to float into hers. "I'm Methodist, girl. And you?"

She caught her breath for a moment. Methodists were bound for hell, some of the old line ministers said so. But she had never quite agreed with that. There couldn't be any religious prejudice in paradise, she thought. No separation of beliefs. No fences in heaven.

"Pentecostal," she said finally. "Do you ever visit other churches?"

"Now and then. But I'm Methodist to the bone. I'm Methodist born, Methodist bred, and when I die I'll be Methodist dead," he bragged.

She recalled him from her childhood days. The memory was vague. Children's games. Passing from class to class in school. She wanted to know more about him.

"What's your favorite color?" she asked.

"Blue," he answered. "Yours?"

"Purple. Got a favorite flower?"

"Bluebells," he responded. "You?"

"Irises. Bet I can guess your favorite sport."

"You don't need a crystal ball for that. It's track, naturally. Do you have a hobby?"

"Singing," she said.

"I like to sing, too."

Leaning against the trunk of the plum tree, he gazed boldly at her. "And you go to Langston, don't you? I see you sometimes waiting for the bus."

"Uh-huh. Started late."

"Me, too."

"I wasn't ready right after high school," she said.

"I had to work a couple of years and save money. But I made it finally." He cocked his head at a proud angle, not quite arrogant.

"I'm glad," she told him.

"I got a scholarship."

"Me, too. A partial one."

"Hey, we have a lot in common. How about that?" He laughed and began fake-boxing at the shadow of the plum tree.

"What do you want to do after college?"

"Work in the courts. Be a lawyer."

"Me," she said, "I'd like to work in medicine."

"You mean be a doctor?"

"Uh-huh."

"Well! That's all right. Doctor Abyssinia Jackson." He gave each syllable of her name its due, enunciating perfectly, his voice ringing.

"You even speak like an attorney," she giggled. "Attorney Carl Lee Jefferson. I can see you now. Three-piece suit, attaché case, ducking down to enter the courtroom you'd be so tall."

"You know," he said, "I never thought I'd finish filling out that monster of an application."

"I know what you mean," she agreed. "Must have written my

name ten times if I wrote it once. What did you answer for the why-you-want-to-go-to-college essay?"

"Tried to write at least a page worth of reasons. That's what my counselor advised. So I described the great statesmen I admired. Mentioned my fascination with the legal process. My leadership abilities. I also added that I wanted to plead cases for the underrepresented. What did you write?"

"A page worth, too. That's about what mine came to. I talked about my work with herbal medicine. My sympathy for the sick. My interest in science and literature."

"I bet you'll be a wonderful doctor."

"Oh," she said, clapping a hand to her forehead, "pardon my manners. I didn't mean to keep you standing at the gate. Want to come in and have some lemonade?"

"Oh, no, I couldn't bother you like that."

"Oh, come on. I fix Saturday lemonade for my parents anyway. Come in and meet them. Every other Saturday they're off work."

"Are you sure it's okay?"

"Sure I'm sure."

"Okay," he said, following her and the gay rush of her laughter down the walk, up the steps past the porch swing, and into the house.

TWO

The broad shoulders of Abby's father hunched over a blueprint sheet at the dining room table. Out of the shoulders grew a head covered with a thick shock of jet black hair salted with sprigs of white. He pulled himself up to his considerable full height at the sound of the screen door slamming shut.

"Daddy, this is Carl Lee."

Her father stood up straight, stiffened in hesitation, then extended a hand to Carl Lee. "Strong Jackson," he said in an uneasy voice.

"Pleased to meet you," said Carl Lee, pumping the older man's hand.

Just then Abby's mother came into the room, set up the ironing board, and plugged in the iron.

"Hello," she said, "I'm Patience Jackson." She stuck a finger in her mouth, then quickly touch-tested the hot iron, which hissed a sizzle of steam.

Carl Lee nodded politely at the caramel-colored woman, who was a plump replica of Abby.

"I'll fix us all some ice-cold lemonade," offered Abby as she headed for the kitchen.

"Sounds good," said her mother, who shook out a balled-up

dress and began pressing one of the five pastel cotton uniforms she had starched and sprinkled.

"Have a seat," said Strong, eyeing Carl Lee skeptically but motioning to the chair next to his at the table.

"What did you say your name was again?" asked Patience.

"Carl Lee, ma'am," he answered. "Carl Lee Jefferson."

He saw Abby's mother and father exchange quick glances.

"Son of Samuel Jefferson?" asked Patience.

"That's me," said Carl Lee.

"In a town this size there could only be one, Patience," barked Strong irritably.

"Of course," she answered, surprised at the unfriendly tone in her husband's voice. She gave Carl Lee an appraisal from his head to his toes, pleased with what she saw.

"Mama," said Abby, walking in from the kitchen and balancing a tray of frosted glasses and a pitcher filled with ice-tinkling lemonade, "why don't you sit down and let me iron those for you?"

"But you have company," said Patience.

"We're all here together. I can talk to him while I iron. Think I can do two things at one time," she said.

"Are you sure you and your friend, Carl Lee, don't want to play a game of Scrabble or chess?" asked Patience.

"I'm sure," countered Abby, arching a quizzical brow at Carl Lee until he gave a swift nod of agreement. She set the glasses for lemonade on the table.

"I'd say no, but my feet are killing me," said Patience, who already had one uniform just about finished.

The skin around Strong's deep-set eyes crinkled at their corners as he gazed affectionately at his daughter, but he noticed, too, that Carl Lee was giving her a look that examined her youthful curves. Gray shadows invaded Strong's eyes, but Carl Lee missed the dangerous glance Strong threw his way. Carl Lee continued to appreciate Abby's beauty as she poured the gurgling cool drink into his glass. Sipping from the glass, he exclaimed, "Best lemonade I ever tasted."

Then he settled his attention on Strong's creation—a blueprint drawing for a chest of drawers for his sister-in-law, Serena. Strong had stroked a design of curlicues at each corner of the chest. He repeated these in the chest legs and around the arched frame of the mirror.

"I know she'll like this chest, Strong," Patience bubbled proudly as she picked up her glass and seated herself at the other end of the table.

"What a talent!" Carl Lee finally said, awed by Strong's masterpiece.

"Perhaps she'll like it," Strong boomed. "It's not every day I get to design and build a piece of furniture for a sixty-year-old bride. Got to make it extra big, you know. She married herself a Texas man."

"From Houston," said Abby, resting the iron on its end while she sipped her lemonade. "I hope he makes Aunt Serena happy."

Patience said in a worried voice, "I do, too. We really don't know him like we know everybody else in Ponca. After all, he's only been in town a year. Why would he leave a big place like Houston to come to a little town like Ponca City, Oklahoma?"

"Marriage brings all kinds of new history to a family," Strong told her. "Births, marriages, deaths. Crossroads of history and time."

"You come into this world, you stay awhile, then you leave, but time and history go on, that's a fact," said Patience reflectively.

"Aunt Serena married!" Abby shook her head in surprise. Aunt Sadonia and Aunt Serena had lived all their lives in the house next door. Sadonia had died in her sleep with a smile on her face a year ago. At the funeral they had laid her out in white. Virginal white. The lovely Sadonia—aunt and surrogate mother to Abyssinia. But Serena, the living sister, had been overwhelmed with grief. She had trembled as she sat, head bowed, between Abby and her parents. Then she had lost her last shred of dignity in the face of death. She had stumbled down the aisle, screaming, "Saadoonia!" Up to Sadonia's casket, crying, "Saadoonia! Saadoonia! My sister, wait. Oh, Sadonia, I'm coming!" And she had tried to climb into the coffin with her precious sister.

Patience had flown out of her front-row pew and rushed up to the altar to drag Serena back out of the casket.

Strong had raced to her side and lifted the bereaved Serena, as if she were a baby, out of Sadonia' s final bed, and carried her back to his seat. His sister-in-law's grown-up legs hung down pitifully, feet barely touching the floor as he held her on his lap. A full-grown infant.

"Just wait, dear woman," he said as he rocked her in his lap. "You're going to get your own casket soon enough! Just wait!"

Strong's words had resounded across the pulpit, up to the choir rafters, and into the grieving ears of the church members, who clapped their hands to their mouths, praying, "Lord, have mercy. Do!"

Later, when Patience and Strong had stopped by the house next door to ask Serena if she wanted to move in with them, the woman's response was an independent "No."

They asked her again and again, but her answer was always the same. "No!" And then she had got married.

Now, inspired by Serena's marriage, Strong talked of old times. Of the Oklahoma land rush when his grandfather, like the rest of the settlers, had run for the land that once belonged to the Cherokee, the Choctaw, the Seminole, the Chickasaw, and the Creek.

"Now, the word *Oklahoma* is Choctaw for 'red people,'" he continued.

"Oh, no," Abby said, rolling her eyes to the ceiling, "there he goes again, talking about Oklahoma. "

"Back in the old days everybody lined up their wagons and ran for their own piece of Oklahoma ground. And because we were mainly farmers then, we had to help each other clear the land, construct barns, and erect homes. Your great granddaddy was a woodcarver and a farmer, Abby. Comes from good stock," boasted Strong, eyeing Carl Lee with a warning, wary gaze.

"It was the red people, my grandfather told me, who finally made life easier," Strong concluded. "After all the killing and battles were over, they mingled, intermarried, and shared the secrets of farming red land."

Strong sketched a few more lines on his chest of drawers, then paused in his drawing to tell more about his family background, conjuring up history from the nostalgic places his memory sheltered.

He talked of the great drought that changed the fields of wheat and corn into a dust bowl, and then the money boom that World War II brought. At last he reached the time when Abby was conceived.

"This young woman you're looking at is very special," Strong continued, pointing a pencil at Abby and giving Carl Lee a threatening look. "Of course, she had an auspicious beginning. You young folks do realize that the date of conception is just as important as the date of birth. The moment of spiritual and physical union has to be right. And the day Abyssinia was conceived was steeped in strange and peculiar wonder."

Abby winked at Carl Lee, who had been listening intently. Even though Abby had been hearing the story for twenty years, and had grown tired of the Oklahoma part of the tale, it still fascinated her when Strong talked about the day she was conceived.

"It was one unusual morning in the dead of December, when

icicles rested on the boughs of trees," her father began. "Then a blooming violet peeked through the snow. The flower shivered and laid its head against the ice.

"Oh, there were signs everywhere, that day more than twenty years ago when Abyssinia was conceived. When Serena asked one of the neighborhood children to go out and select a hackberry limb to dip snuff with, everybody paid attention.

"Serena, who knows that hackberry branches can only be cut in deep spring, when their berries are ripe, and not in the below-zero weather of December, sent a child looking for a hackberry knot. And he found one for her."

"Hackberries in December!" said Carl Lee, settling his tall frame more comfortably in his chair.

Strong continued, "The gray-haired deacon of the Mason Street Methodist Church claimed a robin woke him out of a deep slumber with its bright chirps. When questioned, he said that at his age he certainly knew what a robin singing at dawn sounded like."

"Robins in December!" said Carl Lee. "Amazing!"

"But listen to this. It was Abby's mother, Patience, who smelled the pungent fragrance of honeysuckle and mulberry. Then she came to fetch me at my barbershop. I told everybody to go home. 'Dismissed. Won't be no heads cut here today,' I said. 'My woman's come to get me.' We hurried home through the drifts of snow and ice-slick paths. We decided to have us a baby." Strong took a great gulp of lemonade.

"Now, Strong," said Patience, beginning to blush.

"So you were getting ready for this special girl in December," said Carl Lee, giving Abby another one of his hungry looks.

"Nine months later, September sixth, here she came. Born in the cotton field. A natural baby, baptized by water and fire."

"I know you need water for birth, but fire?" asked Carl Lee.

"One of the embers from the flame branded me." Abby pointed to the small birthmark on her cheek.

"What a day that was," Patience said dreamily, as if she were back in the cotton patch, spread-eagled on the ground, giving birth to Abyssinia and attended by the field women.

Strong set his glass down and resumed his tale.

"After I had driven all the way from the Better Way Barbershop to see what wonder we had created, they told me 'Six pounds, twelve ounces.' Abyssinia, it was announced to me, was born with a healthy pair of lungs. She had a lusty cry all right, this we all could hear even before I went in through the cabin door.

"Abby's Aunt Sadonia was there in the bedroom, plumping up the pillows and changing the sheets. And when Abby had finished sucking at her mother's breast, they laid her in the hand-carved crib I had sculpted with these hands and placed next to my and Patience's bed.

"Then the procession began. First me, the proud father! Then came the curious field workers, entering the bedroom and peeking under the rainbow quilt into which Abby was snugly swaddled. We saw the tiny fists curled up, the small, perfect round head, the dusky-lashed eyes, the tender skin the color of pecans.

"Then Abby yawned and blinked herself awake. Her mother reached over and smoothed down the tangle of dark curls thick as night. But I thought the birthmark on her cheek was her most striking feature," said Strong.

"And still is," agreed Carl Lee.

Strong gave Carl Lee a stony stare at the intrusion. "But I digress. Her Aunt Serena, as I told you earlier, was reputed to be the wisest woman in the town, even though I always thought she was crazy as a Betsy bug. She stooped over the varnished crib and kissed Abby's cotton-blossom birthmark. She stayed there a few moments, peering at the dark-eyed Abby with that birthmark made by the stray ember. Then she straightened her back and began to hum a lilting lullaby. Then she put on her shawl and made her way to the next cabin, still making music.

"The other workers glanced at each other and moved outside to the porch. Enough to talk about for a few days, they decided, for they still had not quite recovered from another extraordinary birth the winter before."

"What birth?" began Carl Lee.

Abyssinia thought she saw Patience grip her chair and flash widened, warning eyes at Strong.

But the storyteller rushed on to end his story. "So they pulled their shawls tighter around them and trudged home to their field cabins. They added more logs to their crackling fires, then sat in their rocking chairs watching the fire rage inside its brick fireplace, safe from the slack jaws of night.

"There they warmed their food, their hands, and their bodies. But they warmed their hearts humming snatches of the lullaby they had heard fall from Serena's lips. They stared long into the blue fire, remembering the baby with a strange birthmark who was conceived when sweet violets intruded upon the snow."

"Oh, Daddy," laughed Abby, surveying the crisp dresses hanging in their pressed pastel cotton colors on clothes hangers. "You do know how to tell a story."

"Well, every word is true," chuckled Strong, now peering closely at his sketch. He jerked his head up suddenly and with a twinkle in his eye said to Patience, "Isn't that right, Mama?"

"How about a game of some serious Scrabble?" said Abby, taking down the ironing board.

"All right," said Carl Lee, rubbing his hands together.

"Why not," said Patience. "I don't have to stand on my feet; I can just sit here and beat everybody."

"That's my department," said Strong, rolling up his blueprint.

While Abyssinia got out the word game, Patience went to the kitchen and brought a bag of red apples, which she poured into the silver bowl in the middle of the dining room table.

The game began. Abby sat next to Carl Lee. Too close, as far as Strong was concerned. They all munched on apples and played their best game. Carl Lee won.

"Let's try one more," said Strong. Carl Lee now sat even closer to Abby. His right arm was hidden. Strong was not sure on which part of Abby's anatomy Carl Lee's hand was resting. At the end of the second game, which Carl Lee also won, Strong said, "Well, guess it's time for company to leave."

Abby and Patience exchanged bewildered looks; the game was just getting good.

Carl Lee stood up, towering above them all, and expressed thanks for a delightful evening. Abby walked him to the door. She noticed the hurt look in his eyes, his puzzlement at her father's stern attitude. She gave him a generous farewell smile.

Once the door closed, her father spoke sharply. "Abyssinia Jackson, keep that tomcat of a boy away from here. Don't want him pissing around here with his arrogant ass!"

"Strong!" said Patience, shocked. "What do you mean using those nasty words?"

"She's grown. She might as well hear them from me."

Abyssinia was amazed. She watched openmouthed as her father paced up and down the room. He continued, "Ever see a tomcat lay claim to territory? Heists his legs. Then commences to pee on all the walls."

"Why do you say that?" asked Abby when she found her voice to speak again. "How could you compare Carl Lee to a stray, mangy tomcat?"

"Okay, okay. He didn't heist his legs, but he was working wonders with his eyes. I know what I'm talking about. I was watching him. It takes another man to know these things," he raved. "Don't want him putting down claims around here. Trying to take over, huh! He's got to know there's a man here, and I ain't letting him get away with a damn thing!"

"Get away with what?" asked Abby.

"I don't want you fooling with him!" Strong shouted, shaking his finger at her.

"But why?"

"Abby's a young lady now, not a child," said Patience, trying to pacify him. "Even you've said that."

"I know one thing, that young man is full of himself. Thinks he's a strong one, all right."

"Who would you have me date, Daddy, a meek, docile man? Carl Lee won't fit that mold. I wouldn't like him if he did. And, come to think of it, neither would you."

"Abby, you might be grown, but you're living under this roof, and you will mind me!"

"Strong, you know good and well she lived on her own in the Barkers' old house for a couple of months before we decided to rent it out to save money for her to go to college."

"But she wasn't taking up with long-legged alley cats, either!" he huffed.

"Alley cat? How can you say that?" cried Abby. "Carl Lee is nice!"

"Road-running, skillet-headed ape," Strong ranted.

"Strong!" came Patience's rebuke. "What's got into you?"

"I never met anyone I wanted to invite over here before," said Abby. She had worked with her root medicine, occupied her time in other ways in the community. She had never paid this kind of attention to the opposite sex before, not in a romantic sense, anyway. She had lived out her fantasies in romance novels and in her imagination. But Carl Lee had exceeded the lingering expectations of her dreams. She smiled involuntarily as she thought about him.

"Now what's so funny?" bellowed Strong.

"Nothing," answered Abby. Her smile fled. The corners of her mouth turned down at the ugly tone in her father's voice. She wondered what was wrong with Strong's eyes. When she looked at Carl Lee's profile, she saw the wonderful curl of his hair, while her father saw a prowling tomcat or a skillet head.

Now Strong changed his method of attack. "We may not have a lot of money, but you come from good Oklahoma stock. "

"What does that mean?" asked Abby.

"Well, you've just got to be careful, that's all, about who you spend your time with, especially when it comes to men."

"I admit I haven't had much practice," Abby began, "but you and Mama seem to know his folks."

Her father's rage gathered momentum like a farm truck running unbraked over a rough downhill road. "That's the problem," said Strong, his face clapped shut like dark thunder.

"That's not fair," Patience said with an exasperated sigh.

"Background will out," Strong shot back. "Daddy trots. Mama trots. The colt's bound to pace."

What was her father leading up to? "Are you trying to say Carl Lee's not good enough for me? Seems to me we've had some pretty rough times, and partly your fault. . . ." She put on a defiant, daring face. Loosened her lips. Glazed her eyes.

Her mother shouted, "Abby! Don't—"

But Abby went on. "How could you—?"

Patience screamed, "Stop it! Stop it, both of you."

Abyssinia clamped her mouth shut. Her mind dulled, feeling

stupid as stone; she was sickened with sadness. She could not believe she was having this battle with her father.

She and Strong glared at each other. In the hot silence, Patience sniffled. For a moment her father's face looked stricken, half mollified. Then righteous anger lit up his eyes in a blaze. A moan ripped its way from his throat, then rushed out through gritted teeth. "I just don't like him!"

He stormed out of the house.

THREE

"Have you talked to Daddy about Carl Lee?" asked Abby on Tuesday morning.

"No, not yet. He wasn't in any mood yesterday. Then he had to go in to work early this morning. But don't worry, I will," Patience said, aware of the look of concern on Abby's face. "Got an early morning class?"

"No, I haven't. Thought I'd get some studying in before this afternoon."

"Do you think you have time to take some of these apples over to your Aunt Serena's before they get too ripe? We have more than we can eat."

"Getting tired of my apple pies by now, is that it?" Abby said with a smile.

"I do believe you make the best pies in Ponca." Patience had to chuckle. "You never get tired of hearing that, do you?"

Satisfied, Abby said, "This is a good excuse to see Aunt Serena. I don't see her nearly as much as I used to since she got married."

"Tell her your daddy and I send our regards," called Patience after the retreating Abby. "She's been on my mind so much lately."

Abby opened her Aunt Serena's front door and ran through the hall filled with irises banked in blue vases. Although she had taken careful hold of the bag of apples tucked under her arm, two or three managed to roll onto the floor. As she stooped to retrieve them, the entire bagful tumbled down.

"Yoo hoo! Aunt Serena!" she called, her load secure again.

"Precious, is that you?" came the joyful response. Abby followed the voice into the kitchen, where she was welcomed with open arms by Serena, a plump high-yellow woman in a canary-yellow cotton dress.

"Stand back and let me look at you. I declare, growing to beat the band. I do believe you're turning into a fair-looking young lady," she teased. She sat back down in her rocking chair and peered through her spectacles. She picked up her darning and said, "I remember the first day I babysat you. Patience and Strong said you were the most precious thing they owned. Precious, Precious, Precious!"

"Oh, please don't call me that old-fashioned name anymore, Aunt Serena," Abby pleaded.

"Precious? You mean don't call you Precious?"

"Abby is what I prefer," Abby gently told her.

"I'll try Pre . . . Abby. Now that you're older I suppose I should call you your young-lady name. But you'll still be every bit as precious to me as you were when Patience and Strong first brought you by that morning with your bundle of diapers, extra dresses, milk formula, and baby quilts." Her laugh twinkled. "What's that you've got tucked under your arm?"

"Red apples for you," said Abby. "Want me to slice a saucer's worth? I'll sprinkle brown sugar over them."

"You' re a good girl, Abby."

By the sink, Abyssinia sliced the apples into wedges and arranged them in a circle on the saucer. She sprinkled them with soft brown sugar. In the refrigerator she found a lemon and squeezed the tangy juice over the wedges. She knew every corner of the kitchen.

At the table where Serena sat rocking and darning her husband's socks, Abby placed the saucer of apples. Serena was humming placidly, caught in one of her reflective moods. "This sewing reminds me of how I used to take you to my quilting bees, downtown shopping, and everywhere else."

"Yes," giggled Abby. "They thought we were mother and daughter."

"Those were the days," said Serena dreamily.

"People said you could tell fortunes and see visions. Did you know that, Aunt Serena?"

"I figured as much. What did you think?"

"I never told you before"—she hesitated—"but when my school friends taunted me about you, I never denied it. I just felt it was all right if you did see visions and tell the future."

"Why'd you think that?" asked Serena as she reached for an apple wedge.

"Because you're all right. So is music, fire, wind, and water."

"Mighty powerful company you've placed me in. Yes, Abby, the future is with us, just like the past is. Sometimes people are looking at something and don't even know what they're studying. The mind is a wonderful thing. Sad to say, most folks don't use a fraction of their brains. Don't see but a fraction of what's there before them." She paused, a concerned furrow knitting her brows. "My eyes are growing dim now, but, Abby, you can do it. You can see beyond what most people will allow themselves to behold. Yes, you can."

"I can?"

"If you want to. You know"—she paused after munching her apple—"the human is an extraordinary creature. Made in God's image, you see. And there is no limit to the amount of good he can do."

"Or the amount of evil," echoed Abby, remembering an earlier lesson.

"Or the amount of evil. That's also true. There is no sin too low for him to sink down to and no virtue whose height he cannot scale."

Her apple finished, Serena picked up the gray-barked hackberry tree limb from next to her rocking chair. She fingered along the length of the limb until she found its corky knot. She wrapped her mouth around the protruding knob and chewed it until it bristled into a tiny brush. Chewing with agitated intensity, she continued to gnaw nervously on the brush as she spoke.

"Always remember, Abby, you have to expect folks to reach for the good. Never expect them to stoop down to evil. Nine chances out of ten, if you look for good, that's what you'll find. But first of all, get understanding."

Serena dipped the hackberry brush into her snuff can and fixed it in her mouth.

"But how?" Abby impatiently wondered.

Serena savored her snuff awhile before answering. "You got to listen a heap of a lot to be good at it. And paint your eyes with compassion, Abby. And sometimes forgiveness. And when somebody does you wrong, forgive but don't ever forget."

"Yes, ma'am." Abby was impatient to ask Serena about love. Her love for Carl Lee grew like mushrooms. Every day there was more affection than the day before. "Aunt Serena, what about love?"

Serena fixed bright eyes on Abby. "Oh, my goodness!" She gave a satisfied laugh. "So you've met a young man. Love you'll have to discover for yourself, Abby. The discovering is a magic all its own. Does he go to school with you?"

"Uh-huh," said Abby, involuntarily catching her breath. Serena laughed her wonderful laugh. Her alert eyes seemed to contain residues of brilliance. Then Serena started sewing and singing.

Always singing when she was in deep thought. Her voice a tuned instrument. A water-rippling, songbird voice.

As Abby sat talking about Carl Lee, she heard the screen door slam. Serena, too, came out of her reverie, and her song stopped. In the doorway loomed her husband, the Reverend Ruford Jordan. Short hair slicked back. Overweight. Squat body. Squinty eyes.

"Hello, darling. Hello, Abby." He ceremoniously swept in and kissed Serena. It was a kiss that excluded Abby. She felt left out and not wanted. A cold tremble shingled her body.

"How long have you been here?" he asked, turning to Abby.

What was it? At the bottom of the honeyed words she felt a fleeting menace.

"Just a few minutes. I brought some apples over," Abby managed to stammer.

"You brought some apples over for us. How wonderful," the minister proclaimed in his booming voice.

"Would you like me to slice some for you?" Abby asked.

"Oh, my wife will." He dismissed her offer.

"Well, yes, Reverend," Serena agreed, rising from her chair. She went to the sink and began slicing the apples. There was an uneasy silence in the room; the laughter that forced its way from between the Reverend's lips was unnatural.

"What's for dinner, my good wife?" he asked.

"Chicken and dressing," she murmured from the sink. This was not the usual Serena. Different. But how? Abby could not put her finger on it.

Is this what marriage does to you? It changes you imperceptibly. Joining with another person, you become someone else. A chill of apprehension oozed down Abby's spine.

"When's the last time you said a good prayer to the Lord?" the minister asked Abby, oblivious to her discomfort in his presence.

Abby twisted uneasily in her chair. She hesitated before answering. "I say my prayers every night, sir." It was an area about which no one had a right to ask. What she did or didn't do with her God was her and her God's business.

Serena brought the apple slices to him. He ate them hungrily, licking the juice from his fingers. Abby's stomach revolted. The preacher's attitude was slick, oily, she thought. Then, as she looked at Serena's bright face, at the glancing light casting a wonderful ray of sunbeam on it, she felt ashamed. Maybe she was downright jealous. Maybe she thought Serena belonged only to her.

Her reason understood her sense of loss, but she was having a hard time dealing with her jealousy, that shadow on her heart. She discovered with a quick lurch that she did not like the Reverend.

He was pompous, even while he sat. His shoulders seemed to her unreasonably high. His head tilted too far upward; his neck was rigid, his movements prepared. He crunched his apple and glanced at Abby as though she were an intruder.

His apple finished, he said to Serena, "Honey, dearest, would you bring me my Bible?"

Serena virtually leaped out of the room to fetch the Bible. As Abby turned back toward him, she thought she saw a malicious glint in his eyes. Disturbed, she turned her thoughts to her earlier realization about the jealousy. Yes, it was true. She did not like Serena's husband because her aunt now had very little time for her.

She had misinterpreted his looks, his very words. She would try to be more accepting, she told herself. She valued her aunt's company so much. She owed it to her family to show herself friendly to this man.

"Where'd you pastor before coming to Ponca, Reverend Jordan?" Abby asked.

"Oh, I had me a big church in Houston," he answered. "Congregation almost a thousand."

"What was it called?" Abby wondered.

"True Vine Baptist Church," the Reverend said.

"Well, why'd you leave?"

"About a year ago, I got a message from God to move on, so I moved on."

"What was it like, this church in Houston?" asked Abby.

"Had a hundred-voice choir. Had ten deacons. Had thirteen mothers of the church. Now that was a congregation!" His eyes glistened as he shared the memories of his great success as the pastor of the Houston church.

Abby noted the unmistakable joy in his voice. She believed he had loved his church and every member. She wished she felt as sure about his love for Serena.

"And you never married before?" Abby asked.

"That, too, was in God's hands. The will of God," proclaimed the Reverend.

"Aunt Serena's really somebody special," commented Abby.

"My wife can sing better than anyone in that hundred-voice choir I had," the Reverend admitted.

"I don't doubt it," Abby agreed.

"Reads the Bible better than any one of those thirteen mothers of the church."

"Dramatically better." Abby nodded.

"A perfect wife for a perfect minister," Reverend Jordan said, folding his hands contentedly in his lap.

Abby emitted an easy sigh, relieved at the joy in the pastor's face when he spoke of Serena. He was all right after all. It had been only her childish jealousy getting in the way of her good sense. She wanted to get to know this husband of Serena's better.

"What did the Houston congregation think of you?" she ventured.

"Bought me a new car every year. A brand new Cadillac. A whole wardrobe of new suits. I was the talk of the ministerial alliance. All the other Texas ministers envied me." He puffed out his chest as he said this.

"And then you had to leave it all," commented Abby.

His face clouded, and Abyssinia shivered as she glimpsed something she could not identify. An unfamiliar shadow hovered in his expression, suggesting cold and mildewed spirits. Even though it was a warm day, goose bumps rose on her arms. She could not breathe; she experienced a feeling of fright. *Damnation, damnation, damnation* was the word that sank its stony whisper into her ear.

Before she knew it she was on her feet. "I . . . I . . . I have to be leaving," she stammered as she scrambled from the room.

In her flight down the hallway she bumped smack into her aunt Serena, making her drop the Bible she had fetched for Reverend Jordan.

"I'm sorry," Abby said, picking up the fallen book and handing it to her aunt. "I just remembered I left something on the stove."

Jealousy. Evil. Knives to the spirit. Poison to the soul. Which had she felt sitting in that room with the Reverend? Jealousy or evil? One or both? she asked herself as she ran back to her own front door. Not understanding just what she had sensed, she went straight to her room. Trying to throw those feelings out of her mind, she immersed herself in the mountain of homework that never seemed to end.

FOUR

At the breakfast table, Strong was unnaturally quiet. Patience seemed wary. Abyssinia ate hot oatmeal in warm spoon-scoops. Then she reached for the butter and spread the yellow smoothness on her wheat toast. She could not help thinking of Carl Lee. Would she see him today at school? Immediately she thought about what her aunt Serena had said about love, "You have to discover its magic for yourself."

To break the awkward silence, Abby said, "I took the red apples over to Aunt Serena's yesterday."

"How was she?" asked Patience.

"She was a little nervous . . . I think. But it's her husband I wonder about."

"What's wrong with him?" asked Strong.

"I don't know . . . maybe nothing," she stammered, remembering her ambivalent feelings about Reverend Jordan.

For a moment Strong looked concerned, too; then his attention shifted to Abby.

"Well, those are old, ancient, grown folks. Been on this earth long enough to know what they want. It's not them I'm concerned about. But you, young lady, are a different matter. You don't know men like I do. I forbid you to see that Carl Lee. He's too aggressive. I can see what's on his mind. "

"Well, I'm seeing him." Abby shouted her defiance, pushing herself up from the table.

Her father stood up, too, then stared across the table at her. "We're not sending you to college to get pregnant by some no-good worthless tomcat boy, Abyssinia Jackson!" Then he slapped her next thought from her mind before it reached her mouth.

She was startled, shocked by the slap. Her father had never hit her before in her life.

"Now, Strong, you promised," sobbed Patience.

"But have you explained the facts of life to your daughter?" he asked, a pained expression tugging at his mouth.

"Strong, she's a young woman!"

Proud tears blinded Abby's path.

"I think you owe her an apology, Strong. And me. You promised me you'd let them be."

Abby gathered up her books and sweater and fled out the door, neglecting to kiss her parents good-bye or to wish them a good day.

Later in the day Abby hurried impatiently from her English class. She pulled an essay out of her binder. A prickling heat burnished her cheeks, and a small frown undimpled her face. She paid scant attention to the chattering sounds of schoolmates coming and going in the crowded corridors. Her eyes and attention were riveted on the term paper she had just got back. The minus on the A leaped out at her like an incriminating mark of shame. She had expected a straight A.

With a dejected slump of her shoulders she leafed through her work looking for grammatical errors. She had carefully gone over the pages after she had typed them. Then she had had Patience proofread them again. As far as she could tell there were no grammatical errors.

A problem with development perhaps? She had spent hours in

the library researching Shakespeare. When she thought of *Romeo and Juliet,* Shakespeare's bittersweet romance, she caught herself picturing Carl Lee's face, his smile, his hair.

She sighed heavily, remembering her father's heavy hand-slap, his bitter words. It was as though he had become another person overnight.

As she put away the term paper, she was suddenly aware of the hustle and bustle of students changing classes. A sudden movement jolted her, impeding her progress down the hall. What clumsy person had bumped into her so rudely? To her astonishment, she looked up to see Carl Lee, his track shoes slung over his shoulder, his books under one arm.

He grinned. "If there were mountains I could climb, you know I'd scale the highest peak, but there are no Mount Kilimanjaros in Oklahoma, Miss Abyssinia." He chuckled deep in his throat and continued, "So would you please tell me what I have to do to make you look at me?"

She smiled back, his good humor lifting her out of her low mood. She had been so absorbed in her essay that she had been unaware of Carl Lee's approach, and, more than that, had failed to notice him strolling alongside her.

"How long have you been walking beside me?" she asked.

He did not answer her question, but continued his flirting. "If there were fire-eating dragons I could save you from, you know what I'd do? I'd slice off their heads with one swoop of my gleaming sword, but there are no prehistoric monsters around here, girl, so would you tell me what I must do to be worthy?" He flashed his strong, wide teeth in a quizzical ear-to-ear grin, his eyebrows lifting in merriment.

Carl Lee. Stretch, they called him on the track field, because he could stretch his legs and outrun anybody for miles around. Now she stopped walking, reached up and adjusted his track shoes on his shoulder, and remembered in a surprising déjà vu flash how he used to chase her down the Ponca roads at dusk and snatch the ribbons from her pigtails.

Now she found herself comparing the young man grinning at her with the mischievous boy who used to tease her. She remembered how his hair had been butchered so short by his father's home barbering job that it bordered on baldness. How his eyes, without hair to balance their size, looked too big for his head.

"Want a lift home, Abby?" he asked.

"I was going to catch the bus," she teased.

"Thought you'd like to ride in my car instead."

"I like being by myself," she said. "Sometimes I think my best when I'm alone."

"Well, excuse me. I was only trying to be neighborly."

"I know. I mean, yes, I'd like a lift, if you'll let me help with the gas."

"I will not," he said, trying to look insulted. Then he added, "That's not why I asked you. I need the companionship. Someone to keep me alert while I drive. "

"Someone to talk to on the road. Is that what you want? A convenience, huh?"

"A pretty convenience," he added, "if that's what you want to call it."

"It's a deal, but only if I can pitch in for gas every once in a while."

"You drive a hard bargain, don't you?" he asked.

"That's the way I want it."

"Stubborn, aren't you?"

"Take it or leave it."

"Always did admire a woman with spunk," Carl Lee said.

"Well?" she asked.

They walked toward the parking lot. She noticed the sparkling chrome first. The car was an old four-door bruised green Chevrolet. What saved it from looking like a relic ready for the car cemetery was the polished and spanking-clean shape in which Carl Lee kept it.

"This is what you might call a vintage model," Carl Lee said as he opened the door for her. She noticed the Langston University sticker above the track emblem centered in the back window. He went around to his side of the car and stacked his books neatly on the backseat next to his tennis shoes. She held on to her books.

"You don't think you're going to study on the way home, do you?" said Carl Lee. "A car isn't the perfect place to read, you know, with all the moving it does. Wouldn't be good for your eyes."

"You've got a point. I can see this car-riding with you will have a few disadvantages," Abby said.

"Anyway, you agreed to keep me company."

"I did, didn't I?" she admitted, and tossed her books into the backseat.

He straightened the pile out neatly, whistling to himself.

Soon he had passed the campus building and reached the outer streets of town.

"Not only can you run like an expert, you drive like one, too," she commented.

He rounded a curve smoothly. "I respect the power of a car," he said. "If you don't, you're in trouble before you know it. Saw a friend of mine injured in a car crash. Broken bones. Teeth knocked out of his head. Turned him into an old man."

"An old man?"

"He needed a cane. Somebody had to feed him. Not a pretty sight. "

"It's true. Injuries can age you," said Abby.

"By the way," he said, "what paper was that you were looking at so hard when I ran into you today?"

"Oh, that. 'Themes in Shakespeare's Plays,' is what I called it."

"I saw the grade," he said, impressed. "You did all right."

"I was a little disappointed," she said.

"In an A minus?"

"I thought I'd earned a straight A. The reason I was looking so hard was that I was trying to find out where I'd come up short."

"Well, whatever is wrong with the paper couldn't be too bad," he said.

"Now, how would you know?"

"You might be short in height," Carl Lee said, "but I have a feeling that's about all."

"Is that so?"

"Uh-hum. I'm the boy who used to chase you, remember? You were mighty hard to catch. So now I'm into track."

They both laughed.

"Well, one thing is for sure," Abby said, glancing at his extra-long legs stretching to the gas pedal, "you'd have no problem catching me now."

"Is that a fact?" The way he said this, warm and genuinely friendly, let her know he was hoping her response had double meaning.

She felt her heart turn over lightly. But she eased her eyes away from him and turned to look out the window at the dusk dropping across the plains and hills, the sun going dim in a velvet sky dressed in evening red.

She started humming to herself. He recognized the melody and began to sing "Blue Moon" in his strong baritone voice.

She picked up the lyrics with him. Her sweet soprano rose along with his rich notes. Abby was conscious of the highway flowing like ribbons behind them.

The russet colors of autumn were everywhere. The leaves fluttered like tender baby birds across their windshield from time to time. She knew that if they stopped the car, they would hear a country serenade. An orchestra of natural sound. The flute voice of the songbirds. The chirping crickets. The uneven rhythm of rustling leaves accented by the singing of tires on highway.

They were even comfortable in each other's silences. They both sighed deeply at the same time. The car followed its sure path homeward.

When they drove up before Abby's door, she said, while gathering her books from the backseat, "Why don't you come by Saturday, Carl Lee, for lemonade and leaves?"

"Leaves?" He studied her mischievous face, perplexed.

"This Saturday I'm cleaning up the yard and garden, and if you'll help me I promise you limitless lemonade," she clarified.

"Are you sure it will be all right with your father?" Carl Lee asked, remembering Strong's uneasiness with him.

Abby's eyes clouded for a moment. A frown nagged at her face.

"I don't know, to tell you the truth. But he'll be in the barbershop all day this Saturday. I did tell him I would be seeing you." She blushed when she realized what she had said. As though the choice were solely hers.

His eyes held hers. "So that's the situation. You want to see me. He doesn't want you to."

Abyssinia held her breath and nodded her head yes.

He didn't say anything for a long while. Then he smiled. "I'll see you Saturday." He watched her start down her walk, her step spry, her head held shy but confident. At last she bounded up her steps and turned around to wave at him. He tooted his horn in farewell and sped away.

Abby avoided Strong for the next few days.

FIVE

Before daybreak, while Abby lay sleeping, something frightened her. A million miniature bumps popped out, disturbing the smooth brown glaze of her skin. A feather brushed along the tip of her spine, bristled at the nape of her neck. She could not rid herself of this pervasive feeling of dread, could not shake the persistent premonition. She held her breath and crept between peaceful dreams and sound sleep. Hid behind shadows. But still it pursued.

In her dream someone dressed in virtue twisted the goodwill of the town of Ponca inside out. The event set the town on its ear. As the nightmare advanced, Abby tried to scream the truth, to tell the trusting people that the thing was wicked, but they opened their front doors anyway and let it in. Welcomed wrong into their very parlors. Her mouth worked at words, but nothing came out. Quiet. Like the silence before the scream of an ambulance.

She woke up in a cold sweat.

When she told her mother what she had dreamed, her mother shook her head compassionately. "You're just like a barometer, Abby. You always could tell when something bad was going to happen. When you were a baby, you ran a fever. Now that you're a young woman, it's goose bumps."

In the light of the day, the nightmare seemed less foreboding.

With her mother standing near and her father in the other room, she really had no reason to feel so dreadful. Then she remembered that Carl Lee was coming to help her in the yard, and she pushed the nightmare to the back of her mind.

At the window she stood watching Strong head for his barbershop. As he moved out of her view, she contemplated the changes that the season had brought. Six weeks' worth of autumn's decayed leaves lay scattered in fiery quietness upon the Oklahoma plains. In the startling translucent light of noon a yellow-breasted meadowlark flitted to a barbed-wire fence and sang of summer gone.

Then Carl Lee was coming down the walk, dressed in blue jeans and a plaid shirt, ready for work.

In the front yard, they raked leaves. Abby struck a match to the first pile, and it went up in flames. They stood together gazing into the flame, then turned around at the sound of Serena's front door slamming shut.

"Hello, Aunt Serena, Reverend Jordan," Abby called. Serena and the Reverend waved. Serena hesitated, as though she wanted to stop and chat a moment, but the Reverend took her firmly by the elbow and led her down the road.

"I sure miss seeing Aunt Serena," Abby said.

"Why, she lives right next door. Why wouldn't you see her?"

"Since she married the Reverend, she rarely has time for me." Abby's voice broke glumly. "Every time I go there he sends her on some kind of chore for him so we don't get to visit at all."

Carl Lee nodded sympathetically. "I wonder where they're going?"

"On some kind of church business, I suppose." Abby gave a dismal sniff.

Suddenly a meadowlark flew over their heads and glided above the flashing bed of fallen leaves they had raked into a rusty pile and set afire.

Abby shaded her eyes and watched the bird fly down the road until he swooped over the figures of the sixty-year-old Serena and her husband. The married pair journeyed hand in hand down a path of jaundiced leaves recently shed from red buckeye trees, hazel alder, American elm, and Oklahoma pecan.

"You really do miss her, don't you?" Carl Lee put a comforting arm around Abby as they studied the couple and the bird. In the bird's whir of retreating wings, Abby imagined the bittersweet hint of drooping lilacs, the death of leaves, and the dried-up sap of naked trees.

"Let's take a break," suggested Carl Lee, trying to cheer her up. "Want to go for a walk?"

"If you want to."

After banking the burning leaves, they started off in the same direction as Serena and Ruford. About a half mile down the road they saw Serena and Ruford turn into a cornfield.

Out of curiosity, Abby and Carl Lee started into the field, too, but they kept their distance. Ahead of them the Reverend released the hand of his wife and went up to his pulpit—a simple wooden crate nestled in the middle of this gold and green pasture.

Abby and Carl Lee positioned themselves far back in the cornfield and sat down cross-legged on the ground. They watched as Serena unfolded her collapsible seat in the front row of cornstalks. Then her pastor husband nodded a silent salutation to his dedicated deacon, a ragged scarecrow, and pulled out his black leather Bible, which was neatly protected by layers of newspapers, and opened it.

"Do you think it's okay to watch them?" asked Abby in a muted voice, filled with vague unease.

"It is like eavesdropping," Carl Lee whispered back.

"How can you eavesdrop in a church?" she wondered out loud.

Neither of them tried to answer that; they glued their eyes on the pair.

Reverend Jordan had told her he had heard a voice in the middle of lightning and thunder one stormy January night and had been called to preach. Looking at him now, Abby felt a shiver tremble down her spine.

Reverend Jordan ascended his pulpit and, shading his eyes against the sun's glare, surveyed his congregation—the cornstalks, which leaned their rustling bodies toward him; the scarecrow, who shouted a holy dance when the Reverend whipped up a sermon strong enough to shake the wind; and Serena, who sat worshipping from her canvas chair.

In the Reverend's survey of his congregation, his eyes did not search the back of the field where Abby and Carl Lee sat and watched.

Now Serena smiled up at the Reverend, her four front teeth catching the sun in her mouth like a glittering harp, and she began to sing.

The two young people leaned forward, listening as the sixty-year-old woman made music from the cradle of her throat. She rocked the tones back and forth, effortlessly stroking the notes until they were the elusive gold and fine rhythm of corn silk caught in the wind:

Our Father which art in Heaven
Hallowed be Thy name
Thy kingdom come
Thy will be done . . .

Serena's whole body reached for the song. She lifted her tightly curled gray head on the deep notes and moved her patient arms, wrapped in their butter-colored skin, on the high notes.

Give us this day
Our daily bread.

Serena's fingers clasped the Bible on her lap as she arched her chest toward the melody, until the song wove its way to a high crescendoed prelude to the sermon.

Abyssinia let out a deep sigh. Carl Lee finally released her hand that he had been squeezing tightly.

There was a brief pause as the entire cornfield seemed to acknowledge the blessing of the gifted singer. Then the pastor heard the words of the Scriptures through his wife. She led him through the twenty-third chapter of Psalms in a trumpet voice:

Yea though I WALK through the valley of the
shadows of DEATH, I will fear no EVIL.

The minister repeated the words, accenting them in different places from the syncopated way she read them.

Yea though I walk through the VALLEY of the
SHADOWS of death, I will FEAR no evil.

Abby and Carl Lee, mesmerized by the drama unfolding before them, uttered not a sound.

The preacher commenced to interpret: "The Scriptures tell us that to live is to walk through the valley of the shadows of death."

"Amen!" came Serena's fervent reply.

"Children, let me tell you that every moment of our lives brings us closer to the doors of the house of Ol' Man Death.

"Yet, if we hold on to God's hand, we have nothing to fear. When the winds of death gather shadows—"

"Preach!" Serena implored mightily.

"—all we got to do is hold God's hand and walk on in His wonderful sunlight."

"Hallelujah!"

Finally Serena led him through the fifth chapter of Revelations. He sermonized the seven horns and the seven eyes of the sacrificed lamb; he preached of brimstone, smoke, fire, and the everlasting torture of hell.

"What drama!" whispered Carl Lee. He reached for Abby's hand, and they stood up to leave.

An hour later, Abby and Carl Lee were busy tending the vegetable garden when Serena and her husband strolled down the ribbon of road toward home. Where the Jordans walked their feet scattered crinkled autumn leaves in orange and russet-red flurries.

Soon the couple entered their gate next door. Serena plucked a bouquet from the irises she groomed inside her front yard. She inhaled their sweet fragrance, looked enchantedly at the blue-violet of their petals, their green, grassy leaves. The Reverend entered the house, but Serena continued along the side of the house and into the back yard, where she reached across the fence and handed the bouquet to Abby.

"Thank you, Aunt Serena," Abby said, studying the deep blue of the irises. Then she caught herself. "Oh, by the way, this is my friend, Carl Lee." Abby thought she saw a small glow in Serena's dim eyes as she peered closely at Carl Lee.

"Good afternoon, my son," she said.

"Pleased to meet you," said Carl Lee. Still she kept staring at him until he said, "Isn't it a nice day?"

Serena seemed to shake herself before giving her standard reply. "Yes, indeed. The Lord sends the sun just like He sends the shadow. Yes, He does." Then she continued in a different voice, "I must feed the chickens now, children. Fine young man. Fine young man," she murmured to herself as she went to attend her fowl.

Still studying the plants, Abby said, "I'd better put these irises in water. Back in a minute." She dashed into the house while Carl Lee continued weeding the garden.

When Abyssinia came out of her back door, she heard Serena's door slam. Through it the Reverend emerged.

"I'll feed Rena," Pastor Jordan said, referring to his favorite pig. He had named the pig Rena after *Serena,* his new wife, because he claimed that the woman and the suckling were the same delicious color of bronze, freckled brown, with pink blushing through it.

From way back in the next yard, Abby and Carl Lee could hear Pastor Jordan slopping the pigs.

"Here, Rena, Rena, Rena, sooey, sooey!"

At the sound of her husband's bass voice calling the pig, Serena, outside near her back door, folded her hands and laughed, her crystal voice flirting with sound. She called to the chickens, "Here chick, chick, chick, chick, chick." She shooed the clucking hens from their nests and collected their brown eggs in a basket of interwoven rushes. She sprinkled finely ground kernels of corn for the Rhode Island rooster, the baby chicks, the speckled pullets, and the matron hens.

When she had got the chickens to run toward her, she made a trail of the chicken feed until she was near the fence again.

"Abby," she called across the fence, "When I wring one of these chickens' necks, I'll fix a plump fryer and invite you and your young man over." She moved closer to Abby's backyard fence. "How're your greens coming? They're standing mighty proud, especially the mustard. But the collards are coming along, too."

Abby said, "Tomorrow I'm fixing mustard greens for Sunday dinner. I'll bring you over a bowl. Just wish I had some crackling bread to go with them."

"Been ages since I've tasted good crackling bread. I'm surprised you remember how to make it," said Serena.

"Well, there're a few ways you can make it. Don't you remember? It was you who taught me how. I grind my corn and sift my flour, crack one egg, and splash in some buttermilk. Then I stir in the pork rinds. And the rinds have to be crispy, just like you told me, Aunt Serena. Rinds crackled from skinned pigs. Then just bake it."

"I'll settle for a slice right now," Carl Lee said longingly, standing up to rub his growling stomach.

"Lemonade is all you get today," Abby told him.

"That's right, I did teach you," said Serena. "I am getting older." She shook her head in humility. "Children, one of the problems with aging is you forget what you oughtn't to forget. And sometimes remember what's not there." She laughed gently at herself. "Let me know when you do bake a batch of crackling bread, Abby."

"Minute somebody kills a pig I'll fix some," she promised.

Serena turned to leave them, then remembering something she stopped in her tracks, and her dim eyes lingered on Carl Lee. "What did you say your friend's name was?" Serena asked Abby.

"Carl Lee," answered Abby.

"Carl Lee who?"

"Carl Lee Jefferson," said Carl Lee.

Serena walked closer to the fence and peered up at him a long time. Then she said, "Uh-huh." She reached her hand over the low fence and patted him gently on the arm. Then saying good day she climbed her back steps and went inside her own house.

"Well, now you've met her," said Abby. "That's my Aunt Serena."

"What a wonderful woman!" said Carl Lee.

"Wish I could be half as wonderful."

"By the time you get sixty, I'm sure you'll be," Carl Lee said in teasing banter.

"She taught me a lot," Abby said in a reflective mood. "I learned so much just being around her. But, as I told you earlier, I don't see her much now.

"She's always busy darning the Reverend's clothes, making him new suits, cooking, washing, ironing, shining his shoes, picking up after him. I don't know why she lets him get away without helping her. My father hangs up his own clothes and scrubs floors more often than my mother. I just don't understand that marriage. Last month, for instance, Serena was painting the outside of the house while he sat in the shade sipping soda. Why, he treats Rena the pig better than he treats her."

"Nothing you can do?" asked Carl Lee.

"Oh, Carl Lee," she lamented, "I feel as if I should see more of her, but how do you make more time? There are still only twenty-four hours in a day. And when her husband's not taking up her time, I'm busy with homework, housework, my parents, or with you. Besides, Aunt Serena will fix the situation. I bet she's just biding her time."

"Maybe you're right," said Carl Lee.

"She's a wise woman. And powerful."

"I can see that," he agreed.

"Hear it, too. It's all in her voice."

SIX

"Aunt Serena and Reverend Jordan have been going to service in the cornfield every night for a whole week now," Abby said to Carl Lee in a worried voice this October evening as she gathered her books and started to get out of his car.

"Any members joined yet?" Carl Lee asked, eyeing Serena and Rufus Jordan walking down the road toward the cornfield.

"I doubt it," said Abby. "Who'd want to listen to a man preach to cornstalks and pray with a scarecrow?"

"Serena does."

"That's different. She's his wife. I wonder how she's really doing. Wish I could talk to her alone, but he's always around, listening to every word we speak to each other."

"Want to take a walk?" He nodded his head after the retreating couple.

"Yes, let's." Abby tossed her books into the backseat again, and both of them got out and stealthily journeyed to the cornfield.

In the dusty dark, night was fast approaching, but soon Abyssinia and Carl Lee had taken their former places in the rear of the cornfield.

Creeping up out of the eastern horizon the full moon rose like a round opal of light, showering the cornfield with phantom artistry.

Corning to a stop low in the sky, the spectral moon began to fringe the husks of the tall stalks with silver. From there it laced strange spangles of light everywhere, so that even the scarecrow standing on duty in the middle of the cornfield glowed with a pearly iridescence. For a moment, watching the light strike patterns in the field, Abby had the impression she was seated in a church watching the play of light through stained-glass windows.

Then, out of the shimmering stillness of night, came the deep voice of Reverend Jordan praying:

For thine is the kingdom
And the power and the glory
forever. Amen.

Abby looked toward the front of the cornfield, searching for her aunt. Although she soon spotted her, she could barely make out Serena's face it was so steeped in shadow. But a solitary moonbeam touched down on the spot where Reverend Jordan stood praying before his pulpit, the silver light transforming him into an awesome-looking messiah.

His prayer ended, now the minister leaned his head to one side. And all was quiet for a few moments. Then he began speaking with an unseen presence whose voice only he could hear.

"You say you want a sacrifice . . . ?" the minister said. "And I shall receive a blessing . . . ? My prayers have not been in vain. What you ask for, that shall I give. My cow, my chickens, my goat, even Rena, my prize pig. You have only to ask, and thy servant shall give."

He lifted his head to the heavens.

Then he inclined his head as though listening.

Finally he spoke. "Rena, you say? You say you want me to sacrifice Rena?"

"Poor Rena," Carl Lee sighed from his place way back in the cornfield.

"That pig's almost like a person," said Abby. "But, Carl Lee, what does he mean 'sacrifice Rena'?"

"Sounds strange. But look, they're finishing now," said Carl Lee as they saw Reverend Jordan take Serena's arm and prepare to leave.

"That's the quickest service I've ever seen," said Abby. "I don't like the sound of this, Carl Lee. Tomorrow I'm staying home, and somehow I'll find a way to talk to Aunt Serena alone. I don't like the sound of this at all."

"I have a feeling you're right. Something's funny. I'll pick up your assignments at school and bring them by for you tomorrow evening," he said, taking her hand.

They hurried from the field ahead of the older couple.

Carl Lee had seen Abby inside her house and had headed his car for home by the time Abby heard Serena's front door open and slam shut.

That night Abby watched a luminous moon from her bedroom window. The moon struck deathly pale against the pigsty in the farmyard. A pallid dagger of light dappled first the farmland then the house in long shadows that shivered from sty to tree, from tree to back porch, and from back porch to the clapboard house. An ugly, ghostly half-light troubled the dark.

At dawn, a glazed-eyed pastor rattled the Jackson screen door with agitated, trembling hands.

"Oh, Miss Abby, Miss Abby, my wife's so sick. She's doing right poorly. I prayed and prayed, but still she's low. Mightn't you come over and stir her up some of your good corn bread?"

"What's ailing her?" Abby asked through the screen door.

"She's just not herself," the preacher said, staring at her as though he were in a trance.

"Well, sir, I'll be over directly," said Abby, worried that her Aunt Serena was down sick with a bad cold. She would go next door, bake the bread, and fix Serena a cup of broom wheat tea.

When Abby arrived at the Jordans' kitchen, she could see strips of skin hanging down from the ceiling on hooks, left to dry. Drops of blood stained the floor. What a mess. She would clean it up after she made the bread and tea and tended to Serena.

"Reverend Jordan, you finally killed the pig," she said to the man standing by the kitchen screen.

Abby found the mixing bowl and the bread pan where she used to find them. She measured the cup of ground corn, the flour, the buttermilk.

"Now that you've killed the pig, Reverend Jordan, I think I'll add some of its skin to the corn-bread batter and stir up a batch of crackling bread." She reached up for a strip of skin.

She glanced at the man. He did not answer. He looked haggard, the hair on his chin stubby, his eyes veined. Then she gave all her attention to what she was doing.

She stuck the strip into a pan and popped it into the oven. Before long the rendered fat bubbled until the skin was crispy. She added this crackling to the batter. She stirred and hummed, then poured the crackling batter into the bread pan and set it in the oven to bake.

"Wonder how she's feeling now? Maybe I'll go in the bedroom and check," Abby said, wiping her hands on her apron.

"Oh, she's sleeping now, Miss Abby," said Reverend Jordan, staring at the stove. "She'll feel better when she wakes up to this good crackling bread."

Abby began to clean up the kitchen. By the time the crackling bread was done, she had washed the cooking utensils and put away the bowl she had used for mixing the batter and had started the teakettle singing. The hot water was ready for steeping the tea.

"You know, Miss Abby, we certainly appreciate this, the wife and I," Reverend Jordan said as she was taking the hot bread out of the oven.

"It's nothing, Reverend," Abby assured him. "Aunt Serena has been like a second mother to me." She placed the pan on the apron of the stove. She picked up a knife and cut a wedge and placed it on a china saucer. She poured the hot brewed tea into a cup. "Reckon she's up? If not I'll wake her. Got to eat crackling bread while it's hot."

She started to the bedroom with the steaming slice on a saucer, balancing the teacup in her other hand.

Through the window in the hallway that separated the kitchen from the bedroom, Abby could see a high wind, unyielding and fierce. It rustled the cornstalks and knocked the shutters loudly against the house. She thought she saw shadows being gathered by the wind. She paused, then shutting that vision out of her mind passed on to the bedroom, thinking that now finally she would be alone with Aunt Serena to ask her how she was really doing, without the Reverend listening to every word they spoke.

"Oh, my God!" Abby screeched. A bloodcurdling wail rushed from her mouth.

The sound of the saucer and cup hitting the floor echoed throughout the old house. Propped up on a pillow was Aunt Serena, her quilt tucked neatly under her chin, her hands folded placidly over her chest, her arms skinless.

On wobbly legs, Abby tiptoed up to the bed. She leaned over and peered into Serena's staring eyes, eyes popped open like a frog's.

"Blink, Aunt Serena. Blink, blink." But Serena's eyelashes were stiff, so she could not blink them.

Abby's gaze traveled down to the slack mouth. "Open your mouth, Aunt Serena. Can't you sing?"

But the silent woman did not answer.

Abby peeked under the covers and jumped back, trembling from head to toe. Serena's entire body was skinless, and the ugly rawness started Abby screaming again. "Oh, my God, have mercy!" she hollered. She drew in a sharp breath and inhaled the aroma of death.

Serena reeked a stench of dead flowers and dust. Gone were her patient "amens," her humble "hallelujahs."

Abyssinia's glance flew around the room, her gaze darting to one thing and then another. She spied Serena's broken cup and saucer.

"Serena?" Dazed, Abby dashed over to the pile of broken china and knelt down to pick up the pieces. If she picked up every sliver, it would steady her hands, unbuckle her mind.

But as she bowed her head between the cracks left by Serena's silence, all she could hear was the obstinate wind and the sorrow of rushing air through cornstalks.

"Serena? Serena? Serena?" she began, talking to the shattered cup and saucer as she tossed the jagged pieces into the nearby wastebasket.

And then she began to pray:

"You whose eye is on the sparrow . . ."

If she picked up every crumb of crackling bread . . .

". . . lend us your presence."

. . . she'd wake up from this nightmare and Serena would be alive.

"You who keeps watch over even the ants . . ."

Her trembling hands reached for the crumbs. . . .

". . . grant us mercy."

. . . and tossed them into the wastebasket.

"Light us a candle in this hour of darkness. . . ."

Now every crumb was cleaned up.

". . . and deliver us from violence."

But still Serena was dead.

"Amen."

After she had prayed to her Higher Authority, Abby got up off her knees and ran home, her feet kicking up swirling clouds of red dust. She dialed the common authority, the police.

A few minutes later the police car skidded to a stop in front of the Jordan house.

From her position on her own front porch, Abby saw the two officers go into Serena's house.

"What in tarnation's all this, Reverend Jordan?" she heard one policeman shout in the kitchen as he looked up at the strips of skin. There was no answer from the minister.

"Check out the back room," this same officer said to the other one.

Then seconds later came a loud cry from the back of the house where the bedroom was. "Christ a-mighty! Come here!"

At the sound of his partner's horrified voice, the first officer dashed to the bedroom.

Now all Abby could hear was a stunned, openmouthed silence.

They shackled Ruford's hands. They shackled Ruford's legs.

Abyssinia walked up and down her porch, her arms wrapped across her waist, and studied the cuffed man as he and the officers stepped out of the Jordan house.

"Never seen anything like it!" one policeman said to the other, wagging his head from side to side, his body shaking from the memory of the scene they had witnessed. They led Ruford to the squad car.

Before she knew it, Abby was moving toward them. Her body on a mission her mind could not quite grasp. She moved with unflinching haste toward the tragic trio of men.

She stopped in front of the advancing group and they halted as if from some strange command. Abyssinia stared at Ruford Jordan.

A wand of anger waved in her eyes. Winter crows crossed her jet black pupils.

Ruford, to his detriment, looked back. The dazed Ruford absorbed the hell sentence in her stare. With the stubborn strength of a damned man, he leaped away from Abyssinia and the astonished policemen.

Although he was tied hand and foot, the police could not catch him. He was leaping down the road like a kangaroo.

One of the officers raced to his car and radioed: "Send help! Send some help! We got an emergency situation out here!" The microphoned words rang out over the neighborhood. People, with the alert wariness of dedicated gossips, stuck their uncombed morning heads out of their doors.

The ember eyes of Abyssinia Jackson followed Ruford Jordan as he took great leaps across the road, foaming at the mouth. Hopping toward hell.

Soon the neighborhood was crawling with police cars, whining sirens, and running policemen intent on capturing Ruford Jordan.

SEVEN

In the dining room the next week, Abby faced Patience, Strong, and Carl Lee with a look of anguish and helplessness that spread like malignant sorrow across her young features.

Abby's pecan-brown face had lost its exuberance. Even the deep dimples which would play themselves into a delightful grin were nowhere to be seen. And the birthmark on her cheek seemed to jump out at them, like a nervous tic. Her voice lowered, her speech slowed, she moved listlessly after the Serena catastrophe, so much so that they wondered if she would ever recapture her dazzle, her infectious joy.

Abby sat wringing her hands, her head down, unable to lift the weight of the discovery from her shoulders, to scrub it from her mind. What had happened to her Aunt Serena was one of the ugliest episodes ever to hit Ponca City or the state of Oklahoma. And Abby had been an eyewitness to the calamity. She had been the first to see what had happened.

"Oh, honey," Patience said, but the words sank down to the basement of her being and rambled around. Patience's hair had turned completely white overnight.

"She was a human being. An example of decency," said Carl Lee, his face knotted up like wood wounds on a tree trunk.

"Why? Why? Why?" repeated Abby over and over again. Her

gaze wandered vacuously around the room; shivers blinked in her eyes. "I'd looked forward to seeing her. To hearing her talk to me, to hearing her sing. Why? Why? Why?" she mumbled, a stuck record.

Her father carefully folded up the newspaper with the screaming headline and tucked it away from sight.

"Abby," her father said, "we remember Serena's song, remember how she sang to you when rocking you to sleep. Remember how she sang when busy." A tortured wind hummed disturbingly in Strong's voice. The horror haunted him.

Patience nodded her head in agreement. A crisp despair lingered in her eye.

Carl Lee gave an anguished sigh of commiseration.

"And to think it happened just before the day I was going to talk to her. Maybe I could have saved her," Abby said.

"If only we had known," said Patience, wrapped in her own quilt of pain.

"Why didn't I know?" asked Abby. Anguish lay low, sharpening knives in her stomach.

"No way in the world you could have predicted this," said Carl Lee. A fury ticked in the dark clock of his face.

"How could he hurt someone so wonderful?"

"Demented," said Strong.

"Mad," agreed Patience.

"There is no defense for madness," added Strong. "Not understanding. Not love. No amount of either is a match for madness."

"He's where all mad folks should be, locked up," concluded Patience. "Just as there is good in the world, so there is unspeakable evil."

"He won't ever be released, I'm sure," said Carl Lee with a shudder.

"But you've got other wonderful memories," Strong reminded Abby.

"Yes, plenty of those. She was a good aunt," said Abby. "But I was not a good niece. I couldn't stop this from happening, don't you see?" She looked at them all with anguish shadowing her face.

"Maybe you were the best friend she had, besides your mother," said Strong.

"I failed. I failed in the worst possible way."

"I don't believe you're being fair to yourself," said Strong.

"I had no time for her. If I had spent more time with her, I could've stopped what happened."

"You yourself used to complain that her husband didn't want you around. You didn't have much of a choice," said Carl Lee.

Abby's tears streamed unchecked down her face.

Carl Lee sought to comfort her by holding her hand. But to his bewilderment she snatched her hand back. Somehow, her guilt was all knotted up with her love for him. As though the time she had spent with him had been stolen from Serena.

"Leave me alone!" she screamed.

"Call me, Abby, if you need me," he said. But she did not respond.

He left.

She was as silent as swallows descending into winter. Blinded by her own grief. She did not see his ache. Deaf, she did not hear the anguish in his voice. But Strong saw and began to measure Carl Lee in a different way.

EIGHT

As she sat in the dining room quilting with Patience and Ruby Thompson, Abyssinia could hear the masculine voices of Strong and Carl Lee drift up from the cellar. The paternal jealousy that had reared its ugly head when Strong first realized Abby loved Carl Lee had been replaced by paternal concern over Abby's grief. Strong would do anything to make Abby smile again. Realizing Carl Lee might be a key to this end, he had asked the younger man to help him make pomegranate wine.

Abby looked down at the cat stretched out and purring by her feet. It was the center of attention for the sewing women.

Patience sat working, her thick, now snow white hair braided in two shiny ropes that draped neatly to her plump shoulders. Her eyes often penetrated Abby's face as if it were through her eyes that she listened, and she always seemed to be listening to Abby these days. Patience stitched careful seams in her cup-and-saucer quilt.

Ruby Thompson, the church missionary, peered through her bifocals as she sewed the underground-railroad quilt. She stitched almost as impatiently as she was known to speak. She pushed a strand back from her finely textured gray hair and tied it into the bun that sat on the top of her head. Her efforts to keep all her hair in the bun were in vain, for little wisps of busy gray hairs danced around her ears and thin face.

Abby watched the two older women sew. Her face seemed ashen

brown, a contrast to her cotton dress tiered in dimensions of blue-lilac, lavender, purple, fuchsia, burgundy. The cheerful colors of her dress only served to make her agonized face stand out more.

The horror of what had happened to Serena had left its mark on her mind like a scar. This devastation showed in her expression. It slowed her movement when she lapsed into memory. Hers was an agitation of the spirit.

The reluctant Abby was encouraged by Patience to join in the sewing. They needed her, Patience claimed, to supply her secret quilting stitch that could not be unraveled.

Patience and Ruby both insisted that Abby had to personally tack each patch. Now Abby sat with them and worked on her own rainbow quilt.

Suddenly a furry ball plopped into her lap, and she looked down and saw her cat settling onto a quilt patch. Abby gently removed the cat, who continued to complain for attention with pleading purrs from her station on the floor.

As Abby sewed her rainbow quilt, she thought about how she had found the cat on one of her recent walks through the woods.

On days when she could not wash her sad thoughts about Serena from her mind, Abby would take long walks into the countryside, where she would stoop to wonder over the cream-colored lilies and the purple fireweed, look up to admire the twittering of skylarks and, if she was fortunate, the braid of the rainbow.

During one of these journeys into the countryside, after she had passed all signs of people and paved roads, she thought she heard a soft meow. It sounded as if it was coming from a bush of heather to the right of where she was standing. Still she was not certain, for the bush was full of song sparrows. There were so many song sparrows perching that she suspected the birds of guarding something there in the bush. A full bloom of starflowers covered the shrub with a pink halo, and the birds. Then one bird dressed up in plumped-up streaked brown plumage started a song with three identical notes that warbled into a lovely melody.

Again she thought she heard a meow intruding between the birds' melody. What was a cat doing around birds?

She moved stealthily forward. The song birds watched her approach and fluttered away to a more distant bush, where they seemed to take close note of her movements.

To Abby's amazement, when she parted the bush, there huddled the most striking kitten she had ever seen, curled up on a sparrow's nest of grass and straw. The creature was a warm ball of ruddy brown fur with eyes that mesmerized. It purred serenely and looked up at her inquiringly.

Abby wondered where its mother was. There was no sign of any other kitten. Had she been part of a large litter which had been abandoned? It was a mystery, for the cat was at least three or four weeks old; it had passed the early period of blindness, and its coat shone sleek and healthy. But where was its mother?

"Hey, little kitty, kitty, kitty," Abby called. She stooped down and picked up the kitten and cuddled it, stroking its back, moving its legs, carefully examining the sinewy muscles and pliant spine beneath the fur. She found no maimed tissue and no broken bones.

The now quiet birds peered curiously at her. But they seemed to be content with her handling of their precious treasure.

"*Meow,*" the cat repeated as she curled herself up into a neat ball, squinched her eyes, and purred deeply, vibrating her kitten motor against Abby's hands.

By some mystical signal, the birds delivered a new song from their elevated perch on the distant bush. The same high notes, followed by a chorus. Then Abby saw the flutter of wings.

* * *

She had taken the kitten home and given it catnip once a week in a saucer of milk she set out on the back porch.

Today the kitten sat at Abby's feet meowing, begging for attention. To entertain her, Abby crushed a sheet of newspaper into a ball. Dipping her hand into her sewing basket, Abby selected bright orange thread, which she tied around the paper ball. Now the cat scrambled around the room with her toy, almost tripping Carl Lee as he entered the room with Strong.

The two men had tested the homemade pomegranate wine and were now bringing the decanter and glasses into the room for the sewing women. Then the men sat down and joined the women as they all sipped the wine. Carl Lee and Strong scrutinized the quilt designs, enchanted with the meticulous detail of threads.

Now Abby was telling Ruby Thompson and the men how she had discovered the cat. The women patted the creature, remarked on her grace, stroked her fur.

The contented cat squinched her eyes and purred.

"What did you name her?" asked Ruby Thompson.

"Opia," responded Abby. "For serenity."

"Tell us again when you found her," asked Patience.

"She was born while starflowers were in bloom."

"When?"

"It was the time when the first stalks of corn began to wilt."

From these spare facts the quilters knew certain things—outrageous color had been present when Opia was born, color locked in the pink, yellow, blue, and green bloom of the starflower. And the cornstalks had been bowed, their golden ears of corn already harvested, stalks waiting to be plowed under the red Oklahoma earth. Late October. Opia was born toward the end of harvest.

"You should have named her Star Eyes. See how her eyes shine like stars," said Carl Lee.

"Or Golden Eyes. Look at the deep gold in them. Shaped like almonds," said Strong.

"What color would you call her?" Carl Lee asked.

"The color of chocolate brown, red-ticked," said Patience.

"Dark Oklahoma clay color," said Strong.

"Maybe the color of Egyptian red," said Abby.

"Egyptian red?" murmured Ruby Thompson.

"I could have called her Bastet. That was what the Egyptians called the cat they made into a goddess. In the ancient Egyptian days, the cats guarded their food supply, the granaries, and kept away rats and mice."

"Why, cats do that today. I don't need a mousetrap with my cat. Mice don't stay if you have a cat," said Ruby.

"But did you know that when a cat died in Egypt, there was a period of great mourning?" asked Abby.

"You mean they had a wake for the cat?" Ruby stopped sewing to stare in wonder at the cat.

"That's about the size of it. The cat was considered sacred. In fact it was mummified just like the rest of Egyptian royalty. "

"What would happen if you killed one?" wondered Strong.

"You could be put to death. Look how long her body is," said Abby.

"Yes, she does look different from other cats," Carl Lee agreed.

"And her whiskers, how long."

"Very sensitive, cats' whiskers."

The women reached to stroke the cat. Opia gave each one her attention, but she would always end up at Abby's quilt, purring softly some cat song deep in her throat. She watched Abby's slow hands create a quilt of rainbow color.

Now and then Abby would study the cat quietly, remembering wilted stalks and flowers just before they lost their bloom, the time flowers bloom their brightest.

NINE

For the past few nights Abby had been haunted by a recurrent dream. As she drifted into sleep, a floating feeling claimed her body. It was then that she sank into the dream like a pebble cast into a lake.

The dream began the same way each time. Abby sat in the front pew of the church and watched a woman march down the aisle in a white veil and a white gown. Abby heard ebbing laughter and wedding music. But to her consternation the face of the bride was hidden from Abby's view. She shifted her body so that she could make out the face, but it did no good.

The spoken portion of the ceremony was so muted Abby could only pick up the rhythm of the sounds. She could not distinguish the minister's words. She listened for clues from the pew in which she sat. She thought she might overhear a name mentioned in whispers by the well wishers who came to celebrate the wedding. But no mouth uttered a name.

The departing bride had reached the church doors and started down the church house steps, yet Abby still did not know who the bride was. She ran after the shadowed face. She rained rice on the newlyweds, trying to steal a glance.

Abby tossed and turned in bed, still dreaming, still seeking. But the secret of the retreating face was circling, circling like the rippling rings on the surface of the lake. The secret features of the missing face were washing, washing in waves away from the cast stone. The ripples moved farther and farther away from the stone just as Abby moved into morning.

Wide awake, she pondered the dream. The elusive woman in the veil and gown disturbed her. She looked out her window at the glancing light of daybreak. She could not grasp the meaning of the dream. Her mind was like the rings of water on the lake. She had drifted away from the stone, her center. Drifted away from some deeper knowledge, some silent part of herself that would not be voiced.

Again she slept. She slept so long that when she did finally awaken, her mother and father had gone on their ways to work at their respective shops.

She took a bottle of milk out of the refrigerator and poured the liquid into a glass. She drew the glass to her lips, expecting the cool, sweet taste of milk, but the liquid was sour. Kept too long. At least it would make clabber biscuits.

Later she moved outside to take in the wash and stubbed her toe on a rock. The aching toe throbbed all morning, and she had to hop around on one foot. Then she broke a canning jar washing dishes. Splinters of glass covered the floor. She swept the sharp pieces into a pile and, taking a wedge of cardboard, scooted them up then dumped them in the trash can. Peeling potatoes for the evening supper, she noticed the spuds were soft and had begun to sprout.

Before she knew it, it was early afternoon. She hastily. brushed her hair, took up her stitching, and went to the porch to wait for Carl Lee.

He was later than usual. He stomped his way along, his head down, his hands jammed in his pocket. . . . He kicked the dust up in angry red puffs around his sneakers. Abby got up and walked to him. At the gate his eyes, it seemed to her, were like still water.

"Carl Lee, what's the matter?"

"I have to leave home." His voice caught in his throat.

"Leave home? What are you talking about?" Abby wondered, puzzled.

"I have to leave home."

"Just get up and leave? But why? Where will you go?"

"Don't know," Carl Lee began. The words lingered in the air, then died.

"What happened?" asked Abby.

Carl Lee looked up to the top branch of the plum tree.

When he did not answer, she said, "You can tell me."

He opened his mouth, but his voice was gone. Her soul sank as she felt pain scraping her heart.

"What happened?" she repeated, tugging at his shirt.

"Something between me and my daddy." His voice shattered into jagged bits.

"What was it?"

He looked down at his dusty shoes. She had to keep him talking. She could feel his need, how desperately he wanted to tell her, but his voice would not cooperate.

"What about school? What about Langston?" she wondered.

"I'm taking a leave. A short leave. I'll find a place soon and be back in school."

"But where? When?"

"I intend to finish school!" The veins in his neck became tight ropes.

"Where will you go and where will you stay, Carl Lee?" Abby throbbed with pain, pain that darted back and forth from her injured toe to her aching head.

He looked steadily at her. "I'll pay my way. I'll finish school." He wanted to say more, but he swallowed the rest of his words.

"Don't go," she whispered.

She was close to him. Her lips wanted to lend their sweetness to him for one moment, the sweetness she drank from his eyes. Just for one moment.

Her heart pounded faster and faster. She came even closer. So close she felt the rough fabric of his jeans. She was all caramel custard in his arms. When he held her, her bones dissolved to cream.

He kissed her. When she caught her breath, he was gone.

TEN

On the porch swing Abby kept the new novel closed. In the distance she heard the cicadas sawing their musical legs together. Sighing deeply, she listened futilely for the birdsong that haunted her every now and then. Hearing nothing from him, she studied the butterflies fluttering over the porches and cars. It was an unusual, translucent day.

She thought about Carl Lee. Missed him. Every day she waited to see his long, tall body strutting toward her. But he did not come. Her days were topsy-turvy, capriciously unfaithful to her. Sometimes the combination of her grief over Serena's death and the absence of Carl Lee weighed her down like a heavy stone.

Inside the house her mother and Ruby Thompson had begun quilting.

"Yoo-hoo, Abby, come give us a hand," Patience called.

"All right," Abby agreed willingly. Now she was anxious to do anything to help mute the troubled feelings that plagued her. Perhaps the quilting could take her mind off Serena and Carl Lee. She was curious about what had happened between Carl Lee and his father. Whatever it was was terrible enough to make him leave home.

As she took her place with the women, their attention was

demanded by the cat purring by the windowsill. Abby smiled slightly in spite of her troubles.

The cat watched chee-chee birds play in the redbud tree and swayed her long tail from side to side.

"Opia sometimes watches the birds for hours at a time," Abby said.

"But she never chases them," remarked Patience.

"Strange behavior for a cat," said Ruby.

"Opia is her own cat, that's for sure," agreed Patience. "That cat, I believe, has her own set of cat rules."

"If human females had rules to live by, I wonder what they would be like?" Abby wondered. "I mean, how are we to carry ourselves around a man, a special man? How does a person act when she's . . ." She hesitated.

"In love?" Patience finished the sentence for her.

"It's not always easy to know what to do, what to say. I didn't know what to say to Carl. Lee when he was so upset about leaving home." A wave of sadness gripped her. "And I haven't seen him for almost two weeks." She sighed heavily. "I wonder why he had to leave his own house?"

"Youngsters do get too big for their britches," said Ruby.

"Not Carl Lee," Abby defended.

"Seems to be a fine young man," said Patience.

"Too big for his britches, I bet you. His daddy might have wanted to be the only rooster in the henhouse," Ruby figured.

"Wasn't any hen in that house." Patience spoke softly.

"But to be put out of your own house and to be angry with someone as close as your father!" Abby remembered the time Strong had slapped her. How uncentered she had felt. "How could I have helped Carl Lee?" she asked.

"I don't know. Maybe there was nothing you could have done."

"The main thing is to be the best person you know how to be. Love yourself first, then you can love and respect others," said Patience.

"Now I can go along with that," replied Ruby. "Take Mrs. Wright over on the next street. She could sure use some of that advice, Patience. I think she has a mistaken notion of what being a woman means."

"Now that's the truth," agreed Patience.

"That woman carries the whole world on her shoulders. She's the breadwinner, the bread baker, the housekeeper, the Laundromat, the doormat."

"A doormat?" Patience stopped stitching and puckered her brow. "I think a woman should be wary of a man who asks her to be his bridge over troubled water and his anchor in a storm. A bridge is something you walk over to get to somewhere else. An anchor is at the bottom of the sea. And we know what a doormat is."

"I hear that all Mr. Wright does is lay around at home and fuss at her for not working faster. I tell you it's like the woman was a mule. He's riding her into the ground. And she's plowing along like that's the way it's supposed to be," said Ruby.

"I heard she was sick a while back," said Abby.

"Flat on her back," said Patience, who had begun to stitch again.

"I guess you'd be sick, too, if you slaved as hard as that woman and never heard a kind word," snapped Ruby. "He's waiting for something, sure as I'm sitting here," she concluded.

"What's that?" wondered Abby, tacking a meticulous straight line down her quilt.

"Maybe for her to lie down with a stroke, helpless," offered Ruby.

"Then she couldn't wait on him, cook his dinner. What good would she be to him then?" asked Abby.

"She ought to ask herself who he's got his eye on. Waiting for her to fall so somebody else can take her place. You work a mule till it won't go anymore, then you get yourself another one. I know some folks who are the same way about a car. They hot-rod and neglect it until it won't run another mile. Then they go shopping for the latest style," said Ruby. "He just might be looking to break in a younger model."

"Wonder why she let herself be used that way?" said Patience.

"Mystery to me. Some folks just don't have any mother wit." Ruby ripped out an imperfect seam.

"Maybe she thinks she's worthless," said Abby. "Maybe she stays too tired to think. She ought to take a break and go somewhere and contemplate the situation."

"That makes a whole lot of sense," said Patience.

"Heard he added insult to injury," Ruby added, tightening her mouth.

"What's that?" Abby asked.

"Hit her for frying his chicken too hard," said Ruby.

"His chicken?" said Patience.

"The chicken she bought with her hard-earned scrubbing-other-folks'-floors money, no doubt. What do you do with something after you've used it?" Ruby challenged.

They did not answer.

"You throw it away," she concluded. "No woman should let anybody use her up like that."

"Maybe she can't break away," said Patience.

"Where I come from there's no such thing as 'can't' and 'couldn't.' 'Can't' got killed and they ran 'couldn't' out of town on a rail," quipped Ruby.

"Abby," said Patience, "the main thing you have to remember when it comes to a mate is that you must love a man who has enough strength to treat you gentle.

"Your daddy knew from the very start that I was in love with two. I told him, 'Honey, I'm in love with two—me and you.'" She chuckled. "You should have seen the look on his face!"

"Daddy's always been in love with you," smiled Abby.

"We have a few problems, but mostly we iron them out. Consideration. Most of the time we're considerate of each other.

"The first man who laid the fire of love at the feet of a woman perhaps singed himself in the giving. Yet I believe Strong offered me the trembling star of fire without flinching.

"From that fire bloomed Abby."

Patience smiled cryptically at Abyssinia. Abby, thinking of Carl Lee, blushed in affirmation as Patience's voice droned on: "When the rain fell in torrents against the roof, his would be a voice that would not leak. His warmth, the binding in my quilt. That's what I looked for in a husband."

ELEVEN

The novel toppled out of Abby's grasp. Was that Carl Lee she saw coming down the road? She squinted her eyes at the approaching figure. Past the grove of plum trees he strolled. It was Carl Lee, all right. Joy danced in her toes as she sprang up from her seat. Arms stretched out, she ran to meet him.

He wore a calico cotton shirt, opened at the chest and tied in a knot at the waist. The shirt exposed a dark brown ripple of stomach muscle contrasting with the blue in his blue jeans and sneakers.

"You didn't leave town!" Her old smile welcomed him.

They stood searching for changes in each other. He seemed taller to her.

"Told you I'd make out okay." He wanted to brush her lips with his.

She said, "Oh, I missed you at school. I missed you, Carl Lee."

"I was gone a few weeks," he answered. "And you'd think I'd been away a year."

"Where were you?"

"Working and finally getting moved. I took a room with Widow Holly." His arms seemed more muscular now. Able to hold her even tighter.

"How do you pay your rent?"

"I work, girl!" Now he was teasing her.

"Doing what?"

"Washing dishes. Mowing lawns. Moving furniture. Any kind of work I can get. Want to go for a walk?"

"Why not?" she said, her eyes gleaming with welcome.

He took her hand, and they started walking down the road.

By habit, they turned into the cornfield. When they realized they were in the place where Serena and her husband used to come, Carl Lee held her hand tighter.

"How'd we end up here?" she asked in a trembling voice.

"Oh, my God," he said, "I'm sorry. I wanted us to be alone and now . . ."

"Hold me," she asked.

He held her tight, soothing her with long strokes of his hand. How she needed him. He drew her down to the ground beside him.

They touched the melody of that trembling music that had begun far back in the corridors of time. Of that flamboyant dance whose steps they had never been taught. Yet, as if controlled by some ancient memory, they moved instinctively, rocking each other, their bodies swaying to meet the warmth that loosened the rigid bones of their spines and softened them into butter.

When their tongues began to search each other's lips for their gentle wine, Abby whispered, pulling back from him ever so slightly, "Carl Lee, I feel so dizzy, and I need you so much. Steady me." Her voice whispered with passion, and she was helplessly filled with a tender yearning whose dimensions had grown so that their depth and height frightened her. But, moving closer to him, she clung to the source of this yearning more desperately, fitting herself securely into the circle of his arms.

He pulled her head back with one strong, gentle hand. "Abby,"

Carl Lee murmured, his dark, flecked pupils, shimmering with luster and light, melting into the cocoa ovals of her eyes. "And I need you. You are my dusk and my dawn. The warm wine of my happiness."

He held her tighter in his embrace. Their bodies flamed like two glowing candles. But when they touched, they trembled as though the fire was not hot enough. As though they wished for something warmer than flame. A spiritual combustion. Something hot enough to forge everlasting tomorrows. Some blood-singed bond as permanent and tenacious as the promise Adam made to Eve.

They kissed again, stoking the coals that had stolen into their fingers, legs, hearts, turning their very veins to furnaces of frenzied ecstasy. They gasped and sighed. The sweet ache was almost too much to bear, the burning heat between them growing more immediate and intense.

His hands searched places forbidden, stroked warm secrets. When she was sure she would be burned alive, she pulled his hand away.

The wind licked her skin in cool baptism.

"No," she said, "don't."

"Please," he begged.

"No, Carl Lee."

"I won't hurt you."

"I know, but no."

He locked his arms around her, and soon they slept, with her head buried in his chest.

The dying cornstalks rustled menacingly, and Abby awakened abruptly, sitting up and immediately remembering Serena and that the last time she had seen her alive was in this cornfield. She opened her mouth to scream, but the next sound she heard was thunder hollering through the sky and lightning skipping after it.

"Carl Lee! Carl Lee!" She shook him.

"What?" he said dreamily.

"A storm is coming!"

"Sure enough?" He sat up and took the sky in at a glance. In the distance thunder grumbled.

"Come on." They stood up and began to run for the abandoned corn shed.

"Hurry." Suddenly water fell from the sky in fat drops, leaving small scabs in the cinnamon dust as it splattered against the warm earth. It soaked the wilting cornstalks so that they drooped and bowed even more. The young couple neared the shed, a welcome sight for shelter.

Safe inside, they sat huddled together. The weather played upon the tin roof as one would play upon a musical instrument. The wind blew corn husks, leaves, and branches across the top in spangles. Then, as the rains increased, the falling of the drops created an orchestra of small drums, cymbals, tambourines.

"The cold weather's setting in," said Carl Lee.

Abby nodded her head in agreement, shuddered, and huddled closer to him.

TWELVE

Snowflakes whispered over the ground. A breeze sent little flurries slipping across the road. Suddenly the last rays of the sun pierced the low-hanging clouds, backlighting the sky in bougainvillea and setting the encrusted snow with silver jewels.

Abby looked up at the January sky casting cold everywhere, accepting the gathering swirls of snow clouds. Then she leaned over her shovel and continued clearing the walk that led all the way to the front steps of the house, preparing for the guests coming to New Year's dinner.

As she worked, she heard the whisper of wind teasing across the stippled snow, snow printed with the tooth marks of tires, rubber boots, and snow chains, and with the scooped-out iron mouth of her shovel.

She nodded to the neighbors whose overindulgence the night before showed in their red eyes and tired faces. Her own mother and father, as was their custom, stayed up until the new year was officially in, then slept late on New Year's Day.

Abby waved at the children making snowmen and scooping snow into bowls for snow ice cream.

Now the winter clouds curled up and churned the atmosphere with flurries of whiteness. The bright snow fell and gradually built up into drifts.

Off the edges of rooftops, icicles, sharp and pointed, dipped and hung, crinkly, from outer windowsills. Children, upon raising a window, could easily pop frozen drippings into sugar water and drink a glass of cool sweet water.

Abby's heart sank as she remembered that when she was younger Serena and she would scoop the snow into a bowl and stir cream, vanilla, and sugar into a creation of quick ice cream, granularly textured and welcome to the tongue.

She watched the children carry their bowls of snow into the house. Eating the snow ice cream in front of a bubbling fire was a winter ritual. She imagined the children savoring the spooned cream and staring into the flames like they were their own grandparents, letting the ice cream linger on the palate, hesitating to eat the last spoonful.

She put the shovel at the side of the house after she had finished clearing the snow and went back inside to baste the turkey baking in the oven with raisins, orange juice, and honey mixed with its drippings. Then she stirred up the ingredients for homemade rolls—yeast, flour, butter, a dash of sugar, a sprinkling of salt, and eggs.

She let the dough rise, and an hour or so later she saw that the rolls had doubled in bulk. She punched the dough down and rolled it out, cutting perfect rolls with a jelly glass, dipping them in melted butter and lining the bread pans.

She set the rolls on top of the stove to rise fluffy again. She scrubbed the kitchen floor shining clean while Opia sat curled up on the living room couch, smelling the delicious aroma of turkey baking in fruit and honey juices.

When she had finished scrubbing the floor, the cat bounded out of the chair and romped through the kitchen. Abby pretended to fuss at Opia, who scampered out of her way.

When the floor was dry, she set the table. A bright red

tablecloth, embroidered orange and pink flowers on the napkins. Frosted glasses. Antique silver-rimmed plates.

There was a knock at the door. She opened it to find Carl Lee looking down at her with a broad smile.

He held two crocks of apple cider, one tucked under each long arm. He greeted her with a warm kiss.

"My, this place smells like Christmas, New Year's, and Thanksgiving all rolled into one." He wrinkled his nose and sniffed. Then he looked down at her. "And you," he said, "smell like the first dew on a spring rose." He tickled her chin. She thanked him for the apple cider and gave him a playful shove.

"Take the cat," she said, "and fetch wood from the woodshed."

Carl Lee and Opia waded through the snow and brought back logs and kindling for the fireplace.

By the time the fire had begun to blaze, snap, and crackle, her mother and father had got dressed, and Ruby, the missionary, had arrived.

Ruby brought string beans and corn pudding. Strong heated up the pot of Hoppin' John he had made the night before. Patience brought out a jar of cha-cha relish.

"A brand new year, a brand new season for the soul. And hope for the heart!" said Strong as they sat down together to begin the meal.

"A happy, wholesome New Year," Patience exclaimed.

"Shall we say the blessing?" offered Strong. "Oh, Lord, bless this food, bless this meat. Come on, children, let's eat. Pass the cha-cha. My wife knows cha-cha is my favorite relish. I relish this relish!" he said, taking a healthy portion and winking at Patience.

"Least it was a short blessing," commented Ruby agreeably. She poured apple cider from a pitcher into the frosted glasses.

Carl Lee laughed his deep laugh and seemed to stretch even

taller than his six feet six inches seated next to the petite Abby.

Strong defended himself as he turned to Ruby. "Never could understand what kind of Christian could spoil good food by taking an hour to preach a sermon at the dinner table. Even the Lord says there's a time and place for everything. The pulpit is the place you preach. The table is the place you eat."

"Strong, you're my kind of Christian man! Pass the turkey," said Ruby.

"I admit there are certain parts of the Bible I heed to more than others," said Strong.

"What about turning the other cheek?" Carl Lee asked.

"You see, the Lord's not crazy," Strong began. "He knows the world is made up of all kinds of people. For some folks turning the other cheek might work. You slap them on one side of the face and they turn to let you smack them on the other side. Me? I never did like playing windmill with my head. For people like me the Lord stuck another passage in the good book: 'An eye for an eye and a tooth for a tooth!' And ain't I a good Christian?"

"You sure are," agreed Patience. Turning to Carl Lee she added, "He's the most fair man I know."

"What about you, Mrs. Jackson? If you had a set of rules to live by, what would you include in them?" asked Carl Lee.

"What would you call them?" asked Abby.

Patience thought a moment. "I'd call them Laws for Lovers. Let me think . . . I think ten rules will do." She began ticking the laws off on her fingers.

"One. Thou shalt let nobody walk all the thread out of thy carpet.

"Two. Thou shalt turn no friend away.

"Three. Thou shalt not bow down to sorrow.

"Four. Thou shalt love thy own image first.

"Five. Thou shalt respect each other as daughter, mother, sister, son, father, brother.

"Six. Thou shalt use wisdom in business.

"Seven. Thou shalt be giving in love.

"Eight. Thou shalt cherish all children as thy own.

"Nine. Thou shalt make thy dreams real.

"Ten. Thou shalt keep thy face toward the sun."

Strong was the first to respond. "Thou shalt keep thy face toward the sun! I can deal with that," he said, looking at Abby.

The cat meowed from her station on the couch. Carl Lee held his breath, thinking about his own problems with his father. He tightened his clasp on Abby's hand for a moment. They smiled at each other.

THIRTEEN

Music from the stereo played softly in Abby's living room as she and Carl Lee helped each other with their homework.

"I think you've got this algebra problem wrong," said Carl Lee. "You've written commutative law of addition when you mean associative law."

"Let me see." She took the paper from him and looked at her answer. "You're right. Oversight on my part. Somehow, when I'm doing algebra, I need full concentration. One part of me is listening to the music and the other part of me is working the problem."

"Music makes me do whatever I'm doing better," said Carl Lee.

"Depends on what it is for me," said Abby. "I can sew to music. Clean house to music. I can prepare my herbs to music."

"Now, take track. If I could just convince my coach to blast music from the loudspeakers whenever I run, I bet I could do the four-forty in thirty seconds flat."

"I believe it," said Abby. "You're poetry in motion when you're running."

"Now that's the truth," quipped Carl Lee.

"Where's your modesty, boy?" asked Abby.

"In my feet."

"And they don't have a lick of shame either. Leave everybody in the dust."

"Why, if I just had me some music on the track, I could run a mile in three minutes!"

"Back to the work at hand," said Abby, looking at the algebra page again. "I'm the one going into medicine, how come you know so much about math?"

He shrugged. "Well rounded. Why do you know so much about forensics? Answer me that."

"Osmosis. Being around you so much and knowing how you think."

"Ready to hear this week's argument for the public debate?"

"Uh-huh." She settled back in her chair, ready to applaud and point out areas that could be strengthened.

Then Marian Anderson's voice came filtering through the room, just as Carl Lee opened his mouth to speak.

"Sometimes I feel like a motherless child . . ."

"Listen to that," remarked Abby. "Now there's a voice. See what I mean about music inter—"

Carl Lee's face screwed into a frown. "Turn it off," he shouted. More quietly he said, "I mean, could you turn it off?"

"What?" she asked. "I thought you could do anything to mu—"

"Please turn it off," he repeated.

"That's Marian Anderson," she answered, astounded.

"I know who it is. Still, would you turn it off?"

"If you insist," she said, still not understanding.

"I'm sorry," he said, "but if you don't mind, turn to another station."

"All right." She got up, walked to the stereo, and turned the knob.

"The problem with songs," he concluded, "is that even after

they're gone, they're still there, the melody still nagging at your mind."

She searched the dial past the classical stations and the country-and-western stations. "What would you like to hear?"

"Oh, I don't know. Anything but that song."

"How about some jazz?"

"Uh-huh."

She turned the radio knob until she found the station that played only jazz music. Miles Davis blew gold from a horn.

"What was it about the song?" she asked, sitting down next to him.

"I wish I'd had a mother; then maybe my father would not have been so mean."

"One time I wished I had another father," Abby admitted, "when a tornado tore down his barbershop and he deserted us."

"That might have helped some, too. But since I didn't have a mother it never occurred to me to wish for another father. I always thought a mother would have made a difference."

"What was your father like?"

"Mean as nails."

"Mean?"

"Mean and mad all the time. He stored his anger inside, and every now and then it came spilling out, mostly on me. I was probably the only person he felt he could express his anger to."

"What was he angry about?"

"About everything. At least it seemed that way to me when I was growing up."

"I heard that your mother died when you were born, but I never really knew about . . ."

"He didn't have my mother there to soften things for him—to be his cushion. In a way maybe that was good. He might have made me and her miserable instead of my mother making all our lives better. When he came home he wanted things as he wanted them."

"He worked downtown, didn't he?"

"Yeah. Chief cook and dishwasher for the Ponca City Hotel. I went to work with him one day. He was going to take me Christmas shopping when he got a break for lunch. I heard his young boss, younger than he was, call him a cucker-headed ignorant nigger."

"How did you feel?"

"Like killing his boss. In my eight-year-old way. With one of the knives left on the counter. My father didn't say a word. I felt ashamed then. For the first time I felt ashamed of my own father. Because he wouldn't do anything."

"What could he have done?"

"I don't know. But that's how I felt. Ashamed! Over the years his wrath grew. He used to leave a list of things for me to do, and if one of them was done incorrectly, he would curse up a blue streak."

"How awful for you."

"I hated to see him come home."

"Did he beat you?"

"Often."

"How terrible!"

"I remember one of the last chores I did in the house." Carl Lee stood up and began pacing the floor.

"Well, before my father left for work he told me to wash the windows. I rinsed them several times with apple cider vinegar water and dried them to a perfect shine, I thought. That afternoon when my father came home and sat down across from me at the table, I watched the pounding of the veins in his temple, the frown tugging around his mouth. I knew he was ready to go into one of his rages."

"What was he angry about?"

"He was staring at the kitchen windows."

"I thought you said you did a perfect job."

"Almost. Not quite. The windows in the front of the house sparkled. But in the rear of the house, in the kitchen where we sat with the last rays of the sun highlighting the smallest smudge, a few thin dull streaks scooted across the panes."

"What did he do?"

"He dumped salt into my corn and told me to eat it. Punishment for not cleaning the windows right."

Abby grimaced. "Salt. How much?"

"About half a cup."

"Did you get sick?"

"No. I have a stomach of iron. The sickest thing was that I hated my father and wanted to love him."

"Was that just before you went away last summer?"

"Yeah."

"So that's why."

"No."

"No? What was it? What made you leave?"

"I don't like to talk about it."

"You can tell me. You can tell me anything."

He stopped pacing up and down the floor and sat down beside her. "I know, Abby, but thinking about it takes me to a time I'd just as soon forget, to a place I won't like to visit." He paused. "Anyway," he said, seeing she expected an answer, "it's not pretty. There's nothing pretty about it."

"What was it?" she asked again softly.

"It was. . ." He looked away from her concerned face.

The words rushed out of him. "It happened late that night before I saw you. Before I told you I had to leave home. I had forgotten to take out the garbage. My father came home in a state of rage. I don't know what they had done to him downtown. I was sound asleep when he threw the covers off me and told me to get up.

"'Get up, get up from there!' he shouted. "I've told you about leaving garbage out. You'll have rats walking round here big as people, gnawing down the house and eating every crumb I bring in here. Get up, I say!'

"I crawled sleepy-eyed out of bed. And I smelled the aroma of something like chitlins or ham cooking in the kitchen.

"I heard my father say, 'I'm going to give you a meal you'll never forget.' I pulled on my pants and stumbled into the kitchen after him.

"'Sit down,' he ranted.

"On the table was a linen napkin that had PONCA HOTEL embroidered on it; a silverware setting of a knife, fork, and spoon; and, in the center, space for a dish. My father took the lid off the pot and placed the meat on a dish, then set it down before me.

"I jumped up, upsetting the chair.

"'No, no, Daddy.'

"'I said sit down and eat!' he insisted.

"'No!' I screamed, staring at the beady dead eyes of the rat on the plate, its tail hanging over the rim. I refused to sit down. I was terror stricken.

"'Sit down, goddammit!' my father said.

"'You can't make me!'

"'You trying to sass me, boy? You must be smelling yourself.'

"He moved toward me and tried to push me into the seat, but I pushed back. We struggled, wrestling, fighting on the floor until my father got the best of me.

"When I came to, my father sat over me with a double-barrel shotgun. 'Now sit down and eat!' he demanded.

"To get up and walk away, Abby, was the hardest thing I had ever done. With the gun at my back, my body numb, my very soul bruised, I stood up. Somewhere I found an invisible rod of steel and iron to hold on to, and I stood up, straightened my back, and walked away."

"And you've been walking tall ever since," said Abby.

She looked at him with respect, a proud glow in her eyes. For a long time they sat quietly, not saying anything. He reached over and took her hand.

"Abby," he finally said, "I'm going to a track conference tomorrow. I'll be gone a week."

"A full week?"

He nodded his head yes and stood up to leave. "You behave yourself while I'm gone, you hear?"

"Please hurry back home, Carl Lee," she said. "Hurry."

FOURTEEN

Abby was immensely touched by Carl Lee's confiding in her about the problems with his father. So much so that the evening of sharing left a strain on her. She was exhausted.

After saying good night to Carl Lee, she took a steaming shower and fell straight to sleep the minute her head hit the pillow.

As the darkest part of night descended on Ponca, Abby's cat climbed out on the picket fence, her coat haloing her body in powder-puff silk. She purred in her softest voice and waited, quietly swishing her sleek tapering tail from side to side.

Before long, the full moon crept with silver feet across the sky's terrain, so carefully and deftly that it avoided stepping on the stars, which had begun their bold and nightly bloom.

The blooming stars fascinated Opia. A satisfied "meow" shimmered from the cat's throat like a subtle, appreciative response to some perfect artistic performance.

The sound of the cat's meowing awakened Abby. Through her window she gazed up at the blossoming stars and smiled sleepily at Opia, who was subdued and charmed by the sparkles of starlight falling over the Oklahoma countryside.

"Opia," she called softly. The cat moved skillfully along the fence until it was adjacent to the bedroom window. Abby reached over from her bed and raised the window a few inches. Opia bounded through the opening and landed on top of the nine-patch quilt.

Abby stroked the cat and wondered about the stars. The stars are always blossoming brightly, even when the sun outdazzles their diamond light so that they appear invisible during the day. Even when storms obscure their shining victory, they're still there.

She stroked the cat and thought. Still they are there. Even when they conceal themselves in shy blue or storm gray, they bide their time, aware of their own special light. Abby and Opia studied the stars until Abby closed her eyes and slipped into a dream.

She dreamed about the wedding of Serena to Reverend Ruford Jordan. In her dream she saw Serena's white dress, witnessed the matrimonial kiss of the devout and devoted husband who had recently come to town hoping to build a church.

As they marched down the aisle, Abby could not help but think that her Aunt Serena was the best possible wife for any minister. She could sing and lead the song service for him. She knew the Bible, her favorite piece of literature.

On the other hand, Serena had never been married before. She wondered if the stranger would make the best possible husband for Serena. Why the spinster would wait until she was sixty years old to marry was the question on the tongues of all the Ponca inhabitants who witnessed the wedding. Perhaps she needed to fill the empty hole in her life left by the death of her sister, Sadonia.

Abby smiled in her sleep, because the most important thing to her was that her Aunt Serena seemed happy. Her face as she kissed her new husband was one big smile bursting at the seams with warmth and fulfillment. Serena's face was a vision of beauty.

Then, suddenly, in her dream, Abby saw Serena's face turn sad. In the sparkling eyes she saw shadows pooled. Around the lips, where a smile used to lie, was painted a pinched, bewildered frown. The melody that was wrung from her mouth now was a dirge of mourning whose notes were the shrieking despair of wounded prey, a snared bird. The bell of her voice was crooked. Lopsided. The sound out of tune. A cacophony of ugliness. A hideous evil lurked beside her. The false and fawning husband grew the horns of a beast. His hand grew five-fingered thorns. His eyes were fields of fire. His lips dripped brimstone. When he spoke his voice hurt her.

"Abby," he said, "there is a price to be paid for all things beautiful. Have you never noticed death on the fringes of a rose?" His voice then crescendoed in ugly laughter.

Abby clamped her hands to her ears, but still she heard his evil laughing distressing the air. She felt herself falling, falling into an abyss of terror and horror and unprecedented evil. Still the evil voice would not leave her alone.

"Have you never smelled the stench of dead carnations?"

Her knees buckled, and she doubled over in spiritual pain.

"Abyssinia, Abyssinia." A gentle voice now. Did she recognize it? She looked up into the sad eyes of Serena.

"I must return to the place I left. I cannot stay with you much longer," said Serena.

"But why, Aunt Serena? Why, why did he do it?" wondered Abby.

"Abby," the older woman spoke, "please remember this. There are some things that just are. Beside a hideous death we see a miraculous birth. Perhaps one could not exist without the other."

"But can't you stay awhile and tell me more? There is so much more I would like to know," Abby pleaded.

"And you will know," said Serena. "But remember this. When you are thirsty, go to the river. Your thirst will be quenched and your sorrow soothed. And Abby, remember Patience. Remember your own suffering. Remember me. We are all taken from the same source: pain and beauty. One is the chrysalis that gives to the other some gift that even in death creates a new dimension in life.

"Abby," she continued, "if you could catch us in the palm of your hand and hold us up to light as you would three jewels, you would see the flickering of a bright shadow. A bright shadow cast by one jewel on the other. "

When Abby awoke, her pillow was stained with tears. A question ran in circles in her mind. Bright shadow? But how much is bright? How much is shadow?

A dry thirst parched her throat. She had been tossed down into the doldrums, that dreadful depression of the spirits.

On this first day of March she had suffered a delayed-grief reaction. She had been waylaid and ambushed by a nightmare.

It had been Serena's face all the time, she bitterly realized. Serena, the invisible one in the wedding dreams that used to haunt her.

FIFTEEN

Now that the winds of March had come sweeping in and the lovely flowers had begun to poke their colored heads out of the ground, Abby became suddenly interested in a new kind of gardening, the cultivation of weeds.

The year before she had prized the yellow snapdragons, the Texas roses, and shooting stars that had bloomed in her front yard. Now she could not abide their brilliance.

She woke up early this March morning and went about her business of clipping each and every rosebud that dared show its face.

It was as though the meaning of beauty had been turned inside out for her. The tulips she tore up from their roots, bulbs and all, and tossed them in a heap. Gladioluses and flags she did not allow in her presence.

But she stayed busy watering the weeds. She tended the ugly, parasitic plants from their small shoots, which spotted the ground like baby grass, until they grew up into great water-sucking, hideous weeds.

The Ponca people could see her this morning, a gray bonnet on her head, a watering can in her hand, busily nurturing the weeds and tossing out any speck of color that was bold enough to raise its blooming head.

She gleaned tangleweeds and stuck them in her pots all over the living room. It was a harvest of beggar's-ticks, crabgrass, and crazy-weed.

Abby sowed the seeds of ragweed, sandbur, and spotted spurge. The stinkweed she especially prized. She set jars of this in all her windows.

Her neighbors worked diligently in their front yards. They watched Abby from the comers of their eyes as they prepared their soil with the rake, the hoe, and the shovel.

The neighbors broke their soil up finely, they raked and hoed and shoveled until the earth was ripe for receiving seed.

The neighbors' yards stood out in sharp contrast to the Jackson yard. The neighbors planted ornamental grass. The lush green of the grass heightened the stark white of the lilies of the valley, the gold of the everlasting marigolds, and the pink and red of roses.

When the neighbors could stand the sight of the Jackson yard no longer, they put down their rakes, hoes, and shovels and gathered around Abby's fence.

Garden workers of all variety congregated and watched her useless work of growing weeds. Grandfathers with snuff tucked in their bottom lips, who savored the smell of fresh overturned soil, came. Old women with slits slashed in their shoes for the comfort of their corns and bunions as they raked and prepared the earth came.

Young girls who wore spring cotton stockings just right for keeping their legs warm while doing yard work came. Young boys whose hair had been allowed to grow a few inches longer than normal for protection against the cool March winds while working outside came.

The gathering neighbors stared at Abby before speaking. When a delegation of them had asked Strong and Patience a few days earlier about the yard, the two parents had both responded that the yard was Abby's responsibility, and, while they did not like to see their place overrun with weeds, they did not believe in infringing upon their daughter's duties. She'll work it out, they said.

The first to speak was the missionary from the Church of God in Christ, dressed in her impeccable white. No comfortable gardening clothes for her. At her own home she even hoed and chopped in her spotless white uniform, as though she wanted to be ready for the Second Coming and did not want to be caught anywhere unprepared. In the field working with the sinners or in the field working with the crops.

"Abby, why are you watering weeds?" the missionary asked.

"You can count on weeds to always be there," she answered, looking up at her gathering audience.

"But what about the flowers?" a snuff-dipping grandfather asked.

Abby tightened her mouth. "You have to put them in the ground."

"Don't we know that well?" said a grandmother, looking at the earth gathered under her fingernails.

"Now weeds, they belong in the ground," Abby explained.

"How could a weed belong?" a long-haired boy asked.

"They come up, don't they?"

"Of course, but that's why we dig them up," a young girl replied.

"Roots and all?" asked Abby.

"You know the way," chided the grandmother.

"And they still come back?" said Abby.

"What?" asked the missionary.

Abby let out an impatient sigh. "If something keeps coming back, it means it belongs. If you can't get rid of it and you keep doing it, who's crazy?"

"Who is crazy?" wondered the crowd.

"Not me, not the weeds," said Abby. "These weeds and I get along fine. They belong here. You throw coal oil on them, they come back. You burn them up, they come back."

"Now that's the truth," the people answered.

"You mow them down, they come back," Abby continued.

"Amen," said the missionary.

"You chop them up into little bitty pieces, they come back."

"That's a fact," said a little girl in her warm cotton stockings.

"You dig them out by the roots, what do they do?"

"They come back!" said her neighbors.

"You plant something in their place and what do they do?"

"They come right on back!"

"Talking about weeds this morning. You can count on weeds . . ."

"To come on back."

"No matter what you do to destroy them, the weeds just . . ."

"Come on back!"

The people went on back to their neat front yards. They went on back to their cultured gardens of heather, jasmine, and honeysuckle. They renewed their battle against the stubborn weeds so their noses could enjoy the pungent smell of flower spice and their eyes could enjoy the civilized sight of color. But now, every time they extracted a weed from their garden, they thought of Abby and her plot of stickers. They scattered prayers with their tamed seeds as they now more gently discarded the rambling intruding weeds.

Later that evening Patience looked across the dining room table at Abyssinia and wrinkled her forehead. She knew that the sowing of weeds was the sowing of futility. The hollow side of hope. And that to cherish weeds was to cherish all that is ugly. To cherish weeds was to collect trophies of twisted triumph.

"Abby, this stew is delicious," said Strong, trying to keep the edge of concern out of his voice. "Would you please pass the sweet potatoes?"

"I think I'll have some more, too," said Patience.

"Butter?" asked Abby.

"Why, you've hardly touched your plate," observed Strong.

"Guess I wasn't that hungry," said Abby.

"We heard about your meeting with the neighbors," Patience said.

At first Abby stared at her in silence.

"Weeds are dependable," she finally said.

"Yes, they are," admitted Strong.

Patience buttered her bread and waited.

"You don't have to expect much from a weed. A weed will never let you down."

"Yes, go on," prompted Strong.

"They're not like people, who come into your life, then die and abandon you!" Abby said in a grating, painful voice.

"Would you have been happier if Serena had never loved you? Had never lived?" asked Patience.

Abby hung her head and began to weep.

"It's all right to cry," said Patience, going over to soothe her.

"Let it go," said Strong. "Tears wash away more than the film from our eyes. Tears can wash away the bitter ache from the heart."

And Abby cried a flood of tears.

SIXTEEN

Strong added bleach and detergent to the bucket of water as he prepared to mop the kitchen floor. Abby and Patience were finishing the dishes.

"Abby, did you know that Carl Lee's father is ill?" asked Strong as he waited for them to put the dishes and pots and pans away so he could start scrubbing the floor.

"I thought Carl Lee was out of town," Patience said, stacking the plates in the cabinet.

"I haven't seen him this week. And he was invited out of state to a track conference. I'm sure he doesn't know about his father. Is it serious?" asked Abby as she shined the last glass dry and handed it to Patience.

"I think so," said Strong.

"What's wrong?" asked Abby. The familiar fear attacked her insides. Were her troubles never to be over?

Patience put the pots and pans away.

"Liver condition. Looks worse than I've seen in anybody walking around. Think you could talk Carl Lee into seeing his father?" asked Strong.

"I don't know." Abyssinia hesitated, remembering what Carl Lee had told her about the problems with his father. She feared greatly for Carl Lee. Her body tensed anew over this upsetting situation.

"He's a sick, sick man," said Strong.

"Carl Lee hasn't seen him since the day he moved," said Abby.

"Just thought he'd want to know," said Strong. "It's a terrible thing for a family to be split up like that. I don't know what happened between them, but after Carl Lee left home, I believe Jefferson understood more about his own shortcomings as a father. Sometimes, Abby, rage is like a flood. If a stream is not large enough to contain rebellious water, the water does not care. It rushes on, heedless of boundaries, tearing down trees, floating away cars, barns, and houses.

"Jefferson's anger," Strong continued, "was like a flash flood, uprooting, overwhelming the natural affection between father and son."

Jefferson, dressed in a dirty felt hat, denim trousers, and denim coat, could be seen outside Strong's barbershop holding up the lamppost, nodding his head in an alcoholic stupor, slipping and sliding his way in and out of drunken fantasies. When he mentioned his son, Carl Lee, the son of his imagination, it was with a pride filled with longing.

"Why, once my boy ran the hundred-yard dash in six flat," he bragged, pulling the wine jar up to his mouth and sucking the bottle lip loudly.

"My boy, Carl Lee," Jefferson declared with jaundiced eyes and quivering lips, "is going to be an attorney, the best in the state of Oklahoma." His words were limping replicas of themselves. Slurred confessions of love he could never state directly and openly to his son. It was an articulate love inarticulately expressed.

It was Strong who saw that Jefferson got home. After he closed the barbershop, Strong would find Jefferson clinging to the curb and now and then lying in the gutter.

Strong would adjust the rim on his hat and stand up taller and say to himself, "There but for the grace of God go I."

Strong remembered the time the tornado ripped down his barbershop. He had been so devastated by his dismay, by what he had thought was the unfairness of life, that he had abandoned his family for a short while and had gone about the world with a tight blanket roll on his shoulder. Looking into this man's face, he saw the shadow of his own. Misery makes us all brothers, he thought as he reached down to lift the man up and struggle home with him.

Abyssinia, returning from the store or from choir practice, would see her father perform this nightly ritual with the drunken man. She was always stunned by the struggle. How unlike Carl Lee the father is, she thought. Strong would nod to her and continue his mission of guiding home the man who tried to drink happiness from a bottle.

After seeing Jefferson safely home, Strong would walk slowly through the star-filled night, savoring his small blessings. He thought of the home he had had sense enough to return to after straying around the country. He thought of Abby, who sometimes favored him with a hot-cooked meal of garden stew and pepper grass greens. And, finally, he thought of the warm arms and gentle affection of Patience, wife and mother of his child, Abyssinia.

SEVENTEEN

It was Wednesday, and the people of Ponca had not seen Carl Lee's father. Strong, on his way home from the Better Way Barbershop the evening before, had thought Jefferson's absence extremely unusual. Jefferson was not in his usual haunts, spilling himself in a blur down the lampposts and over the curbs.

Now people had begun to truly worry. A tension gripped the town. They remembered that they had seen him last on Monday evening. And so they began to search for him in the alleys and out-of-the-way places in the city. They even stopped by the house where Carl Lee was renting a room from Widow Holly to see if Jefferson was there. They did not expect to find him, for it was common knowledge that father and son had not spoken to each other since that fateful day a few months back when Carl Lee had moved out. And anyway, the Widow Holly had told them, Carl Lee was still out of town at his track conference.

When Abby awoke that Wednesday, she sensed impending doom hanging over the day. This feeling of dread was heightened by a driving rain that mingled with red dust against her bedroom window. The sky was crying, she thought, as if in response to the quarreling of thunder and lightning. A hoop of lightning painted everything brighter. The blue of the throw carpet on her bedroom floor turned a shiny, sharper blue. Then the downpour stopped almost as suddenly as it had begun.

This disappearance of Carl Lee's father, Samuel Jefferson, worried Abby. She was concerned for Carl Lee, for she knew that father and son had never come to terms with their anger and their love for each other.

Outside a gentle wind had swept the foreboding clouds back for a while. Now the sky was a blue sheet of silk, not a rippling cloud in sight.

Certain now that the rain had ceased, she put on a gray wool skirt and a cream-white sweater and wrapped a red flannel scarf around her neck. She pulled on her rain boots and hurried out the door.

Purposefully she strode past the weeds in her yard and past her father's carpentry shop.

Then she saw Carl Lee, his tall body drooping, aggravated and lost looking. His long arms heavily laden branches of worry. He's back, she thought, and he knows. He's searched the streets for his father. He is so tall, she thought to herself. He reminded her of a tree walking, his trunk and legs the trunk of the tree, his distressed face a solemn oak mask of dark wood.

"Abby," he called to her. "I was just coming to see if you would help me look."

"Oh, Carl Lee," said Abby.

He reached instinctively for the comfort of her hand. As they touched, they both saw a flurry of movement across the distance in the woods.

"It's the Indian woman," said Carl Lee.

"There, among the trees," responded Abby. "How long's she been standing there?"

"As long as the trees perhaps," said Carl Lee, a curious note on the edge of worry in his voice.

Abby wondered, some foreshadowing thought nudging at her senses. Trees, she thought, that was where his father was, among the wooded area guarded by the Indian woman who watched them now with alert eyes.

As they moved toward the woods, the woman began to retreat. She was a bright shadow in her wonderful array of colors. A bird of light movement.

They followed her deeper into the woods the twigs snapping under their feet. The copper-colored woman moved silently, her steps never betraying her movements. It was only the blur of her colors that served as their beacon.

They followed her past the meandering creek, the elderberry trees, the Oklahoma elm, and the pecan trees. A cheechee bird swooped down in front of them. Then a cloud of birds sprang up from a tree, flapping their wings and singing in the wind.

As they followed the Indian woman, Abby reflected on other times she had seen the Indian woman all over the town, like a statue of proud grace, her multicolored blankets wrapped around her shoulders against the cold and the betrayal of history.

Abby was awed by this daring woman who bragged her beauty with bold colors.

The rapid flutter of a blue jay's wings distracted her for a moment. She pointed to the bird, and Carl Lee, too, turned to watch it cut a graceful path across the sky. When they turned back to follow the Indian woman again the familiar figure was absent. The woman was gone, and in her place stood the most beautiful tree Abby had ever seen.

A rust apple tree stood in the clearing, in full bloom, its bright petals falling on a mound of earth that protruded around its trunk.

Abby stooped down to understand what she was looking at. At one end of the mound was an apple tree branch. At the other an altar of ashes and a shattered wine bottle, its glass broken into chips and arranged into a circle. Then a numbing thought took possession of her. She recalled the times and places she had seen the red woman.

She stared at the mound, and what she imagined set her heart beating wildly. She pictured the Indian digging the red dirt out of the ground with her bare hands. Gently planting the body in the red earth. She pictured her chinking the green glass of the wine bottles into chips. She pictured her placing the apple bough just so. Abyssinia could almost hear the high, shrill sound of mourning the woman made as she rocked back and forth over the mound.

Abby heard a sharp gasp from over her shoulder.

"What?" Carl Lee hoarsely whispered. "What is it?" He knew what Abby had sensed was true. Realizing whose body lay beneath the mound, he did what to him must have been the most natural thing in the world. Because he was a runner, a track star, he started to run. In the stammering silence the wind stumbled.

He ran through the woods. Over heather and honeysuckle he ran. He scrambled through bushes, brush, and weeds.

The birds, astonished at his flight, gave their wings a rest and watched in silence from tree branches as Carl Lee's fast feet flew across the earth, his head swept back by a great wind of pain, his body stretching toward the sky.

He ran back to where Abby knelt by the mound, and yet he could not run away from his burning sorrow. As if he thought that by stamping the ground he could stamp out the pam.

With a burst of speed he again raced, crisscrossing the field beneath poplar and oak. Sending grasshoppers, beetles, and other bugs scurrying out of his way.

He sprinted through a stream. He ran, trying to run the agony out of his feet.

"Stop!" screamed Abyssinia. "Stop it!"

Abyssinia ran to where he stood. His body trembled still as his breath came in jagged gasps. His face ashened into a bruised plum. Sweat beaded the dark curls of hair.

Abyssinia held the bereaved Carl Lee's head in her lap.

Then his tears soaked her skirt like a river of rain. He was weeping, she knew, over what was the ritual burial of his father. Over the grave, some claim, the Indian woman prepares for her husband. But why had the Indian led them there? And what did she have to do with Jefferson?

"It's been so long since I saw him, Abby."

"When was the last time?"

"The time I ran away."

"But you had no choice."

"I could have seen him. At least visited him. But I always felt torn. Torn between this pride of mine and the need to forgive."

"How could it have been any other way?" Abby murmured, stroking his head.

For Carl Lee, Abby's hands were a balm. The touch and feel of soothed pain swaddled in love.

EIGHTEEN

It was late afternoon by the time Carl Lee stopped at Abby's house the next day.

"Do you know the Indian woman came to me early this morning? About three a.m.," said Carl Lee.

"What did she say?" asked Abby.

"Nothing I could understand. She said nothing." He looked out of the living room window toward the woods.

"What did she want?"

"Nothing."

"Where did you see her?"

"In my room. I had a feeling someone was watching me. I used to have those feelings a lot when I was growing up, but every time I would wake up and look around, there'd be no one there."

"But this time . . ."

"This time was different. There really was someone."

"How old were you when you first had these feelings?"

"Oh, I was very young. Two or three, I guess."

"The same feeling you felt early this morning . . ."

"The room felt warm; there was a pleasant aroma there, like flowers or herbs. I can't quite describe it, but it had the same smell—the smell I used to smell the times before, when as a small boy I'd wake up thinking someone was there."

"Are you sure?"

"Sure as I'm standing here. I sat up in the bed. At first it looked like a shadow cast by some object in the room. It did not move. Then I made out who it was. It was the Indian. In her serape, fingering her glass beads; somehow it felt right."

"Did she say anything?"

"Nothing. She smiled, a rather sad yet contented smile, as if she were happy that everything was well with me, like a mother would who must leave her child."

"How?" asked Abby.

"Like a mother," Carl Lee repeated. "But when I turned on the light, she was gone."

"But the smell of her stayed," Abby said, in deep thought.

"And apple blossom petals; I kept them. Want to see?"

"Uh-huh."

He pulled the petals out of his pocket and handed them to her. Very carefully she studied the blossoms. She drew the flowers to her nose. Then it all came together. "The smell you remember—smell anything like these?" she asked, offering him the petals.

He took them and inhaled deeply. "Yes," he said. "Yes. How could I have not known?"

They were silent for a moment; then Abby asked, "What are you going to do about the body?"

"Nothing."

"No funeral service?"

"No. Better to leave him where she put him. Undisturbed."

There would be no traditional community funeral. The long limousine glistening with icy sheen would not carry the body from the church.

"There is such a special peace about the woods," Abby agreed.

"A certain harmony with nature." She smiled when she thought that Jefferson's bones, his blood, his tissue would nourish the color of the bloom of apple blossoms.

Later that evening, after Carl Lee had left and her parents had come home, Abby asked Patience, "What happened to Carl Lee's mother?"

"What do you mean, what happened to her?" said Patience in a tight, uneasy voice.

"I mean, where is she? Did she die in childbirth?"

Her usually talkative parents hushed. The dining room got still and quiet.

Patience cleared her throat, hesitated a little.

"It was a long time ago," began Patience. "I remember seeing her, her coal black hair hanging like silk ropes down her back, a band of beads across her brow. "

"Why, she's always been there, moving like she was a part of the landscape, a part of those woods she walked by and into."

"She didn't always stay in the woods. Stayed right here in town with Jefferson," Abby's mother said.

"She carried the baby quietly all the time she was pregnant. Not a minute of morning sickness. I remember it so well because it was around the time I became pregnant with you, Abby."

"She had a dignity about her. Seems to me like the bigger she got, the prouder she strutted," said Strong.

"Didn't talk much. Like she believed in silence," Patience added.

"That Cherokee didn't even object when the midwife instructed her in the birthing comfort of bed and boiling water. Didn't say a word. When her time came, she just wrapped her shawl around her, left her warm house, and trekked through the woods, where she squatted and gave birth on the naked ground in the dead of winter," said Strong.

"Something she had to do, that's all," said Patience.

"Oh, you could tell she was pleased to be pregnant with that baby all right," said Strong.

"Well, where was Jefferson?" Abby asked.

"I remember the day she delivered the baby boy. Jefferson knew she was in labor. He looked all over town for her, asking this one and that one if they had seen her. He wanted to make sure that she got to the hospital or that at least the midwife was there, but she disappeared on him," said Strong.

"I've never seen a man so perturbed, so worried," he added.

"He finally found her, though, in the woods, just as she squatted over the ground to deliver the child," said Patience.

"To hear him tell it, she was trying to kill the infant. He snatched his child up and brought him back to his house," said Strong.

"Never forgave her, either. He ranted and raved all over about how 'that crazy Cherokee woman was trying to harm his baby,' when actually it was the Indian way of giving birth," said Patience.

"It makes plenty of sense, that method. Gravity is working with you when you squat. But on your back it's an uphill fight all the way," decided Strong.

"How would you know," asked Patience good-naturedly, "since no man has ever given birth to a child?"

"Oh, I can't fault Mama Nature about that," Strong said, a twinkle in his eye as he looked at Abby. "The job you did in giving birth to this jewel was superb."

"Couldn't anybody do anything about the Jeffersons?" asked Abby.

"His temper," continued Patience, still remembering that earlier time. "Jefferson had an awful temper. He snatched the child from the mother before she could nurse him, before the afterbirth could separate from her womb more easily."

"She probably found some roots to fix the problem," said Abby.

"We sent a delegation to see him. But he wouldn't let us in. Soon we stopped trying," said Patience. "The Ponca women have always felt sad and ashamed about that failure."

"Failure?" Abby arched her eyebrows.

"Failure to help another woman when she so desperately needed it."

"Who took care of Carl Lee while his father worked?" Abby asked.

"Next-door neighbors. They had so many children that one more didn't make a difference. Then Jefferson kept the boy himself when he got off work."

"There are some people who say Jefferson found a bottle of milk on his porch every day while the child was still a baby, and it didn't come from the dairy or the store," said Strong.

"She put it there," decided Patience. "She had to. Expressed the milk from her breasts and carried it to her child that first year."

"Folks said it made him strong."

"And tall," decided Abby.

NINETEEN

The missionary, Ruby Thompson, was on her way to sunrise service with some of her neighbors when she saw Abby staring at a tall blue iris in the middle of her weeds. Then the missionary said she thought she saw a cat with an inky tail running through the weeds at Abby's house, but the cat disappeared as suddenly as it had come.

Carl Lee was a block from Abby's house when the neighbors stopped him to tell him about the cat. He just laughed and said, "Maybe it was the Easter bunny."

"I know it was a cat. Don't you think I know the difference between a rabbit and a cat?"

"What's so unusual about a cat walking through a yard? Cats go everywhere. They don't ask permission. They just go where they want to go," said Carl Lee.

"But I saw the cat do a wonderful thing. Everywhere its paws fell, a blossom appeared. I saw the pink star-petaled blooms of heather break out on the end of a patch of green. A patch I had thought was weeds," said Ruby.

"Go on," one neighbor urged her.

"The cat leaped into a tree. And I saw the wild plum blossom. She climbed down its trunk to the ground and ran around the plum tree. Where there were weeds, wild strawberries appeared around the tree base."

"Certainly did!" somebody else remarked.

"The lovely purple tireweed was a sight to behold!" she continued.

Another neighbor continued where Ruby left off.

"She scrambled along the picket fence, and the wild pea vine ran lavender."

"Whose cat was it?"

"It looked like Opia; then again it didn't. It moved faster than Opia. Like a flash of color and light. Yet there was something in its carriage that looked like Opia."

"Well, was it or wasn't it?" Carl Lee finally asked.

Nobody answered.

"Well, what was it about its carriage?" he probed.

"Walked like she was descended from tigers, leopards, lions, and jaguars."

"Stepped like she was sacred."

"Shrouded in antiquity."

"Like she had come through the torture and bonfire of the Middle Ages. Like she had survived the time when they burned cats at celebrations."

"Like she had stared ignorance in the face and lit her eyes with wisdom."

"Like she had fallen from a great height and landed on her feet."

"Or like a moon goddess who hears best at night, when the hunt is on!"

After saying good day, Carl Lee continued on his way to Abby's house. He pondered the news the Ponca people had brought. He had promised Patience and Strong he would visit their church this Sunday with Abby.

Carl Lee now knew much of what Abby was suffering in her loss of Serena, since the death of his own father. His own grief came in overwhelming waves now and then. He realized that the two of them had begun to lean on each other more.

He had never been to a Pentecostal church before. He looked forward to witnessing their services. To hearing the minister's delivery, which Abby had said was more passionate than that of a Methodist minister.

When he got to Abby's door, she was ready. She wore a pleated dress of splendid white. The stark color showed off her dark skin. Her hair was alive with color. Abby had garlanded her hair with one of almost every wildflower that bloomed in Oklahoma.

"God, you're beautiful," said Carl Lee.

"And you are so beautiful," she said, staring into his eyes.

"I heard about this morning," he said.

"Carl Lee," she exclaimed breathlessly, "I wish you could have seen it."

"What was it like?" he asked.

"A balm of beauty," Abby said. "From under a solid rock one cream-colored lily of the valley sprang up, and around its single beauty danced the heart-shaped leaves and bell-hooped flowers of the morning glory. And you know what, Carl Lee, I moved through my yard and I thought I heard somebody whisper, 'Believe in flowers.'"

He kissed both her dimples out of hiding. Then he took her hand, and they walked through the flower-sprinkled yard on their way to church.

TWENTY

The people from the town of Ponca crowded into the Solid Rock Church of God in Christ, where Abby and her family attended this Sunday, even those who did not ordinarily attend this church. The curious people suspected that the flowers in the Jackson yard had something to do with Abyssinia and her cat.

So they packed the pews and waited to hear her message through song. They all craned their necks to get a better view of the Jackson pew. Strong and Patience had already taken their usual seats. In fact, they had been there since sunrise service.

The congregation consisted of a boundless array of saints and sinners who had donned the pastel colors of spring, borrowed from flowers. The women had selected crisp ribbons for their daughters' braided hair. They repeated the color scheme in their elegant Easter hats, which could almost have doubled as flower baskets. The men had stuck handkerchiefs in their suit pockets and etched thin parts in the freshly barbered heads of their sons.

Abby and Carl Lee took their seats next to Patience and Strong just as the minister moved ceremoniously to his pulpit, lined with potted lilies of the valley. His white Easter Sunday robe flowed from his shoulders in perfect pleats. He paused at the podium and looked each member in the face in his sweeping glance at them all. He smiled a radiant smile, the white flash of his teeth sparkling brightly against his dark, tanned skin. He nodded at his organist, who began to play a hymn.

The organ leaped as the organist laid her magic hand to the keys of the instrument and touched some place deep in the souls of the congregation.

The minister beckoned to Abby to come sing; then he sat down. The organist played the best she had ever played. Images all in her fingers. The music came from everywhere.

At the height of her organ performance, Abby stood up to sing. She asked Carl Lee to sing with her.

She opened some new place in her throat and sang:

Who plaits the wind and braids
The rainbow across the sky?
The spirit that moves us
Is standing nigh.
Oh, spirit, sculpture all my ways
And I will sing you all of my days.

The organist followed the song with a glad hand and soon knew its melody. Like a jazz improvisation, she picked up the feeling and moved with it. She found new chords and a brand new bass. Her fingers danced with the song. Abyssinia, her head thrown back, closed her eyes, and Carl Lee followed her words, harmonizing as they always did together.

Oh, spirit, sculpture all my ways
And I will sing you all of my days.

Abby's voice now had a familiar quality that haunted the song they sang:

Who touches honey to fruit
And color to flowers?
The spirit who lives
Is standing by this hour.

As Abby hummed the melodic interlude, something inside her testified in a silent voice: "Thorns sprang up, and I thought they had choked out the seeds, but this morning I tell you I believe in flowers. . . ." Together she and Carl Lee sang:

Oh, spirit, sculpture all my ways
And I will sing you all of my days.

Some small voice whispered in Abyssinia's ear, "The earth sent forth blossoms, seventy times seven times seven. I tell you I believe in flowers."

Carl Lee's voice rang out:

Oh, spirit, sculpture all my ways
And I will sing you all of my days.

The glory in her voice was almost a light that could be touched. Strong and Patience looked at each other and smiled.

Creator, sculpture all my ways
And I will sing you all of my days.

"Seeds thriving among thorns!" Abby's inner voice cried.

"Among injurious seeds. I believe in flowers! I shall gather the flowers and leave the weeds."

"Have mercy!" someone sang out in the back of the church.

The church joined in again:

Oh, spirit, sculpture all my ways
And I will sing you all of my days.

Abyssinia was standing next to the organist now, asking her:

Who gives rhyme to music,
Flight to birds?
The spirit who weaves
Sound to woundrous words.

The organist, in trio with Abby and Carl Lee, witnessed in song:

Oh, spirit, sculpture all my ways
And I will sing you all of my days.

Finally, the church, the entire congregation, concluded:

Oh, spirit, sculpture all my ways
And I will sing you all of my days.

After the service some people wanted to know why Abyssinia's voice was different. Strong and Patience looked at each other. Patience answered, "She has a new song to sing; her voice is made new with the awareness of what miracles spring can bring." But in their deeper hearts Patience and Strong suspected the answer. The voice with which Abby sang had been borrowed from her Aunt

Serena. A bright shadow of a voice. Had they not noticed how she made music from the cradle of her throat? How she rocked it back and forth? How she effortlessly stroked the notes till they were the elusive gold and fine rhythm of cornflowers freed in the wind?

After church Abby and Carl Lee walked in the woods. The trees were so dense that the sun scattered light in intense patches here and there where it penetrated the hanging green branches, illuminating the grass and red earth in spotted lights.

Just where they stepped into the woods an Oklahoma elm rustled gently above their heads, its heavy foliage parting with the breeze to wink light at them.

Although it was a hot, muggy day, the woods were cool.

The light breeze played through the trees and served as a natural air conditioner, filtering the air clean to them from over the gurgling water of the river.

They stopped under the rust apple tree and sat down. After Carl Lee had raised Abby's hand to his mouth and gently kissed it, they looked up to see the bright blur of the Indian woman in the distance.

Carl Lee waved in greeting. Abby, reading the joy written on his face, thought to herself, he has even conquered grief. She joined in the waving.

Carl Lee realized what his father could not. That it was better not to pick certain flowers. Better to leave them where they could blossom fully. Carl Lee knew that the woods were home for the Cherokee woman who was his mother.

He took Abby's hand, and they sprawled beneath the rust apple tree. In the precious quiet, all they could hear was the beating of their hearts. Their doubts and concerns blew away like dandelion puffs before a carefree wind.

It was fine art, the picture of the two of them. Had there been a mirror reflecting the vision of the couple, framing the moment, catching it in one shining composition, it would have revealed the narrow, straight, powerful lines of Carl Lee and the soft, curved, feminine strength of Abby—the pair woven together against a crinkled-leaf backdrop of new green. A sky approaching the deepest blue imaginable with the crimson tinge of the setting sun falling away from them. The wind whispering and nudging the pleated ruffles of her dress, the red earth cradling the unyielding persistence of his solid frame. Abyssinia and Carl Lee. A flower and a rock in human form.

Water Girl

1986

amber: a reddish-brown jewel the color of mountains in Indian summer, a creation of resin from pine trees plunging long ago to the bottom of the sea, buried there for ages, collecting beauty till washed ashore by that ancient midwife Water

Thirst

ONE

Swish. Swish. The golden wings of an eagle whispered high above the backwoods of Tracy, California.

Swish. Swish. The eagle lowered hushed wings. Peering down, he scanned the river, where water sparkled like lace, fringing the late-afternoon mountains.

At a bend in the river where two low hills covered with redwood and pine trees almost touched, the eagle spotted a figure swimming back and forth in an aqua-green bathing suit.

Swish!

He swooped closer, then glided just above a brown girl who moved through the lace-blue water as gracefully as a fish.

Tucking his wings to his sides, he dove down and dipped his beak into the river a few yards downstream.

He drank there until his thirst was slaked, all the while listening to the girl's splashing legs propelling her through the water toward the sloping shore.

She stepped out on the bank. The word *Amber* swirled, embroidered in blue thread across the aqua swimsuit top. She shook the water from her black lamb's wool hair until it sprayed onto her brown shoulders.

Then she walked toward the evergreen trees to change into blue jeans, her feet printing patterns on the dry land while fine particles of sand powdered her wet heels and toes.

As she changed clothes the eagle drew his claws up, threw his head back, shook his wings, and spread them like two golden fans opening in the California sunshine.

Then, soaring over peach orchards, asparagus fields the color of feathery ferns, and Tracy farmhouses with rooster weather vanes catching the light, he followed the barefoot Amber.

She approached a tomato patch of workers running up and down the rows, balancing lugs of red tomatoes on their heads, their long manly arms swinging in rhythm with their moving legs as they hurried to make another quarter. Every cent counted in their hustle to take money home to Mexico before the all too short harvest ended.

Slaving for below-minimum wages, the girl thought.

She passed close enough to see other workers, their backs bent like pretzels as they grabbed the red fruit loose from the prickly vines and shot them in the lugs they pulled alongside them like brown, rough-carved cradles. She saw grimy sweat puddling at the bottoms of their chins.

And the smell of hard work mingled with the hot tomato vines was so pungent, it stung her nose.

"*¡Hola!*" she called in greeting.

"*¿Qué pasa?*" they replied. Then to each other they hooted, "*¡Qué negrita bonita!*"

At her passing they began a mariachi song.

Coo coo roo coo coo cantaré. The sad sweet plaintive sound of Mexico streaked the air until she could almost see serapes, huaraches, piñatas, and guitars.

She looked into the Indian hatchet face of the last tomato picker and glimpsed not an exploited field worker but a flesh-and-bone sculpture of an Inca Indian transported to a Tracy, northern California, tomato field. What time barriers had he crossed?

He lifted his full lug, brimming with tomatoes, straightened his back, and ran down the row with his burden. A map of water soaked his dusty worker's shirt in a trail that led from his neck to his waist.

When she passed him chalking his number on his tall stack of tomato boxes, he shook his sweaty sombrero loose from his coal black curly hair and threw his head back and crooned, *"Coo coo roo coo coo cantaré, coo coo roo coo coo amaré."*

She walked on, the eagle shadowing her high above. *Swish,* whispered the eagle.

Soon she was walking down Corral Hollow Road.

The eagle followed her until she turned onto a grass path studded with fieldstone.

She stopped at the door of a redwood-shingled house shaded by chinaberry trees, turned the knob, and entered.

Dropping out of the sky, the bird looked like a moving sculpture of golden feathers. From his perch on the chinaberry branch, he looked through the dining room window covered with sheer white curtains, valenced at the top. Under the first curtain was another layer of sheers crisscrossed and tied with a ruffle of the same fragile material. Light falling through the curtains gave the room a serene softness.

The eagle saw a family seated at a round pine table, holding hands while the father said the blessing. The father, mother, and grandfather closed their eyes prayerfully, while two twin boys bowed their heads but peeked hungry eyes at a platter of smothered chicken.

Amber sat between the twins.

Behind her, the living room spread out like a page out of some homemaker's decorating magazine.

Amber's mother had scrubbed the oak floors until they gleamed like gold, until the seams in the parquet danced with light. A center rug embroidered with blue trumpet vines hooking themselves into a round wreath added warmth and comfort. The mother had rinsed the enormous plate-glass window in vinegar water and shined it with a soft lintless rag until one wondered whether or not there really was any glass in the pane. Amber often looked out this window to capture a panoramic view of the sea. It was a simple room, sparsely furnished, but alive with light and warmth.

A rocking chair sat next to a little wicker table. When Amber was much younger, her father would rock her to sleep here. A couch, upholstered in a fabric woven from blue and red threads, sat opposite the rocker. Before her father would rock her to sleep, her mother would tell her stories on this couch. From a distance the blue and red threads gave off the color of purple. It was only when Amber was closer, sitting on the couch in her mother's lap, sucking on her three middle fingers and listening to the story of the bear who went fishing in a lake, that she could see where the red stopped and the blue began.

Two straight-backed oak chairs and a music stand centered in front of the oak chairs sat off in the bright corner near the plate-glass window.

Over the brick fireplace, guns, oiled and shined, gleamed down like trophies. On either side of the fireplace along the entire length of the wall was a gallery of black-and-white pictures in oval oak frames, encased in glass—grandparents on her mother's and father's sides. Ancient aunts and uncles. And largest of these ovals was a family portrait. Her mother in a Sunday white blouse and light frilled jacket; her father in a Sunday white shirt and linen suit; her twin brothers, one on each side, dressed in Easter outfits, Amber in the middle, a fantastic ribbon crowning her head, her hair lovingly parted into tiny plaits braided so neatly, so tightly into little pigtails, it hurt to grin. That's why she looked so somber and stern-faced. Everybody else was smiling. She was the only one different, looking solemn.

Now, at the dining room table, she was again looking solemn, sitting between her two younger brothers, the twelve-year-old twins, tall and skinny as two cattails down by Bear River.

While the blessing was going on, Amber's eyes were respectfully closed, her mouth frowning.

"Amen," said her father. David Westbrook immediately rubbed his pouch of a stomach at the sight of the food. David had a balding spot on the very top of his head that you didn't notice until he bowed his head to pray or read. His plumbing customers noticed it when he was on the floor repairing their kitchen sinks.

"Out swimming again?" Jason, one twin, said to Amber.

Twelve-year-old Johnny, still smarting from the beating she'd given them in the swim race the day before, added, "Mama and Daddy found you in a pond."

"Is that why I'm the oldest?"

"What do you mean?"

"Obviously they chose the mermaid before they got to the frogs."

"She called me a frog!" said Johnny, looking for sympathy.

He didn't get any.

The twins were always teasing Amber about being different.

Their mother and father exchanged glances. This was the age-old game all brothers and sisters played on each other. Wanting to be the only one in the family, a brother or sister pretended that another child had been found in a pasture or in a frog pond.

She continued, "Coming back from the river I passed the farm workers," Amber said. "It's a shame." And she began to list the ways in which the workers were taken advantage of.

"Is that so?" David Westbrook said, lifting his napkin and placing it on his lap.

Jason and Johnny mischievously mimicked their father's gesture but with more flourish than he managed, while continuing to eye the main dish.

"Have you seen the places those migrant workers have to live in?" Amber asked.

"Well, I don't suppose it's the Hyatt Regency or the Hilton."

"I'm serious," Amber said, getting heated up. "Not much better than a barn. I don't even think they sleep on sheets."

"I never get called to repair any sinks or showers out there. None of the other plumbers do, either. That tells you they don't have any indoor plumbing for those poor people. So I don't doubt your word, Amber," said her father.

"She's done her research, all right," said one of the twins, eyes still glued to the food.

On the other side of David, Grandfather Westbrook, fondly called Papa Westbrook, served himself a helping of mustard greens. A gray beard hid his chin. He leaned his thickly gray-haired head over and inhaled the tangy aroma of the greens and nodded his approval. "What did you see at the river today, Amber?"

"A golden eagle," Amber said. "But listen to this . . ." And she went on, chattering her complaints.

Papa Westbrook stared out the window. The skin around his eyes pleated into fans. Did his nearsighted eyes see the shadow of eagle wings flutter and rise above the chinaberries?

While Johnny scooped a mound of rice on his plate and Jason reached for the corn bread, Amber picked up the platter of chicken just in front of her.

The twins sighed, dismayed. Amber kept right on talking about the world's problems. She gestured with one hand while the other held the chicken captive.

"Please," said Johnny, looking at the chicken.

"Right," she said as she scooped up a drumstick. On the other side of her Jason groaned. He had wanted a drumstick, and since Johnny had his hand stuck out, he didn't have a chance.

"What I want to know is, how can people be so stupid as to continue to kill one another?" Amber asked.

"Doesn't your head get tired trying to figure all this out?" asked Jason, still yearning for the chicken. Finally he gave up, saying, "You're not our sister. They discovered you in the woods. Some owls raised you, that's why you're so curious."

"Owls?" said Amber.

" 'Who'? Isn't that what owls are always saying?" said Jason, hoping she'd hand him the platter.

"I can think of a lot worse things to be than a bird," said Amber.

"Such as?"

"A jackass."

"Amber!" said Grace, exasperated.

"It's just an animal, Mama," said Amber with a grin.

"Please, please, please pass the chicken," said Johnny, still waiting with outstretched hands. "My aching arms are getting awfully tired."

She handed it over.

"A golden eagle, you say? Didn't we see one just before that last earthquake?" asked Papa Westbrook.

"Yes," said Amber, and kept on talking about cruelty.

Grace, a picture of neat plumpness, a woman the color of gingerbread, shook her head. She used to say about Amber, in order to explain that her daughter had always been a most curious child: "When she was a baby, she stared into the mouths of old men until they told their oldest secrets." Now she said, "Eat, Amber, while your food's hot."

Soup had been known to get cold and chicken to turn into brown jelly when Amber started on one of her long, long monologues, supporting her arguments with statistics delivered between bites of bread and swallows of hot chocolate.

Her flashes of sincere outrage lit up her eyes and deepened the dimples at the corners of her mouth, always reminding Grace of that innocent beauty that could come and go so suddenly, startling her every time she saw it.

"You're just scared of being ignorant," Jason said, pointing a fork at Amber. "Always showing off what you know."

Amber shrugged and started eating.

"'Fraid it's just that colored curiosity that can't be quenched," said Johnny.

"I'm curious about this," said Jason. "How come I can't get a drumstick sometimes?" just as Amber bit into the juicy meat.

Papa Westbrook nodded his head, stroked his beard, and smiled.

David looked at his daughter and said, "Pass the corn bread."

Grace reminded Amber, "Only problem is, the more you read, the more you need to know."

"Small problem. I read *Jet* and *Ebony*, and we talk enough about being black; this is just more of the same, except it's other folks, too," said Amber, setting her fork down so she could start chattering again.

"No, it's not the owl family that abandoned her, it was a mess of squirrels. She's off and chattering again!" said Jason.

Grace cleared the table of dinner plates and served the dessert. The twins watched amazed as Amber's vanilla ice cream, at first sitting so proudly atop the peach cobbler, melted and ran on down the sides of the crust as she continued talking. The crunchy cobbler was flooded with cream until it was overwhelmed, soggy with disgrace. David finally stopped her with a request.

"Amber, I want you and Wade to play a duet for us after dinner. Saw Wade when I was driving up this evening. Invited him over."

"But, Daddy, I was going to read," Amber complained.

"It *was* you who asked me if you could keep company with Wade Dewberry after you turned fifteen, wasn't it? Now you're telling me two months into fifteen that you don't want to be bothered?"

"'Course I do," she said, thinking of handsome Wade and his magnetic eyes, his powerful muscles. "It's just that I have some reading."

Every eye was on her, and she knew it was not only Wade they were thinking about but also music.

After dinner they heard Wade's light scratch on the screen door. And there he was with his husky self, almost taking up the entire door frame. A champion wrestler who played cello.

Papa Westbrook sat in his rocker by the living room window. The twins lounged on the blue hooked rug in the middle of the floor. David and Grace sat on the almost purple couch in the background, holding hands like teenaged lovers, much to the mortification of the twins.

Then all was silence as the duet began. Amber sat with her back straight, then leaned over the flute and began the introduction to "Sacred Mountain, Sacred Tree, Sacred River that Runs to the Sea," her cinnamon-colored lips soft and serious. She bowed her head over the flute and trilled until the music glistened.

Wade, astraddle the cello, began his part slowly, moving the cello bow into the melody, rising in swells. "Sacred Mountain, Sacred Tree, Sacred River that Runs to the Sea."

Then there was a moment between beats, a moment of perfect silence when power gathered. So strong that it touched Papa

Westbrook and locked its fire in his arthritic bones. He found it difficult to sit still, so he rapped his cane against the floor.

"Play, children," he admonished.

To this audience Amber and Wade became a duet of one, their music two waterfalls flowing into one stream. They played for the family. They played for themselves. They played for Music. When Amber puckered her lips and made the flute sing, Papa Westbrook saw a trembling bird dip into the mountainside and shake a lone bush branch for berries.

When she played, she sounded like someone searching for some wonderful and awful secret, something she needed to know and which no one would tell her.

Then Wade lifted his head from the cello, scooped up the wind in his vibrato fingers. A river flowed beneath Papa Westbrook's feet. The twins caught their breath.

Papa wanted to change his walking cane into a fiddle or a trumpet, some instrument, but all he could do was strike it against the floor in appreciation.

At last the notes rose to a crescendo and reached their final resting place.

"Don't know if I could have stood anymore," said Papa.

The group of them chuckled.

After a while Wade asked, "Where's Amber?"

"Disappeared on us again," said Johnny.

"I swear she's got some haint in her," said Jason.

"She's reading; remember, she said she had some book to finish," Papa explained.

"Amber," called Wade as he hurried down the hall after her.

He jingled the little brass deer knocker on her bedroom door.

She opened the door.

"Now you see her, now you don't," he piped.

She laughed, the flute in both hands.

"Can we talk soon?" he asked.

"Yes. Soon," she agreed, one hand on the doorknob, torn between talking to him and going to finish her book.

"I miss you," he said, gently moving her hand from the knob and encircling her in his arms. He kissed her.

"And I miss talking with you, I miss your kisses," she whispered.

She felt his solid strength flow down her spine and into her toes. As rough as he could be with an opponent in a wrestling match, that's how gentle he was with her.

She could stay this way in the circle of his tender embrace forever.

When they separated, she gave him that passionate look. A light in her eyes.

"You know, I don't know any other girl who can do that."

"What?"

"Turn the light on the way you do when you look at me."

"I didn't know . . ."

"Now you do. It's there deep in your eyes, and the only time I notice you turn it on is when you look at me."

"Well, you are a little special to me," she teased.

"The kind of chemistry they don't mention in the chemistry class. We've got it," he said.

"I do miss spending more time with you," she said. "Want to go hunting tomorrow?"

"It's a deal. And when you're finished with that book, I want to hear about everything you're reading."

The soft jangle of the door chimes held her for a moment as he closed the door to her room.

It was a room of rich woods, rose wallpaper with raised rose petals and rose leaves, and pink muslin curtains. The miniature brass knocker on her door with its little brass wind chimes of prancing deer could be gently jingled until the deer danced, her mother's musical way of waking her in the morning or letting her know she was coming into the room.

One of Amber's earliest memories was of watching her mother shine and clean the chimes.

"Make the deer dance! Make the deer dance!" she had shrieked from the crib as her mother rubbed the brass with a soft cloth.

"Anybody who can talk that well is ready for a more mature bed," Grace told David.

"Well, it can't be just any bed. It's got to be fit for a princess."

And they took her looking in furniture stores, but nothing would please them. Nothing would do. They spent all morning looking.

That afternoon, when they stopped by Dr. Goldberg's for Amber's routine checkup, he had told them about a man who built furniture.

"From scratch?" asked Grace.

"Tell him what you want. I'm sure he can please you," said Dr. Goldberg, lifting Amber down from the examination table. "A clean bill of health."

David had written down the number and called up the furniture builder.

"We want a bedroom suite for our daughter, but we want it to be different. . . . What's she like?" David repeated back into the phone, winking at Amber. "She's a beauty, she likes the out-of-doors, she likes the ocean. . . . What size room? The room is a small one, well, not too small. Cozy. About ten by twelve feet . . . Windows? Yes. Lots of light. Windows on two of the walls. . . . How soon can we see the plans? . . . That long? Well, quality takes time. You come highly recommended, Mr. Lockhart. Very well, sir, good-bye."

And they waited. And waited and waited.

"How long has it been, David?" Grace complained one day. "This child's getting so big, her feet are sticking out of the crib slats!" she added, exaggerating.

Then, the next day, Mr. Lockhart, the furniture builder, came by with the plans. Mr. Lockhart, a giant man in workman's denim coveralls. Skin the color of uncreamed coffee. Six feet six, hands like hammers. A laugh like a trombone.

"Is this the princess?" he asked, looking down at Amber.

"The one and only," said David.

"Well, now." He unraveled the plans on the dining room table and stood back. Amber remembered the rustling sound of paper, the smell of blueprints. He was a man of few words. His work spoke for him.

"Oh, look. Come here, precious," David called to Amber, delighted with the plans on paper.

"Color. Color," Amber cried, clapping her hands together, wanting to color the bed, whose headboard was a forest scene of bears and trees, with a footboard of fish leaping from a water scene. Across from the bed, Mr. Lockhart had sketched an oval-mirrored dresser with oak drawers carved in raised flowers. And next to it a chest of drawers with the three scenes of the bed and dresser repeated: the forest scene repeated on the top drawer, the raised flowers engraved on the middle drawer, and water jumping with fish on the bottom drawer.

Lockhart, the artist-workman, beamed.

"Oh, Mr. Lockhart, Mr. Lockhart," Grace said approvingly.

"Why, it'll be ready in another month," he promised, a gleam in his dark eyes as he smiled at Amber, "for the princess of Corral Hollow Road."

Then he bent over and handed Amber an extra copy of the

plans, and she lay on the trumpet vine rug and colored in the furniture with crayons using the colors of bears, water, trees, fish, and sky while Grace served David and Mr. Lockhart little sour-cream cakes and coffee.

Now in her room, filled with its original forest scene furniture, its one-of-a-kind design with the carved oak panels telling visual fairy tales, stories without written words, she listened to Wade's steps leading back to her family in the living room. Then she placed the flute on the music stand by the oval-mirrored dresser and turned immediately to her latest pile of library books.

TWO

The next morning, Amber woke up at dawn. She bounded out of bed and started pulling on her clothes. It was time to go hunting with Wade and her brothers. Dressed as she was in her costume of hunting boots, jeans, yellow parka, knit cap pulled snugly over her ears, a shotgun slung across her shoulders, she looked like she could live up to her reputation as a master markswoman.

Always the first one up in the morning, she took the lead. "Time to go!" she yelled to her brothers. They jumped up out of their beds and into their hunting clothes and gear.

Johnny said to Wade as the wrestler bounced out of his front door in response to Amber's calling, "How do you like being bossed by a woman?"

"Depends on the woman," Wade said with a grin.

Jason nodded to that; obviously the champion wrestler on the Tracy High wrestling team was no cream puff.

"How can she lead me around by her apron strings? Look at her, she won't even wear an apron," Wade explained.

Grace, still in bed, glimpsed out the window at Amber dressed for hunting and she thought about her mother-in-law, Bonnie, who could shoot a hole through a nickel slug at ten paces. And

Amber was as good a shot as Grace's mother-in-law had ever been.

"Just look at our daughter, David," she said nudging her husband awake.

David took one look, grinned, and fell back asleep. This hunting day, Amber heard the lusty crowing of the bowlegged roosters as she and her brothers and Wade trampled through the fresh morning countryside, the dew wetting their boots.

They were on a rabbit hunt this glorious dawn.

Amber spotted the rabbit first. "Look!" And they stretched out like galloping greyhounds, graceful but deadly, and they wailed an attack howl that stripped the limbs from the trees and laced morning fear in the quick legs of the rabbit.

She propped the shotgun on her shoulder. Her slender but strong fingers pulled the trigger. The rough bullet whizzed by the rabbit's twitching nose.

He ran into a hollow sycamore. The nervous birds watched from dawn branches and camouflaged their trembling with puffed feathers. Nothing living was equal to the hot wildness of bullets. The cottontail scrambled out of the other side of the sycamore and stretched out across the field.

Amber ran after him, her braid unraveling, the curl of her hair tangled in the wind. Her boots struck brutally against the earth as she ran. Her knuckles tensed as she clenched her gun. Her face set like female granite.

Wade and the twins ran beside her.

The dry brush swam greenish gray before their eyes as they wove through the sage and tumbleweed. They ran, the thrill of the chase charting their paths. The hot blood pumped faster through their veins as they propped their shotgun butts against their shoulders, aimed, and made their mark.

And the quivering rabbit lost the race with the bullet. Downed.

The surrendered blood of the bunny pulsed into the ground, staining it as red as tomatoes.

The dawn was fully realized. And the sky was a pale bandage of blue cloth. A feeble, washed sun limped over the horizon and sprinkled subdued light across their faces as they studied the rabbit.

Back at the house, Amber yelled, "Hey, Mama!" as they slammed the door behind them. "We caught you a rabbit for dinner. Rabbit thought he could outrun lead, but we got him," she said. "Take a look at this." And Amber dangled the catch by one long furry ear.

She looked up expecting to see what? Pride? But what she saw was a shudder in her mother's eyes and the fleeting vision of a death squad: Amber, Johnny, Jason, and Wade, all lined up in formation with their guns aimed at the helpless rabbit blindfolded and up against the wall of a tree trunk.

"Who got him?" Grace asked, a faint hoarseness to her words.

"Who knows?" Johnny shrugged. "We were all shooting at the same time."

Amber had nothing more to say. She just kept staring at her mother's eyes. Moonstones reflecting strange lights. But when her mother looked at her, she looked away.

"Will you dress the rabbit and cook him for dinner, Amber?"

"Yes."

Amber spread the rabbit out on newspaper on the kitchen table. Found the poisoned slugs and extracted them.

She skinned the rabbit, dug out his insides, cut him in two with the precision of a skilled surgeon. He dressed out to be three pounds. She prepared him with sage, salt, rosemary, and cayenne.

Next she chopped tomatoes and sprinkled them around his proud chest, split in half. Across his quick legs, soon to be succulent drumsticks, she spread minced bell peppers, red onions, celery, and thyme. Time. Time had run out for this creature of the wind.

She placed the rabbit in the Dutch oven to marinate in the savory spices until she cooked it for dinner.

All morning it marinated. Soon it was noon, and Amber's thoughts kept jumping back to the hunt. To take her mind off the new, disturbing thoughts about the death-squad execution of the rabbit, she went into her room and picked up her flute.

The mellow call of the flute drifted on the air and trembled. Her fingers moved like a sure wind, at times joyful, mixed with honeyed sunlight like a rabbit running free on the hillside and at other times as melancholy as a gray dawn or a snared prey yearning to be free.

Through the window as she played, she could see Grace bent over her plants, tending her clusters of small purplish lavender, a living brooch on the bosom of her lavender-colored dress. And when the plant was not in season, she wore tiny dried blossoms. The gentle fragrance encircled her like an invisible haze. The words *Grace* and *lavender* would always mean gentleness to Amber.

Her flute playing finished, she went into the kitchen and peeked into the roasting pan in the oven. The delicious smell of the marinade drifted up, tickling her nose.

Through the kitchen window she saw Wade coming across the road, his back pocket stuffed with a strip of blue.

She met him at the door.

"Want to go swimming?" he asked.

"Sure. Wait while I get my suit." She fetched her swimsuit and headed for the door.

"Where're you going, Amber?" Grace called from the flower garden in the backyard.

"Swimming, Mama."

"No, ma'am. You will not go by yourself. Snakes are out there, Amber."

"Wade's with me."

"All right, then."

They struck out across the meadow, not saying much, just holding hands, listening mostly to the hum of the insects, enjoying the feel of the ground under their bare feet.

Soon they had reached the river.

As they stepped from behind their separate dressing trees, she challenged him, "Beat you to the other side?" And they raced the rest of the way to the river's edge.

She dived in and stroked her way across swiftly.

"Beat by a girl! But they did say you came here swimming; you ought to join the Tracy swim team. They need you."

"They couldn't take it. The girls are already jealous because you're my boyfriend. I hear them whispering behind my back. 'I don't know what Wade sees in her. She's cute, but she never wears fingernail polish. And look at that head. Obviously she spends zero hours on it. The Tracy High wrestling champion needs himself a queen. Now, take me for instance.'" And they both laughed at her mimicry of the envious girls.

"Pay them no mind. If you want to join the swim team, join."

"Well, maybe sometime. Not now. I'd rather enjoy my private victories with you."

They swam some more, then rested.

"You look just like a brown jewel," he said as they lay on the grass, letting the sun dry the beads of water still clinging to them. "I do believe you're half girl, half fish. And if you get any darker, you'll be a molasses mermaid."

"If I hide my feet in the grass, we could pretend they're fins." She giggled.

On the way home they kicked up rocks and ran and romped like jackrabbits.

At the house she stuck the marinated rabbit in the oven, prepared rice, took the rabbit giblets, and made rabbit gravy. "You're staying for dinner, aren't you, Wade?"

He nodded.

"Then do you want to make your famous salad?"

He made a lettuce and cucumber salad, sprinkled with dill weed, dressed with sour cream.

When the table was set, she rang the dinner bell.

Through the family chatter of day's events and crisp salad and flaky rice, the entire table of people seemed to pause a moment when they passed a forkful of the aromatic pepper-sweet rabbit to their mouths.

Delicious.

But they all had sense enough to eat with a studied humility.

Amber kept thinking about the rabbit and about the people in the books she read. Do animals belong to the cycle of cruelty, just as people? she wondered.

Soon Wade winked at Amber and said it was time for him to leave. They excused themselves from the table and went out into the evening air. Holding hands, they walked over to the chinaberry tree and stood beneath it. Then Amber turned to face Wade, a shy light glowing in her eyes. They hugged with such tenderness that they did not want to stop touching. Wade covered Amber's mouth with his until a delicious fire spread through their lips. The more they kissed, the more they wanted to—but when the first star winked at them, they said good night and went their separate ways into their own houses.

THREE

The next day Grace's words were still ringing in Amber's head: "The more you read, the more you need to know."

Her mother had been so right, she thought as she sat at the dresser braiding her hair, impatient to get to her books. This reading was getting to be addictive. She couldn't wait to read what happened next. If it was left up to her, she'd leave her hair standing all over her head. At least that's what Grace claimed. Sometimes Amber was forgetful of herself.

She was trying to read a book on the Japanese concentration camps and braid her hair at the same time.

"I need three hands!"

The scratch on the screen door. "Wade." She had asked Wade to go with her to Susie Yamashita's house.

Instead of finishing the braid—she had about two inches left to go—she threw a rubber band around the frizzly ends and rushed to the door.

"Ready?" he asked.

"They took old folks, babies, everybody with black straight hair and Japanese surnames and threw them behind barbed wire fences," she told Wade as they passed the tomato patch, the wheat field, the statues of hay waiting to be stored in the barn. "Locked them up like pigs in a pigpen."

"You're telling me? I gave you the book," said Wade.

She went on reciting. He let her, knew she had to get it out of her system. By the time she had finished her report, they had crossed through the south end of the Yamashita farm and come out near the front yard of the ranch house.

Japanese gardening with little shrubs and cypresses graced the front yard.

Susie, in a red blouse and blue jeans, waved to them from the front window and soon came skipping out in her sneakers and red socks and big grin to welcome them.

As usual they sat on the redwood steps, with the green junipers potted in redwood planters surrounding them. After talking about the latest song on the radio and the newest dance step, Amber expressed her concern about the Japanese concentration camps.

"Is it true they sent your family off to camps at the start of the Second World War?" Amber asked Susie.

"Yes," said Susie, and she lowered her short lashes.

"Tell me about it."

Susie shrugged her shoulders and blinked her almond eyes.

"Well, where did your family stay?" Wade asked.

Susie blushed. "They were herded to a place without heat in the winter, a place dirty with dust in the summer, given bad food and sometimes no indoor toilets." She swept her bangs and the anger out of her eyes. Changing the subject she said, "Hey, would you guys like some sushi? Mom just made some."

Amber ate the soy-sauced rice, ginger root slivers, and golden eggs wrapped in seaweed. She tried to swallow her curiosity with the food but ended up with a lump in her throat.

On the way home she said to Wade, "Why didn't she tell us

more about those concentration camps?" She kicked a stone so ferociously, it landed several feet ahead of them.

"You're not mad at Susie. You're bothered because it happened."

"Oh, Wade," she whispered, "why is the world so cruel sometimes?"

She began reading the history of the Jews in Germany, Poland, and other parts of Europe. She dared not believe all the sadistic atrocities. They were enough to make her turn her back on the human race. Were they just words with nothing behind them?

"I've got an appointment with Dr. Goldberg this morning," she said to Grace as she vacuumed the round rug in the living room.

"What?" said Grace, who couldn't hear clearly above the vacuum motor. She was busy in the kitchen baking Amber's favorite dessert, peach cobbler.

"I said I have an appointment with the doctor."

Grace rushed into the room and turned off the vacuum motor. "Are you ill?" She felt Amber's brow for signs of fever.

"No, I just have to ask him about something I read in this book about the Holocaust."

"Are you sure that's all you want to ask him?"

"What else?" asked Amber.

"Of course, nothing else," said Grace uncomfortably.

Guess she doesn't like my prying, thought Amber as she put the vacuum cleaner away.

Book in hand, she walked briskly down Corral Hollow Road and turned on Grant Lane. She was so occupied with her thoughts that she did not see the jewel weeds bursting open, showing off their yellow colors when she brushed against them with her pant legs. She took for granted the perfume of wild honeysuckle and the Tracy sky of puffed clouds on clear blue. She kept walking until she came into town and to the Goldberg house.

"I wonder if you'd explain something to me," said Amber, settling herself into the curve of the sofa.

For a moment he looked uncomfortable, but the more she talked, the more interested he became. He answered her questions. Then, finally, he rolled up his sleeves and showed her a blue number tattooed along his arm. Here was living proof.

When she came back to Corral Hollow Road, she went straight to Wade's house and rapped on his door. When he let her in, she plopped down, out of breath, as though she had been running a long race.

"Wade," she said, "It's true. They murdered over six million Jews. Six million people. Lined them up and marched them to the gas chambers. Teenagers and grandpapas and little boys and girls no bigger than the Reyes children down the road. Do you know that?"

"But, Amber, you took the book off my library shelf, remember?"

She went on, "Mouths mined for gold and made into jewelry for sale. Skins of murdered people used for lamp shades. They did experiments on women." These last words lashed out at him, and her voice began to rise even higher, until he could feel it trembling.

"Well, here's your book back," she snapped, tossing it down so roughly it tumbled off the edge of the coffee table and onto the floor.

"Amber, the book's not to blame. Anyway, much as you love books, what are you doing throwing one? Girl, have you gone and lost your mind?"

She bent over and picked it up. "I know the book's not to blame," she whispered apologetically and fled home, the door slamming shut behind her. She was always mortified when she became so overwrought and her anger appeared as rudeness.

That evening the flute was silent.

The next week, standing outside under one of the palm trees lining the Tracy High driveway where the students who lived in the country caught the bus home, Wade spied the title on the spine of Amber's latest book. Above the library numbers he read *Before the Mayflower,* a book of Black history.

A few days later, standing in his window, he saw Amber marching across the road to his house with the history volume in her hand. "Uh-oh, she must have turned the last page in that book."

"If I could, I'd give up reading, it's too darn upsetting!"

"Why don't you?"

"Might as well change my personality. You know I'm too curious. Speaking of being curious, what about your family? I know about the ongoing struggles of all Black folks from reading *Jet* and *Ebony* magazines. I know my own family history, but it occurred to me that I don't know yours."

"Where would you like me to start?" he said.

"With the Dewberry family."

"Oh, like every family we know, I suppose, my folks came from the South. But they came before I was born. So I'm first-generation Californian, the same as you. You just finished the book; you ought to be overflowing with answers by now. What about your family? How do they fit in with the story in that book?" And he folded his arms across his chest.

She began, "On my father's side the first recollection—written recollection—is of my great-great-grandmother slaving for a family called the Westbrooks. They tried to separate my great-great-grandfather from his wife and children. He killed the slave master and was chased across the country by a Ku Klux Klan posse. They didn't count on my female ancestor being an expert with a gun." Amber's imagination soared as she pictured the scene for Wade.

"'The nigger's got a gun,' one night rider shouted as bullets zinged through the air. They said the Klansman lay so close to his horse, it looked as if he were trying to get inside the animal's skin. Trying to hide under the horse's hide," Amber said.

"When that didn't work, he tried to see which way the bullets were coming; when he did, he hollered, 'The nigger's woman! It's the nigger's woman shooting!'

"She hit the bull's-eye. The grand dragon," Amber said.

"How many did they get?" Wade wondered.

"Oh, I forget the exact number. But who knows? Who had time to count? In spite of their courage, Westbrook was injured fleeing Mississippi."

"How was he hurt?" Wade asked.

"Seems one eye was half shot out of his head. With one hand on the reins and the other holding his dangling eye, they rode on into Oklahoma," Amber said.

"Why Oklahoma?" Wade wondered.

"I'm not sure. Probably the prospect of owning their own land. When the government bought land from the Indians, they offered millions of acres to non-Indian settlers who ended up running for the land in the great Oklahoma land rushes.

"The Westbrooks built a home near Ponca City, Oklahoma. Their children had children and so on. My father married my mother, Grace Jackson. Then my father decided to come to California," she said.

"To Tracy."

She nodded. "And we're still here."

"The Dewberry story's not too different. I wouldn't be surprised if half the black folks in Oklahoma came from Mississippi," he said.

"And ended up in California. Still, it's very disturbing, some of this reading. All these details. Like opening fresh wounds."

"Well, what did this last book teach you that you didn't already know?" he asked.

"I'm not sure . . ." she hesitated.

"And it disturbed you," he said.

"Maybe that's too mild. Angered would be more like it. Every time I read about those slaves packed and smothered on a slave ship, squashed together spoon-fashion, dying of disease, thirst, rat bite, and not enough air, it made me want to hurt somebody."

"Then you'd be no better than the rest of the folks. Some didn't make it, but you know that. They jumped overboard first chance they got," he said.

"And some did. Else we wouldn't be standing here." She paused, thinking.

Finally she said, "You know something, Wade, with grand ancestors like those, who came through the water watching ten million thrown overboard and survived the ship crossings from Africa, anyway, who knew about Mississippi lynchings, and lived on in spite of them . . . Sometimes fought back, who rioted, who paid for the right to live. When I think about those folks, I think about staying around here awhile. In fact, I think about living every moment of my life to its fullest until I die. Out of respect."

"Out of respect?" he repeated warmly. They embraced. Gently he massaged her earlobes. And she gave him back a sweet, lingering kiss.

"How about dinner at my house?" he offered.

She accepted.

Mississippi gumbo.

The whole table was quiet as they ate. They paid the highest tribute possible to the cook: rapt attention to the crab, shrimp, corn, chicken, hot sausage, and okra gumbo. Not a word passed a lip. Only food.

After Amber went home Wade heard the flute. For the first time in a long while she was playing again.

Later in the week, as he sat next to her on the yellow bus bumping along the country roads toward home, he read the names of the handful of books in her arms: *Touch the Earth: A Self-Portrait of Indian Existence*; *The Navajos*; *Cry of the Thunderbird*; *Indians of the United States*; *Paint the Wind.*

"Hey, Amber," he said as they parted in the middle of Clover Road, "I'll be in wrestling practice for the rest of the week after school and won't be riding the bus."

She frowned, disappointed. "A whole week? That'll be like a century."

They kissed good-bye.

"All right, then. See you later, Wade."

In her room she read and read, but each book she finished sent her deeper into a labyrinth of curiosity and wonder, and she read long into the wee hours of the morning, propped up in her bed on pillows.

"Amber, it's one a.m. Turn off the light. Go to sleep, dear," said Grace.

If she turned off the light, she did not always go to sleep. She had a flashlight under the quilt and stole a few more minutes.

Now and then she looked up from the page to see the imaginary shadows of Indians through her window. One night when she threw the covers back, she saw stars fall from the dark sky like ashes from the fireplace of God.

There was no one to go to after she finished the books on the Indians. She didn't know any Indians. This bothered her. At least with Dr. Goldberg she got some answers. And with Susie, even though there wasn't much conversation, there was Susie's *presence.* But she didn't know any Indians, and the effect of horror after horror in all the books she had read so far weighed her down, so she withdrew a little into herself.

Early that Saturday morning she played her flute. However, it was a new sound. A warrior wail lifted from the delicate flute and invaded the day.

She was into the pain of all the experiences she had read about.

She did not go to fetch Wade and round up the boys as was her habit on Saturdays so they could get an early start on hunting and swimming.

She avoided family and friends.

At the breakfast table Johnny asked, "When's the last time you talked to Wadell? Aren't you going swimming with him this morning?"

"No," said Amber, using as few words as she could between bites of hot oatmeal.

"Some folks just don't want to be bothered," said Jason.

"Nothing but reading and music and being alone. Not even swimming and hunting with us," complained Johnny.

Amber shrugged.

She excused herself from the table early. Johnny's bushy eyebrows shot up, and a devilish grin lit up his face. "Maybe Wadell ought to personally ask her to go swimming. Who knows what goes on in the water? They say blood is thicker than water but maybe not in this case."

"I believe the young man prefers to be called Wade," said Grace.

"Have you been spying on them when they go swimming alone together?" Jason asked Johnny.

"'Course not. But I bet you this much, she won't be slamming doors in Wadell's . . . Wade's face."

"Would you slam the door in a champion wrestler's face? Our sister might be odd, but she's not crazy."

"Who knows what Amber'll do? She doesn't belong to this family; she doesn't fit. "

"I don't want to hear that again," said David. The ice in his voice shut them up.

"I was just kidding," said Jason. Then he shrugged. "But then again, it wouldn't bother me to leave her be. I've collared drumsticks three times the last three times we've had chicken, she's so preoccupied. I need that chicken, I'm growing muscles for the football team. When I get to high school, I intend to be a star fullback!"

Later on Wade appeared.

"How's Amber, Mrs. Westbrook?"

Grace grimaced. "Sometimes I have trouble understanding her, she's so different."

The melody from the flute drifted out of Amber's room and interrupted Grace's next thought.

"Least she's keeping the music up," said Wade.

"Something new."

He nodded.

Before, the songs had been recognizable ballads and old favorites, but now the sounds were different. Melancholy.

"Mrs. Westbrook, could you tell her I'm here?"

After a long while Amber came out. Her eyes set deep in her head. Her hair in one kinky finished braid down her back, as though she had been thinking and reading and braiding at the same time.

Grace left them alone.

"Amber," he said softly. "How're you doing?"

"Fine. Been busy. Reading. Music," she said.

"What are you reading?"

"Books," she said.

"Oh. Books. Thought we'd agreed to discuss the books. Have I done something wrong? I haven't seen you for a week, but you knew that. I told you beforehand . . ."

There was an awkward distance separating them. She shook her head. "It's just that . . . I mean, don't you ever feel frustrated . . . ? I mean, all this evil, they did experiments on the Jewish women in the concentration camps. And right here in America they operated on one black woman thirty times trying to perfect their surgical skills. And now these latest books . . ."

"Discovering something you didn't know before? Is that what's bothering you?"

"I just need more time to think. I mean, who can we talk to about the Indians? I don't know any. You don't."

"That's right," he said thoughtfully.

Then he said, "Don't you want to take your mind off things a little bit? Why not let's go for a swim?"

"Can't."

"How about a walk, then?"

"I already have."

It was true. He had seen her leaving early in the morning, her backpack strapped in place, a lone figure walking toward the river. He frowned. He didn't like being left out of her thoughts.

"Why are you doing this to me?" he asked.

"What?"

"Shutting me out."

"I just—"

He touched her gently squeezing her shoulders. She leaned against his chest. He was such a comfort.

"I just want to think about it more, that's all. Maybe it's the accumulation of all these horrors and not being able to talk to one Indian. It's got to me."

He understood and yet he didn't. He hugged her tighter, finally let her go, and went home.

Outside, before he could walk even three steps, he heard the flute.

What about Papa Westbrook?

He walked around to Amber's backyard where he saw Grandpa Westbrook stooped over, staring at the avocado tree.

"Who insulted this plant?" the older man grumbled.

Something was wrong with the avocado tree that once grew tall in the garden. Now it turned its leaves toward the ground and would not bear fruit.

He stood up from his inspection of the trunk and shook his gray head sadly.

Wade asked, "Insult a plant?"

"Oh, there are all kinds of ways. Remember the apple tree in the Matthews' old backyard?"

"The one that wouldn't give any apples after they moved away?"

"Remember how the leaves looked?"

"Looked the same to me," Wade answered, perplexed.

"But you didn't get up close and examine the veins. Now there's where you're apt to find the root of the thing."

"Sir?" asked Wade.

"Clogged veins. Shriveling and spotting the leaves."

"But how did the plant get insulted?" asked Wade.

"Don't you remember?"

"No, sir, I don't."

"The new owners tried to chop it down, then changed their minds."

"I see."

"Major insult," insisted Grandpa Westbrook.

"Didn't know plants were so sensitive."

"Just like any living thing. They like good care." One hand

thoughtfully brushed at his gray hair. He continued, "Now, if a plant suffers from an insult, how much then do people suffer from meanness? Wars, genocide, and killing are catastrophic insults."

"Plants and people," said Wade, thinking that in a way Amber was insulted by humanity's wrongs not made right.

"Uh-huh," said Papa Westbrook. "Sensitive."

FOUR

The twins talked between gulps of hot apple cobbler.

"What's she got in that room she's got to keep the door shut all the time?" said Jason, nodding to Amber's empty chair.

"Maybe gold," said Johnny.

"Diamonds?"

"Secret treasures of some kind."

"Something special, that's for sure."

"Under her bed she's got ten talking birds and seven witless cats."

"No, she's got a witch's broom and water for warlocks."

"Oh, it's a mess, that's for sure."

"Have you seen it, Mama?"

"What?"

"Amber's room."

"Well . . . yes."

"How do you like the way she keeps it?"

"It may not be the neatest place in the world," said Grace, exasperated with the chaos of Amber's room. "In a way, maybe it's no concern of mine. I'm not the one who's got to look at it. She does. And if it's a mess, it's her loss."

The boys exchanged glances.

"She's locked up in there again, saying she's not hungry."

Grace Westbrook compressed her lips. Her face rounded and dimpled, as though God had sunk his thumbs in the soft brown cheeks as he held her face between His hands, admiring His creation.

David Westbrook raised his eyebrows and looked thoughtfully at Amber's empty chair, then added in his rumbling voice, "She'll come out when she's good and ready."

"Don't know which I prefer, her tomboy ways or her quiet ones," Grace said.

"We did ask her to go swimming and hunting tomorrow. She said no," said Jason, scooping up another serving of apple cobbler.

"Third Saturday in a row," said Johnny.

"Ask her again. Keep asking," said Papa Westbrook, stroking his gray beard. "When my Bonnie was a young woman, she used to think a lot about things. Serious. But you couldn't find a greater sport anywhere. When she felt like hunting, horseback riding, she could beat the best of us. Only woman I ever saw defy an Oklahoma tornado. Some new adventure will bring Amber out. Just wait. Acts just like my Bonnie. She may not look like her, but she's got her spirit. Now, there was a woman even the tornado wouldn't mess with. By the way, anybody notice how funny the air is lately?"

"What do you mean, Papa?" asked David.

"Earthquake weather," said Papa.

"How do you know that?" asked Johnny.

"Yeah, how do you know?" echoed Jason. "You've only been in one minor earthquake since you moved to California. Barely registered on the Richter scale."

"I memorized the signs," said Papa.

"Papa," said David, "even the weathermen haven't learned how to forecast an earthquake the way they can predict a hailstorm or a blizzard or even a tornado. How come you can?"

"It's in the bones," he answered.

"These tremors don't usually hurt anybody," David said.

"Usually," agreed Papa. "But what happens when 'unusually' is the case?"

David nodded. "You've got a point, all right. Can't measure the damage of an earthquake until it's over. One customer thought he'd gotten away clean after that one a while back, but it had twisted his water pipes up, down where he couldn't see it. Looked all right on the surface."

"Still making mad repairs from the last big one two years ago. That stretch about a quarter mile down Larch Road when you turn off Bear River," Grace said.

"Another big quake or two could split Tracy and the entire San Joaquin Valley in half," David admitted.

"As I told Amber a few weeks ago, I'm ready to go meet my Maker whenever the last trumpet sounds. My bags are always packed. And when it comes to this earthquake business, it's just a matter of time."

"Oh, Papa, what do you mean 'ready to meet your Maker'? You're not going anywhere yet," David said.

Papa answered with a dry cackle. "You've raised a good point, son. I'm kicking but not high, flopping but can't fly. But I'm still here."

Papa went back to sipping his coffee while staring longingly at Amber's chair. He missed sharing talks with his only granddaughter, who always listened to him so acutely and with the same careful attention she offered a seashell pressed to her ear or in the same way she bowed her head over her flute.

"Amber," he said to himself.

"I wonder," said Jason.

The next morning when Amber went on one of her solitary walks, the boys opened her bedroom door.

"Whew!" said Johnny. "Look a here!"

"Books. Talking about books!"

There were books everywhere. A quilt of books on the bed. Books spilling from the chest of drawers and dresser. And books carpeting the floor. They picked up a few volumes and glanced at the titles. There were books about African Americans, Mexicans, and Asians. Books about the Holocaust. American Indian books.

"Got more books than the city library and Tracy High combined," Johnny exaggerated with a whistle.

"Let's get out of here," Jason said, heading for the door and opening it in a rush. "Making me dizzy just staring at all these words."

"Quick. Shut the door. I think I hear her coming!" said Johnny just before they dashed down the hall.

FIVE

Just as her grandfather had predicted, Amber was coming out of her phase of study and silence.

"It's a dirty shame," she said, thinking about the Indians.

She grasped thick branches as she climbed high in the chinaberry tree growing outside the front door.

She looked down Corral Hollow Road to see if Wade and her two brothers were coming, but all she could see was the deserted road stretching to an end and the tall mountains of redwood trees far away.

Now she could hardly wait to go hunting and fishing. The twins and Wade had gone to the store to buy cartridge shells. She had promised she would meet them here by the chinaberry after they returned from shopping.

Suddenly she leaned so far forward in the treetop that her foot slipped and she almost fell. Getting a secure hold on a sturdy limb, she shook her head and blinked. She saw trees dancing. Mountains shaking like Jell-O.

The country air swelled, and the rolling distortion moved closer, disturbing everything in sight.

The chinaberry tree absorbed a shock deep in its root, a shock that spread from root to trunk, to limb, to leaf.

She stared at the house. The plate-glass window was quickly turning yellow. Yellow berries from the chinaberry leaves rained in little thumps against the pane.

"Earthquake!" she yelled, sliding down from her perch.

Any moment the house would come crashing apart, swaying windows and all.

The vibrations continued as her boots hit the ground, then suddenly the quaking stopped, but the air smelled of sulfur, heavy and charged with danger.

She sucked in her breath and waited, dark wide eyes raking the sky, a sky of gray glass.

Then the ground groaned again beneath her feet. She hugged the drunken tree while the gray-glass sky turned to gray slate.

On the other side of the yard, bushes of bunch berry and devil's paintbrush trembled and reeled.

Dazed, she leaned her head against the rough bark of the tree while dizziness swooped over her.

The spasm went on.

From every side she heard the jolting rumble that troubled the tree and sent the glass pane shimmying again.

"Amber!" her mother called from the house. "where are you?"

But Amber was too preoccupied to answer. She was busy digging her boots into the soil, her head cocked to one side, listening.

The unbroken roar of the earthquake knocked shingles off the house. Loosened the red bricks on the chimney until they rained from the roof.

Kerplunk.

She ducked down by the chinaberry to keep from getting hit.

Kerplunk.

Next the earthquake cut a wide swath clear across Clover Road, splitting the asphalt.

"Whoa!" Amber shouted.

But the earthquake spoke again, and as it spoke, the earth rumbled with worry.

"Amber Marie Westbrook!" Grace screamed.

But Amber was concentrating her attention on the earthquake that California legend called the avenging angel of the Indians, a red angel who stepped out of the river now and then to make his presence known.

Kerplunk.

"Go back to the river where you belong," Amber said.

The ground shifted again, ready to gape open and swallow her.

The thought of being gobbled up by the earth paralyzed her, and she could not move even if she wanted to.

"Go back to water," she whispered.

The earthquake, who perhaps wanted to be listened to, finally heard her. And soon, through a great act of will, the earthquake ceased to tremble, wrapped himself in his shawl of turquoise and jade, and started back to the waves of the river.

Before the earthquake could reach the river home, Amber had scrambled into her own home and into the arms of Grace.

"Now, that was more than a tremble," said Grace, hugging Amber to her. "Wonder if your daddy and the boys are all right."

"And Wade," Amber said, her eyes wide as she surveyed the awesome damage. "And Grandpa?"

"He slept right through it. Nothing disturbs his afternoon nap."

The phone rang.

"Probably Daddy checking in now"

"Your daddy's fine," Grace said as she hung up the phone. "Now, I wonder where the boys are?"

"Let's go outside and look." Amber suggested. Amber put her

hand over her brow and looked off down the road. "Here they come, Mama."

"Well, that's a relief," Grace said.

They looked around.

"Looks like we lost part of the chimney, and Corral Hollow Road's messed up," said Amber.

Grace leaned over and picked up a damaged shingle, while Amber gathered the chimney bricks and piled them near the porch.

Next they walked over to the road and inspected the split the road crew would have to repair.

Spiders and long earthworms crawled out of the earth's interior.

"So glad we're all safe," said Grace, watching the boys' approach.

Amber followed her gaze. "Finally we're going swimming and hunting. At last," said Amber, as though somebody else besides herself had kept her from the river and the woods.

Grace thought a moment. She was glad Amber was interested in being with her brothers and Wade again, but the fear of the earthquake made her cautious. "Come on in the house. Another quake might come, and you don't have sense enough to come in out of the rain, even when it's raining bricks!"

"Well, what about later today?"

"Not today. And when they get here, I'll tell them I said to stay put too."

"Wade can't go with us tomorrow. Tomorrow he's got wrestling practice."

"On Sunday?"

"Well, when you're the champ, you have to work when the challengers are sleeping. At least that's what Wade always claims."

"I said no."

She recognized that final note in her mother's voice.

Nothing would budge her. Amber stood looking at the mess the earthquake had made, wondering if it had been satisfied by the time it made it on back to its home where the river dipped into the sea.

She shrugged. She looked over at Grace. Her mother looked like the light was hurting her eyes. Amber knew if she spoke another word of protest, Grace's head would start to ache. Now and then her mother got headaches, migraines, real bad.

Better to go to Bear River tomorrow.

She stepped over the rift in the road and went inside the house.

No is my mother's favorite word, she decided.

SIX

A flood of rose petals, upset by the earthquake, lay stunned on the lawn. The air, which was charged before, seemed to settle itself so the roses could breathe.

Somehow the settled day reminded Amber of her mother. A prim day. A woman's day, a frilly day. An inside-the-house day.

Because of the earthquake Amber was confined to the house. The closest she could get to outside was to stare out the window.

When she was younger, on rainy days she now and then disappeared up to the attic. How long had it been? Years since she had ventured into that musky place, out of the range of her mother's neat glare.

Now, although the attic belonged to the house, it was not like her mother. It was not like the rest of the house. It was more like her room. An outcast in a neat home. The attic was disheveled. In a jumble. Disordered, like the out-of-doors in a way. A wilderness.

One by one she climbed the stairs, puffs of dust flying up around her feet. Nobody had been up here in ages, certainly not her mama with her relentless dust mop, she thought, sneezing as she pushed opened the attic door to enter the small room.

Just a little light filtered through the slatted small window, not enough to see much by and hardly any fresh air at all. She pulled the chain on the attic light; nothing happened. "Bulb's out," she whispered to herself the way people often do in the dark.

Although it was dark, the place was still a minefield. "A-choo!" she sneezed again, hurrying her way to the small arrow of light in the wall.

But before she could reach it, she tripped over an abandoned doll and tumbled. She got up and dusted herself off. Now she more carefully inched toward the window.

If she pushed hard enough on the small slatted window, it would open just a wedge. "There," she said, breathing in the fresh flow of air. The breath of flowers didn't reach this high up, but at least the air diluted the dust.

In the middle of the collected clutter a fringe shawl covered a thick trunk. Here she sat in the semilight, her chin in her hand, elbow on her knee.

Where to start?

She looked around. Old paintings, old hats hung on nails; one of a set of high-heeled shoes, looking orphaned away from its mate, pointed a golden pinched toe at her; an ancient table whose surface she once crayoned pictures on sat patiently in the corner; her first baby bed looking ready for occupancy, reminded her that time moves on and that she was fifteen now. All of these wonders lived in the attic.

The place comforted her. In the attic nobody had cared if she left her crayons out, or if the high-heeled shoes she hiked around in while wearing her mother's old-fashioned skirts were left out of their boxes.

In the old days, when she was tired of playing here, she had always sat and daydreamed on this very trunk. She had called it her throne.

The trunk. Why not start here? She had taken the trunk for

granted. It had been her special seat. And she had thought of it only as a place to sit. Not a trunk.

"Why, I could be sitting on top of a treasure!" She slid off the trunk and knelt before it. She pulled the shawl away. "Padlocked!"

It was the first time she had ever seen anything under lock and key in this house.

"Why?" she wondered out loud.

She pulled a hairpin out of her braid and started working at the lock.

Her fingers trembled with curiosity and frustration, and she dropped the pin more than once.

But she was persistent.

On and on she turned the pin, this way and that.

By the time the lid's lock, rusty and old, gave way, her braid had undone itself and stood out like a kinky halo around her head.

"What have we here?" she said, peering in. "A bundle of old scrapbooks!"

She opened the one on top, a brown, fragile loose-leaf binder. On the first page she saw her daddy dressed in an air force uniform, his head held high and proud.

She paused a moment, considering him. No wonder Mama married him. He's so handsome. The bald spot had not claimed the top of his head yet. She turned to the facing page. Across from that photo she discovered a picture of her mother in a frilly evening gown, in the standard pose for a high school prom, a carnation pinned on her bosom, a flirting twinkle in her eyes. Why, she looks like she never had a migraine in her life, Amber thought.

She kept rummaging until she came to the scrapbook at the very bottom of the box. More pictures. "Now, wherever in the world did Mama find a ribbon that large?" she wondered out loud, studying the school photo of herself taken at the kindergarten door. Somebody had written on the back: "Amber's first official day of education." The writing seemed to be that of her mother's neatly controlled hand.

Her father's scrawl turned up every now and then, especially on the backs of her twin brothers' snapshots. There Johnny and Jason were, babies, looking like two black-eyed peas in a pod, one's arm over the other, sound asleep in an oversize blue bassinet. But which one was which?

Even back then they looked mischievous. As if saying, "Guess who?"

When had their mischief begun?

She couldn't remember. They'd always been a bother as much as she loved them. Even before they were born they had been a bother, acting up as they did in the middle of her Easter poem. Easter service, her first public appearance at three years old, and what did they do? Sent her mother into labor. The boys were on their way. She never did finish that poem. She had gone with her parents, refusing to stay with the other church members who offered to babysit for her. She had to see. They had to rush from Sunday school to the hospital, the rest of the Easter poem still turning in her head. She was sitting with her father in a hospital waiting room instead of thrashing bushes for Easter eggs. At last Dr. Goldberg announced that the twins were born. Hand in hand with her father, they hurried to the hospital's plate-glass window, and what did she see?

Two boys. Their bald heads looking like two Easter eggs.

She turned the page. A picture of her in a christening dress.

"My lands, I look so serious."

Wonder when this was taken? The picture was so fragile, the edges peeled into her hand. Is there a date behind it?

She was afraid to handle the photo too much, afraid it might crumble all to shreds in her hand.

Maybe she'd better leave well enough alone.

She started to turn the page. Carefully—but her thumb brushed the picture.

There was something under the photo. Like padding.

She fingered the thick surface.

Probably nothing. Maybe another picture, her at one day old, right after she was born?

Her curiosity leaped, catlike, to the top of her head, then sprang down to her searching fingers.

The christening picture came out easily enough. She quickly turned it over to find a date scribbled in bold blue printing on the back.

She looked down at what was left on the page, expecting to see the baby picture.

"Well, it's definitely not a picture," she said. Left on the scrapbook page was a folded piece of paper. Yellow with age.

She unraveled it.

The ink was faint, smeared with water drops or teardrops. She screwed up her eyes, trying to decipher the lines.

After a moment she could make out the first word, but she needed more light.

She walked over to the little shuttered window, where the light flowed steadier and stronger. Now there was light enough, all right.

It was a letter. Dated back before she was even born. Ancient.

Probably a love letter between her mother and her father.

Thinking of the handsome young man and the pretty young woman of the photographs, this possibility of passion notes between her parents fascinated her. She leaned over closer to the window light. Now she could see better.

"Dear Aunt Grace and Uncle David . . ."

No, it was not *between* her mother and father, it was *to* them.

She read on.

Her eyes skipped to the bottom of the page.

Oh, it's from cousin Abyssinia when she was in med school, a thank-you note for their wedding gift.

Then it was not a secret love letter from her father to her mother or vice versa. She yawned and started to fold the letter back up, but out of the bottom of her eye she thought she saw the word *pregnant.*

Pregnant?

She quickly spread the paper out again and leaned toward the light.

"We are pregnant, expecting a child (a girl, we think) around the last of February or the first of March. . . . We wonder if you might be interested in taking this baby?"

The first of March . . . A girl? *But that's when I was born. . . .*

As the impact of her discovery slammed into her mind, she crushed the yellow paper in her trembling hand.

"Maybe my eyes were playing tricks on me," she whispered, and she spread the paper out again. She studied it over and over. "Oh, it's true. It's true! They lied to me!"

There was a place in her, on the left of her brain, where rage and pain lived. It was the place most affected when she witnessed oppression, when she read about the ill treatment of anybody. Now that place in her mind quaked with anger.

"They threw me away! Like an old hand-me-down dress!"

She could not deny the evidence of her own ill treatment. And it was not found in one of her books or in *Ebony* magazine but in this single sheet of paper kept hidden in this dark attic.

As she studied the yellow paper the rage and pain distilled into a tiny drop of liquid. Then the single jeweled tear slid down her face and silenced her moving lips.

And then, as if by reflex, as though she had a hold on something hot, some yellow flame, a burning insult, that echoed the outrage of every persecuted group and slammed her head with a pain reminding her of the one she felt for the Blacks, the Jews, the Japanese, the Indians, her grip loosened, her hand opened swiftly, and the paper fluttered to the floor.

Her mind could not easily deal with the discovery. She focused on a golden narrow-toed shoe, everything else in her vision's periphery blurred. She was crushed. A compacted chest. No breath. A half-hypnotized invalid. What was that sound? It was coming from way up high. You can't get any higher in this house than this. Is it raining? Why, it never rains in the summer. When she peeked through the attic slats, it was only raining sunbeams. Yet on the ground, where the sunbeams splashed, the red petals of June roses had fallen like red petals of rain.

SEVEN

Amber, Jason, and Johnny coming out of their driveway were dressed and set for the Saturday hunt and swim.

They waved across the road to Wade, who hailed them from his open screen door.

He wished he could join them. He wanted to talk to Amber. She hadn't spoken much since yesterday, the day of the earthquake. And last night she had been shut up in her room. He sighed. Given the last few weeks, her silence was not all that unusual. But yesterday when they were getting ready to go hunting, he thought she had come out of her stupor.

"Well, at least she's getting out again," he said to himself with relief, then he yelled out loud, "Amber, catch something for me, a rabbit big enough to make the stew kettle smell. Remember what I told you, Johnny, a wrestler needs good nourishment. Right, Jason?"

"Have a good practice," the boys called.

Amber, her aqua swimsuit tucked in the back pocket of her jeans, adjusted the shotgun across her shoulders. Then she balanced the huge pack on her back.

When she and the boys got farther down the road, she turned around to wave to Wade, but he had already disappeared back into his house, preparing to get to wrestling practice on time. She waved to Grace and Papa, who were still standing on the porch.

"Leading the way again," said Grace. They thought she looked more like her old self once more. with Jason and Johnny bringing up the rear.

"What you got in that backpack, Amber?" one of the twins good-naturedly asked as they hiked down Corral Hollow Road. "A couch?"

"No more than I need," said Amber. She felt as though she were carrying a mountain of pain on her back. She didn't feel very much like joking with anybody today.

Grace, at her station on the porch, squinched up her eyes. It seemed that Amber's backpack looked larger than usual.

"Eyes are acting funny," she said, shaking her head.

"What?"

"Nothing, Papa." Then, "I had to bite my tongue to keep from telling Amber to stay. I'd trust the boys more in an earthquake than I would Amber. Sometimes she just doesn't show good sense, something to do with that curiosity of hers. . . ."

"At least she's up and out, away from her mom and those books. Be thankful for small blessings," Papa said as he turned to go tend the garden. "I can't believe I napped right through it."

"As you say," Grace repeated, "be thankful for small blessings."

Before long, after passing through the evergreen forest and a variety of redwoods, Amber and the twins came upon Bear River.

It took Amber only half a minute behind the sweet gum-tree to step into her swimsuit.

"Get ready. Get set. Go."

All three dived into the water at once. A great splashing filled the air as arms and legs flew through the water.

"Told you she learned to swim before she could walk," said Jason as Amber beat them to the other side.

"Didn't I tell you she's not our sister? They found her in a pond," said Johnny, floating on his back.

"What's the matter, Amber, lost your sense of humor?" said Jason at the stricken look on her face.

The look gave way to a half smile.

They dog-paddled, did the butterfly stroke, the breaststroke, splashing and kicking until their fingers and toes were waterlogged.

After a while they stopped swimming.

It was a bright day for hunting, and the air smelled of river and pine.

As they began the hunting phase of their Saturday outing, as usual, Amber led the way, her shotgun ready. Her piercing eyes spied the rabbit first. And their guns went up.

As the shot rang out she remembered a shudder in Grace's eyes and had visions of the rabbit up against the wall, herself the chief executioner.

After the rabbit was downed she knelt over him. But there was none of the old jubilation. The surging sense of triumph followed by proud laughter was missing.

For a moment her brothers thought she was praying, she was so still over the dead bunny.

"Here, take him on home," she said, handing the rabbit to Johnny and looking away. "Think I'll pick some wildflowers. Thought I saw some jewelweeds over there."

"All right," said Jason, looking taller and skinnier than she remembered. Johnny, beside him, looked like his mirror image. In unison they turned away from her in the direction of home.

Soon her brothers were in step, walking briskly down Bear River Road.

For a long time she stood watching them move down the road until she could not see them anymore.

Then she turned and started walking in the other direction, her backpack secure.

EIGHT

Back at the house on Corral Hollow Road, Grace lay napping. Breathing softly, she dreamed of her children. One of them, with back turned, was fading from sight.

Suddenly she sat straight up in bed, strict as stone. A foreign wind whispered through the screen and shivered along the nape of her neck.

In the distance a car rumbled down Corral Hollow Road like a prehistoric monster clearing its throat.

Her frayed voice erupted, "Jason!" and she thought she heard a dark burst of thunder, but the sky was still. "Johnny! Amber!"

Now she pulled the white cotton sheet off and sprang to the floor.

She ran through the archway separating the bedroom from the living room and stopped as though a force had broken her flight just in front of the screen door.

The sound of running feet coming down the road from the direction of the river filled all the jagged corners of the house.

Danger hitched a ride on the hurried feet of the runner.

She shaded her eyes and looked down the road. Instead of three children she saw only two.

A channel of air whisked in from the screen door, but it did not cool her. A gust of weeping heat.

She carefully glued her eyes on the advancing figures.

She recognized the approaching gingham shirt. The particular gait. The careful sling of the gun over the shoulders. She could make out who it was running down the road from the river now. It was Jason.

One hand fluttered over her heart, and the other hand hesitantly touched the screen-door handle.

"Jason, what happened?" Then, before he could answer, she asked, "Where's Johnny? Where's Amber?"

"They're coming. Nothing . . . nothing happened."

Did she see glinting shadows in her son's eyes? Something she could not put into words hung in the air. She glanced nervously down the road at her other son trudging along, the rabbit in one hand.

"Johnny?" Grace said when he reached the house. "Is everything all right?"

"Sure, Mama," he answered.

"Where's Amber?" Grace asked as the twins hung their guns over the fireplace.

"Oh, she'll be along."

"You know I don't like her left alone. You know that." Sighing because she thought she was again falling into that everlasting habit of being overanxious about her children, she said, "I think I'd better lie back down. I had the most disturbing dream."

"What was it?" Jason asked.

"I thought . . ." she began, then stopped, throwing up her hands. "Just a stupid dream." She walked back into her bedroom shaking her head.

About an hour later David Westbrook pulled up in the driveway.

Grace got up and put on a pot of coffee as Papa came in from gardening. She sat out a can of condensed Carnation milk, and a little porcelain glass jar of sugar.

"How was your day?" she asked.

"Okay, except I had to repair that Taylor woman's toilet again."

"Again? What's this, the tenth time?"

"Uh-huh. You know, the tenants never were home when I went there before. Today they were. Now I understand."

"What?"

"When a three-hundred-pound woman sits down on a toilet stool, it's been used. Where's Amber?" he asked.

"Must be at Wade's," Jason said.

"Time for her to come home," David said. Grace dialed across the road. "Hello, this is Grace. Would you tell Amber it's time to come home for dinner? . . . Oh. . . . Thank you. Good-bye."

She hung up the phone, puzzled. "Now, where could that child be? Too late for her to be out."

"Somewhere quenching that colored curiosity, no doubt," Johnny said.

"Where could she ever be?" said Grace.

"She'll be here by the time the table's set," David said.

"I do wish she wasn't so adventuresome," Grace complained.

"No such thing," David said.

Papa Westbrook nodded his head in agreement. "Well, she does go too far sometimes. Remember the Priscilla Redwine incident?" Grace said.

"Priscilla Redwine? How could anybody forget Amber and the Priscilla Redwine episode?" Jason and Johnny chimed.

"Who was Priscilla Redwine?" asked Papa.

"Let me tell it," said Johnny.

"No, I will," Jason said.

NINE

A couple of years ago Grace Westbrook and Mrs. Dewberry, Wade's mother, had been discussing Priscilla Redwine, the woman everybody claimed couldn't have children.

"Why can't she have babies?" Amber had asked.

"They took all her equipment away," Grace said.

"What?" asked Amber.

"Womb. Ovaries. Both breasts. Where would she put a child? What would she nourish it with?"

"Cow's milk?" Amber asked.

"She might. Me, I don't believe in heifers nursing children," Wade's mother had said.

"I thought a heifer was a cow who never had a calf."

"In this case I mean a cow that never gave birth to a human."

"Oh."

"Babies who drink cow's milk are always up in some doctor's office. And the hospital stays full of bottle babies."

"So where'd she find this baby she keeps wheeling up and down Corral Hollow Road in that carriage?" Grace had asked.

"Nobody knows. Best little child in the world, though. Never once heard her cry. Not a peep," Mrs. Dewberry said.

"So it's a girl, then?"

"Judging from the pink frills and ribbons on the carriage, it's got to be."

"Ever see the face?" Amber wondered out loud.

"Never."

"Think some unfortunate young girl had it and left it on Priscilla's doorstep?" Mrs. Dewberry asked.

"Must," said Grace.

Other Tracy people were not as kind as Amber's and Wade's mothers.

Amber had heard snatches of enough mean conversations from the gossipy females to verify this lack of kindness.

"Who would have Priscilla Redwine even if she did have all her organs?" one woman asked.

"Night gets dark," the other one replied.

"You act like a man loses his memory when the sun goes down. I don't care how dark it gets, how's he gonna forget a face like that?"

"Well, honey, you're not married, either."

"I'm biding my time. Waiting for Mr. Right. Know I'll get me a man before she ever will. Face all wrinkled like chitlings. Talking about ugly! Why, my feet look better than her face."

For some time the country folk had been wondering about Priscilla Redwine. Always talk, talk, talk behind her back.

Still, every day the sun was out, Amber could see Priscilla pushing that baby carriage. Whenever anybody approached, she would cover the child up.

"Don't come near us with your bacterias," she would fuss the minute adults looked like they were about to get too close to the buggy. "Get your old folks' germs on from around this innocent child's breath!"

And then Amber would see Priscilla running for home, pushing the carriage and flying down the road as if ten demons were after her. She would run in her front door and close it. People could hear the locks clicking. Then, after peering out the windows, she would draw the curtains shut. And that was that.

Two hobos walking down the road figured it out.

"I doubt if anybody's in that buggy, anyway. Mighty strange we never hear the baby cry. All babies cry, that's a universal fact."

"Something dirty's in the milk all right," the other hobo said, after thinking carefully about the situation and readjusting his bedroll on his back. "Ain't nothing in that carriage but air and blankets."

"Anyway, everybody knows Priscilla Redwine is a little touched in the head. Crazy as a California earthquake. Her daddy was an undertaker. Living 'round dead folks'll drive anybody nuts."

"Wasn't only dead folk. Dead elk. Dead eagles. And dead owls. Redwine, best taxidermist in the county."

It was true that after Mr. Redwine the mortician died, Priscilla closed the doors and turned the laying-out room into a living room. People had to take their dead elsewhere. They could no longer walk past the mortuary window where they used to inspect the dead lying out in their caskets, dressed up for viewing with stuffed deer, hawks, and bears' heads staring down at them from the walls. Now Priscilla stood in her window for herself where she could look out toward the sequoia-covered hills and mountains as she rocked the baby in her arms.

Well, a few months went by, and still nobody had seen Priscilla Redwine's infant.

Then Amber thought, *Wouldn't it be wonderful if she was the first person in the countryside to see Priscilla Redwine's baby? Now, that would be quite an accomplishment.*

The minute she thought it, she had already begun to prepare to do it. She wanted to tell Wade, but the thrill of keeping it a secret and a surprise changed her mind.

In order to accomplish the feat she had to study Priscilla's habits.

Amber noticed that whenever Priscilla came outside, she always had the baby with her. You see Priscilla, you see the carriage pushed in front of her.

Every day, just about, Priscilla went to the store and bought fresh vegetables, a carton of milk, and a jar of baby food. She also never failed to buy her favorite chocolate-chip cookies.

The baby was eating well; the grocer had told everyone. But he had not seen the baby's face, either, although the pair frequented the store daily. The baby's little head and entire body were covered up as a protection against pneumonia, flu, and TB.

"Funny how that baby never protests all those blankets weighing down on her head," said the grocer, lacing his hands over his fishbowl belly. "Always sleeping. Guess Priscilla waits till it's nap time to do her shopping so she's not disturbed by all that hollering."

"Maybe she feeds it some of her chocolate-chip cookies," somebody said.

And that's when Amber got the idea of how to get into Priscilla's house. She knew that Priscilla had a yen for chocolate-chip cookies. Amber would sell her some, hot from the oven. The last time Amber had sold the Redwines cookies was when Mr. Redwine was alive. And he always bought two dozen, claiming Priscilla would eat the entire twenty-four cookies in one sitting.

Amber smiled, thinking about how she would be the first person in Tracy to see the child. Then she would tell Wade if the baby's cheeks were fat, if her eyes sparkled, if she smiled back at you when you tickled her chin, if she had ten fingers, ten toes, and if she looked anything at all like Priscilla Redwine.

As far as Amber could tell, the only time Priscilla was not with the baby was when she took her nightly bath. Amber discovered this after watching the house for a week.

It took Amber a week to determine that the lights went off in Priscilla Redwine's house every night at nine fifty-five precisely. Then it took her another week to discover that the bathroom windows were steamed up at about nine thirty every night. So the best time to see the Redwine baby was between nine thirty and nine fifty, a twenty-minute span.

Getting inside was the difficult part.

That afternoon, after Priscilla had done all her grocery shopping and was settled in for the evening, Amber rang the door bell.

Priscilla answered the door, babe in arms almost smothered in pink blankets.

"Yes?"

"Miss Priscilla, I have some chocolate-chip cookies fresh made. Just popped them out of the oven."

Priscilla's nose had already identified the delightful aroma.

"Let me get you some money. How much?"

"Same as usual. Dollar a dozen."

"I'll take two dollars worth, then."

Which is what Amber knew she would say. Amber quickly stepped inside the house at this opportune moment. The fragrant cookies in front of her, like so much bait.

"If you're busy with the baby, I can hold her for you," Amber said, and she reached for the bundle.

Priscilla backed away, pulling the baby closer to her. "Wait. No, wait." She checked her dress pocket, jingling some change.

Oh, no, I hadn't counted on that, thought Amber, that she would have the change on her person.

Priscilla counted out one dollar.

"You just want one dozen, then?" asked Amber, holding the change.

Priscilla thought a moment, looking from the baby bundle to Amber, who wanted to hold the baby, and then to the cookie bag dangling in Amber's hand.

Then she decided, "Well, just a minute. Stand right there. I'll be right back." And she hurried away, keeping the baby on her hip.

The minute the woman was out of sight, Amber unlocked the window by the door.

When Priscilla came back into the room, her eyes seemed to stray to the window. Or did they? Amber guiltily wondered. Priscilla shifted the baby to her other hip and handed Amber a dollar bill in exchange for the cookie bag.

"Thank you, Miss Priscilla."

"You're welcome," answered Priscilla as she shut the door, clicking the double lock.

At the dinner table that evening Amber could barely contain herself.

"Why're you so fidgety?" Grace had asked.

"Oh, nothing," said Amber.

The twins turned their eyes upon her. Their noses sniffed the air, smelling danger, adventure.

"What's up, Amber?"

"Nothing."

"Why're you so excited?"

"I'm not excited."

"The few times I've ever known you to eat everything on your plate and ask for seconds is when you're excited about something. Something secret," said Johnny.

"Leave Amber alone," David had said. "She's got a right to be reflective."

And that was the end of their interrogation and just about the end of dinner.

After helping her brothers clean the kitchen Amber joined the family for a game of Monopoly. After she had acquired as much money and property as she could, she said good night and turned in early to read her novel until it was time.

But she could not concentrate. She could not follow the plot of the story. Her eyes kept straying from the page and to the clock on her nightstand.

After a few long hours it was nine o'clock.

She tiptoed out the back door and went racing down the road until she came in sight of Priscilla Redwine's house. She slowed her pace. It was only about nine fifteen, so she had fifteen minutes to wait. What would she do for fifteen minutes?

She stationed herself in the backyard under the loganberry bush where she had waited so many hours before to ascertain Priscilla's schedule. She had waited more patiently then, but tonight she was as impatient as ants.

And she felt guilty. Entering somebody's house without permission was serious business. Although her father never hit her, she was sure he would scalp her alive if he knew about this adventure.

But then she thought about being the first person in Tracy to see Priscilla's baby, and her guilt took a backseat.

She looked up and saw the bathroom light go on. Then it's time, she said to herself. She stealthily crept to the front door and, bending low, soon reached the window she had unlocked earlier.

She raised the window quickly, then heard a door shut somewhere inside the house. Had she come too soon? Was Priscilla Redwine just brushing her teeth and had come back to check the baby before taking her bath? Was she coming to recheck the doors and windows?

Amber held her breath.

Then she heard the bathwater running and sighed a sigh of relief.

She stepped inside the house and carefully closed the window.

Now the baby.

The house was as still as a mortuary at midnight.

Not a sound could she hear. She had hoped for a cry or at least a baby giggle.

To get to the bedroom where she supposed the baby was, she had to go through the kitchen. Kitchen cabinet doors stood open, exposing row after row of baby food jars unopened.

She gave an involuntary gasp. If Priscilla was hoarding all this baby food she bought every day, what was the baby eating?

She kept walking and soon forgot about the baby food when she spied the crib in the bedroom. And in the middle of the crib rested a bundle.

She sped to the baby bed.

There was a baby in there, all right. The hobos had been wrong about that. This was much more than air and blankets. And certainly too big for a doll.

She pulled the pink, frilly blankets aside, and her eyes almost popped out of her head. She was petrified with amazement. Her tongue froze in her mouth, and her throat turned to a cavern of aching ice that would not thaw.

"Who???" she finally whispered when her throat relaxed.

"Who?

"Who?" sounding like an owl who-ing hoarsely in the evening.

She had seen stuffed bears, stuffed elk, and stuffed tigers before, but never in the entirety of her life had she ever seen a stuffed baby.

She leaned over the crib and peered closer. The baby eyes were black with lacquered lashes. The cheeks plump and dimpled. The tender arms as soft as cotton to the touch.

"Who?" said Amber.

"Who, who, *who,* WHO!" She finally screamed so loud, the whole house shook. She jerked her hands away from the crib bars so violently, she upset the entire cradle. The stuffed baby rolled on the floor and kept staring at her with her lacquered eyelashed eyes.

"Who!" Amber took off running, vaguely aware that Priscilla Redwine's bathroom door was opening.

She didn't stop to look at the woman. She didn't turn around. She ran through the kitchen with its cabinets of unopened food. She ran through the living room and reached the front entrance.

She unclicked the locks and jerked the door open, almost pulling the knob out of its socket.

She ran down Corral Hollow Road hollering, "WHO? WHO? WHO?" and on into her driveway, forgetting her stealthy plan of careful deceit to tiptoe home through the back door with none the wiser about her little secret trip. Forgetting about how in the morning she was going to smugly describe the Priscilla Redwine baby to Wade and to all who would listen with open mouths.

"WHO?"

Running. Running. Running to her own house.

Her front door swung open, and her father, mother, and twin brothers stood with their eyes stretched, taken back by the image of Amber running toward them hollering "WHO?"

Her father caught her, held her, stroked her head, and asked, "Amber, Amber, what happened? Did somebody bother you? Calm down and tell me, baby, what's wrong?"

But all Amber could say was, "WHO? WHO? WHO?"

It had been Wade who dashed across the road and who finally calmed her down so they could hear what happened. In a strange way it had happened just as she had planned, with Wade and the others listening with open mouths. But it took all of them, including Wade, keeping a steady eye on her that made even the telling of it possible.

That was another time. Now the family sat in the living room waiting for Amber and wondering where she was. Jason's retelling of the Priscilla Redwine story only reminded Grace of the fantastic lengths to which Amber would go to soothe her curiosity.

"An insatiable appetite for knowing," Grace decided.

"You must admit, though," David said, "some good came out of Amber's detective work. It did get that Priscilla Redwine some help. Social workers and doctors galore."

"For truth?" said Papa, enchanted by the episode that had taken place before his arrival. "That's my Amber, all right."

"But where is she?" Grace wondered.

"Seems to me that the Priscilla Redwine incident started with a walk too. And look how long she was gone that time," Johnny said.

"Gone for hours and we didn't even know it. Slipping out each night to time that woman," Grace said.

"But where is she?" Grace insisted. "Lord, I hope she didn't go on one of her unusual hunting trips."

"We already did the hunting, Mama," said Johnny. "I tell you, she was headed home. She'll be here soon."

"She'd better," said Grace, a motherly threat in her voice. She was remembering with clarity that extraordinary hunting episode that day last year.

TEN

"We have a tomboy on our hands, I think," Grace said from the couch, looking up at the gun rack with its one empty place. Evening shadows dappled the shining oakwood floor and bounced against the brick fireplace. Grace was thinking of another Saturday morning when Wade was away at a wrestling match and the twins had gone with him. "A girl born with adventure in her blood."

Amber had gotten up that day last year, frisky as a pup, and declared that she was going for a walk, claiming that even the very pine trees in the distance beckoned her to come and enjoy the day.

"Go ahead," Grace had agreed reluctantly as she folded bathroom towels and other freshly dried laundry. "But don't go hunting alone. I don't like the idea of you out by yourself with a gun. What if you accidentally shot yourself?"

"I won't, Mama. Haven't you said that I am a fantastic markswoman?"

"Yes, Amber, you are. And you're careful too. It's just that sometimes your thirst for adventure frightens me. Heaven knows, I'm not sure why. You're so bold, if you met up with a bear, I declare I'd have to pray, 'Lord, please have mercy on the bear.' But then again, you don't have sense enough to be afraid of anything."

"Look, Mama, no gun," Amber said, showing her that the

gun was still in its rack over the living-room fireplace.

She embraced her mother and soon had bounded out of the front door. Instead of taking Corral Hollow Road, she struck out across the field. On the far horizon cows, like mobile brown shrubs against the hillside, chewed their cuds and fussed at flies with their tails.

As she ambled through pastures she watched blue jays pipe through the air, their flashing wings riding the wind. All around her life quivered: the ghostlike gum trees throbbing with the shrill dronings of cicadas and the small sounds of bugs hurrying and fat bees humming.

A jackrabbit leaped up in the field and went bounding through a maze of sage.

And then she saw the prize she would take home. She got down on her belly and moved as quietly as an Indian in a Western movie.

Before she could say *lightning*, she had it.

Holding her treasure in one hand, she started back to her house.

There, she found Grace sitting in the living-room rocker, humming to herself. She tiptoed up from behind and covered her mother's eyes with one hand.

"Mama, I got a surprise for you. Can you guess what?"

"Will you give me some clues?"

"Yes."

"What color is it?"

"Guess."

"Blue?"

"No."

"Green?"

"No."

"Yellow?"

"Yes."

"Is that the only color?"

"No."

"Lots of colors?"

"No."

"One more color?"

"Yes."

"Purple?"

"No."

"Black?"

"Yes."

"So it's yellow and black. Inanimate?"

Amber hesitated. "Yes, it's dead."

"Yellow and black. Hmmm. Inanimate. What could it be? Is it something to eat?"

"No. You wouldn't."

"Oh. I know what it is!" Grace said, clapping her hands together. "You've brought me a flower. A lovely yellow flower with black eyes. A black-eyed Susan. Oh, Amber!" And she jumped up from the rocker and turned around with a delighted smile on her face.

But her joy quickly evaporated. In one hand Amber held a headless three-foot-long rattlesnake.

"Amber!"

"Oh, Mama, it can't hurt you."

"Put that dreadful thing down."

"But it's dead."

"Obviously, but how . . . ?"

"I killed it."

"What? How?" Grace gave Amber one long, despairing look and threw up her hands. "No, I don't want to hear about it. Amber Westbrook, you go to your room till your father gets here. And get that thing out of my sight."

"Oh, Mama."

"'Go, you hear?"

"Land's sake. It's just an old dead snake."

"And you killed it. What if that viper had bitten you? And there you'd be out in the middle of nowhere dying from snakebite."

"But it didn't bite me. And I killed it."

"Lord, have mercy. What did I do to deserve this fate? A tomboy daughter with not enough sense to leave some of God's creatures be. Just wait until David gets home. You just wait." And Grace went to her room, saying, "I feel a migraine coming." She lay across her bed mumbling, "A daughter who hunts snakes . . ."

Amber had been so pleased when she first saw the snake. She had gotten down on her knees and flattened herself out, slinking along on her belly Indian-style, quiet and quick, until she came right upon the rattler.

From the back of the diamond-checkered serpent, she shot out her hands as quick as lightning and grabbed his tail. With a swift flick of her wrist, *pop,* she had whipped the snake's head off his neck.

She had gone home to show off her trophy to her brothers and Wade, hoping they were back from the wrestling match, but they were not there. Then she had seen Grace and impulsively decided to play a little mischief on her mother, but it had backfired and now she had to spend a boring afternoon in her room. Thank God for books; otherwise she would be as dead as the rattler from boredom.

She went outside and buried the snake and came back to her bedroom and picked up a book to read.

From down the hall she could hear Grace mumbling to the air, "A daughter who hunts snakes . . ."

"She's just brave, that's all," admitted Jason begrudgingly as he held up the wall between the living room and the dining room.

"I wish I could have seen the look on Mama's face when Amber shook that old snake at her," said Johnny, his long frame stretched out on the round rug so that his feet hit the hardwood floor and his head rested against the soft hooked carpet of flowers.

David, who sat next to Grace, looked a little worried but tried not to show it. "I'm giving her a piece of my mind when she gets home this time."

"I'd like to see her snake out of this one," said Jason, stretching out next to Johnny.

"Think she could be at Wade's by now?" Johnny asked.

Just then, a familiar scratch at the door. They all jumped, but it was only Wade. "Amber here yet?" he asked.

"Oh, Amber, Amber," whispered Grace, "where are you?"

ELEVEN

"I was hoping she'd be here by now," Wade said. "After today' s practice, smelling sweating wrestlers and squeezing my opponents' rusty necks into nelson holds, I'm ready for the sweet smell of women and something more delicate for my fingers to do. They're itching to touch the cello strings. I thought Amber might want to play a duet after dinner."

David stared stonily at his watch and drummed his thick fingers on the couch arm. The evening shadows now lay across the room, as heavy as his thick arms.

"No, she's not back yet," Grace said, holding on to her sense of humor. "That curiosity of hers is enough to kill a cat. Probably lingering somewhere on her way home, trying to satisfy it."

"She knows about curiosity and cats for sure," Wade said.

"Legendary curiosity," said Papa.

"Don't we all know it," Johnny said. "We've got the nosiest sister in the whole town."

"More like the whole state," said Jason.

"Speaking of curiosity and cats, I remember the last time we went to the river together. She told me the Minerva story," Wade said.

"The who?" asked Papa.

That spring day weeks ago, an evergreen branch from a giant sequoia swayed like a natural fan above Wade and Amber. From the murmuring river a balmy wind blew. Beneath the tree where strawberry begonias blossomed, they sat on a cushion of crushed flowers. She unwrapped the lunch she had packed and handed him a vanilla-wafer sandwich of salami and sweet pickles.

For a while they had munched the sandwiches silently and studied the soothing colors of crimson primrose and golden alpine poppies bordering the river.

When they had crunched on the apples and nuts she had brought for dessert, they had buried their garbage and had thrown the shells toward the river. Suddenly a mouse skidded from under a clump of flowers and scurried away with a nutshell that had a little meat left in it.

"Now there's an industrious animal," Wade had said, laughing.

"How adorable he looks with his cheeks fat with the nut. Good thing no cats are around."

"Uh-huh," he answered lazily.

"Wade?" Amber's voice took on a new lilt.

He turned to her, all ears.

"Have you ever looked at the cat-and-mouse game with the mouse's eyes?"

"No," he said, "I don't have beady eyes." Then he kept silent. When she looked like she was looking, something about her face reminded him of Papa Westbrook when he was telling one of his tall tales.

"You know," she said, chewing on a blade of grass, "while the cat walks around proudly with its hunting chest stuck out saying, 'I smell a rat,' the mouse is squealing and fluttering his tail, shrieking, 'I smell a cat!' Minerva was such a mouse."

"Minerva?" said Wade.

"Now, Minerva was a fat mouse," Amber explained. "She liked to eat."

"What did she eat?"

"Spiders and creepy crawling things like grubs and caterpillars and centipedes. But she pined for the chance to get inside somebody's kitchen. She wanted to nibble on cheese. Not your ordinary American cheese; she craved cheddar cheese. Rich and tangy. A sharp cheddar cheese is what she yearned for. And although she had never before eaten this cheese, she had heard of its incomparable quality. Minerva, after all, did have impeccable taste.

"Minerva would vary her diet sometimes by eating tree bark, roots, nuts, and field seeds. These were common enough mouse foods, but then her cheese tooth would start bothering her, and she'd begin craving the more elegant cheddar, that gourmet dish for mice.

"Minerva's mother, however, was quite concerned. She had said often enough, 'Minerva, don't be meddling around People's houses.' Minerva's mother despised People and often referred to them as that disgusting, heartless human race of animals that are always trying to stamp out the whole family of mice with their poisons and traps.

"Minerva's mother was a concerned mother mouse who looked after her offspring with a discerning eye. Tried to teach Minerva mouse about the perils and pitfalls of life."

"Just like all mamas," Wade added.

"But as the old folks say, 'Children will be children.'

"One evening, I guess it was about seven o'clock, Minerva got an awful fancy for some cheddar, the deep yellow sharp variety. She ate a few grubs, but they didn't satisfy her. They weren't the right texture. They only whetted her appetite for cheese.

"Remembering her mother's earlier lessons, Minerva thought about all the reasons she should not pine for the forbidden food. First of all, she didn't want to upset her mother. Usually Minerva was an obedient daughter. Then again, she knew that to go cheese searching was a dangerous undertaking."

"Uh-huh," Wade said.

"You see," Amber said, "there were all sorts of mishaps awaiting a too adventuresome mouse. For instance, the possibility of encountering a mousetrap, that steel-jawed contraption that would gape its mouth and close its fangs on a mouse tail or a mouse toe."

"Dreadful!" Wade said.

"Yes. Thinking about it made Minerva shudder. Then there were those absolutely impossible People, who would resort to all sorts of strange behavior at the sight of a mouse. Women who screamed loud enough to burst a poor mouse's eardrums. Grown females who jumped on milk stools and held their dresses above their knees like little girls. The male People would come out and try to rescue the women doing their stool dance of fright by killing the mouse.

"Minerva's cousin, Alfredo, had been cornered, shot at with a pistol, beaten with a kitchen chair, and left for dead on top of the garbage heap.

"There were dire consequences to be considered. And the last hazard of all was that most mangy nuisance, the cat.

"Even though Minerva had never seen a cat, her mother had once described one for her."

"What did the cat look like to the mama?" Wade asked.

"'The cat, my dear Minerva,' the mother began, 'is a mangy creature with sharp knives for claws. Indeed, one clawed paw can hold a whole mouse in its viselike clutches. What makes it even more contemptible is that it lives with that awful breed known as People.

"'The cat has a roaring voice. The *meow* is a whining sound like a high-strung wind out of the north, pouncing down on the ears, enough to make one quite deaf.

"'The cat,' Minerva's mother continued, 'has long stiff hairs hanging off its dreadful mouth. When it makes the high whining sound, the hairs tremble with a terrifying quiver. And it's always showing off for the People by taking advantage of helpless mice.'"

"How awful for the mouse," Wade said.

Amber went on with the story. "'You never can tell what color the eat's going to be, either. Some come black as night. Others white as cotton. Some are motley-hued. Some are three-colored cats with cavernous mouths. There are huffy orange striped ones too. So don't count on an exact complexion. A cat can be any one of several colors.

"'The tail is an instrument of deception. He swishes it from side to side. That's supposed to be a sign of contentment. Don't believe it. I've seen them swish their tails from side to side while slapping and pawing a mouse.

"'Always beware the fat tail. It usually means the cat is vicious. Now, if you see a fat tail accompanied by hair sticking up all over the body like a moving brush with bristles, look out! That's a mean, ornery animal. Known to victimize and prey on some poor mouse.

"'But you know you're doomed when you smell the eat's breath. It is as hot as hell. The tongue reminds you of the fires of hell. It is red. And when you see the cat's tonsils, it's all over.

"'Now listen, Minerva, this is very important.' And the mother mouse stared the daughter mouse squarely in the eye. 'Before you see the claws, the whiskers, the color, you can smell the cat. As I have told you, his breath is hot and rank. It reminds you of stagnant pools where skunks have lingered. When you smell the cat, it is warning enough. Do not come out of hiding'—Minerva's mother pointed a cautious finger at her daughter—'for you smell a cat.'"

"The mama mouse had the situation covered," Wade said.

Amber continued. "Now Minerva had listened intently to her mother's warnings of woe about the cat, and she was appropriately terrified, but her desire for cheddar cheese ran unchecked even though, as I say, she had never tasted a piece before.

"About a week before that, her mother decided that Minerva was old enough to hear about the death of Minerva's father. He had met a fate similar to her cousin's, except it was a cat who got him. It was a cat who ate him.

"Minerva tried hard not to think about cheese. But every time she looked at the gnawed hole her father had burrowed into the People's house, she thought about a nice piece of cheese. It was an irresistible longing. And every time she saw that particular shade of deep yellow on a butterfly, on a fallen autumn leaf, on a daffodil, her mouth watered in uncontrolled drooling.

"She wanted to tell the other mice, but she was too ashamed of this compelling urge.

"One day while she was out scampering near a woodpile, she had the most extravagant yearning for cheese. No words of caution seemed to stick in her mind. Not the lesson of the claws as sharp as knives. Not the picture of the screaming women whose husbands used chairs and guns as weapons against mice. Not even the gaping horror of the steel mousetrap could quell this surging passion. The only possible answer to her great desire was a nibble, at least one nibble, of cheese."

"She was hungry for cheese, all right," Wade said.

Amber said, "Now, it was late in the day, when the sycamore cast shadows from the tree branches on the house walls, and the wind had come out of his cocoon in the sky to holler down the corridors of the alleys of time. But Minerva had her urge. She became a hunter. She would have her wedge of cheese. Her morsel of gold.

"A quick glance told her that Mr. and Mrs. People were home. There were two Fords—one red, one blue—in the driveway. She could not, however, smell the cat, but she saw long, gray hairs lying about. Somewhere a cat crouched.

"Minerva would not be stopped. She scampered from the

woodpile and hid under a tire of the red Ford parked in the driveway.

"From where she sat curled up beneath the tire, she could more clearly see the hole her father had bored in a wall of the house. She didn't think about what had happened to her father, though. She thought only of the smell of cheddar.

"The coast looked clear. She ran across the vast open space between the car and the hole in the wall, making herself as small as possible. There was terror in each quick step she took, but the need for cheese was stronger. Before she knew it, she had come to the hole. She had second thoughts. Should she turn around and go back to her woodpile?

"A furtive movement behind her sent her scurrying into the hole in the wall.

"Inside the hole. Now she was between the outer and inner walls of the house. She found she was trembling from fright, but she had made it this far safely. She sniffed. Yes, she could smell cheese. She made herself perfectly quiet. Listened. There were People around, but they seemed to be in another part of the house.

"Minerva tiptoed to where the hole opened on the inside of the wall of the house and looked out on a shiny green linoleum floor. Her nose told her there was water about.

"She could smell some meat sizzling in an oven. She was in the kitchen then. That was good. The kitchen was where the cheese was kept.

"She took a deep breath and wheeled from her safe position behind the wall. She sniffed the delicious perfume of cheese. Then she spied it. It was right next to her.

"She rushed to the wedge of cheese, but part of it was laced with steel and wood. 'Steel,' she whispered to herself. 'This is a trap.' But some of her mice friends had told her that if a mouse was very careful, she could safely nibble a little of the cheese.

"Minerva moved adroitly and so did not spring the trap.

"She peered and saw how she could grab a bite without moving the mechanism of steel.

"She bent over and tasted the cheese. 'Scrumptious!' It was the best food she had ever tasted.

"She carefully bit off another piece. 'Ummm. Heavenly.'

"She ate more and more. The trap did not budge.

"Her little mouse stomach was almost full.

"As she was preparing to take another bite she heard a shrill scream that caused her to dig her toes into the linoleum, but the linoleum was not solid ground, was not dry land, and so instead of clinging to earth, she went skidding across the slick linoleum floor, away from the escape hole."

Wade caught his breath. "Poor mouse."

"In the distance," Amber continued, "she heard heavy, running feet.

"Now she remembered in minute detail the description her mother had painted for her of the screaming woman on the familiar stool with her dress pulled up. These, then, were the husband's footsteps she heard advancing.

"Soon he would be upon her.

"Minerva got her bearings and began to scamper back toward the hole.

"Out of nowhere she smelled a peculiar odor slap her across her face. Just as she reached the hole she saw a ball of stiff gray fur blocking her way.

"There before her hunched a steel-gray cat with flickering green lights for eyes, ready to pounce.

"Minerva came to a screeching halt on the glass-green floor again.

"Everything was in a spin. She could hear the whirring screams of the woman, like the cries of a siren in her ears. The green floor swirled under her like the sea. The husband's pounding feet had abruptly stopped.

"She was doomed. She could see the cat squinch his green eyes, the powerful cat claws reach for her, the humped back bristled with brushlike hairs. And then she looked up into the red-hell tongue of the cat. Minerva knew her life was over. She would end up like her father."

"She's done for, for sure," Wade said.

"Suddenly she heard a loud crash, a chair came whizzing by her head like a bullet, but it missed her and hit the cat. The cat, fur flying, went howling and screeching, the fat tail skinnied and drooped. The cat, now reduced to a mewling pussy, slinked away, hurt and humiliated.

"Minerva gathered her wits about her. The unfortunate cat had left the hole free.

"She flew to her escape through the hole in the wall and waited within the inner compartment. When it was safe, she fled as swiftly as she could back to her woodpile.

"There Minerva found her mother waiting, her face scowling anxiously."

"Frightened half to death, I bet," Wade said.

Amber, nodded and continued, "'My dear Minerva!' her mother cried with a trembling voice. 'You had me worried to death. What a fright I have had. Where have you been?' Then her shrewd mother eyes spied the cheese crumbs around Minerva's mouth and knew.

"'Oh, Mother,' Minerva said, her own shaking body quieted by now, 'I have been on a wonderful adventure. I have seen the cat and I have tasted cheese.'

"'What!? Haven't I taught you better? What possessed you?'

The hasty questions came tumbling one after the other. 'How could you? It must have been h—'

"'Heavenly,' Minerva said, thinking of the cheese, her eyes rapt with beads of joy as she giggled.

"She savored the taste of cheese still on her tongue as she revealed to her mother all the flavorful dimensions of the tangy, golden cheddar.

"'But the cat?' Her mother sighed.

"'Oh, my dear Mama,' Minerva said, shrugging off the hazards of the hunt, 'one cannot fully appreciate the joys of heaven unless one has suffered the horrors of hell.'"

Wade ended his rendition of Amber's cat story.

Grace settled her eyes on him and said, "Some story. I must say, Wade, that doesn't help matters. It only serves to prove my earlier point. Like that mouse, Amber's too adventurous. A girl who stalks snakes. Out there alone with a gun. In the middle of earthquake weather. She could have an accident. No telling what other dangerous tricks she's got up her sleeve. I'd feel much better if I knew she was in her room reading about adventures instead of out there creating them."

"I tell you," said Papa in defense of Amber, "nothing can take the place of a real-life adventure." David was silent.

"I'm sure Amber's all right, Mrs. Westbrook," Wade said finally. "Think I'd better get across the road. My turn to set the table for supper."

TWELVE

A few hours later Wade looked up from playing his cello to see the sheriff's car pull up to the Westbrook house.

"It's late," he whispered to himself. When he'd begun playing, it was still light. Now it was dark. "Something's wrong."

The Westbrook porch light was on. The black-and-white star-shaped insignia stamped on the car door and the dark, somber uniform Sheriff Wilson wore as he marched stiffly up to the Westbrook house were distress signals to anybody who lived on Corral Hollow Road. The sheriff only showed up when there was trouble.

Although Wade could not hear a word, he could see Grace standing in the doorway wringing her hands in her apron. Then the sheriff went inside and closed the door behind him.

Wade stared at the silent cello and bit his lip. "Sheriff's at the Westbrooks'," he announced as he went into the kitchen and took his seat at the supper table.

"Wonder what's the matter," said his mother.

"Probably nothing," his father said.

"Probably nothing," Wade repeated.

His mind could not stay on his dinner but kept darting back to the Westbrook house.

He was startled out of his reverie by a bald, hammering knock.

His father went to the door.

Wade, glued to his seat, could overhear the conversation coming from the front of the house.

"What can I do for you, Sheriff?"

"Just want to know if you've seen the Westbrook girl. She's missing."

"Missing?"

"Didn't come home this evening."

"Sure she's not down the road visiting someplace?"

"Her mother's called everybody she could think of."

Wade's mother got up and went into the living room. Wade could not move. The voices drifted to him as though from another world. It was as though some giant wrestler had him in a vise. The giant wrestler squeezed him so tight, he paralyzed his arms and legs.

His mother spoke. "My God, it's way past dark already."

"May I talk to your boy?"

"Wade!"

Wade broke loose from the giant's grip of panic. He walked into the living room.

"Seems the Westbrook girl's missing. You seen her?"

His mouth flew open, but the invisible wrestler had set up a new match inside his stomach. A full nelson to the guts.

"No, sir. I haven't talked to her since yesterday. Right before the earthquake when we were supposed to go swimming and hunting. But after the earthquake Mrs. Westbrook wanted everybody home. And then she waved good-bye this morning when I saw her going swimming and hunting with her brothers as I was getting ready to go wrestling practice."

The sheriff scratched his head. "She never reached her house, evidently."

His father said, "Anything we can do, Sheriff, let us know."

With that the sheriff left. The family returned to the table, but everybody was too full of worry to finish eating.

As they bussed their dishes to the sink his father said, "I pray to God Amber's all right."

The vigil began.

Wade and his father went across the road to talk to David, who paced up and down, wavering between jumping in his pickup to go look for Amber and staying near Grace in case the sheriff brought back news or in case Amber herself appeared with some sensible excuse for her absence. At this point he'd even take a stupid excuse for her absence. Worry was taking the place of rage.

"Amber, where are you?" Wade whispered as he stood under her chinaberry tree. The giant panic wrestler was back, and his grip was awesome; he bent Wade's head down to his chest.

Then Wade heard the sheriff's car lurching along the road, headed back to where they all stood waiting in the Westbrook yard.

The sheriff said, "Went down to talk to the Reyes children. They hadn't seen anything unusual. Think we'd better get everybody we can to go searching."

David, now spurred on by something specific to do, dashed to his pickup with the twins. Wade heard him mumble, "Maybe she's had an accident and is lying somewhere on the side of the road, hit by a car."

Papa Westbrook looked like all the air had been let out of him. He sat next to Grace.

Wade and his father hurried across the road and hopped in their truck.

Mrs. Dewberry joined Grace and Papa Westbrook on the porch bench. A giant inkwell had splashed over the sky and snuffed out the sun. Here and there stars spotted the stained dark, and the grim-faced men in their pickups turned on their headlights and pierced the somber paper of night with high-beamed slashes as they scoured the roads that Amber might have taken.

As hours passed and the search continued, Grace's eyes seemed to sink to the back of her head, fill with water, and run over.

Her weeping was an eerie accompaniment to the odd symphony of car and truck motors and tires whining.

Finally the men reported back to the Westbrook house.

Nothing.

An avalanche of helplessness swept over David, his shoulders stooped over the phone as he dialed the doctor's number.

"Dr. Goldberg, David Westbrook here. No, it's not just my wife's migraine. I'm calling about Amber. She's missing, and my wife . . ."

David hung up the phone and went to sit by Grace, who looked grayer and grayer in her lavender, her hands trembling the way tomato vines quiver when the Tracy wind is up.

On the opposite couch Wade, the twins, and Papa shuddered.

Wade's parents stood in the doorway, helpless.

A set of squealing tires signaled new hope. But it was only the doctor with his black bag and hypodermic needle.

After Dr. Goldberg left Grace stretched out on her bed like death, her weeping eyes now closed in drug-induced, temporary peace.

There was nothing left for anyone to do now but go in their houses and rooms and wonder, "Where is Amber?"

THIRTEEN

"Where is Amber?"

The second day of her daughter's disappearance, Grace imagined all manner of horrors.

Was Amber dead by accidental shotgun wound?

Dead by rattlesnake bite?

Assaulted by demented murderer?

Sometimes Grace was consumed by rages and shook her fists at the sky, threatening to skin Amber alive, if she was alive. But those four words—*if she is alive*—soon smothered all her anger and left only agony.

The migraines disappeared. There was no room for anything but her loss, not for headaches or back pain or colds or sore throats. Every other pain diminished in the face of this paralyzing trauma.

"Where is Amber?"

If Grace had been a photographer, she would have shot pictures of gnats swarming, hissing vipers, and the parched skin of earth just before an earthquake. She was beside herself with grim visions and totally uncentered. The cooking pots looked wrong. The gas flame never flared brightly enough for her eyes so full of darkness lately, and so meals burned.

She forgot the ratio of flour to shortening and lost the recipe for her favorite crust. The twins took cautious bites out of each serving of apple cobbler and lay their forks down.

David ate only to sustain himself and so paid scant attention to biscuits hard as rocks, burned beans, and scorched rice.

Papa Westbrook stared off into space from time to time and whistled to himself, *Sacred mountain, sacred tree, sacred river that runs to the sea* in a minor key at the dinner table, where it was totally inappropriate.

Across the road evening was falling in the Dewberry living room. A bougainvillaea sunset fringed with crimson flames spread its fire through the plate-glass window by which the cello was stationed, and then went out.

Wade sat down to play the cello.

First he rubbed the catgut bow hairs with the sticky rosin until they were tacky enough.

He massaged the bow until he remembered how water sparkled like jewels in the tight curls of Amber's black lamb's-wool hair when she surfaced after diving.

He had sat down to play the cello.

Before starting, he tightened the pegs. His strong fingers turned the wooden knobs until he created from memory Amber's flute fingers strumming mountains, trees, and rivers into being. He worked until the wires sang in tune.

He had sat down to play the cello.

Before he could begin, he oiled the ebony fingerboard, the spruce belly, the maple scroll, the graceful body.

He polished until he was dizzy with Amber's hips, the curve of her legs dripping with beads of water, her swimsuit clinging as she stepped out of the river.

He had sat down to play the cello.

But the bow was quiet.

He remembered that the fingers pulling the shotgun trigger and whipping the snake's tail belonged to the same hands that called forth notes from the flute. And the sweet sound of her voice telling about the curious Minerva mouse was the voice with the *who?* cry caught in its throat, describing the Priscilla Redwine baby. And everywhere he looked, and especially when he looked at his cello, he saw her.

He had sat down to play the cello.

Quest

FOURTEEN

Amber followed the path of the river deep into the forest. The weight of the heavy backpack slowed her down as she walked through ferns and over fallen trees.

In the backpack she carried a knife, soap, toothbrush, matches, a few cooking utensils, a sleeping bag, gown, jeans, socks, shirt, and underwear. Her swimsuit was folded up in her back pocket, and she toted her gun across her chest.

Beyond these things, she carried questions and the need to know, strewn like bright pine branches balanced on top of the backpack.

"Why didn't they tell me I was not theirs?" she asked the air.

"Why did cousin Abyssinia abandon me? I mean, my real mother, Abyssinia, abandon me? Mother? But what about Mama? Oh, it's all mixed up." She just wanted to get someplace and think. Although there had been plenty of talk about the relatives in Ponca City, Oklahoma, the name Abyssinia was just one of the kin. Amber had never even seen her.

When she got near that part of the river that dipped into the sea, a golden eagle spread his wings, casting a long shadow over her path. And when she stopped at the place where she had decided to camp, the eagle sat down on the tree like an animal vacationer at a human zoo and stared at her, his long talons wrapped around a eucalyptus branch. He did not move his powerful wings for an hour as he watched her claim her place in the woods.

When she had finished unpacking, the mist came down and lifted the eagle up from the eucalyptus to the hills and carried him far beyond the mountains.

She looked all around her at the pine and sequoias swaying in the breeze, the fragrant bushes of sage and rosemary, the red-blushed clouds half an hour before sunset.

Her backpack no longer weighed her down. She was ready to go walking; walking is when she did some of her best thinking. She needed to think and walk during these last minutes of dusk.

She started off in the gathering twilight, moving away from the river, taking in the seascape of a wild tangerine sun plunging toward the violet and scallop-waved ocean. Now she kept hiking and looking up, naming the wheeling and perching birds, discerning their songs, their feathers. Did they have any answers, these innocent birds?

She looked at the blue jay who passes truth to her baby birdies by instinct and asked, "Blue jay in the sequoia, can you tell me why they hid the truth from me?"

"Brown wren above the pine, why?"

"Robin in the evergreen, why?"

"Thrush in the bunchberry bush, why, why?"

Then some sixth sense directed her eyes to the ground, and her heart thumped up in her throat and hung there.

A mass of crawling creatures writhed and wriggled before her feet.

She could not get around them.

She heard something fall, thudding to the ground behind her. She could not go back, either.

They blocked her path. Raised their dangerous heads and swayed their hooded eyes at her.

Mama snakes, daddy snakes, and baby snakes dressed up in their diamond backs and glittering scales.

The hackles on her neck rose and her muscles locked.

The creepers set up a clatter of rattling.

"Oh, Mama," and Grace's warnings came back to haunt her, "Snakes are out there, Amber."

Why, oh why had she laughed at her mother?

But she's not your mother, the snakes seemed to say.

They rattled in front of her. They rattled behind her. Why had she laughed at her mama, who was scared stupid of snakes, who couldn't even stand to look at a worm.

I tell you, she's not your mama, the snakes mocked.

Some part of her was aware of clefts and abysses in the customary wood sounds. Chirpless birds. The crickets in the tall grass had stopped cricketing.

The dry rattling mesmerized the whole forest until it made dumb every other sound.

Nearest her, one snake licked his hot tongue at her; fangs shot out like a flickering fork of fire.

Whose child are you? You're not your mother's daughter. Not your daddy's girl. Not your brothers' sister. You don't know. You're ignorant!

Instinctively she jumped high and grabbed a tree branch, hoisted herself up, and swung her feet over the limb out of the way of the family of snakes.

Her breath had left her body and was still crouching in the middle of the swarming serpents.

Just when she was about to retrieve her breath she heard a hiss. She looked above her and spied a grandfather snake wrapped around a thick branch. He looked about nine feet long and three feet thick.

Ignorant. Ignorant. Ignorant. Not your mama's girl.

She fell backward out of the tree into a clump of bushes away from the snakes and started running.

"Snakes, get out of my way. My way. My way. My way." She was her own hollering echo.

She ran and ran. Somehow she got back to the campsite.

She was shaking so, she had to sit down and hold her head in her hands.

After a while she could hear the sounds of the forest again.

The birds were chirping. The crickets singing. She removed her head from her hands and listened intently, but she could not hear any rattling.

She started whistling. At first the whistling came with hardly any breath in it. Without any tune anywhere near it. A halting sound. Her skipping heartbeat began to steady itself as she half whistled on. By the time the whistle became as clear as a whistle should be, her pulse had gentled itself and night had wrapped a soft black cloak around her.

She knew that if she had started exploring a half hour later, she would not have seen the nest of snakes. It would have been too dark.

She dared not venture out again unless it was to go back home.

Home.

She rolled her sleeping bag up and put it in her backpack but quickly took it out again.

Home? *You're an outcast. Abandoned. A daughter under false pretenses.*

Besides, she wasn't letting any snakes make her go back home. Besides, it was too dark. But when she thought about the rattling snake nest, she wasn't too sure. Maybe when morning came . . . It was pitch black. She could hardly make out the river and the sea. Besides, where was home?

She unzipped the sleeping bag and settled down. Was it fear of the dangers she had walked into or a blinding anger that she had been abandoned and lied to all these years that infected her eyes and made her cry? After a while tiredness swept all other considerations away, and she fell sound asleep.

In her dreams she heard sharp bird talons and saw a beak striking again and again against yellow-and-black flesh, slippery-skinned and fanged with poison.

Soon after the strange dream, the morning sun climbed to the edge of the earth and hesitated.

She woke up itching and scratching. *I've been snake-bitten,* she thought. But when she looked down at her skin, she saw that she was covered with a fine rash.

"Poison ivy," she moaned.

As she sat up in the sleeping bag the bright sun showed her the poison vines tangled among the innocent mint and sage.

The rash broke out in whelped stings over her face, arms, hands, and stomach where she had scratched during the night.

She made a poultice of mint and mud, but still the fire of the poison ivy taunted her fingers with promises that if they only scratched a little, they could put out the fire, but whenever her nails dug into her skin, the poison fire smirked and spread its stinging torture even more.

She stopped scratching and thought of a fire for tea; this thought exaggerated the itching. But she gritted her teeth, told her fingers to be still, and went to fetch water from the river.

Where the water dipped into the sea, she saw the blue color of it begin to change. The water sparkled brightest here and began to churn itself from light blue into indigo fringed with white foam until the water flowed clear indigo. She saw stones at the bottom of the river and little schools of fish flashing in and around the stones as they wiggled through the crystal stream. The sight of the water made her more thirsty. She leaned over and dipped the pan into the indigo blue.

On the way back to her small camp, she saw the eagle bent over a long, looping serpent. Then he lifted the rattler in his claws and climbed the sky.

So one of the snakes had stalked her and slinked around, ready to poison her, but the eagle had watched and swooped down and made the preyer the preyed-upon.

"Well, that's the end of snake worry," she said as she gathered kindling and dead wood for the fire "with an eagle like that watching."

For tea she picked wild mint leaves and slipped them in the pot of water. For breakfast she found the spotted brown eggs of pheasants.

For lunch she caught a perch, seasoned him with sage, and smoked him over her fire.

For dinner she ate dandelion greens, the roots of cattails, which tasted like white potatoes, and juicy blackberries whose dark sweetness dribbled their syrup down her chin. She saved a few berries to rub on her skin as a repellent to the mosquitoes.

At day's end she settled down and listened to the river at the spot just before it poured into the sea. The incense of evergreen enchanted the forest, while the eagle beat his wings against the twilight sky. Soaring until the holiness of mountain, river, and tree disappeared and only the image of the eagle remained on the retina of her eye.

Before turning in for the evening, she took a soothing bath in the river. The fire of the poison ivy was beginning to smother itself by now.

As she dipped and ducked, soaping herself, she remembered other dips she had taken with Wade and her brothers. A scavenger of shame sank its crabby claws in her heart: she was remembering the betrayal and the symphony of the snake. *Whose child are you? You're not your mother's daughter. Not your daddy's girl. Not your brothers' sister. You don't know. You're ignorant!*

FIFTEEN

At last the sound of water lulled her to sleep, and she dreamed of the ocean and her place under the trees so intently, she imagined she was a water drop merging with a drop of pine sap. Then, turning, she welded herself to herself. Her breasts first. Then her spine, into one long, rippling cord until she was almost whole. A marbled miracle.

When she was brown, shot with gold, an emerging jewel snuggling the seed of herself deep into the lining of her mother's watermelon belly, when she curled herself into a prenatal ball, when she had done all this, she felt the power of herself.

Her ears opened like seashells. All during her centuries of nine months, the loudest whisper she ever heard was this: *Yes, yes, and yes.* Laughter, and always the whisper: *Yes, yes, and yes.*

The yeses now and then took on new form, and she was visited by the most extraordinary music coming down to her water home—an intricate, embellished voice rich in notes but with the echo of music sung through water. Somebody was singing just to her, in a voice as sweet as a flute. And she dreamed the song of herself.

It was while she was listening to the coda of the song that she almost discovered the thing that she knew she did not know. Some truth so ancient, so basic, it was as though some part of her had always known it. Voices. A woman's. A man's. But the husky voice was not David's, and the first voice was not Grace's. Both like talking music. Maybe the male and female voices of God?

Later, when she had walked through the fire that singed her naval after she had come up out of the water, she saw faces too vague to discern. The faces of . . . They were bending over looking at her. Just when she thought she had their faces almost clear, they wept and turned their heads. Then, like two kites escaping out of sight beyond a tree or over a hill, a strong wind snagged them, lifted them up higher, and turned their heads away from water.

Her eyes searched for them, but her sight could not hold them. They did not look back at her but stepped like leaves into the mouth of the wind.

SIXTEEN

Two days passed, and Amber was no closer to understanding that most baffling puzzle. What happened? Why was she abandoned? Then she thought about the dream. Were the people in her dream her cousin Abyssinia, her mother-cousin Abyssinia, her father-cousin Carl Lee?

To herself she said, "If I am not my mother's child, my daddy's daughter, grandpa's Amber, the sister of twins, then who am I?"

She thought and thought. She collected free corn.

She fished and smoked catches of bony perch and spiny bass. But still no answer.

If she could just have her flute. Maybe it would help her think.

Search for answers through the medium of music, an inner voice seemed to say.

How to do that?

With the flute, it answered.

"But the flute is home," she said.

The voice was still.

She would sneak home when everybody was asleep and get the flute out and come back to the woods.

But the snakes—she could only go home when it was daylight.

She could do it; wasn't she always the first one up? The rest would still be sleeping if she went early enough.

At the first blush of dawn she started out. When she reached home, the house slept the deep sleep of ignorance, unaware of her presence.

It only took her a minute and she was gone again.

She played the flute, with the sound of birds composing in the background. With tumbling water splashing between notes. With the wind in the pines haunting her breath breaks.

She played all day, stopping only to eat. And the flute, too, seemed to ask why, one thought with her mind.

She played and played; she played the sun out of the sky; she played until her lips would no longer quiver. And she passed out in her sleeping bag, the flute tucked in beside her like a baby. Down and down into the softest sleep.

In her dream she heard a flute playing high rondos and lilting minuets all around her forest bed. She lifted her head from her midnight dreams, perked her ears, and listened.

The soaring notes beckoned her. She unzipped her sleeping bag, threw the top cover aside, and stood up.

A ribbon of sound pulled her.

Whose child are you, out here alone and alone? the flute seemed to say.

There across the moonlit path, there in a clearing of fallen logs covered by a wild rambling of bougainvillaea blossoms, she saw a sight that made her gasp.

A troupe of deer—does, bucks, and fawns—stared at her with wide velvet eyes.

One taller than the rest, with antlers like a crown, held a silver flute in his hand. "Come, my Amber," he said in a voice as smooth as an oboe. "You love music and you love knowing. Come, and I'll play you your answers."

Her nightgown flowing behind her like a veil in the wind, she slipped down the path toward the buck until she stood among the purple flowers a few feet away from the deer.

She was so close, she reached out and touched a fawn. His whole body trembled under her gentle strokes.

Then the tall one motioned her to a nearby log. When she was comfortably seated, he lifted the flute to his lips. And the music came, sprinkling awe everywhere. For a moment the wind did not blow. Even the moon turned her head and listened with a silvery smile playing around her moon mouth.

A mother is the one who loves you.

A sterling sound flew from the flute. It lingered on the pine needles and tumbled into the flowing water, then drifted away on the churning foam where the blue became indigo.

A daddy is the one who cares.

Soon the sound lifted itself from the river and the sea, and returned riding on the back of the wind.

A brother is a dear rascal, a bother you cannot do without.

When the music came circling back, the deer began to move.

First in rows of threes.

Then they paired off and skipped into an intricate ballet of steps. Their hooves touched the ground and rose up. The fawns galloped in the middle, hooking hooves in hooves. Graceful in their spotted coats dappled with moonbeams.

Amber had never seen such prancing choreography, and neither, evidently, had the flowers. For all around her the bougainvillaea leaned breathless color toward the dancing deer and blushed with rouged petals of excitement.

When the music and the dance reached pure rapture, the handsome deer nodded his antlers.

And Amber stood up.

The sound of the flute pulled her away from the blushing flowers and in among the deer.

Her feet floated beneath her. And she touched each animal as she circled the dance forest floor.

The wind blew a steady hum through the pine trees while the deer backed away to let her dance alone in the center of the clearing.

And the flute-playing buck trilled a seamless sound, without pauses for breath.

And she danced on and on, weaving in and out of the circle of deer.

Soon the high music dropped from the top of the pines and sequoias and drifted down around her feet and settled on the forest floor.

When the music stopped, she found herself kneeling before the crowned deer.

When she looked up again, the forest was clear. The animals had gone. But when she looked down, she saw patterns of hoofprints in the dirt and grass.

The dawn woke her up. Her spirit soared. As she unzipped her sleeping bag new music played in her head.

She remembered the lyrics and what they declared:

A mother is the one who loves you
A daddy is the one who cares
A brother is a dear rascal, a bother you cannot do without. . . .

SEVENTEEN

It was the third day and she was exhausted. Her spirit was happy. A window had been lit in her mind, and when the truth hit it, it sparkled and sparkled. Yet the energy it cost to light the window, the all-day-long and into-the-evening playing of the flute, cost her.

On this third morning she rested and thought and thought. Now she was not so angry with her parents who had raised her but toward the ones who had left and abandoned her; she wasn't sure how she felt. That would come later.

"I'm going home," she said. And home to her was Grace and David, the twins, and Wade.

At the water's edge she brushed her teeth. The stones in the water seemed to reach under her lids and paint her eyes with the morning gold of legends. And the sound of the waves washing over the sand and stones was the sound of water speaking.

It was as though these three days had opened a spiritual place in her mind and she was open to night and day dreaming. Ready to receive the speech of deer and water. And this morning the water spoke to her.

The water said, "I am the smell of sweet decay. The current of old order, established before man made his footprints in the sand near the sea. The river knows. The river knows about fish and about man. I was there when man swam with fins, when his skin was silver scales. When he lost them and stepped out of the sea. When his skin was all colors and he owned everything his eyes could see. I am the dark smell of life. When the river flows briskly, its water is as murky as mud. They say water changes everything it touches. Even metal will wear down when troubled by water. Hill and mountain. Given time, water will erode rock into sand. And when I wish it, I move to music. I swell to music, and sometimes I rage, intrude upon the land, swirl, churn, surge, and roar. Now and then I cry acutely, shroud myself in fog and grieve.

"Now I know music. I have washed stone for thousands of years and tasted sulfur in my mouth. Now I know music and the river aroma of eternity. I am water and I know everything."

"You say you know everything," Amber said. "Then tell me about the Indians."

"I will tell you about the earthquake."

"Yes."

"One day long, long ago, the earthquake who lives beneath the river, just where I dip into the sea, became lonely and decided he would venture out of the water and onto dry land to see what wonders the earth held.

"But in order to come up, he had to break through rocks beneath the sea. Then through the crust of the earth until he was swimming up to the waves. When he got there, he walked on the sea until he reached dry land.

"The people ran when the earthquake came toward them. Even the rocks, steady as they had always been, were shaking with fright. The mountains, long known for their courage, trembled at the sight of the earthquake coming out of the water.

"The earthquake was so happy to touch the shore, he skipped under the valley, danced through the insides of the mountains.

Touched roads and unzipped the dark fabric of the earth.

"Now, the earthquake was dressed in clear red. If you were a tree or a rock or a mountain, you could see his stately presence. If, however, you were a mere human being, you could not imagine his appearance. You could only feel his presence by the way his movements shook everything in sight. By watching a rock, a tree, a mountain, you could feel him moving through everything.

"Even though the earthquake was huge and looming and large, he was innocently ignorant of his capabilities and effect. So what if the earth trembled beneath his feet? What does a human feel when he stomps his giant feet across the ground the ant is crawling on? Nothing. So it was with the earthquake. He was so immense, he did not appreciate his largeness in respect to the rest of the world. He was. And that was sufficient reason to do what he was supposed to do. An earthquake quakes in much the same way that a storm cloud storms. Because it has to. Surely the gray cloud does not care who it whips with vicious downpours stippled with thunderbolts, whether man-killing sharks or openmouthed babes, it goes about its business of storming.

"The earthquake was about its business of quaking.

"But there was one group of humans who were not afraid of the earthquake. The Indians. When the earthquake quaked, they offered up a ritual dance. A presentation of praise and welcome. A bright dance at once joyful and hospitable. They made fires. Feasted. And danced until they were dizzy. And all around the celebration the mountains moved and bounced. The rocks pranced. The trees wiggled and joined in the jubilee. It turned out that the mountains, rocks, and trees only needed someone to show them how to appreciate the earthquake. The earthquake laughed and felt like a high celebrity in the midst of these festive folks.

"And then, at the very height of the celebration, the Indians were cut down by an enemy tribe. The earthquake began to cry when he saw the hearts of his friends pierced by weapons. Their tepees destroyed, their feasting pots bubbling with food overturned, their lifeless bodies strewn all over the countryside. The slaughter took a century, but to the large earthquake whose sense of time was different, it seemed like a day.

"He went back to the water. He went back to where the river dipped into the thirsty sea. He cried so hard, his tears mingled with the river's until a mighty flood came. After he had cried out all his sorrow, he fell asleep. And he slept for years. But whenever he wakes up, he thinks about his Indian friends and begins to pace up and down the river until he squeezes rocks in the palms of his hands, knocks the interior apart, and comes up through the earth's core. He swims up from the river bottom, strokes his way onto the land, and begins to stomp up and down the earth, frightening every creature in sight. Uprooting permanence.

"Defying order." The water ended her legend.

Amber sighed.

"Then tell me about myself," she said.

"You are the girl of many mothers," the water said, then spoke no more.

"What?" said Amber.

But the water had finished talking.

"Well, anyway," said Amber, "I'm going home. Right now."

Quenched

EIGHTEEN

On the third day, Wade saw Mrs. Westbrook waving him over, and he hurried across the road.

"I can't find Amber's flute," she said. The usual air of lavender that traditionally sealed itself around her was absent, making her seem less herself.

"What do you mean?" asked Wade.

"It's not there. You know she kept it in her bedroom just beside the dresser. I went in to dust her room this morning, and it's gone!"

"Gone?" said Wade, thunderstruck. "Are you sure Mr. Westbrook or one of the twins or Papa Westbrook didn't move it?"

"I asked them," she said. There were both tears and laughter in her voice.

"The flute."

"Wade . . ."

He looked at Mrs. Westbrook, and he couldn't breathe. "Excuse me," he said. He flew across the road.

His cello stared at him in its usual place in front of the living-room window.

The flute melodies that had made him toss and turn in his sleep during the early dawn—had he dreamed them or not? "Sacred Mountain" flute sounds had drifted in through the curtains.

Something squeezed his heart, and this time it wasn't the phantom wrestler of panic.

Out of the living-room window he saw Sheriff Wilson drive up in the Westbrook driveway.

When the sheriff pulled away, Wade saw Mrs. Westbrook go out to her garden to water the lavender.

Just then his mother came into the room and stood next to him, also watching Grace tend her garden.

"Why, that's the first time I've seen Grace in that garden since . . ." his mother said.

Wade looked at his cello.

Then he turned to his mother. "Mama," he said, "I'm going for a walk."

He heard music coming from the river, closer and closer; the sound grew. He walked toward the sound, a ribbon of melody pulling him toward it. There was another sound. The sea. He was following the river to the sea. And the magnetic tug of the combination of music and sea was irresistible.

He heard the flute, but it was not played like a flute.

It was played like a bow and arrow. "Sacred mountain, sacred tree, sacred river that runs to the sea."

He followed the trail of notes, a river of sound, through the path by the water. It had been a long time since he had been this close to the sea.

He brushed aside hanging branches, stepped over feathery ferns, walked through needles of light lacing through the trees.

Now the notes were more crystal, more urgent, more near. And all around him he saw trees reaching so high they threatened to scrape the sky. Music so tall, it could create light and stars and full moons.

A doe and her speckled fawns gamboled across his path

unhurried, as though they were used to seeing only friendly creatures this far in the woods.

Then he spotted her walking toward him, her backpack in place, her lips on the flute, a long kinky ponytail tied almost neatly, so he knew it hung in a question-mark curve down her back.

He stood still. She saw him.

She pulled the flute from her lips. She was all grace and sureness. A cinnamon face of sparkling ebony eyes and a splash of white, white teeth.

When she reached him, they clung to each other.

"Amber, Amber, Amber," he said. Mirth ran out of him like a laugh locked up too long.

"How could you leave?"

"I had to."

"Why?"

"First I have to tell you about the attic."

"The attic?"

"What I discovered there. You see, I'm not who you think I am or who I thought I was. I'm not my mother's and father's child. When I was a baby, I was abandoned. I'm not Johnny and Jason's sister." And she went on to describe to him the contents of the letter from Abyssinia and Carl Lee.

"You were adopted?"

"Something like that. And I'm not my grandpa's Amber."

"And nobody ever told you? That's mean!"

"I thought so. At first."

"And now?"

"Now I don't know. I had these dreams about my folks and everything bothering me lately. Earthquakes, Indians, what my folks mean . . . The dream . . . Part of the dream was the legend of the earthquake who lives in the river. Nobody had ever told it to me before in full detail."

"No, come to think of it, I've never heard it explained. But tell me, Amber, how can you dream a legend?"

"I can't tell you how. I just did."

"But wait. Tell me the dream about you and your folks. Did it explain your birth?"

"In a way. The water spoke. 'I am the daughter of many mothers.'" And she tried to imitate the female voice of water.

They walked hand in hand now. Going home. Before long, the sea was far behind them and only the river and the trees were left.

And then suddenly the earth trembled.

Earthquake!

Above their heads the giant pines wagged back and forth.

Then all of a sudden, pine needles and pinecones started raining through the air, and the evergreen and troubled fragrance of the tall sequoia trunks swayed dizzily all around them.

Through the lace-light of quivering trees they started running as fast as they could. Alongside the river as it flowed tumbling toward the sea, they scrambled.

They fled toward home, moving frantically as the trees rustled and bent all around them, their cones flying through the air like shingled baseballs.

"What an earthquake!" she gasped, breathless with hurry. "When I have children, I will not let them play cowboys and Indians if the Indians are always the villains."

"What?" said Wade.

"I'll explain later," she said.

The earthquake roared.

"Is it going away?" asked Wade, trying to gauge the trembling of the ground as he ran.

"Perhaps it's just started."

They looked into the water as they skirted the swelling, complaining waves. The river spoke in an ancient language. Now out of breath, they tiptoed past it like eavesdroppers. The wind began to rise. And it sang.

When the river began to answer the wind more violently, and the earth shook more powerfully beneath their feet, they crept along, silently praying each step of the way.

Finally they reached Bear River Road.

"We've made it this far. Won't be long before we're home," she said.

They kept pushing on toward home as the earthquake quaked, and the eagle dipped his shadow away from the sea, then led them on.

Already Amber could imagine herself sitting in the living room on the round blue trumpet-vine rug, her brothers on both sides of her, her parents sinking themselves in the palm of the purple couch, her father rubbing the couch's shoulder with one hand and holding her mother's hand with the other. When the smell of lavender cut the air like incense, that's when she would tell them how much she loved them and why she ran away. Then they would tell her the whys of her birth, and her grandfather would wisely nod his head in agreement with Amber's right to know. She could hardly wait.

"Home," said Amber, so softly that Wade had to strain his ears to hear, her fingers tightly laced in his, so close. So near to the magic of love and water and eagle and home. So close to home.

The Golden Pasture

1986

THERE WAS A BOY STOOD TALL IN THE WORLD on his way to becoming a man and he looked for mountains to climb and horses to tame. But there were no mountains in his part of the world, so he looked for horses to tame, and found them grazing in a golden pasture. Then he said to himself, "A mountain's a task you fix for your spirit, a wild horse the challenge to your soul." Then he looked up into the blue. To the eagle climbing the cliffs of the wind, to the hands of the sky brushing clouds across its face. To Father Time setting out the sun every morning and every evening bringing it back in. And as night fell cloaking the world in darkness, the boy decided, "I'll be that steadfast in all I begin. And if some days I fall down, if my dreams get broken, I'll dust me off, mend my dreams and start all over again, and say how lucky I am, for I am young and full of chances." There was a boy stood tall in the world on his way to becoming a man, who woke at sunrise and said, "I'll reconcile my work and leisure, pleasure, joy, and duty, for if I lie down in a golden meadow, I do not waste this beauty. I bask in the wonder of mistletoe, fireflies in wheat fields, songbirds in trees, and horses who romp in these pastures. I am a young man running through high weeds, riding up tall mountains, taking my time in the climb. I have taken an oath with tomorrow, and I plan to meet me there looking back at the boy standing tall in the world on his way to becoming a man."

Part I

Snow

A Cherokee woman, her head wrapped in thick layers of red cloth, her chubby body protected by a multicolored wool coat, hurried her way through the snow.

She skipped, slowed, stopped, and checked her bearings in the snow-powdered woods. These fields were so snow-powdered even the trees and shrubs and little scurrying animals wore coats of snow.

A golden-faced woman, her jet black hair hidden under the red head wrap, she moved on, aware of snow white trees, snow white bushes, and snow white snow rabbits leaving little paw prints in the powder.

In places the wind had drifted the snow until it was as high as her protruding, bulging waist.

Now and then she stopped, gasped and stooped over, hands holding her belly like a basket of gold clasped close to her body.

The shawl-like fringed coat hung in such vivid colors around her that she looked like a huge peacock bird with feathers of wool skipping and stopping in the snow.

This continent of snow appeared secluded, in its own time warp, far from the cars that fled down Loganberry Road in Ponca City, although Loganberry Road was in fact only a half a mile away from where she picked her way through the snow.

What was she looking for?

The right place.

She had to reach it in time.

The place she wanted was not an anonymous hospital bed with nurses holding thermometers and hypodermic needles. She did not want a cold stethoscope anywhere near her.

She hated the idea of the steel tools the doctor used to force a child's head out of the birth passage. She had seen the forcep marks on enough newborn babies' heads.

She wanted the child to come into the world all on its own. To have a sense of control even as early as birth.

She had not wanted Ponca City Hospital, a common place with orderlies dressed in green running in and out of her labor room.

No, she did not want to hear the sharp irritation of high-heeled shoes on the tile floors smelling like antiseptic.

Nor did she want the crackling of emergency loudspeakers calling for doctors.

She did not want the sound of death and pain and suffering anywhere near her this December day.

She had grown tired of arguing with her husband about what she didn't want when he took her to Ponca City Hospital for her checkups.

That was not the world she wanted to bring this child into.

She searched for a quiet place. A place of uncommon beauty and peace.

It was here. She had seen it many times before. She had visited this birth room which she herself had prepared.

Bent again with pain, she stopped and held on to the trunk of a pecan tree, the limbs bowed down with snow. Now a skeleton of a tree.

No, this was not the place. She moved on.

She passed beneath a stately elm, its snow arms outstretched.

She brushed against the slender bones of honeysuckle bushes, seeing where the snow quilted the exposed branches a seamless white.

No, this was not the place. Yet.

A bushy-tailed red fox moved nearby, cunningly. He watched her.

He stayed a distance behind her and followed. Tracking her, keeping count of the times she stopped to clasp her golden belly, and the duration of each wave of pain.

The fox watched, a smile lingering just under his fox snout around his fox lips.

At the edge of the forest into which the woman had stepped, a tall dark man almost the color of night stood wrapped in a heavy brown wool coat.

He put his hand up to his brow over which a white wool cap sat and peered off into the woods. He did not see what he wanted.

So up and down he walked, along the edge of forest, his eyes glued to the ground, searching.

He had been looking about ten minutes when he found what he had been searching for.

Tracks.

The right size.

He started running. Lightly at first. Following the tracks. Then fear squeezed his heart. And he hurried his footsteps.

Now he was panting, his breath flying in and out of his chest in great gulps and gasps.

He passed under the snow-laden pecan tree, past the Oklahoma elm, by the wild blackberry bush.

"Oh, my God," he whispered, "let me be in time."

He followed the small tracks on and on.

And then he heard a tiny chant lifting up through the snow air.

"Thank goodness!" he said, running on more quickly following her footsteps.

Again the snow began to fall, so quietly he didn't notice it at first. Then it was flying around his head, glueing his eyes almost shut.

He stumbled along.

The female voice hit a high, piercing note just as he went flying and falling over an old pine-tree stump.

"Shoot!" he fussed.

He picked himself up and forged ahead.

Soon the snow was so thick he had a time finding his way.

"Not now! Not now!" he said to the snow. But the snowflakes grew fatter, fell faster.

"Snow flurries!"

The snow covered up the woman's tracks. And the snow muffled her singing.

He pricked his ears and continued picking his way toward that song.

Then the wind blew and moaned.

He stopped because the sound of the wind covered her voice.

He trembled. "Even the wind's against me," he fussed.

He knew his woman, his wife, would not think of the noisy wind as moaning but only as Mother Nature singing and humming.

Then the wind stopped.

He pricked his ears and listened.

Now the sound of his wife singing was as pure as the newly driven snow.

It was her all right. Rose Branch Jefferson. His wife. Pregnant and alone.

What he called alone, she would call her solitude.

Ponca City Hospital, where he had registered her to go for the birth, where everything was safe and sanitary, she had called the last stop before you get to the funeral grounds. She could not understand birth and death being in the same building. She said.

How is it that love gets so twisted, so misunderstood.

The differences in culture and background had attracted them to each other, but these differences also pulled them apart.

Then the wind started moaning again and he couldn't hear her.

He had lost her, he thought, his heart falling, but he kept on walking, hoping somehow he'd find her.

He turned to the left and soon came upon a bridge, but it was slick with ice. The bridge was a walnut wooden crossing over a frozen stream where fish hibernated under the frozen glass of the water, waiting for spring to come.

Then just on the other side of the bridge, he spotted her peacock-colored wool coat brilliant against the snow. She was stooped over near an old oak tree, probably the oldest thing in the woods, it was so large.

"Rose Branch!" he called.

Why didn't she answer?

He heard her singing muted and low. Her chanting came in gasps now, no longer like a crystal thread of music but in short notes like snippets of strings.

He could see her squatting down, her back to him, facing the tree.

He heard a frail cry. The baby had come.

What was she doing bending over the child like that?

He couldn't see. . . .

"Don't you kill my baby!" he hollered, alarm in his voice.

He started running across the bridge. Then he tripped and careened, sliding, skating across the treacherous ice.

He slid on his bottom, gasping from the freezing cold.

He skidded until he ended up on his end on the other side of the bridge.

He picked himself up and ran to the bent-over Rose Branch, hopping through the snow the last part of the way.

She tried to cover the baby.

"You're smothering him," he yelled. He was furious at her for being out here, trying to leave him out, trying to keep him from his own child. At the same time he was excited now that he was upon her and could see it was a boy.

"Give him here!" he demanded.

The woman glared at him, but she was too weak to protest.

Besides she had to finish her job. She bit the umbilical cord in two.

Drops of red blood on the snow white snow.

Red petals of life.

And he snatched up the child and went swooping across the snow, the child, like a little wood creature, tucked under his woolen coat and arm.

Still bleeding, Rose Branch crawled up into the hollow of the oak tree. It was dry there. She had prepared it months ago just for this time. Deer hide covered the cave. There were deer hide blankets and lots of straw to keep out the cold. It was much warmer in her cave than outside in the snowy woods. A keg of nuts and dried rust apples and dog tooth violet bulbs sat in the corner. For water, she would eat the fresh snow.

Of course she had planned to nurse her child.

From the open flap in the oak-tree house, all she could see was this tall husband, moving like a crow more stealthily now, over the ice on the wooden bridge. Away from her. Her child tucked under his coat, held close to his breast, cuddled just under his heart.

She wanted to lie down in her cave and just rest. But she still had more work to do. She had to deliver the afterbirth.

She squatted again.

Inching closer, but staying out of her eye range, the sly fox watched.

Soon a wave of pain hit her and she delivered the afterbirth.

"Bury it, bury it, bury it." The old familiar chant crowded her head.

But she could not move, she was too tired from the strenuous labor and the shock of Samuel Jefferson catching her and taking the child like that.

Through heavy eyelids she saw the snow clouds part. The sun would come out and warm the woods and melt the ice and snow on the walnut bridge.

The fox waited behind a nearby hickory tree.

When he saw this Rose Branch drifting off to sleep, he scrambled soundlessly to the tree cave, sniffing the afterbirth.

But Rose Branch's mother ears were so finely tuned she could distinguish the difference between a fox's feathery steps and the smallest shift in the wind.

Like any new mother, she could have heard her baby turning his head in the middle of the night.

And so she heard the fox's paw, the fox's smile and her eyes flew open.

She stared at the fox with an expression that looked beyond him and on into the next world.

The fox drooped his tail, yapped and barked, then scurried away, just a-running.

Rose Branch got up and finished her business of burying the afterbirth and reciting the chant that would protect the spirit of the child from scavengers of all kind, animal and human.

"Safe passage, safe passage along life's journey."

The Bond

When Samuel Jefferson got back to his house on Loganberry Road, the entire town of Ponca showed up on his doorstep to see the baby.

Missionaries and ministers. Saints and sinners.

A little of the snow had fallen onto the infant's coal black hair and the Ponca City women, to protect him against getting chilled, bathed him in warm olive oil and gently brushed the waves of his sleek hair until it shown like blackberries or black patent-leather curls.

After hearing Samuel Jefferson's story about his Cherokee wife alone out in the snowy woods, a group of Ponca women, led by Patience Jackson, went out into the forest to search for Rose Branch but they came back to sit by the warm blaze crackling in the fireplace, saying they could not find her.

During the next few days, nursing women, who were still breastfeeding their own babies, took turns nursing the infant born in the woods.

Samuel Jefferson's Ponca City neighbors were so generous, he didn't need to buy a thing. The women brought old and new baby clothes by.

A few days later, when bottles of mother's milk started appearing on his doorstep, he assumed the nursing women had expressed milk from their breasts and left the bottles there.

When he thanked the Ponca women, they stared at him blankly. He chalked it all up to that community pride those women had such an abundance of. Why thank them when they considered it their duty?

"What are you going to call him?" asked Patience Jackson one day. She was a plump brown-skinned woman, pretty and practical.

Patience had recently married Strong Jackson. Of all the Ponca City women, she had been the most consistent and diligent visitor to the Jefferson house.

Her husband Strong understood her need to help.

They had been busy trying to get Patience pregnant. In fact, she was sure she had just conceived. If her calculations were right, then she'd have the baby in September.

She went about with a secret smile of knowing, thinking about the possibility of her own child as she practiced motherhood on this baby boy, changing his diapers, burping him after he finished his milk.

"I don't know," Samuel Jefferson finally responded to her question about a name. He thought of naming the baby after his father, but he and his father, Grayson Jefferson, hadn't seen eye to eye in a long, long time.

"Well, do like the old folks used to do. Wait until you have a sign," said Patience, rocking the baby boy, swaddled in baby blue blankets, back and forth.

After heeding what Patience had said, he looked for signs, but he didn't see any.

His father would have called him blind. There were signs all around him.

Sun was peeking through the December clouds one morning when he picked up the milk bottle left again outside his front door.

Later that day, when he poured the last drop from the large milk bottle into the smaller baby bottle, he noticed this etching on the big bottle's bottom: The Carlton Bottling Company.

"That's his name. Carlton," said Jefferson. "Well, Carlton sounds too plain. Carlton Lee. That's it. Carlton Lee. Carlton Lee Jefferson."

He finally wrote his father, sent the letter off to Golden Pasture where his father's ranch was. "Dear Pa, you finally have that grandson you wanted so bad. His name is Carlton Lee Jefferson. I hope you're proud. Your son, Samuel Jefferson."

Over in Golden Pasture, Gray Jefferson finished watering and grooming his horses.

Before he knew it it was time to meet the mail rider. It was a distance to the mailboxes, and since he had a few items to pick up in town anyway, he jumped in his truck and must have reached the gate just after the mail rider left, for there was a letter waiting. The red flag was up.

Leaving the motor running, he took the letter out of the box and let the red flag back down.

He shut the gate and got back into the truck. Immediately he opened the envelope from his son.

When he read the letter's short message, a curious smile crossed his face and he said, "Well now."

The thick-haired, clean-shaven Gray sat the letter on the seat beside him. Then he stuck his mighty hands on the gear shift, moved into third gear and sped the truck along the gravel road until he intersected the Oklahoma highway.

He didn't stop in town at all. He just kept on coming. He drove on into Ponca City to see this Carlton Lee Jefferson.

Around noon, Gray pulled up to the small wood house, white

now because it was covered with December snow, and parked his truck.

He took giant leaps across the snowy lawn and banged on the door before entering.

He spoke quickly to his son, Samuel, and headed for the baby crib.

He leaned over, unwrapped the baby blankets and examined his grandson from head to toe.

"Why he's grinning at me. I believe he knows who I am," said Gray, rubbing the blackberry curls on the baby's head. "And he's got a dimple in his chin just like mine," he exclaimed proudly.

He wrapped the child back up.

With his tall frame, he looked like some wonderful brown giant hanging over the crib and tickling the cleft of Carl Lee's chin.

"Oh, look at him smile," said Gray.

"That's just a ghost smile," said Patience Jackson, over in the corner near the stove ironing baby clothes. Hadn't she heard the older women talking about the angels playing around the corners of babies' mouths?

Gray Jefferson paid no mind to that. His grandson was different.

And every time Gray spoke, the baby grinned.

Samuel Jefferson proceeded to act jealous.

"You heard what the woman said," Samuel growled. "'It's just a ghost smile.'"

"Of course I heard what she said, but I also know what I'm looking at," said Gray.

At the sound of Gray's voice, Carlton Lee smiled again.

"Where's the child's mama?" said Gray.

"She disappeared. Probably died off in the woods somewhere. Must have been suffering from childbirth-sickness. When

I found her, she was trying to smother this poor critter."

Gray, not believing that last part, glared at his son.

"She'd still be home if you'd treated her right."

"Now don't you come in my house starting any confusion, old man. This is my house!"

"I still say that Indian woman would still be here if you knew how to cooperate sometimes and learned how to show a little affection. Black folks and Cherokees have been marrying and getting along for as long as I can remember. It's worked for centuries, what's your problem?"

"Out of my house. Out!" screamed Samuel.

At the sound of his daddy's quarreling voice little Carlton Lee started squawling.

"See what you've gone and done," said Gray, picking the baby up and whispering to him. "Now, now, Carl Lee, my little Carl Lee."

The baby hushed.

Patience Jackson who had opened her mouth to ask the men to quit fussing out of regard for the child said, "Well, shut my mouth!" she was so amazed at the newborn's response. She couldn't wait to tell the women in the Ponca City quilting bee about this smart baby who knew his own grandfather's voice from anybody else's.

Samuel Jefferson didn't say another fuming word. He too just stood in awe of the magic Gray Jefferson had worked with the baby, Carl Lee.

Sometimes love plays games. It leaps and hopscotches over the heads of fathers and sons and matches up fathers and grandsons.

Such was the case with Gray and Carlton Lee.

And when her ironing was done, Patience Jackson rushed off to tell the amazing news: a baby boy born in the snow, coming into the world already acquainted with his own grandpa.

At last when Gray kissed Carl Lee's brow and finished cooing over him like an old woman, he reluctantly jumped in his pickup and headed down Loganberry Road on his way to the highway that led to Golden Pasture.

When the door closed behind Gray, Carl Lee started crying, crying his heart out, as though he felt his grandfather had abandoned him to his own father.

Samuel Jefferson picked up his son and rocked him, suspecting there was a bond between grandfather and grandson that would never ever be broken.

Part II

King of the Horses

In Golden Pasture late one Thursday afternoon, twelve-year-old Carl Lee bent over the sink at his grandfather's kitchen window preparing lemonade and looking out the window onto the backyard.

He watched Gray and Billingsley carving hickory wood statues in the half shade of a blackjack tree. Billingsley was Gray's best friend. A rodeo partner from the good old days.

As he squeezed the lemons in the glass pitcher, he thought his grandfather and Billingsley looked like two old benign buzzards, with their backs humped by time.

Carl Lee was a thin boy, with warm brown eyes offset by thick bushy eyebrows looking like two black wings.

His skin was clay brown. There was a dimple in his chin.

And when girls looked at his hair they thought of peppercorns and blackberries.

He stirred honey into the lemon juice then added water.

"Who would have thought," Carl Lee said softly to himself, thinking of a time when Gray's and Billingsley's backs were straighter, when they sat taller in the saddle and rode fifty to a hundred miles a day in the thick heat of Oklahoma hills and New Mexico mountains rounding up wild horses for the Boley Rodeo.

According to stories his grandfather told him, the horses

ran, hysterical with rage, galloping over prairie grass, up and down gulleys, stamping up red-dirt clouds, unsettling clay dust, jackknifing, kicking holes out of the ground, trying to escape the roundup.

He turned to the refrigerator to add ice to the lemonade, still listening to the voices of the older men.

"Yessir, we rounded up some bad horses for the Boley Rodeo, all right," his grandfather was saying.

Gray Jefferson, dressed in a pair of blue overalls and a denim shirt, scraped at the wooden figurine he sculpted. He was so tall, his head barely cleared the blackjack tree he sat under. A big man, husky even though his back was stooped just a little bit. The more than twelve years since Carl Lee had been born had aged him. Now he was grizzly-bearded, a white halo of hair sticking out around his head. Hands, gnarled knobby with age but still heavy with power.

"Remember that four-legged scoundrel, Broken Bones?" said Billingsley.

"Broken Bones? Do I remember? Who could forget? Went beyond his name. That mustang broke bones all right, but he didn't stop there. Broke bones and backs!" hooted Gray.

"What year was it he tore down the corral, wrecked a car, broke rail fences over the rider's back, and sent that poor cowboy out on a stretcher?"

"Any year he came, he cut up. He didn't have any special time for acting up. You've got to have crickets in your chimney to climb up on anybody's wild New Mexico mountain horse."

"Yet we lived to tell it."

"Still . . . ain't nothing like the Boley Rodeo," said Gray. "You can raise hell in peace."

"Remember the year that Thunderfoot . . . ?"

"Who wouldn't."

"Horse never should have been caught and sent to the rodeo," said Billingsley.

"He's. . . ." Gray halted as Carl Lee appeared. "Lemonade, just the ticket for a dry gullet," Gray said, accepting the ice-crackling pitcher. As he wiped the sweat from under his hat band, he added, "Heard the palomino calling you, Carl Lee."

"I think he wants to be saddled, Grandpa."

"Either that or he's having a bad day. Horses, like people, do have bad days, you know. Maybe he's feeling cranky with a headache."

"A headache? You mean horses have headaches too?"

"They have heads don't they?"

"Big heads," said Carl Lee.

"Big headaches."

Carl Lee said, "My lands," then stretched out on his back under the redbud tree next to the porch where he could relax in the shade and watch the grasshoppers springing and krickety-kricking across the buffalo grass, thinking about what size aspirin a horse would have to take. "The size of a plate," he imagined.

The palomino called again.

He had promised his grandfather he'd be able to recite "There Was a Boy" before he rode again. Gray had taught him not to break promises. "A man's word is his bond."

How did the poem go? Under his breath he recited, "There was a boy stood tall in the world on his way to becoming a man, and he looked for mountains to climb and wild horses to tame. But there were no mountains in his part of the world, so he looked for wild horses to tame, and found them grazing in a golden pasture. Then he said to himself, 'A mountain's a task you fix for your spirit, a wild horse the challenge to your soul.' Then he looked . . . looked . . ." He couldn't remember the rest.

Out loud he said, "You know something, Grandpa, if I had my

way, they'd conduct school in a yellow pasture and compute arithmetic problems on horseback."

"Be kind of hard on the teacher, don't you think?" said Gray whittling away at his stick of hickory wood.

Carl Lee said, "If I could trade places with the math instructor I'd compose problems asking for the circumference of a corral, the area of a horse's stall, the number of meters from the stable to the house."

Carl Lee's mind drifted and in his dreamworld he listened to the rhythm of the Southern drawl coloring and seasoning all his grandfather's and Billingsley's words.

He liked to hear these two heroes talk their old fogey talk as he called it, for their voices were as rich as a country landscape and ripe with stories.

His grandfather, who came to Oklahoma by way of Mississippi, had a storehouse of Mississippi stories about alligators, and Oklahoma stories about Indians and horses and rodeos.

Carl Lee especially enjoyed hearing about the black cowboys and the Boley Rodeo. He had wanted to ride in the Boley Rodeo for as long as he could remember. But each year Gray said he was too young, too inexperienced; everybody knew you had to be thirteen. And that was an exception; most folks didn't ride until they were fifteen years old. Old men, thought Carl Lee.

But Carl Lee was anxious to prove himself. He couldn't wait any longer. Thirteen was half a year away. An eternity. And next summer he'd be thirteen and a half, already an older man when the Boley Rodeo rolled around again.

He wanted to perfect some horse tricks but the palomino was too tame for the rodeo. Didn't have a lick of spirit.

He couldn't figure out yet just what he could do. He wanted to participate in the rodeo this Labor Day. Do something so wonderful they'd have to call him "cowboy" instead of "cowpoke."

But the palomino was too tame.

The late sun was making him doze.

He'd never figure out anything lazying around like this. But he closed his eyes anyway.

His grandfather's sidekick startled him out of a daze by tapping him on the shoulder and handing him the thing he had sculpted. "Here's a saddle, son," said Billingsley.

Then his grandfather showed him the hickory horse. The saddle fit just right.

"Why, thanks," he said lifting himself up off the ground. "Better quit kicking against bricks and go inside and study!"

That Thursday after school, Carl Lee, astride the palomino, trotted along the road toward home, accompanied by his two school friends, Jessie and Norman, who rode their palominos, one on each side of Carl Lee.

"You know something, Carl Lee, I heard my folks say your grandpa keeps a secret horse in the stalls somewhere," said Jessie, one hand up trying to keep his big hat from swallowing his narrow head. "They say the horse came from Arabia or someplace strange like that."

"I heard the same story," said the tobacco-colored Norman. "And they say if you listen closely, at three o'clock in the morning you can hear the sound of your grandfather and that secret horse galloping over the earth where there aren't any fences. Hooves pounding like drums."

"How do you know it's a horse?" said Carl Lee.

"Maybe it's some other wild animal they're talking about."

"Nothing sounds like a horse running but a horse running," said Jessie.

"Now that's the truth," Carl Lee admitted, looking at the palomino he rode not only to school but every chance he could get, sometimes even from the house to the barn.

"I heard it myself," said Norman in a quiet voice.

"Heard what?" said Jessie.

"The secret horse."

Carl Lee and Jessie turned to look at him.

Norman had a strange sound in his voice. He said, "Once I stayed up late one night just to see if I could hear Gray Jefferson riding that secret horse. I heard something, but when I looked out the window I didn't see a thing except the moon. It was a funny feeling, looking at the moon and hearing that galloping sound and not being able to see horse nor rider. It was a quiet night, except for that.

"It was clear and the moon was full. There was something strange in the air. A funny, funny feeling," said Norman.

"Funny feelings? I know exactly what you mean," said Carl Lee. "I get one when I look at the No Trespassing sign in that forsaken corner of our ranch."

"What's that?" his friends chimed in unison.

"Certain off-limits areas on the ranch," said Carl Lee.

"Off-limits?"

"Anyway nobody goes back there," said Carl Lee, catching himself and wanting to change the subject. Maybe he had talked too much.

Carl Lee chewed on a blade of alfalfa grass and studied the golden coat and silvery mane of his palomino. He didn't want to talk too much about his grandfather's business. But already, he could see his own curiosity mirrored in the eyes of his two friends.

Norman said, "My grandpa says your grandpa's the best cowboy in the county. And I never heard him compliment anybody before in my whole life. In fact, nothing I do can please him. He's the orneriest old cuss in Oklahoma."

Jessie said, "My grandpa's just the opposite. I can't do a thing to get him mad. I have tried him. Nothing. I can't raise even a growl from him."

"How'd you like my grandpa's knuckles upside your head? That grayheaded son-of-a-gun's got hands like rocks," said Norman.

"At least you know what the parameters are. You know what I mean?" said Jessie.

"What's this big word, parameters?" asked Carl Lee. "Oh, he heard it in his social-living class. One way parents and grandparents show love is by demanding that the adolescent act in a responsible manner. 'Letting you teenagers know what your responsibilities are,'" he said sounding just like a teacher. "Stuff like that. Those are the parameters."

"Hey, you got it. Almost word for word, Norm," said Jessie.

"I haven't had that class yet," said Carl Lee.

"You will," they assured him.

"My grandpa's parameters are his heavy hands," said Norman.

Carl Lee nervously brushed at his blackberry hair. "Your grandpa sounds like my father," he said to Norman. "Mean."

They paced slowly ahead, silently thinking about parents and grandparents and growing up.

Parameters, Carl Lee thought; is that what he was missing from his own father? His father's parameters were set by cursing, swearing, and threatening.

Ever since Carl Lee had reached adolescence, the relationship with his father had become more strained.

Almost as though his father feared something. But what? That Carl Lee was almost a teenager? A sure sign he was growing up, becoming a man? Maybe his daddy wanted him to stay a baby. He had been nicer when Carl Lee was younger.

"My mama's dead," Carl Lee said to his friends. "She died when I was born."

"Oh, man," said Jessie. "I can't imagine not having my mama."

"Me either," Norman said.

"I know," said Carl Lee.

Carl Lee longed for a mother, like everybody else had. Still he wasn't an orphan. It would be hard to be an orphan in a place like Ponca City, where the neighbors knew your every move.

"Count your blessings," his grandfather had said, and that command echoed in his head every time he wanted to feel sorry for himself.

"I'm no whiner," he decided.

When boys got past twelve, they pretended their tear ducts had dried up.

But sometimes at night their tears still flowed. However, none of them ever talked about this.

Instead they said, "You know that Alex down yonder on Deer Creek Road? He's the biggest crybaby you ever did see."

"Alex is always looking for something to cry about." It was all right to be a crybaby, but not where people could see you.

"Yeah, you know he's going to tune up and cry when his chin drops. Face so long he could put a bridle on it and eat oats out of a churn. Saw him yesterday weeping about having to milk the cows at four in the morning. That high-behinded boy might not ever grow up!" said Norman.

"Either that or he's gonna turn into a girl. High behind and all."

They were silent. That was one of their greatest fears, to turn into a girl!

They thought about it every time they cried like a girl at night in their private beds.

"You know something," said Carl Lee, following their unspoken line of thought, "my grandfather says it's all right to cry sometimes."

"He did?!"

"Sure did. Said many's the day he's cried like a baby, and he's sure he'll be crying about one thing or another if he gets to be a hundred. The world can be a sad, sad place, according to him."

"Well, nothing womanish about that old cowboy," said Jessie.

"No, my grandfather doesn't have to apologize about anything," said Carl Lee.

"That must be the way to live," said Norman. "Not too many 'I'm sorry's.' And no backing up in your life. Cry if you feel like it. But laugh most of the time."

"Any time you got family in the world, you're going to have some crying days, that's what my Grandpa claims," said Carl Lee.

"I see him in church every Sunday, but I'd like to really meet him, sit down, and talk to him," said Jessie.

"Me, too; when are you going to invite us over?" asked Norman.

"I don't know," said Carl Lee, thinking. He liked having his grandfather to himself. Always when he was at home with his dad, he got no attention except an awful lot of fussing from his father about the sloppy way he washed dishes, or the five or six blades of grass he missed with the lawn mower. His father didn't like him asking a lot of questions either.

Asking questions. That was Carl Lee's favorite pastime.

When he was three and four he drove his father crazy asking, "Where does the wind go when it blows away? What color is a thought? And Daddy, where do mamas go when they die?"

Asking questions, looking for answers. And the next door neighbors let him be an unofficial part of their family of nine kids. But next door he was just one among many. And with nine kids they didn't have time to answer all his questions. They could barely keep up with questions from their own flock. So he stopped asking.

Sometimes his grandfather answered questions he didn't even know he had.

At his grandfather's he could ask as many questions as he wanted.

At his grandfather's he was king of the horses.

"I don't know," Carl Lee said to his friends again, not wanting to sound mean and selfish. "I'll let you know."

"Hey, Carl Lee, I'd like to come and hike in that No Trespassing pasture," said Jessie.

"Me too," said Norman.

"No way. Grandpa wouldn't like it," said Carl Lee.

"Don't you ever wonder what's back there?" they asked Carl Lee. "How can you stand not knowing?"

Carl Lee just shrugged; they had come to the entrance to his grandfather's ranch. He turned his horse off the main road.

"Well, I guess I'd better be moseying on along," he said. "See you."

His friends and their horses soon disappeared in the distance. He headed his horse along the fence until he came to the wooden bridge that crossed Opal Lake. As always, he tightened the reins so the palomino would stop.

Today the lake air thickened with the croaking of bug-eyed frogs and the noisy quack-quack of the ducks that lived in this blue lagoon stretching the entire length of his grandfather's forty acres.

Opal Lake, fed by an underground spring, flowed as clear and iridescent as the lights in an opal. Water plants floated on the crystal stream and long-beaked birds hunted the surface for the little water bugs forever skipping across its top.

On the shore, a mallard duck craned her long brown neck at her brood and the ducklings flexed their webbed feet, lifted their thin, reedlike legs higher, and waddled after their mother into the swimming stream.

All the ducks on Opal Lake were just losing their flight feathers, which fell away on the shore and in the stream. But the most dramatic change affected the drakes, the glorious male ducks with the iridescent colors, who dropped their rainbow feathers in the water, their bodies signaling summer by copying the ordinary brown of the female.

Carl Lee dismounted and walked down to the water.

He picked up two floating colorful drake feathers, stuck one in his cowboy hat, and carried the other back up to the bridge to his horse. He placed this one on his horse's saddle, then continued along the fence until he came to his grandfather's gate.

Clop-clop, clop-clop. the palomino paused for a moment at the mailbox that marked the place the path turned, then moved on, proudly swishing his golden tail and wearing the glorious drake feather Carl Lee had fished out of Opal Lake. There was no sweeter sound on earth as far as Carl Lee was concerned than the sound of horses' hooves beating against the earth. A perfect rhythm.

Such grace, such balance. He even liked the way horses held their heads.

Soon Carl Lee and the palomino came to the part of the gravel path that branched to the house and then veered off on to the barn.

The ranch house, made of red bricks compressed from Oklahoma red clay, stood on a small rising. The brick fortress, shaded by southern pines, looked secure and as though it had stood there forever.

"He's home," Carl Lee sighed with relief, seeing his grandfather's Ford pickup parked at the end of the driveway. A little way from the house stood the barn made of wood. And every summer, they whitewashed it.

Beyond the trained plants of the enclosed ranch yard, beyond the leaning picket fence, the mesquite and sagebrush expanded his view. Untamed buffalo grass and wire weeds carpeted the way to the horse stables. And the warm wind brought him the raunchy, sweaty rich odor of horses, musky and compelling.

He led the horse between the house, past the vegetable garden of okra, greens, tomatoes, peas, corn and toward the barn.

"Whoa," he said.

He dismounted and stabled the horse in the barn. He let out to pasture the two cows which supplied enough milk, butter, cream, and buttermilk that they never had to buy dairy products from the store.

For a moment he stood and watched the cows slowly roam the fields, their cowbells clanking gently.

Walking back to the house on the other side of the barn he passed the chicken coop fenced in with chicken wire circling the yard for the chickens and roosters and the three turkeys that strutted and gobbled there.

Even before he could reach the house, he knew what they were having for dinner. The aroma was unmistakable: pinto beans. And if they were having pinto beans that meant hot-buttered corn bread to go with it. And maybe a gallon of loganberry juice to wash it down. Early spinach from the garden made into a crisp salad.

The only thing he was never sure of was dessert. He couldn't smell it cooking. It was always fresh fruit, finished off with a glass of milk. And his grandfather was full of surprises. Once they had fresh cantaloupes and it was too early for cantaloupes. His grandfather had gone all the way to Langston to a special produce market to find the round, luscious fruit. Mexican cantaloupes.

His grandfather was as unpredictable as a Mexican cantaloupe on an Oklahoma table at Christmas.

This lazy June day he was thinking about how wonderfully unpredictable his grandfather was as he dashed up the front porch steps and opened the screen door.

The living room testified to the fact that there was no woman within miles of the ranch. This front room was solid and comfortable. Hardwood floor but no rugs. Knotty pine walls that needed no painting. A brick fireplace. An old stuffed sofa, kind of a green color and lumpy, absolutely perfect for kicking off the boots and lounging. There were no little starched doilies on the sofa back or sofa arm to worry about sliding off and onto the floor. And no fluffy laced pillows that could only be used to look at.

Across from the sofa sat a rocking chair that his grandfather liked to sit in and read his paper and think and watch television. A brass floor lamp for light stood like a sentry next to the rocking chair, and two end tables of oak wood sat on each end of the sofa.

"Grandpa," Carl Lee called, "I'm home."

"I've been in the kitchen, carrying on with the pots and pans," Gray boomed, coming into the living room. "How was school?"

"So-so," came Carl Lee's usual answer.

"Well, Horse," one of Gray's fond names for Carl Lee, "want a snack before you get started on the chores and homework?"

"Maybe something to hold me before dinner," he said, putting his backpack of books down on the lumpy green couch and following his grandfather to the kitchen.

The no-nonsense kitchen went with the living room.

It was practical, including in its simple design a white Wedgewood stove, a Sears, Roebuck white refrigerator, and ample counter space.

This cooking and eating room repeated the walls of knotty pine seen in the living room. Pots and pans hung down from the ceiling, and a sturdy oak table and chairs sat in the center of the green linoleum floor.

"Something to hold you before dinner," Gray chuckled. "That's what I thought you'd say. We've got leftover potato salad, and," he opened the refrigerator with a flourish, "the makings of a rodeo sandwich."

A rodeo sandwich was anything you could round up to put between two slices of bread.

Gray reached in the refrigerator and pulled out a boiled egg, a yellow chunk of cheese, lettuce, tomatoes, sliced beef left over from a Sunday roast, and one solitary fried chicken drumstick. He sliced and piled all this onto the bread and made Carl Lee an enormous sandwich. So big it was a chore to wrap the lips around the whole thing. Then he made one for himself. Just as hearty.

They ate with Carl Lee talking between bites and swallows about the assignments Miss Monroe had given him for the English class, memorizing that long, long poem due by the end of the summer session and writing an essay called "How I Think Golden Pasture Got Its Name." The essay was due right away.

"I wonder how she thinks up all these memorization and writing exercises," said Carl Lee.

"That's her job," said Gray.

"And what did you do today?" asked Carl Lee after draining his glass of ice-cold milk.

"Same old, same old, groomed the horses, mended a few fences, started dinner, talked to Billingsley."

Carl Lee didn't consider Billingsley competition the way he considered his younger friends, Norman and Jessie. I'm the only young person I want my grandfather paying attention to, he thought. Billingsley was too old to be anything but comfortable around.

Carl Lee glowed with happiness. Summers with his grandfather were the grandest times of all.

He walked to the whitewashed barn and began his evening chores.

He rubbed down the five horses, swept out the barn, spread the straw out in the stalls, evenly. And went to the well, a well that drew its water from the same underground crystal spring that swelled Opal Lake.

He let down the bucket and lifted up the coolest, sweetest water in Oklahoma. Using the tin dipper that had hung on the well wall for generations, he drank a long draft then carried the bucket back and forth from the well to the animals' troughs, watching the fuzzy-tongued cows lap up the cool water until their thirst was slaked and there was water to spare.

He enjoyed the country so much he thought the chores were a new kind of fun.

Maybe it was the way his grandfather set things up.

He wasn't sure.

Even Gray's lectures turned out to be stories and fairy tales. He didn't know anybody who was as lucky as he was when it came to grandfathers.

When the chores were finished, he started to his room to study before dinner. In the living room, he picked up his books off the lumpy green couch.

His grandfather was relaxing in his rocking chair chuckling and reading *The Golden Pasture Gazette.*

"Great day in the morning!" he said rustling the paper as Carl Lee walked past on his way to his room. "Listen to this. A man divorcing his wife said he wanted the house and all the horses. Claimed the woman was too citified. He caught her a rabbit and asked her to cook it. And she asked, 'But how do I get the feathers off?!' He said he should have known something was strange when right after the honeymoon she took a bucket and went out in the barn to milk the horses.

"Not many women left like your grandma; that woman could do anything," claimed Gray.

Carl Lee looked over at his grandmother's picture. She had died before he was born. The photograph was one of those where the eyes followed you around the room. And she had a hint of a bittersweet smile on her chocolate lips as if she listened to the conversation too.

"She sure was beautiful, Grandpa," he said admiring her picture with the black woolly hair brushed neatly into two spirally buns twisted to the side of her head above two perfect ears.

"By the way," Carl Lee said turning back around, "did the man get the house and the horses?"

"No," said Gray, folding up the paper. "The woman got the horses and the man got the house. You tell me, is that justice?"

"Now that would make a good writing assignment," said Carl Lee, turning to go down the hallway to his room.

"Remember what I told you, Carl Lee," said Gray.

"Jot your ideas down. Or else those words will grow wings and just fly away. You know it's the lead in the pencil that puts an anchor on thoughts. They're not liable to get up so easy and run away. Why words are just like horses—harness them on the page. Claim them."

"Oh, Grandpa," Carl Lee chuckled.

"All right, I'm telling you," said Gray good-naturedly.

"Imagine how you'll feel if a thought you had flies to somebody else's head. Next thing you know some other student's claimed it and gets the credit, just because he's had the good sense and foresight to write it down."

With Gray's words ringing in his head, Carl Lee continued down the hall.

His room included a bed with a mattress like a rock.

"Boys need firmness for their backbones," Gray had claimed.

A small table and chair that served as a desk sat under a window looking out over the pasture. In the corner across from the desk stood a chest of drawers with an oval mirror hanging above it.

Everything in the room was blue. A blue bedspread, a blue hooked rug, and blue walls.

Horse pictures he had found in magazines decorated the walls.

As he sat at his desk covered with several scratch pads, a mug of pencils and pens, he thought he'd get started on Miss Monroe's composition first. She was always expecting the best. And nobody liked to see her frown. When she frowned the whole classroom got dim. She had said they were to write a short essay on how they thought Golden Pasture got its name. "Make up something," she had said. "It doesn't have to be true."

He picked up his pencil. Opened the composition book. But he didn't write anything. He sat still and let his mind wander.

He kept thinking about the name "Golden Pasture."

How to get a golden pasture in summer. Maybe plant alfalfa in row after row. The kind that produce yellow flowers.

He started jotting down his ideas on a piece of yellow scratch paper.

Bury yellow iris bulbs?

Scatter daisies?

Or design a field of goldenrod.

Wait! Plant something as common as daffodils.

To get a golden pasture let the buffalo grass, mowed and sickled, collect the Oklahoma sun.

He looked out his bedroom window over the fields and fields of alfalfa. He knew this variety would give acres and acres of yellow flowers as the summer progressed, but there was also another way to get gold from alfalfa.

He wrote "alfalfa" on the next line of his yellow pad. Once the alfalfa was ready to be cut and dried, he knew they would bale it. Then leave the stacks in the fields to dry.

When all of this became hay, he would look out over the meadow and see the haystacks of gold.

This possibility from common straw excited him. Oh, but let the sun hit straw, it turns to gold. And the smell of gold is honeysuckle or the aroma of hay when it's kissed by the sun.

He said to himself, You are lucky if you take off your boots and stand barefoot, your toes tickled by the straw, in the midst of a golden pasture.

"I'll keep that part," he whispered, scribbling down the thought on his scratch paper.

His mind kept traveling back to what Gray had said. Thoughts have wings—if you don't put them down they fly away to the next person. Why one day you might hear some other student standing up in the classroom reading something you thought. Jot things down. That's what Gray had told him. It was supposed to be a joke. But Carl Lee wondered if it really was.

He went back to thinking about Golden Pasture.

He would pretend the town of Golden Pasture got its name from the yellow flowers of alfalfa plants and the stacks of hay in the Oklahoma fields.

Every writing assignment starts in the mind first, Miss Monroe said. Now all he had to do was organize his notes and thoughts on paper.

Then he'd read this draft to his grandfather who always listened with a smile on his lips.

He started writing, *You're lucky if you ever get the chance to take off your boots and stand barefoot in a golden pasture and let the hay tickle your toes. That's what the founder of Golden Pasture did when he saw the wild alfalfa fields blooming like gold all over Oklahoma as far as he could see. . . .*

It was easy. All he had to do was put the words down until one word followed the other. Until the words faithfully echoed his thoughts.

Once he got started, he said to himself, this could be fun, even if he did hate summer school.

"Thank God, it's Friday," he whispered after writing a page worth on Golden Pasture.

He closed his composition book, laced his hands behind his head, and looked out over the fields.

At last his eye settled on the No Trespassing sign. "How can you stand not knowing?" His friends' question echoed in his head.

Well, it wasn't the easiest thing in the world. Many's the time he wanted to strike out over to the No Trespassing pasture anyway.

But his grandfather might turn into somebody like Norman's grandfather. He didn't ever want to experience Gray's heavy hands.

It wasn't the hands that scared him, it was Gray's being upset with him. His stomach churned just thinking about it.

Through the window that No Trespassing sign beaconed at him like an odd-colored string of rodeo lights dressed up in neon.

It might as well have said, "Come on."

He wouldn't. The only thing stopping him was the frown he knew would cross Gray's face.

With a father like he had he didn't need his grandfather against him too.

Sitting at this open window he heard the quack-quack of a drake calling to a duck and her ducklings down by Opal Lake.

"The grandfather wind is stirring," he said.

When it blew, even slightly, he could hear duck and frog sounds from the lake more clearly. And the wind, older than memory, puffed his cheeks and blew the fragrance of the southern pines that swayed over the brick house so gently yet so resolutely that the pine scent wafted through the bricks and sifted through his open window. Pine perfumed the air, reminding him of other aromas.

He remembered two distinct scents: the smell of his father's anger and the fresh fruit aroma of the apple woman.

That musky combination happened a long time ago, but the memory came back to him through his senses.

"Who?" his father had said to him years ago. He could remember the incident just as plain, as plain as the nose on his face and the smell in his mind.

"The apple woman," Carl Lee had said.

"I told you there's no such person; how many times do I have to tell you that?"

"There is. She smells like apples, and she looks like a golden goddess!"

Samuel's ears perked. "You dreamed it."

"I didn't."

"What does a golden . . . goddess look like?"

"Look like? Oh, Daddy she's got skin like gold. Gold bird feathers stuck in her black hair. Gold glass beads around her neck. Daddy, gold shimmering bracelets up her arm."

"Where'd you see her?"

Carl Lee giggled with joy, thinking, *My Daddy's talking to me.* This was the first time in a long while Samuel had asked him questions and listened so intently to him. *Oh, we're actually talking.*

"At my window. I saw her at my window."

"When?"

"Sometimes when I wake up. The smell of apples comes through my window and there she is," he piped in his little boy's voice. "An arm full of apples. I watch as she eats them."

"Didn't she offer you any?"

"Yes, but you told me never to take food from a stranger."

"That's right," said Samuel, a troubling shadow piercing his eye. "But you dreamed it. You dreamed the whole thing," he whispered;

however, his whisper was a hoarse shout that got lower and louder.

Catching this tension in his own voice, Samuel forced patience in his tone. "Sometimes when we're waking up in the morning we get our dreams and our real world all mixed up. You see, Carl Lee, I'm real. I'm the most real thing in your life."

Carl Lee stopped giggling, sorry he'd ever told Samuel about the golden woman and the essence of apples.

Then his dream and reality really did get mixed up. He flinched remembering the last time he saw the goddess.

She came and stood by his window, her arms filled with rust apples, a smile lingering softly around her golden mouth; something else invaded the air of the dream.

He smelled it first as a scorched stench that overwhelmed the familiar apple aroma. Sweat. The acid scent of anger.

Then he heard it. A shouting at the window. The golden goddess' smile turned inside out.

Her weeping jerked him upright in bed. He jumped up to go to her aid.

But when his feet hit the floor, the only person standing at his window was his father.

"See, I told you," Samuel had said. "There's nobody here. See. There's nobody here but me. And a bird or two," all the time picking up the golden feathers off the ground below the window. He kept saying this: "Nobody here but me."

Now, sitting at his grandfather's window looking out at the No Trespassing sign, Carl Lee let the scent of pine replace the remarkable aromas he remembered.

He shivered. He couldn't figure out why there was so much pain in the recollection of that long ago morning, yet he could not conjure up that last encounter without concluding that somehow his father had kept his dream from him by running it away.

Time to rest that memory and think of something else, he sighed to himself.

No Trespassing indeed.

Then he turned away from this pair of windows: away from the window with the sign beckoning him and especially away from the memory window in his mind.

"Better halter that horse and harness another one!" he spoke, so loud he startled himself and any golden witness who might have been listening.

No Trespassing

"Mail rider's come and gone," Carl Lee said spying the red flag sticking up on the mailbox.

His sinking voice echoed so low, his horse whinnied. When his jean-wet thighs involuntarily clamped tighter around the palomino, the horse shivered.

The mailbox, waiting on wooden legs, was a sign post for the path that led to the ranch house. The box, carved in the shape of a horse, bowed its dull head under the heat wave as though it had something even hotter in its belly.

Trying to delay what he might discover inside, Carl Lee slowly lowered the red wooden flag shaped like a horse's ear.

As he reached for the flap that opened the gray mouth of the box, he mumbled, "Probably another threatening letter."

Sweat poured from his forehead until his face glistened as wet as his clothes, still dripping from his swim in Opal Lake.

At least three times a week his father sent a letter to Gray in Golden Pasture threatening to pick up Carl Lee, claiming he needed his son in Ponca City to look after the house, as though the house were a person.

Carl Lee opened the mailbox.

Anxiety dizzied him until his ears rang and he couldn't see

right. Water in his ears. Shadows in the mailbox.

And in the center of the darkness a sharp rectangular white-hot stone.

The horse stood perfectly still.

A butterfly landed on the horse's ear and he quivered the ear and swished his palomino tail. The sound broke the spell and Carl Lee could hear the crickets again. And his eyes cleared.

Now he could make out the white envelope all right. He grabbed the letter from the box and raked his glance across the handwriting.

"Doggone it!" he said to the horse. "Why can't he leave us alone this one summer."

Last summer his visit had been cut short by five weeks when Samuel swooped down and dragged him away from chores in the barn and fields, leaving the horses and cows unfed and the water bucket overturned in the pasture.

Quickly, Carl Lee stuck the letter in his wet shirt pocket.

Realizing his mistake, he yanked it out, but it was too late. The letter was soppy wet with the ink lines all running together.

"Can't read this anyhow," Carl Lee said. Furiously, he tore the soaked letter to pieces and chucked the whole mess in the bushes.

His father never wrote directly to Carl Lee. He talked around him, about him in letters to Gray, but rarely directly to his own son. Carl Lee resented that.

Many times Carl Lee'd thought of throwing the letters away, hating to see the frown that crossed Gray's face as he would read the disturbing messages.

For a moment, it felt good, tearing that letter up like that.

He thought, My father is like the winter. Why I can't even remember the last time I saw him laugh. A face all torn up like a tornado. A smile dead as the alfalfa grass in winter. A spirit buried under the pine-tree ground.

As he got, closer to the house, he saw the familiar Ford. "Oh no, Daddy's here," he whispered.

Soon he heard the dreadful sound of quarreling.

Trouble. "Whoa," he whispered. He pulled on the reins and the palomino snorted, then was quiet.

Now the quarreling ceased.

Carl Lee's ears perked up, and he moved a few steps closer to the house where he stilled the horse in the shade of the southern pine tree.

It started again.

The voice of his father. The voice of his grandfather. "He's coming home to Ponca City now!" Samuel, his father, shouted.

"No way," said Gray in a voice tough as pig iron.

"He's in the middle of classes and in the middle of summer."

"I'm the daddy and what I say goes."

"I agree," said Gray after a long pause and in what seemed like a lighter tone of voice.

Carl Lee's stomach bounced. "How could Grandpa agree with him?" he whispered to himself as he tied the horse to the porch.

He quickened his steps up the stairs. *Too soon. Too soon to go home.* Then Gray clarified what he meant. "I agree that what you say goes. And I'd like to remind you that what you *said* in May was that Carl Lee would spend the whole summer here in Golden Pasture."

When Carl Lee opened the screen door he saw his father, all six foot seven of him, swaying like a tall tree in a fierce wind. He saw his tree tall father bend over and take a drink from a bottle of cheap wine.

"Hi, Dad," Carl Lee said, but there was no joy in his voice. He was not glad to see Samuel Jefferson.

"I'm taking you home," said Samuel, who looked past him as he spoke; he never ever looked at Carl Lee when he was talking to him.

"I'm not going," Carl Lee said. "You can't even take your ownself home." He crossed his angry arms, his heart stampeded under his wet shirt.

Gray set the rocking chair in motion.

Samuel took another swig from the wine jug, draining it before setting it aside. Then he said, "Been swimming in Opal Lake. Thought you were supposed to be in school."

"I was," Carl Lee said, befuddled. Maybe his father did look at him. But how? Out of the corner of his eye? "Yeah," he said absently answering his own question.

"Yessir! Don't be getting grown and surly now, Mr. Big Britches. I'll make you wet those blue jeans sure enough. And it won't be from the water in Opal Lake."

"I got a fool for a father," Carl Lee said, unable to bridle his tongue. He turned to go change his wet clothes.

"Don't you turn your back on me. Just like your mama! Don't you turn your back on me!"

Gray started to rise from his chair to intervene between father and son, but before he could do anything to stop him Samuel hurled himself at Carl Lee, knocking him to the floor.

"I'll teach you!" Samuel snarled and swung at Carl Lee.

Carl Lee's head spun with pain. Angrily, he twisted away and jumped up swinging. A reflex. He knocked the staggering Samuel back down.

When he realized what he had done, shame swamped him. He wheeled.

"You will mind me as long as you're a son of mine!" Samuel hollered after Carl Lee as the boy ran from the room and down the hall.

Carl Lee bent over in his desk chair by the window holding his bruised head in his hands. His head felt as big as a horse's.

"Leave here, Mr. Sam. Right now," Carl Lee heard his grandfather saying.

"You're teaching this boy to disobey me?" said Samuel, swaying to his feet.

"No," said Gray. "But I bound you this—he's said he's not going and I second that decision. He's not going anywhere with you drunk!"

"The whole world's against me," Carl Lee heard Samuel whine. "I can't even have my own son to myself." When Carl Lee came out of the bathroom, he saw his father, nursing a black eye, whirl and go stumbling out of the house and down the steps, weaving across the yard and out into the field toward the No Trespassing sign.

"Most likely, he'll sleep out in the field and be gone by morning," Gray said in a sad voice.

"Why does he act like that?" Carl Lee asked, still upset.

Gray didn't answer him at once. A look of longing and sadness etched the lines deeper in his face. "Maybe he resents you coming out here, being with me. He always wanted you just for himself. Even from birth."

Gray finally sighed, "When will he learn we can't build a fence around our feelings or the people we love."

"Love?" said Carl Lee, irony mocking his voice.

Carl Lee brooded. Maybe Samuel wouldn't be gone in the morning. Maybe Samuel would come back from the No Trespassing pasture to raise him out of his sleep before daybreak.

"Maybe in order to cool things down, I'll have to cut the summer short and go home to Ponca City." Then, remembering last year and Gray's anguished phone call to Ponca City when he couldn't find Carl Lee in the fields that fateful afternoon that Samuel had forced him home early, Carl Lee recommitted himself. "No," he said, "this time I'm standing my ground."

After chores, Carl Lee didn't do much homework, he kept staring at the No Trespassing sign and hoping that his father would leave him in peace in Golden Pasture.

That night in his dream he hit his father so hard the pain' woke him up. The moon beaming through his window showed him a fist swollen fat from hitting the iron rail of his bed. The oppressive heat and his aching hand kept him in a sweat. He tossed and turned on the firm mattress for what seemed like an eternity before falling back off into a deep sleep.

He didn't know how long the rooster had been crowing when he woke up.

Terror drove him as he hopped out of bed and ran out of his room, down the hallway through the living room and opened the front door to look out.

His father's car was gone.

The Appaloosa

Now it was Saturday again, a week since the fight with his father.

As Carl Lee went about his daybreak chore of milking the cows, the long shadows of morning lay softly against the Oklahoma landscape. A subtle patchwork of shade subdued the blackjack trees, keeping out the light until later.

The birds broke the quiet stillness, a choir of them, calling gently, sweetly enchanting the air with their warbling.

The rooster faithful to the dawn shadows crowed intermittently and strutted up and down in his chicken coop. His red comb crown catching the first glint of the Saturday morning sun.

The patient nesting hens, fat with feathers and the confidence that comes after laying an egg, spread out their feather dresses proudly over their straw thrones and clucked noisily.

When Saturday was half gone, Gray said, "Carl Lee, I'm going into Boley. I'll be staying overnight. We're celebrating Billingsley's birthday.

"Billingsley's gonna be seventy-two," he announced. "The old tribe of retired cowboys will be doing some serious partying this evening. In fact I intend to wear myself out. I'll be too tired to do anything after it's over but sleep.

"And you know, Carl Lee, I don't celebrate and drive."

He picked up a bottle of his personally prepared loganberry wine that he aged especially for parties.

"So," Gray promised, "I'll spend the night and be back first thing in the morning. Before the dew dries in the northwest pasture, I'll be home."

"Don't worry about me," Carl Lee said. "Have yourself a good time, Grandpa."

As evening fell, Gray prepared to leave.

"Hey, Special Pony, how do I look?" Gray said. He was dressed in a straw hat, a long-sleeved shirt (a leather beaded necklace peeping through his collar opening), and a pair of cowboy britches. His boots had been polished until they gleamed.

As old as he is, my grandpa's still handsome, Carl Lee realized with a shock.

"You'll pass, mighty handsome for an old mule," he teased good-naturedly.

Gray grinned.

The steady rumbling of his grandfather's old truck starting up was a lonely sound.

It was strange being at the ranch without Gray.

The cows mooed to let Carl Lee know he wasn't completely alone.

And the five horses in the stable whinnied as though saying good-bye to Gray.

Carl Lee couldn't think about horses without thinking about his grandfather. Gray had taught him to ride the summer Carl Lee was five years old.

That summer Gray had placed him on the gentlest pony for that first riding lesson. Carl Lee was so proud he rode until the June bugs came out and then fell asleep in the saddle.

Carl Lee also remembered that later on that summer, the first week of September was the occasion of his first trip to the rodeo in Boley.

That Labor Day they had put the five horses in the horse trailer and hooked the trailer to the pickup. Carl Lee couldn't get over how well mannered the horses were. Standing in the trailer quiet as shadows. In fact, their quietness on the long road to the rodeo was as amazing to him as the fact that horses sleep standing up. Perhaps they too were full of anticipation. The rodeo. A place where any horse could strut his stuff. Ever since he had been five years old, his steady dream was to perform in the Boley Rodeo.

Carl Lee had learned how to run fast by watching the horses.

"How'd you learn to run like a horse?" his grandfather had asked him.

"I think like a horse," the five-year-old Carl Lee had responded.

"How's that?" asked Gray, the answer stopping him in his tracks.

"Four," answered Carl Lee. "I think I have four legs instead of two."

And he had demonstrated for his grandfather. Racing from the barn to the house.

Scratching his head, Gray said, "Twice as many legs, I guess that multiplies your speed all right."

And Gray had told everybody he knew, "My grandson really owns four legs instead of two, you just can't see the other pair."

He had a lot to be thankful to his grandfather for, Carl Lee thought as he went into the kitchen.

After warming up and eating some of Gray's hearty stew of potatoes, beef, onions, and peas—and the skillet bread that went with it—Carl Lee washed up the dishes.

He reached in the refrigerator and took out the slice of stone mountain watermelon, placed it on a saucer, sprinkled salt on it, and settled down in his grandfather's rocking chair. The melon tasted red ripe and juicy sweet.

After he finished his dessert, he washed the saucer and his hands.

He went and got his Bible and started scripture searching in preparation for leading a discussion in Sunday school the next Sunday.

He started at Genesis and had been through the entire Bible when he came upon the first chapter of Revelation. He stopped at the third verse because it sounded like something his grandfather would say, "Blessed is he that readeth."

"Shoot," he said, putting the Bible down. "I wish Grandpa would come on home tonight."

Then he chastised himself for being selfish. Didn't his grandfather devote every summer to him? Surely, he could allow him one night out with his friend Billingsley without having Mrs. Nervalene Robinson come a mile down the road to stay with him. He was too old for Nervalene Robinson to babysit him on Billingsley's birthday as she had done in years past, and while she was there making dumplings or corn-bread dressing or some other dish Gray didn't have in his corral of recipes.

"Maybe I'll watch a little TV," Carl Lee said to himself. He got up and turned on the TV.

There was one of those game programs with dollar bills flying through the air, lots of audience applause, and contestants hopping up and down with joy, carbon copy giggles in their voices every time they got a correct answer. On other nights that he had watched he was entertained by their happy shenanigans, but tonight they just looked like somebody had wound them up.

He turned the dial again.

An old-fashioned movie. An ancient cowboy rode into a ghost

town on his palomino horse, and as he dismounted and tied his horse to the railing along the board sidewalks, he talked slow to the sheriff.

The old cowboy made Carl Lee think about his grandfather and how lonesome he was although Gray hadn't been gone a good two hours.

He turned the channel again.

A scary Alfred Hitchcock movie. He loved Alfred Hitchcock movies, but not tonight. He turned the dial again.

Nothing satisfied him. He flicked the switch to off. He was restless. And even rocking in the rocking chair pretending he was his own grandfather didn't soothe him. He kept getting up and looking out the window.

The day was leaving. The sun falling over the horizon.

The ranch sounded strange and quiet. Even the cows had stopped mooing. And the five horses must have been standing up, asleep in their stalls.

Now what?

He could review his homework. He went to his room and picked up that poetry book.

He opened the book. Then he closed it.

No, he wasn't in the mood for memorizing that poem. He looked out of the window.

A full moon stared him straight in the face when he studied the sky.

And the blackjack tree outside in the yard squatted in its own shadow.

The moon's reflection shone down and made the green alfalfa fields look scary. The fields glowed like phosphorus.

Everything added to his loneliness.

Then he realized much of the happiness around the ranch had

a lot to do with his grandfather's presence. It was not just the old brick house, the fields and the trees, the cows, or the whitewashed barn that he enjoyed. Why, the sound of Gray's voice at night was like a light turned on in the dark.

Yet, as he thought about it he realized, it was more than the baritone bass of Gray's voice even.

He pictured the fast-slow movement of Gray's hands when he was frying skillet-hot-water corn bread. Something as simple as that. It made home, home.

He heard something cornered howl far away. And he shivered.

An owl flew past his window. Like a winged cloak in the dark.

Get a hold of yourself, he said.

Then there came the most eerie scream. The sound of crying, distress, but it was not a human voice.

It sounds like its coming from. . . .

Yes, it was coming from the direction of the No Trespassing sign.

An animal was hurt.

But what animal?

Something cornered? Some dangerous thing he had never seen before?

There was danger in the woods.

Some wild bobcat at his throat?

A rattlesnake striking thigh-high above his boots on a dark night was a danger.

But he had been on coon hunts before at night. And it was pitch black when they hunted possums. Surely he wasn't afraid of any old rattlesnake.

But Gray had been with him those times. This was different.

No it wasn't a cornered animal, he thought, listening closer.

But what was it?

He was rooted to his chair.

Then the eerie cry again.

He gripped the chair's arms. If Gray was here, he'd know what to do. The two of them would put on their boots, grab their shotguns, and ride over to see what was the matter.

But Gray was gone, over in Boley, dressed up, partying. And he was here, a boy of twelve, alone with things hollering in the night.

The sound inched under his hairline and stuck there. Lay desperate in his ear.

Oh, the wailing.

The cry of hurt.

He couldn't sit still.

Soon he was up walking the floor.

The call of pain. He had to help.

He decided he wouldn't take the palomino. He would run over to that No Trespassing place and see what that was.

After all, he could run almost as fast as his horse. He pulled on his boots.

The call came again, higher and more eerie.

He went into his bedroom and took his shotgun off the wall.

"This will never do; I can't run fast with this old gun," he said out loud.

He hung his gun back on the wall and hurried out the bedroom door.

He ran through the kitchen. Whatever was hurt, he was going to help. He couldn't take much more of that strange screaming.

Out the back door he flew, over the alfalfa phosphorous green fields, out past the alfalfa into a patch of wild indigo and wild sunflowers around a blooming redbud tree, over the planks bridging Opal Lake, running with the frog and cricket sound in his throat too, and through a copse of blackjack trees.

He ran on and on to the sound of the wavering, haunting cry.

He ran until he wanted to cry out for breath.

He paused only to unlatch the gate with the No Trespassing sign on it and pass into another field.

He ran on toward the sound.

A big lonely southern pine blocked his path just as a huge horned owl with a span of wings as long as he was tall flapped in front of him.

"What?" hollered Carl Lee. Then the creature took off steering between a pair of oak trees and on out of sight.

Into the night the raw cry of pain flew and stuck in his ear again.

And he was running toward whatever was making that sound.

Then he was upon it.

The crying thing.

It sat in a meadow, edged with goldenrod. Next to the goldenrod he spotted yellow primroses and daisies, all yellow and proud.

In a field already blooming in golden alfalfa flowers as though a special sun shone on this alfalfa field, a sun that did not beam any place else, he saw the most beautiful creature his eyes had ever beheld.

"An Appaloosa!" Carl Lee gasped. He was brown all over except on his back and on his hooves. "A raindrop horse," he whispered, noticing the white area on the loins and hips, the patterning of round spots like clouds.

The horse lay crying in the middle of this golden meadow, crying the most eerie cry.

What was wrong?

He ran to the horse and examined his legs. No leg was broken. And then he saw the nearby hole in the meadow.

He looked at the horse's black and white striped back hooves.

Right away, he knew what had happened; the horse's right back foot had stepped into the hole and he had strained a muscle trying to pull it out.

The Appaloosa had gotten down and couldn't get back up.

He would have to help the horse up. Take him to the barn near the house, put him in the stable and take care of him.

But he had no harness, no bridle.

He spied a honeysuckle vine running along the nearby fence.

He ran to the honeysuckle, pulled out a long piece of vine, and made a wreath to put around the horse's neck.

The vine made excellent twine and he let one long piece of honeysuckle rope trail down from the wreath. And this became the bridle.

He soothed the horse, talked to him, coaxed him with firm but gentle voice as he pushed, helping the horse rise.

Still crying the horse pulled himself up and followed Carl Lee without resisting him, led by the bridle of honeysuckle.

The Appaloosa walked along behind him dragging that hind leg.

Past the oak trees, the southern pine and on through the unlatched gate, past the copse of blackjack trees, across Opal Lake, and the redbud tree in blossom, the limping horse followed Carl Lee until the ranch house came into sight. They passed the house and went straight to the barn.

He knew what to do for a pulled muscle. Hadn't he seen his grandfather take care of horses before?

Pulling a muscle was one of the most painful accidents to happen to a horse, next to having a broken leg.

Knowing this, Carl Lee continued to talk gently to the horse as he led him into the barn. The other horses neighed and seemed to look on from their stalls with compassionate eyes as Carl Lee helped the Appaloosa.

He knew the treatment for a pulled muscle.

The thing to do was to walk the horse awhile. He had already done that, bringing him from the golden pasture.

The other part of the remedy was to put heat on the muscle of the injured hind leg.

Although it was well past his bedtime by now, he stayed up tending the Appaloosa with liniment heat packs, whispering encouragement in his long ears.

Between applying the aromatic heat packs, he laid straw in an empty stable. Spread it around until it was even. The stable now was ready for the Appaloosa.

Soon the horse stopped crying.

Then Carl Lee led the horse to the straw stable. He didn't want to leave the Appaloosa in case he started crying with pain again and had to have the liniment packs applied again, so Carl Lee curled up alongside him in the straw and fell asleep.

He woke up from a deep sleep when he heard a rooster crowing.

And another sound.

The sound of his grandfather calling him.

"Carl Lee! Carl Lee!"

Carl Lee had a time orienting himself. Where was he?

Not in his bed. He smelled straw, the sweat of horses, and the intense fragrance of honeysuckle.

It took him a little while to realize he was in the stables. With the horses! With The Horse! The Appaloosa!

Wait until his grandfather heard!

He didn't holler back at his grandfather. He didn't want to startle the Appaloosa. He palled the raindrop horse and left the stall, securing it behind him.

He ran out of the barn into the growing sunlight. "Here, here I am, Grandpa!"

"I went to your room. Your bed hadn't been slept in," Gray said worriedly.

"That's because I wasn't in it. I slept in the barn."

"What?"

Carl Lee told him all that had happened. And about the beautiful horse.

Gray stood there, stunned into silence.

"You mean the Appaloosa?" Gray asked when he found his tongue.

"Yes, that one." It was then Carl Lee realized he might be in trouble for going into the forbidden area, but he had thought only of an animal, out there hurt and alone. Now what would his grandfather do? His voice lumped in his throat and he shut up.

"I don't know about this," Gray said shaking his head after what seemed to Carl Lee like a century.

"Now let's go see him," his grandfather said.

They walked inside the barn.

Carl Lee brought some hay over to the horse and fed him.

Gray stood there still looking amazed at the way the wild horse responded to his grandson.

After a while he just shook his head, not saying much.

"Grandpa, can I keep him? Can he be my horse?"

"I don't know, son. He's wild. He needs to be out in the open pastures, with a bigger fence than we have for the rest of the horses. That's why he had his own acres over there. It took forever, but I fenced him in."

"Please, Grandpa. . . . Oh, please, I think I'll die if I can't have him."

"Well, no you won't. But we'll see."

Gray was trying to figure something out. But Carl Lee was so excited he couldn't pay much attention to his grandfather. The

Appaloosa! The wonderful Appaloosa! He couldn't stand it.

"'We'll see,' oh, Grandpa!"

"That's enough for now," Gray said with sternness in his voice.

Then he continued, "Obviously the horse likes you. Maybe because you helped him when he was in pain. . . ." He scratched his gray head. "But I wouldn't try to ride him. He's bucked and busted more men than . . ."

"What?" asked Carl Lee.

"I said I wouldn't try to ride him."

"He can't be ridden, Grandpa, he's got a pulled muscle."

"We'll see. We'll see," Gray kept saying, as they headed to the house.

In the kitchen Carl Lee peeled potatoes for breakfast and after they had sizzled crisp in the big black skillet, they sat down to a meal of old-fashioned hash browns with onions, scrambled eggs, buckwheat flapjacks and Alaga syrup, orange juice, and broomwheat tea so strong you couldn't see the bottom of the cup.

Gray finally said, "Why you're just like your daddy in a way. He was crazy about horses, too. Except that boy always did have fits."

"My daddy a boy?" said Carl Lee.

"Even I was a boy once upon a time," Gray said with amusement.

"Your daddy had these crazy spells. Crazy about horses like I said. You got that from him naturally. That's for sure! It was a horse that made Samuel show his mettle. I thought I had Samuel figured out as the laziest, most no count teenager that ever passed through adolescence. As he got older he only got worse. But now I think maybe I was wrong for thinking that way."

"Grandpa? You wrong?"

Gray took a sip from his cup of broomwheat tea. Then he

added, remembering some old incident, "And Samuel was right. Once, your daddy loved a horse. I should've let him keep the horse after we caught him, but I wanted to show him off in that darn rodeo. He was a king, that horse."

"What horse? What are you talking about? What happened?" Carl Lee asked, sopping the last morsel of flapjack into the Alaga syrup.

"Oh, the horse became part of the rodeo. . . . And. . . . Never mind the in between part," he said, cutting the story short noticing Carl Lee's ready feet pointing toward the back door. His bottom on the edge of the chair itching to leap up and run-see about the Appaloosa.

"The upshot is Samuel and I never saw eye to eye about that incident. The horse ended up not his and not the rodeo's. But not free either. To a horse like that freedom means being wild. That's something Samuel understands."

Gray emptied the last of the broomwheat tea from his cup. "Your daddy was wild. Samuel, Samuel, running wild, wild as any horse that bucked, stomped, and escaped the roundup in the New Mexico mountains out yonder. Staying out late, drinking rotgut and tanglefeet wine. Chasing women like a stallion chasing mares. The only time he got his mind together was when that horse appeared. I've never seen one man make over a horse the way Samuel did over that long-ago stallion. And the horse liked him. Wouldn't let any other rider come near him except Samuel.

"Samuel didn't want that horse in the rodeo though. Said it was a shame and a disgrace for the horse to be in the same arena as some of those peasant ponies and nobody nags."

Although Carl Lee was interested in hearing about his father's teenaged years, he thought he heard the Appaloosa bleat with pain. He scrambled out the back door, forgetting about washing the dishes and taking out the garbage, barely hearing Gray's last words.

"Your daddy's never forgiven me. Never. Never. Never forgiven me for the horse named Thunderfoot."

Cloudy

The Sunday morning crickets continued their soft June calls, vibrating as Gray milked the cows and Carl Lee groomed and brushed the horses. The cricket sound of peace and summer and all that's right with the world lay over the ranch like a net. Through the holes in the net Carl Lee heard the cheechee birds, the mockingbirds and starlings, and meadow larks.

Chores over, breakfast finished, they bathed in preparation for church.

Now they were in Gray's sparsely furnished bedroom getting dressed.

"Can't I stay home just this one Sunday?" Carl Lee begged as he ironed the white shirts they were to wear.

"No, partner, we have social commitments too, you know," said Gray, his thick fingers searching his box of cuff links. He selected two twist-shaped cuff links, a pair of silver lassos.

Carl Lee knew by Gray's tone there was no talking his grandfather out of going to church.

"I'd never hear the end of it. Next thing we know all those nosy women in the church would be arriving with baskets of food, snooping and sniffing around, claiming I need another wife."

No getting out of it then. They were definitely getting ready to attend the Golden Pasture African Methodist Episcopal Church.

He finished laying out the clothes on his grandfather's bed.

His grandfather's iron bed still had the last quilt his dead wife had patched on top. The quilt served both as a decorative spread in summer and as warmth in the winter.

Otherwise, it was a man's room. But one that was orderly. Shoes and boots lined up in the closet. Shirts and ties on one side. Cowboy clothes, coveralls, and overalls hanging on the other.

Gray handed Carl Lee a pair of cuff links in the shape of spurs and they finished getting dressed.

"Here we are harnessing ourselves in these contraptions just like any other horse or mule," said Gray, standing in front of his bedroom mirror. With a grimace he perfected a knot in his navy blue tie.

"Let's see, my young stallion," he added, checking to see if Carl Lee's light blue tie was straight.

It was, but he gave it an extra twist anyway.

"Well, we're early as usual."

Gray picked up his old King James Bible and Carl Lee went to his room and fetched his newer Bible. They headed for the truck.

"I sure do wish I could spend the day with my horse," said Carl Lee, as they roared across Opal Lake's bridge.

"I know how you feel," said Gray.

"Can I name him?"

"Name him?" echoed Gray. "What would you call him?"

Carl Lee was quiet for a moment remembering the first time he saw the Appaloosa. The raindrop horse. He recalled how the brown horse looked with the splashes of silver on his withers and the black spots dappling his loins and hips like storm clouds on a moonlit canvas.

"I think I'll call him Cloudy."

"Cloudy?" said his grandfather, amazement in his voice. After a while he said slowly, "I like that."

"Cloudy," said Carl Lee.

Soon they were rolling into Golden Pasture. They stopped in the middle of Main Street and then parked in front of the white wooden church. They walked up the red-brick steps leading to the entrance.

Once inside they pulled off their hats and walked down the aisle.

The congregation was singing "Bringing in the Sheaves," and Jessie and Norman scooted over so Carl Lee could sit next to them in the pew occupied by the younger people.

Gray went farther to the front and sat next to his old friend, Billingsley, a bald-headed man as tall and muscular as Carl Lee's grandfather.

Billingsley's head looked like a full moon shining in the middle of the day.

Carl Lee mischievously wondered if Billingsley shined his head when he finished shining his boots.

He felt a drake's feather tickle his insides at the thought of Billingsley busy shining his head, making the rag pop as he polished his scalp until it sparkled.

He was so full of excitement about the horse that seeing Billingsley's bald head gave him a kind of emotional release. He wanted to laugh so bad his stomach hurt holding it in.

"What's so funny?" whispered Jessie, noticing Carl Lee's belly jiggling up and down.

"What's up?" echoed Norman.

Once he got over being tickled about Billingsley's head, he thought the two old friends looked dignified and as if they knew everything important there was to know in the world.

Too, he wondered how he would look when he got that age, if his head would be bald like Billingsley's or with hair full and white like his grandfather's. And however it looked, he wondered if his head would have as much sense in it as theirs.

Now he threw himself wholeheartedly into the singing, "We shall all rejoice when bringing in the sheaves."

His voice was almost deep, not quite. He was presently a tenor on his way to being a bass. As he sang, he remembered what his grandfather told him: "Put some authority in your voice when you make music, but color it sweet."

The notes of the song flew to and from the pews of women whose perfume drifted like flowers in the air. The sweet rhythm rained over the younger girls sitting next to their mothers, their ribbons on their heads like colorful streamers.

And the voices floated along his own row among the congregation of boys in white shirts and ties, just like him, but no coats. Boots shined. Short hair, some cut the old-fashioned way, by setting a bowl on the boy's head and cutting around it. But all the short hairstyles boasted neat parts and were brushed back until each hair lay in its own pasture.

After the song ended, Reverend Honeywell preached a sermon about the four horses in Revelations.

"Revelations, sixth chapter; fifth and sixth verses. 'And when he had opened the third seal, I heard, Come and see. And I beheld, and lo a black horse; and he that sat on him had a pair of balances in his hand . . .'" But Carl Lee's mind was on his own horse, and so he didn't pay much attention to the minister's sermon.

Before he knew it Reverend Honeywell was saying the benediction, "May the Lord watch between me and thee while we are absent one from another. Until we meet again, let the church say, Amen."

"Amen," the congregation sighed.

Carl Lee walked out of the church and into the light and onto the red-brick church steps with the rest of the congregation. He spoke politely to everybody, but he didn't want to linger very long. And his eyes kept making silent pleas every time he could catch Gray's glance.

After only a few minutes of standing on the green lawn with Norman and Jessie watching the ribbon-haired girls and calling them delicious names like "Golden Cookies," "Nutmeg Honeys," and "Sweet Chocolate Drops," Carl Lee was ready to go.

Gray, sensing Carl Lee's anxiety, talked only a few minutes to the widow women.

"Oh, Gray, your grandson's going to be as tall as you are, I declare!" said Nervalene Robinson, the mother of the church who used to babysit Carl Lee when he was younger. Now she was somewhere in her nineties, peering at Carl Lee through her bifocals.

"Yes, the boy's amazing. A pedigree. Why, he sprints as fast as a race horse. He's as sure-footed as a quarter horse. Got the hindquarters of a Lipizzan, runs as smooth as a Morgan, and is as handsome as a Clydesdale." Gray stuck out his chest.

As anxious as he was to return home, Carl Lee smiled in spite of himself. He didn't know what to think of his grandfather's comparing him to horses, but he liked it.

On the other hand he knew his grandfather's comparisons could be cutting too. When Nervalene Robinson asked him, "And how's that son of yours in Ponca City doing?" his grandfather didn't bite his tongue but looked Mrs. Robinson straight in the eye and said, "Still cutting up. A wild ass on the loose."

When the astonished Nervalene Robinson, leaning on her cane, looked at him with her mouth open, he said, "It's in the Bible. A wild ass on the loose. Hosea, eighth chapter; ninth verse."

At that, Nervalene Robinson gave a relieved little laugh. His grandfather said good day then turned and said a few words to Billingsley, but they didn't talk long either.

Finally, Gray was saying his farewells and heading straight for the blue pickup, his Bible tucked under his arm.

As they motored down the road toward home, Carl Lee sat on the edge of his seat. Way after while they were passing over Opal Lake's bridge. He barely heard the frogs crowing and the crickets fussing at the heat.

And the sound of the drakes quacking in a chorus was muted. Once the red-brick house came into view, he let out a great sigh.

Gray had barely parked when Carl Lee busted out of the pickup and ran straight to the barn. Cloudy was up and moving around, but he still limped a little.

Carl Lee cleaned out the Appaloosa's stall and strewed new straw.

He walked the horse a bit.

Then he applied more liniment cloths.

"Pretty soon, he won't need those hot packs anymore," said Gray, leaning over feeling the horse's leg.

"He's healing fast all right," Carl Lee agreed.

"I bet in one week, you'll hardly know he pulled this muscle," said Gray.

"He's gorgeous," said Carl Lee. "The most handsome horse I've ever seen."

"He's a magic horse all right."

"Magic?" said Carl Lee, lifting his eyes from packing the liniment cloth to the horse's withers. All right then, he decided, a handsome magic horse. That was Cloudy to the tee.

"Hey, mustang, don't you think you ought to take off your church clothes?"

Carl Lee, in his excitement, had forgotten all about that. He ran into the house and changed.

A week passed and Cloudy had lost his limp.

Carl Lee found a halter and a bridle in the barn and put them around the horse's neck. Then he walked him all around the barn and across the alfalfa field, but he stayed away from the No Trespassing area.

Gray was yelling something.

"What?" Carl Lee yelled back.

"Yes," Carl Lee answered, "he let me put the halter on him."

From where he stood in the fields he could see Gray hitch up his britches then scratch his head in wonder and yell something about "You're your daddy's son, all right."

At the end of the next week, Carl Lee experienced the spirit of Cloudy.

Every time he tried to mount him, the horse tossed his mane, shook his neck violently in warning, and gave a belligerent snort.

After much coaxing, Carl Lee finally mounted the horse and rode him a short distance.

Again he saw Gray near the front steps yelling and waving his hat.

"What?" said Carl Lee.

"Yes," Carl Lee hollered back, "he let me mount him and ride him."

At last he saw his grandfather hunching his shoulders and shaking his gray head until Carl Lee thought it would roll right off his neck.

Later that day they put all six horses out in the pasture. Standing near the fence, now covered with wild raspberries and wild blackberries, the horses lounged in the shade of a redbud tree. Then they moseyed on down by the lake, flicking the biting flies from their backs and constantly whipping their long tails like motorized flyswatters.

Carl Lee and Gray brought two chairs out to the pasture and sat under the tree watching the horses drink from nearby Opal Lake.

Carl Lee's hand flew up and rubbed a tickling burn on his neck. "Darn mosquito."

Gray said, "Mighty sneaky pest the mosquito."

"Sneaky?"

"The way he lands so light on you. Won't put his weight on you like a bee or a wasp. No. The mosquito lands so light you can't feel him, till he's through, that is. When he's sucked his fill of your blood, he takes off, singing his mosquito song. Reminds me of some people I know. Just as treacherous. You don't know you've been stung till they've done you in."

"Maybe they ought to have a repellent for those kind of folk," Carl Lee said.

His grandfather gave a belly laugh. "Insect repellent for people?"

"Why not?" said Carl Lee, letting his imagination run.

"I only heard of insect spray to keep off bugs. If they had insect spray for people, I'd buy up a store's worth," said Gray. "There are folks out there so sneaky they'll try and sell you a horse with no legs.

"But back to this insect spray to keep off bugs. We didn't have any spray in the old days. We used smoke and blackberry juice to keep the biting mosquitoes away. Still works today," he said reaching for a bunch of wild blackberries, squeezing them through his strong black hands until the juice ran down. Then he rubbed his skin until it stained even darker.

Carl Lee followed suit. The berries stained the skin around his fingers too, creating a new hue. He was a red-clay boy with the juicy darkness of the berries blending in with his color.

Inevitably, the conversation turned to horses. "If only I had the eyes of a horse," said Carl Lee. "If I could just look forward and backward at the same time, just like Cloudy. . . ."

"I like your eyes just as they are," said Gray.

"The horse pays well for that ability. Although one eye can look in front of him and the other can look behind him, he has a blind spot. Can't see what's right in front of his nose. Same thing with a jackass."

Then Gray went on to add, "Your daddy's got a mind like a jackass's eyes. He's still in mourning over losing too much. But he can't see you at all. The miracle standing right there in front of his eyes." A sadness claimed his face, and then all at once his old eyes brightened as though a hidden candle was lit in them. "But I remember one miracle he did work. One rodeo night."

"I have to tell you about the night your father worked a miracle. The night he saved a horse's life."

Carl Lee stared into his grandfather's eyes. The look and the sound of Gray's voice took Carl Lee back through time until he too was at the rodeo in Boley watching the events unfold.

"It was raining that night at the Boley Rodeo. The rain started at first in little sprinkles, just misting. The grandstand overflowed with folks from Maine to Mississippi from California to Kansas. And the star of the show was Thunderfoot. Thunderfoot was an Appaloosa that was captured wild, sold to the rodeo—and no man could break him."

"Where did he come from?" asked Carl Lee.

"Whoa boy! That's another story."

Gray continued.

"The horse was beginning to look haggard, to show the effect of being trotted around, mistreated from rodeo to rodeo. And this night a rider named Hellhound came to Boley expressly to ride Thunderfoot.

"The crowd ached for action, thirsted for a taste of Thunderfoot's blood.

"Earlier in the day Samuel heard Hellhound say to a

wrinkled-faced cowboy in a broken-down hat, 'I'm going to break that horse tonight if I have to kill him.'

"The news flew like cheechee birds, *Hellhound's gonna break that horse tonight if he has to kill him.*

"The message got around from barbecue pit to barbecue pit.

"Hellhound's boasting could have been the sauce the rodeo fans put on their ribs, his words stayed in their mouths and flavored the food and the atmosphere of the rodeo gathering.

"Now Hellhound was an ornery cuss. He would do anything to break a horse.

"Used his spurs like a butcher knife.

"Left horses bleeding and sometimes blinded.

"And he only rode once a year. It was always an occasion. He'd wait until a horse had built up a reputation for himself and then he'd appear.

"He was invincible, they say. But Samuel thought he was a coward.

"'We never should have sold this horse to the rodeo, Daddy,' Samuel said. 'You should've let me keep him!'

"Hellhound waited until a horse had been worn down by the other less skilled riders, and then he would come along like some long-lost hero out of the Oklahoma hills bragging, boasting about being the greatest bronc buster in these here parts.

"'Show me the animal I can't ride. I want to see him,' he ranted.

"An uneven match as far as Samuel was concerned.

"'Hellhound's more animal than any horse I ever met,' the teenaged Samuel said to me.

"Hellhound always wore yellow, perhaps to match his yellow eyes. The yellow was different, as if he had dipped his outfit in a special vat of dye whose color he borrowed from a yellow flame.

"That night he looked fairly incandescent.

"When he talked directly to Samuel or breathed in Samuel's face, Samuel had to turn away or move so Hellhound was standing downwind from him.

" 'That's how he conquers wild horses,' Samuel whispered to me. 'Stuns them with his stinky breath.'

" 'I am the baddest cowboy that ever crouched in a saddle!' Hellhound swore.

"Hellhound made fun of anybody a horse threw. 'Look at that baby, ought to be home still nursing his mama,' he said of a Guthrie man whose back got busted.

"The crowd had reached a frenzy of excitement. They always saved the most special event of the day until last, way past sundown.

"The clowns clowned more that night. People drank more, bringing their own red home brew, a fermentation of raisins, potatoes, and anything else that'll mix with a pound of sugar and yeast. After they had run it off for two weeks, it was so strong it'd tear your head off.

"Half the folks in the stands were drunk from that red tanglefeet, so alcoholic and strong it'd tangle your feet and your mind.

"Then they did what the old-timers advised never to do—they split open stone mountain watermelons, the sweetest kind in Oklahoma, and mixed drink and melons. A bad combination. In an atmosphere like that anything might happen.

"Not wanting to miss a thing, I stayed as sober as Reverend Millhouse over in the holiness church.

"The bulldoggers finished their bulldogging, the steer wrestlers finished wrestling their steer, and the bareback riders bucked and hopped off the backs of their horses in one piece either with no bones out of place or with backs broken.

"A storm threatened.

"Over the heads of the rodeo crowd angels roller-skated in

the sky. The sound deafened the ordinary confusion.

"And the clouds whipped up a show that kept all their attention and their faces tilted up.

"Then the wind started.

"If the wind is the breath of God, He must have been having a coughing fit that night. Even the thick windows of the cars that get to the rodeo early and line the fences of the arena trembled and shook, and the weather-beaten railings circling the arena rattled so hard they fell away like toothpicks.

"In the meantime all the horses, bulls, and steers kicked the sides of their chutes with a banging noise, adding to the clamor.

"The loudspeaker clacked, filled with static. One old-timer said, 'I'm leaving this place,' as he picked up his gear, eyes on the sky. Samuel understood then why some folks won't turn on anything electrical when a storm's in the area. Old-fashioned folk turn off all the lights and sit quiet. Won't even answer the telephone. 'When God's working, I don't need to be busy,' the bowlegged cowboy said on his way out of the stands.

"There was something syncopated and dangerous in the air.

"That night was as different from regular night as daylight and darkness; dawn and dusk; midnight and morning. It was a night fit for the hounds of hell. It took night to its extreme. Who could rightly compare it to any other night they'd known?

"At first it was just drizzling, with the loud noises from up above.

"At the same time the loudspeaker announced, 'And now for the event of the evening, we have Hellhound riding Thunderfoot.'

"I was standing right next to Thunderfoot's chute with Samuel. As was Hellhound's habit, he was lollygagging around the grandstand so the people could see him. He always took his time about going to the chute.

"The rodeo fans leaned forward, a terrible quiet descended momentarily and hovered over the arena.

"Hellhound mounted Thunderfoot, and the horse bucked and snapped, kicking up his heels, wild-eyed beyond his usual rage.

"The horse, feeling the devil on his back, whirled and bucked fiercely. Thunderfoot performed so spectacularly, he was getting the best of Hellhound who at this moment was hanging on for dear life.

"Hellhound, wall-eyed with worry, was intent on not being bested. He began pulling his dirty tricks, cutting the horse with his spurs. Blood flew like rain. And people commenced to crying, grown folk hugging their bottles of tanglefeet and just letting the tears fall unashamedly when they thought Thunderfoot was finally done for.

"Then the sky split open with white lightning, and a sound like a giant horse, some mythical ancestral, granddaddy of all horses, stampeded from a cloud causing thunder so loud it distracted Hellhound. In that quick moment, Thunderfoot whipped Hellhound to the ground.

"In a halting gallop, Thunderfoot ran to the side of the arena where Samuel and I watched.

"On the other side of the arena, Hellhound picked himself up and started running after the horse, determined to get back on him and finish the job.

"That's when Samuel bolted into the arena, caught up with Thunderfoot and told the horse, 'I'll save you.'

"The Appaloosa, his coat slippery with blood, was so grateful he forgot to kick. His eyes streaked red with fire held the kind of terror that perhaps only a proud, untamed horse knows.

"But he obeyed Samuel.

"And that horse let the tender rider mount him.

"Thunderfoot and Samuel looked like two phantoms in the wind, under cover of a cloud. The rodeo fans couldn't tell who the rider was. But the horse, now he was obvious. Nobody moved like Thunderfoot.

"But Thunderfoot was so injured, he couldn't run as well as he used to and Hellhound was gaining on them.

"The crowd, up out of their seats, urged Thunderfoot and his rider to escape.

"'Go!' they hollered in one wave of sound, but some of the thunder had been bled out of Thunderfoot.

"Then just when it looked like Hellhound might catch Thunderfoot and his mystery rider, the fans decided to get in the act.

"Outraged, they stormed out of the stands and swooped down on the shameless Hellhound and collared him. They couldn't let him hurt Thunderfoot anymore. The horse had thrown him fair and square. The horse had won. There in the pouring rain, the rodeo fans kicked and cursed Hellhound, perhaps for all the other proud horses he'd violently subdued with his spurs. They beat the Oklahoma stew out of him. That varmint. And left him in the middle of the arena with his yellow suit in tatters.

"Hellhound dragged himself up out of the mud and swore one day he'd get even.

"He never showed his face again in Boley or any other Oklahoma rodeo.

"It is said he went to the New Mexico mountains searching for Thunderfoot, sure whoever took him had freed him back to the mountains. They say today he roams the world still looking for the wild Appaloosa determined to finish the job he started."

Gray sighed, bringing Carl Lee back to the present and the smell of the alfalfa pasture and the sweat of the horses.

Carl Lee, thinking about Samuel saving Thunderfoot, was so excited, he couldn't breathe for a moment. "Grandpa!"

His own father a hero!

He looked toward the horses at his own Appaloosa.

But Cloudy was grazing, so Carl Lee couldn't see his eyes, but he imagined Cloudy with that penetrating look in his brown eyes, a look that Carl Lee decided must be the way horses look when they smile.

The Legend of Thunderfoot

August came galloping in like a band of horses.

There was only one more week of summer school left. Every chance he could get away from studying Carl Lee spent in the barn or in the pasture with Cloudy.

Today he was joined in the barn by Gray and Billingsley.

"Grandpa," said Carl Lee, who was rubbing down Cloudy while the horse nibbled at the hay, "since I'm going to ride in the rodeo this year, I need as much information about it as I can get. I want Cloudy to be a star. How does he compare to Thunderfoot and some of those other famous horses I hear you and Mr. Billingsley talking about?"

"Going to the rodeo, yes," said Gray as he inspected the stables for cleanliness, "riding in it, now I don't know about that. We'll have to see how you do in school and what kind of show you're doing for us, right, Billingsley? You see, B.B., he's keeping his horse trick a secret; when are you going to let me in on it, Carl Lee?"

"Won't be long, Grandpa, I promise," said Carl Lee.

"Oh, go ahead, tell him about one of the rodeo stars. Tell him about Black Out," suggested Billingsley.

Gray shook his head.

"Then tell him about Broken Bones. Now there's a story."

"No," said Gray, inspecting the bottom of a stall, secretly pleased at the neat arrangement of clean hay spread out evenly.

When his inspection was done, he started to say no horse stories today, he was feeling tired; but looking at his grandson, standing there rubbing Cloudy, with that curious expression in his eyes, Gray had a change of heart.

"All right, then," he said, selecting a bale of hay and making it into a seat.

His older buddy and Carl Lee did likewise.

"I'll tell you about how we caught the greatest rodeo horse of them all—Thunderfoot.

"It was a cloudy day when we came across Thunderfoot. We had been running this pack of wild horses for a week. It was in the far mountains of New Mexico. These broncs were the hardest bunch we had ever run. And like I say it had been cloudy, cloudy. Storms and rivers of water pouring from the sky. I thought the horse I was riding was a fast horse, since I had caught him years ago and tamed him myself, but there was a horse in the bunch we were trying to catch who could run circles around mine. It was the darndest thing I ever saw.

"There we were wet to the skin, soaked on down to the bone. And we didn't have sense enough to stop. It was like we were being driven by forces outside our control. We were obsessed with catching this horse.

"It was hard to even get a look at him. He looked like a thunderbolt out of nowhere, a bolt from the blue, as transitory as smoke, a brown slash of earth cutting across the land, a fugitive on four legs. But that glimpse only served to pull us on, riding behind him. He took us over some rough, rough territory and some only God had seen. Landscapes I thought I dreamed, mesquite bushes, sagebrush, tumbleweed, mountains shaped by mist, so dense they looked purple until you got right up on them.

"And once I saw gushing water flowing out of a stone right on the rib of the mountain. That was about the time we lost the third person on our team." He was silent for a minute, as though paying his respects to the lost cowboy. Then he continued.

"They say in some of those places the earth just opens up and swallows a man and his horse. But that's an Indian legend more ancient than I am. Still we never saw Hopkins again. We searched a whole day for him, but to no avail. Then as was the unwritten law of cowboys in the wild, we went on with our pursuit.

"We chased that phantom of a horse, his mane flying out behind him, his court of horses bringing up the rear. Racing along almost as fast as he was, they had to be sure-footed to keep up with him.

"I bound you, I saw in Thunderfoot's entourage one of every kind of horse in these parts.

"It looked like he had personally inspected every tribe of horses in the area and selected the fastest, sleekest, most magic thoroughbred out of each family to ride with him.

"I saw a palomino, an albino, a Morgan, and a mustang, but he led them all—this raindrop horse, this Appaloosa—this Thunderfoot.

"I tell you, he was a legend. Once, when we stopped only for a moment, we saw him standing on a ledge, standing far off looking at us as if to mock us for our tiredness.

"We had stopped to eat, but when I saw that beauty staring down at us from his high ledge, I told Billingsley, 'come on!' And we left food, plate and all, and mounted our horses and started off again.

"Before we could blink an eye Thunderfoot had disappeared from the cliff. Everything about that day was fleeting, as transient as the clouds.

"Sometimes the wind would blow the clouds and the storm would move. But the horse was following the clouds.

"When we'd lose sight of him all we'd have to do is look up in the sky and see where the darkest cloud was and that's when we'd get sight of him again.

"Then off we'd go, dashing through the red mud, the hoofs of the horses ahead pounding the ground, making their own kind of distant thunder.

"Six days later, we were still chasing. The folks at home told us later they thought we had fallen off a canyon and become food for the buzzards or that we had toppled into one of those holes the Indians tell us separate this world from the one below.

"We were lucky, only one of us had disappeared. We weren't quitters; we raced on. That horse was in our blood by then.

"It was get him or die out there in the New Mexico mountains, struck down by lightning or sliding through the slippery mud off into a canyon.

"And we had to have him.

"We didn't stop for anything. We ate from the saddle. Hardtack and biscuits and hurried sips of water from our canteens.

"It was often dark when we passed under thick brush there through the New Mexico mountains, following the storm as we were. Things took on shadows and shapes they did not ordinarily have.

"I'm not sure why the horse headed for the makeshift corral we had made in that canyon.

"He started directly for the wedge.

"Maybe he was still following that cloud.

"I know he was too smart to be hedged in. The cloud was so low, it looked like the horse was descending from it.

"I don't know. Maybe there was something wrong in the sky. He didn't seem tired. He made an error.

"He turned down the cliff, following the cloud, headed for the canyon, shrieking. The most unearthly, lacerating bellow.

"Then that awful echo: the wild band of horses, answering him.

"Pretty soon, he was at a point where he couldn't turn around.

"We had him.

"They were hemmed in.

"I can still hear the raw horse sound of anguish today. The horse hollered in a voice that was almost human.

"Round and round he stamped. Trapped. For the first time in his life."

Gray paused, changed positions on his seat of hay.

"We brought him back to the rodeo at Okmulgee. They couldn't tame him there.

"Then what happened to him, happened to many wild horses that wouldn't be broken: he was sent around on the circuit from show to show. He became the highlight of every rodeo from Okmulgee to Muskogee. Thunderfoot, the horse that wouldn't be broken. The horse that broke the riders. The horse that gave the ambulances a reason for lining up.

"In spite of his haughty anger and wildfire temper and the violence he heaped on any rider crazy enough to mount him, Thunderfoot was loved by many.

"They had horse dolls carved in his likeness. Horse blankets with his image on them. Pennants and flags featured Thunderfoot, that mane stretched out, the way I remembered him when we captured him. A free raindrop of a horse descending out of a cloud."

Gray paused, then continued.

"It's a sad thing, the love-hate relationship the rodeo public has with horses that won't be broken. Most of them were ridden until they were crippled, or otherwise injured and then there was only one thing to do. Shoot to kill."

Gray shook his head.

"A bitter end. They send dead horses to the meat packer. After the butcher gets through. . . . Think about it. Something beautiful you found in a canyon, running free, ending up on somebody's kitchen shelf in a tin can labeled dog food. Life's a riddle.

"But Thunderfoot was lucky. Samuel stole him before he wound up dead. He was one of the ones who would never be tamed, at least not that way, although people kept hoping he would and wouldn't be, rodeo after rodeo. They took him from town to town, but he still wouldn't be ridden. It would take a miracle to tame him. But like I said, Samuel took him."

"And Samuel, my own father, stood up to Hellhound," said Carl Lee.

"Hellhound never knew who did it, but he vowed to kill the horse and the man next time he came across them."

Gray went on, "Samuel loved that horse. Maybe he recognized something of himself in Thunderfoot. Some free spirit that hated taming."

"You say he stole him; what if the rodeo committee knew? . . ." asked Carl Lee.

Gray explained, "The rodeo committee had a special meeting and decided the horse had had enough. They said whoever took him was justified."

"What happened to Thunderfoot? Where did he go?"

"That's something your father may tell you one day."

After saying that, Gray got up off his bale of hay and walked slowly toward the house, deep in memory. His friend Billingsley silently stepped beside him.

Carl Lee rubbed Cloudy's mane and thought about Thunderfoot. A horse made tame.

Fear

Carl Lee and his friends, Norman and Jessie, sat cooling their boots on one of their favorite after-school spots, a stretch of fence nestled in the low valley, surrounded by the low hills of Gray's ranch. Behind their horses tethered to the posts, the golden alfalfa fields bloomed.

Honeysuckle spiced the air. Yellow blossoms stuck up their gay heads in the wild dandelions too.

"I was afraid I wasn't going to make it," said Carl Lee.

"Well, looks like you did, and with flying colors too. I thought Miss Monroe's teeth were going to fly out of her face, she was grinning, showing all thirty-twos so hard when you recited that poem. Show off!" Jessie accused.

"Oh, get up off him," said Norman. "You weren't too bad yourself reciting that poem. 'Listen to that enunciation,' Miss Monroe said, eyes lit up like two candles, her smile so bright the whole classroom almost got blinded. You didn't miss a word, you even paused at the commas. You both make me sick!"

"We might make you sick, but I don't see you crying," Carl Lee grinned. "Let me see that report card," he demanded.

Norman was up and off running. Plump as he was, he had some speed. He gave them quite a chase. But Carl Lee caught him and held him while Jessie took the card out of his pocket and looked at it.

"An A!" Jessie whistled.

"Yeah, in Miss Monroe's class, but check out the C in math," said Norman, sprawled on the alfalfa, out of breath from running so hard.

They counted their winning grades and their so-so marks; nobody had anything to be ashamed about.

After they finished horsing around, they crawled back up on the fence.

"We didn't have anything to be afraid of after all, did we?" asked Carl Lee.

"Yeah, but fear comes anyway," said Norman. "I'm afraid I'll be five feet all my life, even though I know I'll grow some more."

"Fear's like that all right."

"I'm afraid my daddy will die," said Norman.

"That my mama will," said Jessie.

"That my grandfather will throw me off the ranch," said Carl Lee.

"That one day the world will blow up before I can get to see it."

"That no girl will ever want me."

"That some girl will!"

"That my daddy will say I can't ride in the rodeo," said Carl Lee.

"He wouldn't do that," said Jessie. "Would he?"

"Anyway, how would he know you were going to ride?"

"My grandfather wrote him a letter and told him I might ride this year," said Carl Lee.

Nobody knew what to say about that, they could only wait and see.

"How will you know what he'll say?"

"Oh, he'll write and let us know." Carl Lee shivered.

Every letter he'd taken out of the mailbox from his father had been a threat. He didn't know what would be worse, receiving a letter before the rodeo or not receiving anything at all so he could just hope his father wouldn't respond, meaning he didn't care one way or the other.

They all thought about this awhile, then Jessie went on to discuss fears in general. "I'm afraid I'll do something awful and embarrass myself to death."

"I wonder what girls are afraid of," Carl Lee said.

"Now that Mary Jane Morgan couldn't ever be afraid of failing anything, as smart as she is, could she?"

They discussed this for a while.

After they had exhausted what each girl looked like in the class and who they thought was the prettiest and the smartest, they ended up talking about horses.

"What is it that horses don't do ordinarily?" Carl Lee asked Norman and Jessie.

"Well they don't talk," Norman said, scooting his hat farther up off his brow.

"They don't play the piano or the flute," said Jessie. "That's not what I mean. What spooks a horse?" said Carl Lee.

Just then he saw the ugly hobo he'd noticed just last week slither past them down the road.

"Who is that man?"

"Looks like a creature from the deep," said Norman.

"He's got yellow fox eyes." Carl Lee felt spiders walking up his neck. Where the man's feet walked, Carl Lee imagined he saw fox tracks. He hopped off the fence and mounted his horse. "Guess I'd better be moseying along," he said uneasily, still eyeing the man as he slinked out of sight. The talk of fear had spooked them all.

Still, he hurried his horse home, not bothering to stop and wade at Opal Lake. Not bothering to check the mailbox with its red flag lifted. He hurried past the cows mooing in the pasture.

"God, it's hot! Alfalfa smells so hot it's almost cooking! Like . . . fire!"

He sniffed. An acrid stench smothered the air, and by the time he approached the hill leading down to the ranch house, he saw a curl of smoke coming from the direction of the barn where the alfalfa hay was stored.

The barn. The horses!

"Cloudy!"

By now he heard the horses shrieking.

"Fire! Fire!" he called.

His grandpa ran to the porch, looked at Carl Lee hightailing the palomino to the smoking barn and hollered on his way back in the house. "Stay back, Carl Lee. I'm calling the fire department!"

Carl Lee knew he was supposed to stay away from the barn fire, but he couldn't help himself. The bales of hay exploded like firecrackers, and the dark smoke billowed in pluming clouds.

He leaped off the palomino and ran to the barn.

He pushed open the door, and he knew somehow that the scarecrow bum had started this, but how? Trespassing, napping in the hay, falling asleep with a cigarette in his sagging mouth, a cigarette whose ashes sparked the fire.

"Coward of a bum!" Why hadn't the bum called for help or at least saved the horses while there was time.

Carl Lee put his arm over his forehead and tried to peer through the thick smoke.

His eyes stung.

Every time he took a breath, he coughed.

The horses shrieked, tossed their manes and stamped around in a tight circle.

Any second and they would stampede and kill each other, but they would not pass through the fire, even though there was a narrow passageway they could make it through to safety.

"Come on! Come on!" Carl Lee hollered.

But the horses only screamed louder.

Through the dense smoke, and the terrible pop of hay bales exploding, he could make out Cloudy.

He ran over to him, trying to remember what he had heard Gray say a long time ago—that's right, a horse's greatest fear is fire. His grandfather had told him, "A horse won't ever cross a path of fire."

What to do?

The pathway to safety was narrowing every second.

He leaped on Cloudy's back and covered the horse's eyes with his hands. Then dug his heels in Cloudy's side.

"Go, boy!"

And Cloudy, through a great act of trust, moved forward.

But already the flames had narrowed the passage until there was hardly any room left.

Was he to die here with the horses, then?

He dug his heels harder in Cloudy's side and let out a yell that spurred the blinded horse forward even faster.

At last they were leaping past the tongues of fire. Out of the fire's mouth.

Into the fresh air.

Behind him, Carl Lee heard a crash and the beams of the barn came thundering down.

He could not get back into the barn to rescue the others.

He and Cloudy circled up and down in front of the barn, agony streaming down Carl Lee's face, and Cloudy still screaming.

"If only I'd had more time. If only I hadn't stopped to horse around with my friends I'd have caught that bum and saved the horses," he said to his grandfather as the firemen with their long hoses swished water on the flames.

Now he and Gray stood on each side of Cloudy rubbing the shivering Appaloosa, smelling the stench of burnt horse flesh, helpless as they listened for the silenced voices of the screamless horses trapped inside.

The hired carpenters, overseen by Carl Lee, had raised the last hammer and rung the last nail into the last plank on the new barn.

"You've done a good job, my young contractor," Gray said to Carl Lee standing back looking at the new structure. "We won't worry about the outside painting yet. We'll get to it next summer; the wood preservative staining the panels will have to do for now."

"I'm wondering something, Grandpa," Carl Lee said as he hauled a bale of hay to the new stable. "Can you ever get a horse used to fire?"

"I doubt it," said Gray nervously fingering the letter Carl Lee had brought up from the mailbox.

"But I thought you said anything was possible."

"It is. But fear's powerful. We don't easily go against our instincts. And that's a truer truth for animals."

"But if a horse could get used to fire. . . ."

"It would save a lot of horse lives. As you yourself witnessed, they panic because they can't shut their eyes and run on through fire to safety," said Gray.

"Yes," said Carl Lee remembering, "they trample each other. And then they get burnt up."

Carl Lee wondered about the ugly bum who started the fire.

"I guess that bum's far away from here by now," he said.

"If I catch him anywhere near this ranch, I'll fill his behind full of buckshot," Gray said angrily tearing open the letter.

Carl Lee braced himself for his father's message. Was this letter the most threatening, the most cruel letter of all? What was inside? Would his father forbid him to ride in the rodeo?

Gray read out loud quickly.

"Dear Papa, I'll see you both at the Boley Rodeo. I won't be able to visit you all after the event. I have to be to work the next day. But I'll pick up Carl Lee the Sunday before Attucks School starts as agreed. Your son, Samuel."

"Well now," said Gray. "Your daddy hasn't been to the rodeo in a long time."

Carl Lee barely heard his grandfather, he was so busy trying to figure out the letter. He thought, *It's not a threatening letter.* Still you could never tell about Samuel. He often promised one thing and did another. Samuel might come to the rodeo drunk. And then he'd forget any promise he had made. Carl Lee prayed he'd show up sober.

Every day Carl Lee rode Cloudy. Then he would run beside him so fast until he could compete with the horse for speed. He thought about horses and fire and the additional pressure of having his father a spectator. Would what he did please his father? Or would he be the laughingstock of the event with his father laughing the loudest?

Running as fast as a horse was the first part of the performance he wanted to give at the rodeo.

But he had a feeling it wouldn't be enough. Wouldn't be spectacular enough.

The rodeo was a rough, rough place. A place where life and limb could be lost so easily. A place where ambulance sirens screamed and reputations were made and broken in a swirling second of hot clay dust and ice-cold sweat.

And the cowboys and rodeo fans were tough judges. They were used to the wonderful, the exciting.

It would take something quite extraordinary to get rodeo fans up out of their wooden seats.

Otherwise, why take up space in the schedule of events?

He wanted to do something so wonderful even his hard-to-please father would applaud.

Carl Lee thought about all these things as he raked straw and toted buckets of water to the horses and cows.

After his chores were finished, he sat on a bale of hay thinking, his head bent and supported by one hand, looking like his own grandfather.

Thinking, thinking, thinking.

August continued to blaze a trail across the meadow. The August sun touched the tips of alfalfa grasses and buffalo weeds, turning them into hay.

When Carl Lee ran beside Cloudy he sometimes sent fox squirrels, minks, rabbits, raccoons, and possums scurrying in the August woods.

Watching from their branches or winging through the sky, the chee-chees scolded and starlings twittered until they sang the lightning bugs out at dusk. The lightning bugs flitted, glowing green, and winked at the boy and the horse practicing way past dusk beneath the country sky.

On many evenings after it was too late to ride Cloudy and run beside him, Gray found Carl Lee sitting on that bale of hay thinking with the barn light on. Then late one night, he went into the barn and Carl Lee was up off the bale of hay working away at something.

"Kind of early for you to be in here, isn't it?" asked Gray. "Not practicing this midnight?"

"Later," said Carl Lee, carrying the joke further. "What are you making with that leather, Horse?" asked Gray. He was standing in the barn door opening, the full moon glinting off his shoulders, watching Carl Lee snip and cut intently, concentrating on his work.

"I'm making some sunglasses for my horse," Carl Lee answered.

Gray chuckled. "I like your sense of humor."

But he noticed Carl Lee wasn't laughing; he was taking another piece of leather down from the barn wall and measuring it.

"But why are you doing this?" Gray asked.

"To find a way through fear," said Carl Lee, looking up from his work.

My goodness, thought Gray, he's grown over the summer. I think he's at least three feet taller. And talking more manly.

"Well, it won't be long before the sun is up. Better come in soon and get some rest," said Gray, just before walking back toward the house.

Many evenings, Gray stood on his porch and watched Carl Lee and Cloudy practicing in the field. The boy sometimes running alongside the horse.

Today his friend, Billingsley, joined him. "Why that's the most fleet-footed boy I ever saw," said Billingsley watching the boy and the horse running, riding, and playing in the pasture.

"Won't be long before rodeo time," said Gray.

"Will he make it?" asked Billingsley.

Gray shrugged. "I keep telling him I don't know, but we'll see."

Soon it was a week before the rodeo and Carl Lee thought he was ready.

He brought out the horse blinders and showed Gray his stunt, perfectly timed so that with a flick of his wrist he released the blinders to cover the horse's eyes at just the right moment.

He had been extraordinarily careful; he had to be doubly careful not to let the horse get hurt.

"But how?" asked Gray, amazed.

"Practice, Grandpa."

"Do it again," he asked.

Again, Carl Lee and Cloudy performed the stunt. When he was sure Carl Lee could do it over and over again, as many times as he and Cloudy chose, Gray tossed his hat into the air and let out a great yell of joy.

"Cowboy!" Gray hollered. "It's rodeo time!"

Rodeo

From the cab of the pickup Carl Lee could barely make out the outline of Cloudy riding quietly in the green trailer behind them as they jostled along the road to Boley.

Gray was quiet too, thinking.

Carl Lee followed suit, gazing out the window at the redbud trees and counting the miles from Golden Pasture to the rodeo and wondering if he would still be a cowpoke when the day was over. Or if he'd be a cowboy recognized by the small world of rodeo people.

Finally, he saw the sign proclaiming "Boley, Oklahoma, population 512."

"Not on Rodeo Day," he whispered; on Rodeo Day the population ran into the thousands.

The town wasn't big enough to hold all the spectators and participants, so the dusty campers spilled out into the countryside.

He read the license plates from Kansas, Texas, Arkansas, California, and New York.

"Made it in good time," said Gray.

They pulled into the grounds at the same time as the rodeo clown was parking his truck.

The clown, already in makeup, settled his spike-haired chartreuse wig on his head as he climbed out of his vehicle, a pair of itchy-looking, neon-green underwear on for costume. He leaned over and tied the strings on a pair of red-and-orange-striped boots.

"Seems like it took us forever," said Carl Lee.

"That's because you're anxious. What if you had to come as far away as the clown?" his grandfather said, maneuvering the truck along the rodeo drive.

"Where's that?"

"Comes from the place where Bill Pickett, the cowboy who invented bulldogging, is buried. A little place called White Eagle, Oklahoma."

"White Eagle? That's five miles outside Ponca City!"

"Uh-huh. Ponca City, the place you were born," said Gray nodding his head. "That makes the clown almost a homeboy for you then, my young cowpoke."

"It's a small world," admitted Carl Lee.

"And getting smaller."

After they had unhitched the trailer within the rodeo compound, they parked the truck in a line with the rest of the five-mile-long parade of cars, pickups, and station wagons that had come to Boley especially for the rodeo.

Excitement was in the air. People lolling on hoods and fenders. A glad wail of music caught them in the act of wagging their heads.

Men in broken-down straw hats barbecued ribs and rabbits next to their cars and trucks, drinking that Red Mule and White Lightning, hollering at one another across smoke and husky slurred laughter.

Pecan Street. The main street in Boley. Barbecue stands and fish stands as far as Carl Lee could see.

"Hey man, you riding Broken Bones today?" the green-haired rodeo clown, adjusting the baggy pants of his lime green underwear, hollered.

The snaggle-toothed cowboy grinned. He had been taken out on a stretcher one famous year by Broken Bones when the newly arrived mustang, wild from the Oklahoma hills, wrecked a row of cars lined up near the rodeo fence, then broke the railing on the rider. Broken Bones had given him amnesia. The first thing the cowboy had said when he woke up in the hospital was this: "What happened?"

"Hey man, what happened?" a tobacco-spitting cowboy in a stained felt hat asked the unfortunate rider, slapping his leather chaps.

Hoorahing, is what Gray would call it. Fortunately, the rider had recovered fully, else hoorahing would be out.

Harmless joking. Never see a fight, people just hanging out, having too much fun and eating each other's food in generous samples. Spiced with good-natured joking: "How do I know what you're giving me is coon or not? Look like dog to me!"

"This ain't no dog. This here's barbecued coon. Still got his foot on him for proof. See here." And the man examined the coon's foot, satisfied. "Hey, Gray, you and your grandson wrap your lips around some of this here coon. Want the foot?"

As Carl Lee and Gray walked the five miles to the rodeo chutes, they stopped often, tasting other Oklahoma recipes of barbecued coon, frog legs, catfish steaks, roasted goat, and garfish.

Through it all, there was talk of the latest horses brought in from the Oklahoma hills. "I'm just itching to break in Time Bomb."

"Either him or Knock Out."

"Give me Thunderfoot in the 'rena any rodeo day.

I'd swop every bad bronc in the bunch for just one chance to bust that sonofagun."

"Yeah, but he ain't here."

Everywhere they stopped the cowboys were raising plenty of hell in peace.

As they neared the rodeo arena, Carl Lee eyed the ambulances lined up outside the fence, ready to take hurt cowboys away. Would he end up in an ambulance like the man they hoorahed about "What happened?"

Outside the chutes, fenced in by weather-eaten wooden slats, cracked in places, he led Cloudy out of the horse trailer, rubbed him down, brushed his coat until it shone, then he laid the special blanket on the Appaloosa's back.

He stayed near his horse in the chute, listening to the other horses kicking in hollow bangs inside their small stables.

Soon, most of the milling people had entered the grandstand and taken their wooden seats. Other spectators clustered around the outside of the fence ringing the arena. But Carl Lee did not see his father.

All through the hot day ranchers, cowboys, cowgirls, wives, husbands, and cowpokes watched triumph and rodeo disgrace as cowboys left the arena, arms upheld in victory or taken out on stretchers.

Through the dust in the arena, Carl Lee could see the sunbeams dying in the powdery particles; he looked up and saw the sun hanging red and low over the grandstand. It was getting to be evening and Carl Lee's own test was nearing. His father had not shown up. He didn't know if he felt relieved or sad. At times both. Relieved that Samuel hadn't arrived ranting and raving drunk to stop him from performing. And sad that his father would not be there to cheer him on.

"Bulldogging!" the loudspeaker clacked. The noise escalated, the bulldoggers stood three feet deep at the ready. The wooden booths were jam-packed with grinning, joy-drinking men in straw hats.

These were the riders who rode in the bulldogging tradition of

Bill Pickett. Riding alongside the bull, then diving on him. Catching the bull by the horn and twisting his head, taking him on down to the ground. Biting the dust.

The bulls snorted, then lunged their thick heads, hurtling men through the air, eliminating cowboy after cowboy until there was only one left in the ring to confront the rankest bull in the stadium.

The rankest bull in the rodeo cannonballed out of a chute near Carl Lee. Rolled his great, fantastic eyes, wicked and red. Shook his head full of horns scored by scars.

The cowboy, shadowing the bull with his horse, finally made the dive, leaped aboard the bull's back, grabbed the awful horns, and held on.

"Go, man! Look at that cowboy handle that bull!"

"Go, man!"

The crowd roared the bulldogger on. He stayed clamped to the bucking back, his free arm raised.

The bull twisted in spirals, soaring upward, then plunging to the earth, still wheeling.

Then the cowboy was over the hump of the bull, working with the horns, then riding him on down to the earth. The bull was beat. The clowns caught the bull's attention. And the cowboy was home free.

Carl Lee looked all over the stadium, but his father was not there.

"Wild horses couldn't pull me away from here," a rodeo fan said, taking a swig of his corn whiskey and leaning out of his wooden booth.

"Quit drinking too much tanglefeet. What you think that is?" asked his partner when a New Mexico wild horse busted through the chute.

"Straight from the mountains, they didn't stop to wipe the dust off his withers. Look-a there. Horse still got the mountain mud on his hoofs. What? What's he doing? Kicked the saddle out of the rider's hand? A cowboy-maker. A cowboy-breaker.

"Look at him go, acting like Thunderfoot."

"He can go, but that ain't Thunderfoot."

"Ain't nobody crazy. We know Thunderfoot when we see him."

Gray cleared his throat, turned his head, looking up at the sky.

The man, still sipping at his fire water—or tanglefeet as his partner called it—said, "Remember the year Thunderfoot sent ten men to the hospital. Sirens sounded like one long song."

Carl Lee could make out Billingsley sitting over in his jam-packed wooden booth, leaning across the railing, studying every move the horse made. Now and then he would look over at Gray and nod or shake his head.

Just then, Carl Lee saw his father enter the row on which Billingsley sat and sit next to the older man. He looked . . . sober!

"Look, Grandpa, Daddy made it."

Gray looked over to the stand where Samuel sat and said, "The last time your daddy came to the rodeo was the night he saved Thunderfoot."

There was a huskiness to Gray's voice and a wistfulness as he looked over at Samuel. . . .

Then Gray followed Carl Lee's gaze back to the arena. The wild mustang couldn't be tamed; he bucked, he fought, knocked the horseman off, and laid on his own back, kicking up his thrashing four legs and screaming the way wild horses scream. As if to say, come near me, you son of a buzzard, and I'll kill you.

The Boley cowboy was not frightened; brazened with bravery he tried the horse again and succeeded in mounting him. The horse broke out running, bucking, jerking, twisting and turning, trying to rid itself of the determined cowboy.

The wild horse whipped that cowboy from side to side. But even though his hat fell off his head, he stayed on, swaying with each thrust. All of a sudden the horse skidded to a stop and threw his thick neck back with such force, he catapulted the cowboy, sending him sailing through the sky, head first, toward the grandstand. Looked like the horse took wings as he galloped away leaving a red plume of dust behind him.

The cowboy landed so hard he forgot to roll. He toppled to the ground with one foot folded up under him.

"Another two-legged pedigree bit the dust," somebody in the crowd hollered. Broke his leg.

Somebody must have told the ambulance driver, because the siren started before the cowboy had hit the ground good. At least it seemed that way to Carl Lee, who grimaced as he watched the ambulance attendants running out of the arena with the injured cowboy on a stretcher.

I wouldn't want to be in his boots, Carl Lee thought. "Can't ride bucking horses like we used to in the old days," grunted a bowlegged cowboy, a Camel cigarette sagging out of one corner of his wrinkled mouth. Outlined against the full moon, he looked like a walking raven.

The whistle blew.

Then it was Carl Lee's turn. He cinched the Appaloosa, setting the saddle high on his withers, then led him through the chute.

Carl Lee stroked the Appaloosa's long ears, which pointed and twitched as the horse listened to Carl Lee's encouraging whispers.

The crowd, led by his father's bass voice, was saying something Carl Lee couldn't make out. Perhaps, he thought, they're admiring the horse's saddle blanket covered with silver stars that Carl Lee had stitched.

Of course there was much to admire. Carl Lee had banded his

blackberry hair with brilliant drake feathers fished from Opal Lake, and his cowboy shirt sparkled too, decorated as it was with the same spangle of stars patterned on Cloudy's saddle.

As the cowboys and cowgirls called and hooted in the stands, the aged and experienced rodeo hands hung around the sidelines, talking among themselves about the possible hazards of allowing a twelve-year-old to ride in the rodeo.

"I tell you that's got to be the horse. Only one like him in the world."

"It can't be, but it sure in hell looks like him."

"That kid might fall off and break his neck; I don't care if he is Gray's grand."

"Well," one man said slow as a mule tired from a two-day haul, "I bound you if he's Gray's grandchild he must be pedigree."

"Even thoroughbreds have to be groomed. What I want to know is, is the boy groomed yet? Especially for a horse like that?"

"What's he gonna do, cry if he fall?"

The old hands couldn't tell anything by studying Gray's face. He was so still, you would have thought God was breathing on him.

When Carl Lee finished whispering to Cloudy he stepped away from the horse, crouched down on the ground beside him, balanced forward on his toes, feet splayed, ready to sprint.

Then he called, "Cloudy!"

And the horse was a cloudy, bright sky of movement, a graceful arc of rhythm moving down the path. Carl Lee ran beside the horse like a night sky in liquid motion, the fringes of his leather pants flapping behind. The mane of Cloudy flying in the wind like a flag of freedom or liberty or something grand that horses are proud of.

Running. You could see the horse in Carl Lee.

Running. You could see Carl Lee in the Appaloosa.

The people had never seen anything like it before. A man-boy who could run as fast as a horse. A horse in rhythm with the boy.

Running, they reached the end of the corral and spun around, still running, in a circle, in unison, a dance between a boy and a horse.

Turning on the last beat, Carl Lee leaped onto Cloudy's back, secured his feet in the stirrups, and without pause raced toward the place where Gray stood waiting at the end of the stadium.

This time as Carl Lee rode Cloudy it was as though they flew, melded together. When Carl Lee turned his head to the left, so did the horse. This turning was a signal to Gray to light the circle of fire.

An "O-O-O!" went up from the crowd as the design of fire, in the shape of a star, blazed over the dusky rodeo just as the lights in the stadium went out.

For a moment the astonished onlookers were quiet. "Cloudy!" the boy yelled.

"Cowboy!" the crowd shouted in one great wave of sound.

"Cowboy!" called Gray.

Moving down the path straight to the jagged hoop of fire, Carl Lee pulled the blinders over the horse's eyes.

At just the right moment, he whispered in the horse's ear, "Jump!"

The crowd held its breath.

Then in one mighty leap, like a cloud or some other water image of a boy and a horse, they penetrated the flame.

Cheers engulfed the stadium as Carl Lee and Cloudy emerged unscathed on the other side of fire.

The doubting old hands took in the whole picture: the boy with feathers in his blackberry hair and his horse standing with a ray of light from the first evening star showering down on them, outlining a stage of dust and dirt enhanced by a natural spotlight.

The spotlight was an illumination emerging from a cloud; the star displayed the pair, the boy and his horse, in radiance.

Even Gray had lost his inscrutable expression as he observed the way the night star showered sparkles over the trembling horse and the victorious boy with the band of drake feathers around his head, holding the reins with his right hand, waving triumph to the applauding people with his left hand.

Gray seemed to be the only one in the stadium who heard thunder far away.

As Carl Lee reigned in his moment of glory, he spied a fan slouched over in the same pew as his father. The stranger was about six seats away from Samuel. Something about the man. . . . The shrouded posture. Cunning, like a fox. Treacherous. Up to no good. Hunched over under a raggedy cloak of evil.

Staring at the man, Carl Lee felt a spur in his chest.

A light rain began to fall.

He started to turn away from looking, but the imaginary spur stung him again. And by reflex his mouth opened trying to figure something out as the rain swept down harder. He looked through the curtain of rain. And then he knew. Why that's who that is. It's the bum! The bum who started the fire!

The yellow-eyed man raised up slowly out of his seat.

"Father!" Carl Lee shouted.

Now the rain beat a noisy pattern. He repeated his shout, "Father!"

And his father heard him and followed Carl Lee's pointed finger.

Samuel stood up and got a good look at the terrible cowboy.

"Hellhound!" Samuel bellowed.

Hellhound turned, recognized Samuel and hesitated, looking from Samuel to Carl Lee's horse.

Hellhound waved something in his hand. Pointed it first at

Samuel, then at the horse, trying to decide which to aim at first. He ranted, "I told you I'd find him! I'll kill that varmint for sure this time." And coming to a decision, he aimed a silver pistol at the horse.

The arena full of fans quieted. Nobody said a mumbling word. Nothing stirred in the danger-charged air except the innocent drone of falling rain.

A shot rang out.

A bullet whizzed past Carl Lee's nose. As he ducked, he saw his father leaping across the bleachers, intent on stopping Hellhound.

Slippery with rain, Hellhound slid out of Samuel's grasp and aimed again.

This time there was nobody to stop him. Samuel couldn't move fast enough.

Then the sky thundered with the sounds of the hooves of a thousand phantom horses stampeding overhead. Light swept the darkness.

A bolt of lightning shot out of the sky and struck Hellhound so hard, it knocked the boots off his feet. A barefooted dead man tumbled into the arena and lay there, his burnt mouth filling with sloshing rain.

It was as though the creative hand of God reached out of the sky and scratched Hellhound off the face of His world.

As Carl Lee saw the ambulance attendants dragging Hellhound off the arena, he realized what the crowd had been yelling when he first brought Cloudy out of the chute and excitement had deafened his hearing. They had been screaming, "Thunderfoot!"

"Thunderfoot?!" So that was it, he realized as the rain started to fall in torrents. Their love of this one horse had brought them all—Carl Lee, Samuel, and Gray—together.

Now, as the rain poured harder, his father and Gray helped him dismount.

His father shook his hand as they stood by the horse Carl Lee knew as Cloudy and his father knew as Thunderfoot.

In a look that spoke louder than words, Carl Lee's eyes echoed, man to man:

"Now we have ridden and freed the high spirit of the same horse. Up and down the world we have come."

When Carl Lee caught Samuel's rare smile, he thought, *He's listening to me.* The glow in Samuel's eyes reminded him of the light jumping in and out of the crystal stream. An opal flashed in Carl Lee's chest, and he saw himself forever holding a horse's reins, leaning over the waters running clear and free through Opal Lake, and picking up the brilliant feathers of a heritage.

From the feathers, from his fathers, iridescent and grand, he would memorize the man texture and the male colors for all his years to come.

Horses and Men

Carl Lee and Gray were riding home.

"Why didn't you tell me about Thunderfoot?" asked Carl Lee.

"I thought your father should tell you," answered Gray.

"So, why didn't he tell me?"

"Because he's an angry man."

"But why?"

"Because I told you. Samuel's like that horse. He's been fenced in. Someday he'll find his spirit again just like Thunderfoot did with you."

The Golden Witness

A harvest of oak leaves blew steadily across the alfalfa fields. Some fell into Opal Lake and floated like big, bright butterflies in the stream.

Samuel stopped his car to look out over the pasture strewn with autumn leaves. Then he continued driving along the dirt path leading to the ranch. He was coming to fetch his son and take him home to Ponca City.

He parked his car and walked across the wire grass path. He listened to the sound of the yellowed leaves from the redbud tree crunching under his feet. A cow mooed patiently somewhere in the pasture. A tamed horse whinnied down by the stables.

Then, as though dropped out of the sky by a golden spirit, a solitary leaf touched his cheek and continued its flight to the ground.

Now he was beneath the southern pine trees where the summer sun bowed its head and waited for fall.

Today he was sober. Today his heart was steady. He put his hand on his father's door and entered the house.

At the desk in his room, Carl Lee waited, his packed suitcase on the bed. He looked out the window and studied the trembling leaves, so orange they looked as if they had been kissed by fire.

"September's come to the golden pasture," he whispered.

It was time to say good-bye to Cloudy.

It was time to talk farewell words to Gray.

It was time to go back to Ponca City. With the father who sometimes couldn't see the miracle standing right there in front of him. With the father who had once been a hero.

Carl Lee decided he would remember the best that his father had been, even though he realized there were sure to be a few difficult times ahead. Maybe hidden beneath a spirit as icy as an alfalfa field in winter, Samuel Jefferson, the one who saved Thunderfoot, had a soul as warm as a golden pasture in summer.

Carl Lee had crossed another threshold, knowing the world was full of summer and winter people. In winter he'd remember summer.

Looking out over the meadow, at the trees changing color, at the sky taking on new shapes of clouds and gathering the wind to its chest, Carl Lee wanted to linger there forever, but he stirred, hearing footsteps falling, coming down the hall.

There were many things to remember. This summer he had become a man.

He had a heritage. A backbone.

He had Thunderfoot.

He had a grandfather who crowned him king of the horses.

He had a hero for a father.

The footsteps came closer, but he did not get up yet. Something held him there for another moment. Then through the open window, down, down out of the open sky, over the fields and lake the sound descended.

As though whispered by a golden witness, he heard this, the faintest of echoes, fly in through the window:

"Safe passage, safe passage along life's journey."

And the sound sparkled, like an opal in his ear.

Journey

1988

And there shall be no night there;
and they need no candle,
neither light nor the sun;
for the Lord God giveth them light:
and they shall reign forever and ever.
—Revelation 22:5

Once upon a time
Sages believed the tarantula's bite
Created the most compelling urges
Those bitten would not be still or
keep quiet
They spoke in and out of turn in
spite of themselves

PROLOGUE

In the deep blue lap of night, Meggie Alexander, a nutmeg-colored infant with a birthmark in the middle of her forehead, lay in her cradle trying to braid the moonbeams trailing through her window, but the misty light kept slipping through her fingers.

Then one evening when the frost on the fig tree looked like stardust, a dappled brown tarantula with a lightning stripe across her back crawled into the dimples of Meggie's hand and tickled her.

Meggie giggled.

The tarantula, taking this giggle as a welcome sign, sighed a long string of silk and started weaving picture stories.

Although tarantulas have not been known to spin webs and hang from cradles and doorways, Meggie's tarantula was different. She spun gossamer tales that thrilled the baby and relaxed her at the same time.

When the child's eyelids drooped heavily, the spider knew her bedtime stories had worked their soothing magic on each shimmering spoke of the round, round web.

The pleased spider stopped weaving in the middle of a spoke and knelt down on her eight legs so she could admire the way the jasper stars twinkled against Meggie's nut-brown skin, bathing her face in blue shadows.

Meggie was a change-of-life baby.

Her mother, Memory Alexander, had thought her childbearing days had passed her by. She was fast approaching fifty when the baby's blood first whispered in her ear and her husband, Michael Leon Alexander, was on his way to fifty.

"Old people's children come here looking wrinkled and ugly," Midnight Alexander warned from the rocking chair in her room, richly smelling of fresh paint, liniment, and vitamins.

"I hear you, Mama," Michael Alexander had said, standing on a stepladder busily painting one half of his mother's room iris-lavender.

In the comer, a corncrake Midnight had insisted on bringing from Oklahoma ruffled his short wings and hollered in a cage, wanting to be out slipping through reeds around some muddy lake.

"I can't believe you're going to put death and birth in the same chamber," Midnight Alexander had complained to the pregnant Memory. "Something all broke down next to something new. I'm like some old worn-out car. Fix one thing, something else breaks. Tamed the arthritis, now diabetes is bucking. I tell you you'd better free my corncrake and carry me on to the old folks' home today, my bags are packed."

"We couldn't bear that," said Memory, pausing, her brush dripping iris-blue in tiny specks on the golden oak floor.

"Anyway, just last year at ninety you were still going out to the pasture feeding the cows," said Michael.

"That's the problem," Midnight reflected. "I should have stayed there last winter and kept my mouth shut. No, I had to go tell you about taking the ax and breaking the ice so the cattle could drink. Next thing I know I'm spirited from Oklahoma to California, sitting up here listening to my bones talk back to me. I never heard them then when I was taking care of my own business on my own farm.

Old people should work as long as they can. All these years I've been waiting for a grandchild from you two and just when I've resigned myself to not having one, since you're both too old and Memory ready to go through the change, you come up pregnant. I repeat, old folks' babies come here looking wrinkled and ugly!"

But Meggie didn't come here looking wrinkled and ugly. She came here nutmeg-colored, smooth-cheeked, dimpled with a small birthmark in the middle of her forehead.

She was coming in as Grandma Alexander was going out. Grandma Alexander took one look at her brand-new grandchild and said, "Well, sir, I've been waiting ninety years for this.

"Carry on," she whispered just before she closed her midnight eyes, gave up the ghost, and became pure spirit.

Meggie was born screaming into the light that November morning; her grandma, on her way to heaven, stopped to gather morning glories in a garden of stars and did not yen for earthly candles as she gathered the flowers to her breath. Time, watching her, struck twelve bells that fateful evening. Midnight passed between today and tomorrow.

"Carry on."

And carry on they did as though it was a chant threading through their lives: "Carry on."

Memory, in age two generations removed from Meggie, had a storehouse of wisdom saved up to pass along to her daughter.

The gray-haired Memory, the silver-haired Michael walked, exercised and continued to work—Memory as a junior high school teacher, Michael as a captain in the medical corps of the army. Continued to work to keep old age, heart attacks, rheumatism, and high blood at bay and to keep their minds alert.

"Snow on the chimney; fire in the oven. Feel so good I just might live to be one hundred," Captain Michael Alexander acknowledged his snow white hair and flexed his muscles as he heated up Meggie's formula.

"Me too," said Memory, rocking the infant and thinking, here's all the children we ever wanted rolled up into one, and judging from how passionately Meggie hollered for life, it would take two centuries worth of wisdom to raise her,

Another frosty night so cold and clear the stars looked like chips of ice in the midnight sky, the midnight spider returned to the nursery. Hanging from her loop of silk she touched the crinkled wisps of Meggie's curls.

And the black locks sprang back as they were. "Wish my brown hair would bounce like that," whispered the tarantula.

But it was Meggie's giggle that inspired the best picture stories.

From the living room, party sounds drifted into the nursery.

"New house. New baby. All cause for celebration!" cheered Meggie's parents to the happy guests.

The sounds of crystal glasses breaking in the blazing fireplace echoed down the hallway.

"Hear that? That captain daddy of yours is home on leave, and he'll be leading people in here any minute to admire your sparkling eyes," said the spider to the baby and she scampered surreptitiously to the linen closet.

There the tarantula worked, standing up on her eight legs, mixing her poison, and scooting her many eyes around in her head.

When the tarantula got finished fixing her poison, she sat down and spun her silk like a lady, sewing and humming.

Finally the celebration wound down.

"See you at church on Sunday," somebody hollered in parting.

"Where'd you find that baby? She's absolutely too stunning for this world, and with that mark in the middle of her mind."

"Middle of her forehead," said Meggie's mother.

"That's what I said. Middle of her mind," claimed the old visitor, once the bosom buddy of the recently departed Midnight Alexander, leaning on her crooked cane.

"Sure some ancient fairy didn't leave her on your doorstep?"

A laugh from the other departing guests. The slam of a car door.

The old visitor was spending the night on the couch.

She asked, "Where do you keep the bedsheets?"

The spider stopped weaving and listened for the answer, her heart dropping down to her eight knees.

Her one worry was discovery of her residence on the top shelf.

"In the middle drawer in the linen closet," answered Michael Alexander.

The woman with the crooked cane did not stretch arms up to reach the high cedar shelf where the spider worked.

The spider, undisturbed, finished weaving her silk and looked around for a tasty mosquito or a tempting fly.

It was dinnertime and she was hungry.

After she ate two biting flies and one fat moth, she waited for the parents and guest to go to bed, longing to see Meggie.

In the meantime, the spider took a short nap herself, sleeping with three of her eight eyes open.

Finally when the embers flickered in the freestone fireplace and the only sound was the November rain falling in fat sparkles against the windowpane, the spider, pulling her ball of silk behind her, threaded her way into the nursery.

Because she had no bones, she was as lithe as a feather.

She threw a line of silk like a lasso and, shimmying up it, heisted herself over the cradle railing and began spinning a new web with the ease of a native spider.

Meggie giggled.

Too loud.

The spider stopped her calligraphy.

And Meggie stopped giggling.

Somebody stirred.

And then the sound of footsteps.

Uh-oh.

At the slightest warning—a cough from the grown people's room, or a slipper slapping across the floor—the spider untangled herself from the cradle slat and flowed down like brown-legged river water. There on the floor she buried herself in the carpet, becoming inconspicuous, looking only like a shadow or some innocent stain.

The orange-brown color of the rug reminded the tarantula of the copper leaves on the ground up in Eucalyptus Forest where she once danced in the wild.

The two of them were coming, Michael and Memory Alexander, to check the baby for wetness or hunger or illness.

"Was that a cry or a laugh?" Memory asked.

"Sounded like a laugh to me," said Michael.

"What could she be laughing about? Anyway, she's too little to laugh, she's only old enough to smile."

Because they did not expect to see anything like it, when the parents looked into the cradle at Meggie, they did not notice the intricate almost invisible web.

"Oh, she's all right," they cooed.

Memory took off Meggie's wet diaper.

"Hand me the powder, Michael," she said.

When Michael reached into the pocket, there was only air.

"No more left," he answered.

"Impossible," said Memory. "That pack's supposed to have six cans of talcum!"

"See for yourself," said Michael, taking over to pin the baby's diaper on Meggie, not clumsy as the spider would have expected since they don't teach diaper skills in the army.

"Imagine that! Shortchanging us!" complained Memory. "Why, that corner store merchant's as crafty as a spider and as crooked as its web!"

The listening tarantula took the insult personally. And the devil got into the tarantula.

Before the mama followed the daddy back down the hallway, the spider somersaulted down her silk string to the floor beside the near-sighted Memory, knowing full well the woman couldn't see her.

"Old lizard lady!" the spider hissed.

Memory looked down, but she didn't see anything. It was all the tarantula could do to keep her fangs from sinking into the woman's skinny toothpick ankles.

"A walleyed heifer!" pouted the spider.

When the house had quieted down again, and she could hear all the people snoring so hard they rattled the windows, the spider talked to Meggie about Memory's offensive remark.

While she chattered, with her spider-dancing mouth, she wove a web from one side of the cradle to the other, generous with her silk. A spider speaking in tongues.

"People're always saying things like 'spiteful as a spider.' Yes, we have been called creepy, crooked, crafty, and cold.

"And folks don't discriminate.

"They throw us all in the same spider bag, from my wolf spider cousins, to the black widow clan, and the labyrinth branch; even the sack spiders and the brown widows and red widows get mashed together in the name-calling.

"No respect, even though we protect the earth from crop-eating locusts and disease-carrying mosquitoes.

"I don't mean to brag, but I've been present at all the cataclysmic events in this here old world. Witnessed earthquakes, tornadoes, whirlwinds, and typhoons. 'Course I put down my spinning wheel and laid low, what do you think?

"I get so sick and tired of common folk trying to put their nobody feet on my queenly head. Me? I was present in the first world. Furthermore," the spider boasted, squinting her crooked eyes, "I come from a *loooong* line of royalty and famous people. Millions of years ago I saw the first rainbow. I ruled as the Egyptian historical arachnid. Cleopatra's last confidante. I'm somebody."

The sun was rising, the night over, and through the nursery window colors gathered.

The spider then finished her patterned story, and while Meggie giggled at the odd ways the lines curved and leaped just over her bed, the spider sucked in her waist, climbed up her silk hose of a dragline, and looked out the window at the sky.

"Look a yonder! A colored bridge to heaven!" the spider exclaimed. "A rainbow. Now, there's a pleasing pattern!"

And Meggie wanted to braid the watercolors into a shawl for her shoulders, a quilt for her cradle.

The tarantula crawled down out of the bed just as the mama rounded the comer shaking a warm baby bottle in her hand.

Mornings, alone and quiet in the closet, the spider measured her worth; she was of benefit in general to the earth, but also of benefit in particular to this house. More than once she had heard Memory Alexander remark that the house stayed free of flies and mice, "And not a cat around."

Memory Alexander had been repeating this observation for over a month. "House free of flies and mice and not a cat around."

It was over a month ago, the day after Meggie's grandmother took herself on up to grandma heaven, that the tarantula had discovered Meggie's house.

Meggie asked, "How?"

"The discovery went like this," said the tarantula. "I had me a cousin, a wonderful black widow woman named Johanna Hopkins. After we'd come down from Eucalyptus Forest carrying our poisons and our silks, I said to the black widow that I had reserved a place to stay.

"Reservations?" asked the black widow.

"Then an argument broke out over who would stay in your house, Meggie.

"'I think I should be the one,' said the black widow, her natural selfish self-centeredness loomed. "'No,' I said, 'because in the process of making my reservations I already investigated.'

"'Investigated?' asked Johanna, who could be all venom and mouth. Mouth, lord, that widow could talk.

"'Yes, ma'am. And I already determined the carpet's the color of a tarantula spider,'" I said most proudly.

"The black widow, putting her hands on her spider hips, rejoined, 'I only believe what I see and none of what I hear; you've got to show me!' and she climbed the wall of the house herself and took one look in the window and wholeheartedly agreed. When she saw the rug, she said, 'Well, shut my mouth!' and she left quicker than a jumping spider rumored to jump twenty times the length of its body.

"The last thing I saw of my cousin Johanna she was moving through the high grass, heading for higher ground, reeling in her loneliness, in search of a black widow mansion in Eucalyptus Forest under some fallen tree trunk where she'd feel right at home."

"The end," said the web.

Next time the tarantula visited Meggie in the nursery was a stormier night. The wind had its back up and sounded like a train traveling, clickety-clack, raka-tak-tak over the house.

The spider wound down out of the closet on her silk rope and ambled along the wall and into the nursery.

Thunder echoed and stomped in giant boots across the sky.

Thin, steel-threaded winds choo-chooed at the windows and screeched in a language that only babies and spiders understand.

The tarantula lifted one of her hairy eight legs and tickled the baby in her dimple.

Meggie woke up and giggled.

The tarantula said all spidery-voiced, "I don't know why grown folks act so scared of spiders. They ought to take a lesson from babies. Why, in the entire state of California have you ever heard of a baby killed by a spider? 'Course not! We understand each other. But grown folks getting pinched by me and my cousins don't smell a bit like sweet anise and talcum powder."

The spider shrugged. "They smell like fear."

"Can't stand fear, it makes me want to bite somebody," said the spider with humor.

"Fear, fear, fear," giggled the baby in spider language, not quite understanding the emotion, having never experienced it.

"Why, I'd make a perfect babysitter," continued the spider, and she began to weave another allegorical web.

"Better'n a guard dog," she added.

"Guard dog," mimicked Meggie.

The spider crossed her many legs. "Imagine somebody coming into the nursery with me in here. I'd only have to hunch my hairy back and nod and they'd scram!"

Then the storm rubbed the electrical lines against the tall old oak trees lining the street and blew out all the power, so even the night-light didn't glow enough for Meggie to see the web story the spider had written. Clouds had strangled the pumpkin moon, so no light from that source either.

When the circling clouds loosed their hold on the winter night, and the sun rose, the spider wanted to stay longer in the warm and fragrant bed.

But footsteps swished and she bade Meggie good-bye and scampered down and on past the slippered feet of the sleepy-eyed Memory and dashed up the ajar closet door and onto the rose bed of cotton sheets.

There she kicked her eight legs against the rough closet wall doing a hot spider dance.

The spider heard the mother say, "Gicchy, gicchy goo," to Meggie, then add, "My precious, how bright your eyes are, just like you've seen a little magic."

"Of course," murmured the spider under her breath, doing an easy eight-step, "I'm the magic."

Her dancing done, the spider got into her most creative mood. She began a large project, her most ambitious to date.

An intricate web. Its breadth so vast it would, when finished, cover the entire top shelf.

The tarantula got so involved she took a holiday from Meggie.

And every day Meggie boo-hooed and called unceasingly for the spider until her voice grew hoarse.

"The baby's got the croup," the tarantula heard Memory Alexander say to her husband.

"Croup, my eye!" hooted the spider, "she's pining for me."

Finally after the spider had finished crocheting her best web she went back to the crib for a visit.

And just in time. Meggie was beginning to become less fluent in the spider language and could say words like "mama," "daddy," "bottle," and "water."

Meggie's hair was even bouncier and thick enough to hold in

place for fat braids. About the head she looked like a doll-sized version of her mama.

"You've grown, honey," sighed the spider, admiring the three braids like a triple-threaded rhythm on each side of Meggie's head.

"And so have your webs," Meggie answered touching the sticky silk perfection.

When Meggie smiled, not giggled, at the silk pattern, the spider could see bumps where teeth would emerge.

This depressed the tarantula, but she tried not to let it show. Meggie's innocence, the spider knew, could not last. The dimples in her hands were not as snuggly deep. She had grown an inch.

"Why, keep growing like this, you're gonna be as straggly as your mama. An Amazon girl."

"Tell me a story," Meggie cooed.

And the spider wove the story of her black widow cousin, Johanna Hopkins, who vowed to set a record by marrying the most husbands in the territory, the ancient black widow game of husband trapping.

"You've heard of one-upmanship? She practiced one-upwidowship. Why, the woman had seven husbands in one month!"

"Am I a People or a spider?" asked Meggie, intrigued by the black widow's shenanigans.

The tarantula waited a long time before responding; it was the hardest question she had ever answered. "You're a People," said the spider.

The baby caught her breath sharply as if she wanted to turn her sigh to silk and couldn't.

Resigned to her lot in life, Meggie fell into a baby-soft sleep. The spider squatted in the story web listening to the rhythm of Meggie's breath blowing against the web and smelling the licorice aroma of sweet anise.

The tarantula became mesmerized by the whisper of wind

which was Meggie's breath, the way it pushed the crocheted web of Johanna's seven husbands back and forth, back and forth.

Hypnotized.

Next thing the spider knew, Memory Alexander stepped into the nursery and froze at the sight of the poisonous spider hovering over her innocent child.

The light ebbed pale in there.

But the shadow of movement disturbed the spider, bringing her out of her reverie.

Now the tarantula was fully awake.

She felt what was coming right down her boneless spine.

She stayed very still as the nearsighted mother inched closer to make sure she wasn't mistaken. . . .

Certain now about the hairy creature, Memory Alexander hollered; the force of her lungs untangled the intricate web, and seven husbands fell like gossamer wings over Meggie's face.

"Tarantula, my spider," Meggie, now awake, cried in their language, frightened for the first time in her life, not for herself but for her friend, the storytelling spider woman.

Memory Alexander snatched her baby from under the silken veil and for a brief moment clutched Meggie close to her like a sack of whole wheat flour with eyes.

Abruptly, she sat the baby down on the floor and found her weapon. A prior month's *Life* magazine.

Smash.

"You can run, Mrs. Spider, but you just can't hide," Memory Alexander chanted as she lifted the *Life* magazine to issue out Death.

Meggie, sensing how precious little time was left, spoke to the spider in a singsong voice, like a harp was caught in her throat: "So much I wanted to ask you, Mrs. Spider; how to weave the wind into scarlet ribbons. . . ."

The spider, hearing Meggie, hunkered down dodging the magazine.

Smash.

Meggie continued, "I want to borrow the watercolor blue from the rainbow to dye my yarn for the colored shawl."

"Run on, but you cannot hide," the mother repeated.

"I want to leave a spell in the threads purple as amethyst in autumn."

Smash.

"Run on, but you cannot hide," the mother repeated.

"How many strings would it take, I wonder?" asked Meggie in that music voice.

The tarantula moaned, her time running out, answered, "Five or six." Thinking of all the lessons she had meant to teach the child she managed to respond, "Meggie, get yourself a guitar, a loom of strings, an audible loom. Meggie, be a queue-jumping, jaywalking woman.

"Shimmer when you jump, glitter when you walk."

The message echoed in Meggie's ear.

Smash.

"You can. . . ."

From way off Meggie could hear the spider holler, "But whatever you do, Meggie, let nothing, nobody, separate you from the light."

The mama couldn't understand any of this.

Smash.

"Run but. . . ."

Finally the spider, in a beaten voice, said, "They say babies develop amnesia. . . ."

"You just can't . . ." continued the mother.

Smash.

"Hide."

"But I know better," sighed the spider,

The spider's last words were these: "When Meggie's"—*smash*—"searching for the blue-peace shawl, reaching to braid the light"—*smash*—"she's thinking of me."

ONE

In the coming sunrise every wildflower flourishing in ditches and unkempt places, every blade of thirsty grass drinking dew before day, every web shimmering on the straggly backyard fences, and every sigh of dusty wind seemed to be waiting for Meggie to wake up.

No voices in the gathering waiting spoke at first; sound seemed content to be one with the resilient wildflowers, part of the landscape.

Finally a solitary voice broke open and started to speak one, two, three words, like a too-early rain, starting to fall, then stopping halfway down from the sky. The voice was gone. Something was trapped here.

"Get up, Meggie!" the male voice spoke, then was silenced.

Fifteen-year-old Meggie, sound asleep, twisted and turned, balled up in the bed like the outline of a question mark.

Then some compassionate archangel dressed in white gauze with a crown of morning glories on her snow white head whispered, "All our days are numbered, Meggie." And the angel sat down and gently turned her spinning wheel.

In her dream, Meggie mounted a silver sky, climbing the stars, stepping up one to the other, skipping up a hill of stars that glowed like bright crystal stepping-stones lighting her way to heaven.

Then the archangel's spinning wheel turned into a glistening mahogany guitar and she bent her silver head over the strings as she strummed.

The guitar's sweet twang interrupted Meggie's skipping rhythm and her feet hesitated.

The broken voice freed itself from the trap, and abruptly Meggie's eyes flew open when she heard it, more startling than the guitar, repeat, "Get up, Meggie."

Now that her eyes were open, the male voice was gone. The stars had disappeared. Her feet were bed bound, No grandmotherly angel strummed a sacred guitar.

It had not been her father's voice. He was overseas on army assignment and would be gone at least a month.

The male voice in her dream had a chuckle in it same as Billy Watson's used to have.

Now she would only hear that voice in her dreams.

It was the morning of Billy Watson's funeral.

Billy Watson, her original gingerbread boy. Her chocolate Boy Wonder. Her buddy, her friend.

Meggie untangled herself from the purple quilt and the blue sheets, disturbing her mongrel dog, Redwood, so named because his coat was the color of redwood. Redwood yawned himself awake at the foot of her bed. And the sleepy-eyed Jehoshaphat, a fat tortoiseshell tomcat with golden eyes, nicknamed Fat for the last syllable in Jehoshaphat and because he was fat, uncurled himself from the curve of her elbow.

"Time to leave already," she said eyeing the clock next to the handsome portrait of her father in military uniform and her mother in schoolteacher dress.

"Redwood, you stay home with Jehoshaphat today, you hear?" Her mother had flown to the Panhellenic Council of the Sigma

Gamma Rhos, AKAs, and Delta sororities up in Oregon State and wouldn't be back until Sunday night.

Redwood whined, sad-eyed and droopy-eared, a little unhappy about obeying this order to guard the house when he wanted to be at Meggie's heels.

Time to leave this room of cotton textures and rainbow colors, Meggie thought.

No time to play her guitar while sitting in her concert chair, an avocado green chair planted beneath the cotton curtains in cool colors scampering and running down her windows.

How her thumb ached for the mahogany guitar waiting mutely on the comer chair.

She got up and didn't take time to make her bed. She left the chenille pink bedspread tangled all up with the pale blue sheets and the purple crazy-patch quilt.

"Billy, Billy Watson," she said to her mirror as she pulled the comb through her thick hair. When the mirror didn't answer her, she stopped with the comb in midair, leaving the great curls to riot mournfully all over her head.

Thickly sighing, she plodded to her closet and, pushing aside the blue jeans and assorted sweaters and shirts she usually favored, chose a checkered black skirt, a cotton black high-collared blouse, and slipped into a pair of tight, rarely used, toe-pinching ebony patent-leather flats.

On her slow walk to Billy Watson's funeral, her mourning turned to rage. And with the storm of emotion came a terrible, lumbering energy. Her heavy steps carried her forward in spite of herself.

The cement sidewalks didn't help her mood either. She wanted earth under her feet and a jungle of trees for her canopy. She wanted to be up in Eucalyptus Forest with Billy Watson romping through the wild wheat meadows and listening to the corncrakes call back and forth. But Billy Watson, who had had a sixteen-year-old's chuckle in his voice, and who had lived three streets over on Hilgard, had been found shot to death by some trigger-happy fool.

"Billy, Billy, Billy," a corncrake's song scampered in her ears as she found herself staring at the long black hearse squatting like a grotesque cockroach in front of the church.

The sound of Billy's name made her hand tremble on the doorknob to the sanctuary of Perfect Peace Baptist Church.

"Why? Why? Why?" she asked the wind.

Getting no answer, she turned the knob and entered.

The choir, robed in black, hummed some old mournful song.

The song sagged. "We Shall Overcome" sounded like we never shall. The key dragged. The words didn't believe themselves. They would not soar. Dried-up hope. Let down dignity into a drought-dry well.

Meggie stood watching the people packed in the church blur into a crowd of dark somber dresses and suits, and the sight of the casket wouldn't let her sit down. A scalding rage ran from the top of her head down to the bottom of her feet.

Every time she tried to sit the sight of that silver casket pulled her up and the sound of the corncrake calling Billy's name like a bell burst in her ears. She opened her mouth and couldn't close it. And the grief-ring in her voice made the mourners unbow their heavy heads.

She raved, "Why, more young folk than old're getting buried, and you're talking about 'Yea though I walk through the valley of the shadow of death . . .'? What are we going to do about this?" Meggie asked of each face raining grief. "We don't want to walk through the valley of the shadow of death. We want to run up the hillside in the sunshine of life."

Dennis Bell gave a coughing kind of laugh. Peelheaded Dennis, the son of the Battling Bells, sat shyly on the back bench, alone and detached from the funeral mourners. A strange teenager with a limp in his mind, Meggie thought. An old young man who always did the opposite of what good sense dictated. Something awkwardly lopsided in his lanky arms, his hanging shoulders.

"Got dropped on his head as an infant," Meggie's mother once explained with frustrated compassion.

"How?" Meggie had wondered.

"In one of those infernal battles that the Bells pitched. Crib shattered. Instead of crying Dennis was lying there on the floor, wet as a turtle, diaper hadn't been changed since the battle began early that morning. Dennis, just grinning up at us, his rescuers, like he was the king ant at a July Fourth picnic.

"Bells, drunk as skunks, had fought 'til they dropped, selfish, mindless of the child, cold and wet and helpless in that house of Scotch-drinking and angry-at-the-world, sorry parents."

Remembering all that, Meggie turned and gave Dennis a sympathetic look that shut him up, that made him scoot down lower in his seat and sink his head deeper into the well between his shoulders.

At the front of the church Reverend Hawkins, all humped over, crouched on his knees in private conversation with the Lord, asking, "Dear God, what shall I tell these poor people?"

He got no answer from the Higher Power, but he did hear Meggie's cry. He couldn't get a prayer through, but Meggie's lament caught his ears. Slowly, he pulled himself up off his aching knees.

"Church, some of us are not holding up so well," he explained to the congregation in sympathy for Meggie's sorrow.

"Daughter, you're just grieving," he said tired, tired of preaching so many funerals for the young. It was all a riddle. Cancer-riddled bodies. Bullet-riddled boys caught in the crossfire of gang fights. Drug-riddled ODs. Suicide riddles.

"Come on up, Miss Meggie, and look into the casket," Reverend Hawkins offered forlornly.

"I'm not," said Meggie. "I'm not looking in any more caskets at people my age. It's not natural. The only people supposed to be in the shadow are the old folks. I gotta think of some other way to live with my memory of Billy.

"Billy, Billy, Billy," she rasped, eyes brimming, transfixed by the sleet gray casket.

Just then Reverend Marvella Franklin, sitting over in the Amen Corner so inconspicuous folks usually missed her until she opened her mouth, stood up.

"Evil walks and death stalks," she began hesitantly. "Carry a light in your heart," she whispered.

The whirling words ran Meggie on out of the church house. And she roamed the streets, wearily searching for something she could not name. She went to the places she and Billy Watson had frequented and finally to the Bay Wolf Barbershop.

The barber standing on a small mountain of unswept hair just looked at her in an understanding way and nodded for her to take her seat on the stool where she usually waited for Billy.

Pretty soon the men seemed to forget the lonesome girl lingering so sorrowfully over in the comer beneath the calendar of dark movie stars and brown beauty queens.

They talked about Billy Watson.

Talk. She was sick of it.

But she listened anyway. Maybe some answer abided here, here at Bay Wolf Barbershop where Billy used to chuckle and join the men in careless and serious conversations.

All of a sudden Peter Watson, Billy's wino uncle, swayed in the doorway declaring, "They say Reverend Marvella Franklin got a prayer through."

The Right Reverend Lee Arthur Huntington, who had a habit of bringing up the controversial issue of "can a woman preach?" shook off his barber's bib and rubbed his smooth freshly shaved, fig-colored chin.

Eyes flashing with defiance, these words ran out of Reverend Huntington's mouth and settled in the ear like a deep itch: "God called Paul, he didn't call Paula! Called Elijah, not Eliza. How many times do I have to tell the ministerial alliance to keep that woman out of the pulpit; don't be giving these women the power to preach?"

"You can't give what you ain't got," said Billy's wino uncle.

"What?" said the reverend.

"It's God's to give. Not man's. If He can make an ax talk, how come He can't make a woman preach?"

For Meggie, the answer to every question could be found in the results. Could she or couldn't she preach, this Reverend Marvella Franklin?

"Tell you one thing," said Billy Watson's uncle, sour wine making his speech slur, "when she opens her mouth up yonder on the Perfect Peace pulpit every devil in Berkeley takes off to beyond the city limits on the outskirts of town. Never mind that when Moses climbed the mountain the devil slid up there behind him. When Marvella Franklin climbs God's mountain she brandishes arrows, sticks, and godly stones. A snake ain't got chance one. She can look at you and read you. Why, she looked at me once and didn't a drop a liquor cross my lips for a month. What you got to remember in this old world is that the devil's alive and everybody ain't sanctified!"

"What's her text?" asked the mailman, taking Reverend Lee Arthur Huntington's place in the barber's chair.

"Choose," said the wino.

"Choose?"

"A one-worded text. Who ever heard. . . ?" Reverend

Huntington didn't finish his sentence; disgusted, he walked on out of the shop, down-turned fig mouth muttering something about the Bible saying let the women be quiet in the temple and shaking his head as he waddled, making a beeline to his own storefront church, to make sure the Missionary Group of women meeting that afternoon stayed ten feet from his pulpit as they studiously thumbed through the Bible in their course of interpreting it.

This "can-a-woman-preach?" conversation was reported to everybody who came to get a haircut. Needless to say Perfect Peace Baptist Church would be crowded come Sunday morning.

What did Marvella Franklin mean at the funeral when she said, "Carry a light in your heart," Meggie wondered, and what does that and the oddly titled text, "Choose," have to do with Billy Watson?

Meggie was sitting in the front pew at Perfect Peace when Reverend Marvella Franklin brought the Sunday message.

"Evil walks and death stalks. Carry a light in your heart. If the light's in your heart can't anybody keep you from it. Can't anybody turn it out. Not even PG&E. If they cut off your electricity because you can't pay your bill, you've still got the light. One day when I was feeling mighty low I went down to the river where nothing talked but the water and picked me up some stray sprigs of wood and built myself a fire where I could listen to God speak without interruption. One day you might not be by the water, you might not be by a place you can gather wood for an old-fashioned ordinary altar of fire, but if you carry a light in your heart this you can rely on, it will always be there. When you pray say these words: 'Most holy creator, God of the trees and everything that walks and swims and flies, stand by me!

"'God of thunder, God of fire, lightning, water, and cloud, deliver me in times of trouble, stand by me in times of joy, stand by me when the world begins to understand. Hear my plea, bend an ear to me, most mightiful, powerful, heavenly Creator stand by me.'

"And Church, that is my prayer, Now if I, stooped over as I was with agony, could straighten my back and choose, anybody can choose. My whole life was a river of pain. Couldn't anybody grieve and grumble more woe-be-gone than me. If you looked at me long my face would cloud up.

"First I tried to handle the hurt by myself. Woe to the person ever told me No. When I got through cursing them out and walking up and down their back with spikes, you could run a truck through where their feelings used to be. I was a dangerous woman! Sow the wind, reap the whirlwind.

"When I searched outside myself for consolation I fell in with all kind of false prophets, Bible-thumping bigots, wrongdoing rabbis, and money ministers, When I went to the so-called authorities for help I ran into jackleg politicians, wheeler-dealers, henchmen, finaglers, and wire-pullers. It was about power. Wanted me to bow to them. Anybody knows me knows I don't bow down to nobody but God!

"God is the archconsoler. I say God is The Authority.

"And the joy you've got waiting, even the rainbow can't hold. . . . Can taste the blue skin of a blueberry and the inside-out purple beauty of a fig. I say you can hold music in your mouth and rest inside a note."

She broke out into one of those low husky shouts, her feet doing a sanctified dance, while the church members' voices popped up here and there waving her on, saying, "Amen."

"Now somebody might leave here thinking I don't like preachers. . . ." Her voice dipped. "I didn't say that. But not everybody up in the pulpit is anointed. You want to know why this woman's preaching? When the only power I ever respected called, I answered. Yes, I was *called* to preach! I know you've been talking about can a woman preach?

"Some of you even saying now if a woman can preach next thing they'll be claiming is God's a woman."

Now she declared so quietly some church members involuntarily scooted forward in their pews, "*God can be whatever God wants to be!*"

She went on and tied the sermon together, talking about choosing, then she ended it with these resounding words falling quiet as small sprinklings of nutmeg whispering into a bowl of whipping cream:

"Choose to live.

"Death dealing is the devil's duty.

"The devil's still swishing his long reptilian tail, hooding his ruby snake eyes, walking up and down seeing who he can devour, strewing banana peels on the steep path of life trying to see who he can trick into slipping. Be aware!

"Carry a light in your heart. Some of you're already shining like neon. Don't even need batteries; you've got everything you require to keep the light going. And God makes no mistakes.

"Choose.

"Carry a light in your heart and live!"

Meggie wondered, what's all this got to do with what happened to her Billy Watson; he couldn't have chosen to die, Billy with that chuckle in his voice.

Carry a light in your heart, the reverend woman had said; what on heaven and earth did she mean?

TWO

The sunlight glittered on teenagers of all variety and colors and shapes that decorated the stucco-dotted campus at Berkeley High on Monday morning.

Redheaded skinny ones sprawled near the acacia bushes by the music department. Fat as butterball ones ate Snickers and Bit-O-Honey candy bars, joyously littering the grounds with the wrappers, enough of the sticky sweetness glued to the waxy paper to draw armies of grateful ants.

Muscular jocks, black as molasses, white as vanilla, dribbled basketballs back and forth in the outdoor court by the gym. Eyeglassed bookworms, raven-haired young women, some with skin gingerbread-brown, others—Japanese, Vietnamese, the strengthening color of delicate rice powder—pored over their texts on the landing near the English and history wing.

A little late for school, Meggie dashed up the history building steps, Redwood shagging along behind her.

"Stay," she admonished Redwood at the propped open classroom door.

The once blonde Miss Blount preened as she adjusted her eyeglasses on her head. "Today, class, we will discuss the Black History unit, starting with the first slave who arrived in Virginia."

Blount was always losing her spectacles.

Now Blount interrupted her lecture with, "Where are my glasses?" a question full of accusations, thinking as she did that one of the mischievous students had sneaked them off her desk and hidden them.

Meggie knew that at home Blount was the same way, for the teacher lived next door to Meggie, giving the girl ample opportunities to observe the woman's lapses of memory.

In class Meggie often wiped tears of laughter from her high cheeks, trying not to giggle out loud at the glasses sitting on top of Blount's head where she had pushed them and forgotten. Why didn't the woman just buy her some bifocals and be done with it?

Where were those tears of laughter now?

Today the laughter wouldn't come. Meggie only felt like tears.

Nobody told Blount the glasses were on top of her head. She'd find them. Eventually.

"So let us begin the unit on slavery," repeated Miss Blount with that smugness and sense of superiority people who see themselves as winners sometimes exuded like acne.

Meggie looked into her classmates' faces and all the students' eyes mirrored flustered frustration. The white ones reflecting guilt, the black ones shocked indignity.

Only Dennis Bell, who was once dropped on his head as a baby, smiled contentedly.

Meggie said from her seat in the back row, "I'm about ready to vomit. I'm definitely going to barf up breakfast if I read another chapter about slavery and everybody I know my age is too."

The teacher looked at that mark in the middle of Meggie's forehead and the room temperature elevated. Stifling, felt like fireballs charging through the air. If you moved wrong one would hit you. Miss Blount wiped sweat from her brow.

Meggie, her bottom lip trembling, her midnight eyes fiery, was not thinking about Blount. Meggie wanted to go back and straighten out history. Rake a slave master over with his own chains. On the Middle Passage dump the ship captain in the bloody Atlantic and drown his evil white ass. Let the limbs descend from the trees and whip every lynch mob into the ground 'til nothing but their stubby heads was left.

"I want there to be so many prominent successful black folks nobody can be proud about being the first black congressman, the only black woman nationwide radio announcer. It's an insult, not a source of pride, to be sitting up bragging about being the first and only. It's all right to be the first, but it's a disgrace to be the only. Whoever's the only ought to be bringing more people into the light. First and only creates too many unnecessary jealousies between folks who ought to be working together anyway. I want there to be so many black stars in American skies you can't possibly count them all.

"When it becomes nothing special to be excellent, which we are, maybe a few more of us can lift up our heads and stop acting like we've forgotten our own yesteryears."

Students started sitting up straighter in their chairs and murmuring "That's right. Well?"

Miss Blount, when faced with this kind of unheard-of reality, tensely gripped the white chalk so hard it broke in two and fell to the floor.

Miss Blount said, not addressing Meggie's words, tension making her voice fragile enough to crack, "Meggie, why is that dog hovering in the doorway like a slobbering idiot? I told you not to bring that hound into this schoolhouse.

"Park that mutt outside!"

At the disrespectful reference to his pedigree, Redwood barked and raised the hairs on his shaggy back, then went dashing up to

Miss Blount who jumped back, clutching her chalk to her chest.

"No, Redwood," said Meggie, calling the dog back.

"You don't have to bite her. Something already took a chunk out of her brain."

Meggie swung out of her seat, walked over, and knelt in the classroom door, patting Redwood.

"Those who do not know history are doomed to repeat it," said Miss Blount quoting one of the history-book historians.

"They're doomed to repeat history whether they know it or not," said Meggie from the doorway.

Somebody said, "Yeah, we read about how these young black boys get roughed up and killed, but maybe nobody cares because the same episode keeps on repeating itself. Just the other day I read in the newspaper—"

"I'm sick of slavery and I'm sick of things happening to us. I don't want to hear about anything else happening to black folks. We need to be responsible for what we do to each other today, not for what our forefathers and foremothers did or suffered. Whoever shot Billy Watson must have known about those other injustices, but did that stop them? No."

"I know who done it," said Dennis Bell out of the blue; because he was a little deranged nobody ever paid Dennis Bell any mind.

"I saw. I know who done it," said Dennis Bell.

Might as well have been the wind talking, nobody even looked Dennis's way.

"Well, a lot happens to black people just because they're black," said Miss Blount.

"We were getting hurt back then and we're still being hurt today. And it's not because we're black. We've just been conditioned to think that's the reason."

Redwood barked an "Amen," as Meggie continued.

"We need to look where we're going; looking back we often stumble and fall, can't see what's right there before us. Like what this present generation needs."

Blount looked from Meggie to Redwood then back to Meggie.

"What this present generation needs is more respect," Miss Blount clipped, white chalk all over her black skirt.

"For instance?" Meggie challenged.

"Like showing respect for the people who have to look at you. Appearances."

"Respect?" said Meggie. "I respect the goodness in people, no matter what their age or the color of the eyes looking at me. But I don't respect idle ignorance from any source. If the TV talks to me wrong, I turn it off. If I pick up a lying book, I lay it down."

"We can show respect by the little things we do. Take appearance," Blount continued.

Then Blount aimed her words at the class. "The way *Nutmeg,* I mean Meg, goes around looking it's hard to tell the animals from the humans."

The classroom hushed. Miss Blount, who had one day overheard a student refer to Meggie as Nutmeg, because she sometimes acted nutty or different, had stepped over a dangerous line and didn't know it or didn't care.

Now Miss Blount swept her gaze over two of the Rastafarian-haired students and her voice became an ugly weapon.

By the way she wrinkled her mouth, Meggie could tell she was thinking about a nest of snakes.

"*Nutmeg* lets the wind comb her hair. *Nutmeg* lets the sun iron her clothes!" Blount said, pacing up and down in front of the blackboard and summing up her point.

Sometimes the students couldn't believe the teachers' stupidity and some of them, tired of being taken for toads, dropped out.

Others grew film across their eyes and only saw what they needed to see. They buried these rejections and insults in a graveyard of their minds.

By the time they graduated they had entire cemeteries as underground, mummified cities, never to see the light of day.

"That's it!" angry Alton Gillespie shrieked. A freckle-faced boy with chestnut hair and cedar-green eyes, he didn't think he was able to stomach another sarcastic word from four-eyed Blount.

"How could you talk about Meggie like that?" he said, his voice incredulous.

"You know something," he said, getting up out of his seat, "it takes some respect to keep from cursing you out."

"Sit down, Alton!" Miss Blount commanded.

The whole class held its breath wondering if Alton would sit down and if he didn't what Blount would do.

Blount and Alton glared at each other. The fireballs just waiting for somebody to make a false move skipped up and down the aisles.

Then the bell rang. And the class let out a sigh of relief.

The outraged teacher, fuming audibly, looked down the roll book, stopped at "G," then scribbled a mark against Alton Gillespie in the ledger.

"Glad that class is over," said Alton as he joined up with Meggie and Redwood to walk to the chemistry lab.

"I don't know who's worse, Blount or Spellman."

"Boy, am I blessed," Meggie sighed, rolling her eyes up in her head, "and to think I live on the same block with both of them."

Alton and Meggie had the same chemistry professor, Mr. Spellman, who had been voted the most-hated teacher in the entire school. Spellman, an oily-voiced professor of cynicism.

"Can't stand the man," said Alton.

When they entered the classroom Spellman, skinny, skinny and the color of a brown rifle handle, was standing like a sergeant in front of a battlefield of desks with sinks and Bunsen burners.

A tension that had started in Blount's room continued building like an electrical storm you could not see, only smell, like the acrid fumes from a Bunsen burner.

An unseen cloud of sulfur hovered over the chemistry lab.

Experiment fifteen, the hardest assignment in the chemistry class so far, had been difficult for Meggie. But she had struggled with the problem until she chanced upon the right answer. She had meant to discuss the chemical reaction with Alton, but they had been so busy reacting to the wrath of teachers they had used up all the time between classes.

Now Spellman marched up and down the rows assessing each student's experiment. If the experiment was correct, he gave no praise, but if it didn't look right, he mercilessly embarrassed the person.

Now, a stiff grin on his nasty lips, he stood rigid in front of Alton, shooting his mouth off like a shotgun.

"You don't have the equation right. You're not at home in your mama's kitchen making chocolate chip cookies, you know, where an extra pinch of sugar won't make a difference."

Then these sharp words shot their way out of his cabbage-breath mouth: "How's what you're doing going to turn out right, Dummy, if you've written the formula wrong?"

Spellman's tone of voice, picked up by every alert ear, sounded like a machine gun mowing down children yearning to learn.

Spellman snatched at Alton's paper so he could hold it up to ridicule in front of the entire class.

Before Meggie could catch her breath, Alton clobbered Spellman so hard the older man fell between the two aisles of Bunsen burners, his mouth jerking.

"For heaven's sake," said Meggie, going to Alton's side.

"You make me sick," Alton said coldly to Mr. Spellman.

Slowly Mr. Spellman collected himself up off the floor.

He pointed a finger at Alton and sputtered, "Boy, you're on your way to the penitentiary. You're trying to break into the jailhouse."

"At least it's not the cemetery," said Alton, "'cause if I ever hear my name in your mouth again, Mister, you are on your way! They won't have to call the ambulance, they'll dial directly for the hearse!"

That very afternoon in the principal's office, while Spellman was making sure Alton got suspended, Spellman developed voice problems.

"Pupil's name?" asked the principal, writing out the suspension order.

"G-G-G-Gillespie," Spellman gasped with difficulty.

A tightness around his vocal cords. It was as though all the teenagers Spellman had mistreated had their hands around his throat trying to choke the living breath out of him.

By the time school let out everybody knew Spellman had been whisked to the hospital where the doctor found signs that he'd never talk clearly again. He decided to resign that same day and to retire on disability.

On the way home Meggie and her classmates wondered aloud what had made Alton so angry, but when Meggie looked into their eyes, she could see the recognition. Alton had physically fought against what they all recognized but often couldn't articulate. The uglies.

Spellman gave you the uglies.

THREE

Often Spellman, who lived directly across the street from Meggie, would get home from school long before she did, but today on her walk to Vine Street she saw him sitting in the American Savings and Loan building. No doubt seeing about investing his upcoming retirement check, she thought as she watched him through the immense plate glass window. Fidgeting in the heavy slat-backed bank chair, Spellman pointed to his useless throat and passed notes back and forth across the desk to the seated officer who serviced his account.

A teacher certainly can't pass notes back and forth to the students, thought Meggie. A teacher needed a voice, that's for sure.

"That Spellman sure loves money," Meggie said to Redwood.

She knew that greenbacks were a necessity in a world where money kept hunger away, kept a roof over her head. But the green she loved most was the green of trees, the green of grass, and the green of bushes.

The color, the texture of green things, filled up her thoughts as they journeyed home, and before she knew it they were turning up her street.

Three elderly men, including Spellman, lived in the cobblestone building known as the Rhinehart house on Vine Street across from Meggie's place.

One of Spellman's housemates, a ferret-faced man, whose once mouse-colored hair had turned to silver, looked through the slatted dusty blinds at Meggie and Redwood as they arrived at her door.

He was *The* Mr. Rhinehart and his marbly eyes glinted and jumped as he watched the teenager and her dog.

Meggie's oaken front door led into a small Tudor, painted cinnamon-brown with copper-orange shutters. A cinnamon-bricked chimney looked like a hat on the edifice. The attic window glanced out on her front yard alive with September hues of dusty green: bay leaf bushes, Japanese bamboo, gardenia, cypress hedges, and a cedar tree whose silver-sheen branches brushed the walls of the house.

Every plant needed a little water, every dusty garden waited thirsty for a late October rain.

An almost-green lawn, kept trimmed by Meggie, stretched out like a carpet around an emerald-colored pine tree.

Admiring Meggie's long legs and her irrepressible vigor, the old man said through a set of yellow false teeth, "Teenagers carry the fountain of youth everywhere they go," but he said this meanly. Since he had no grandchildren, he lacked the softening influence of grandfatherly love, an influence that sometimes moderates the reactions of the old when they consider the young.

Teenagers danced sure-footed at the physical peak of life, Rhinehart thought resentfully.

"Such a robust and hearty girl," he said bitterly, sweetly, envy like venom in his voice.

Mr. Rhinehart rubbed his tobacco-stained hands together but carefully so he only gently touched the pain that blazed in his knobby, calcium-laced knuckles.

Meggie fished the key from her back jeans pocket and unlocked the black oak door.

As she and Redwood entered, filigrees of golden light from the oval stained glass set high up in the door spangled across her sweater like angel's hair.

Jehoshaphat dashed inside just before she let go the knob. The tortoiseshell cat was so happy to see Meggie and Redwood he danced fat-legged on the cocoa couch and the winged chair, then scampered light-pawed from the standing brass floor lamp to the stereo left turned on to reggae music. Jehoshaphat danced almost in time to the reggae music showering them with notes from an acoustic guitar.

Meggie threw down her books and tried to dance too, rippling an air guitar, swaying her knees, dipping and locking. Her hips did not rock steady as a heartbeat though. Her timing was off. Redwood sat on the couch and just swung his tail and panted, too tired from fooling with People to move.

Meggie, if not in rhythm with the beat, did listen to the message of the Jamaican group singing, asking,

Let's reach for tomorrow,
Today's not all we got.

Turning off the radio and followed by her pets, she went into the bedroom.

Here was her special place. The lavender room enjoyed a southern exposure. To harvest the benefits of the southern sun, Meggie had hung crystals, waterdrop shaped, in the three-paneled window. Afternoon rainbows pierced the jewels just so.

Looking at the way light danced through them she remembered why early Indians called crystals the bones of the ancestors.

She kept one window panel open and it stayed that way, October rain or September shine. Today from this open space the natural incense of outdoor air drifted inside. The air, so full of the sun, smelled like the gardenia bush beneath her window.

In the corner on the avocado green chair her mahogany guitar still waited.

But now she needed sleep more than she needed music.

She curled up on the bed, Redwood near her feet, Jehoshaphat resting in the crook of her arms.

She slept fitfully.

Thirty minutes later she woke up and stroked Fat, who looked as if he'd dreamed about catnip and girl kittens and butterfly-chasing. Surveying the chaos of bed covers, she thought she must have dreamed of monsters and ogres chasing her in a Billy Watson nightmare, her bed was so messed up.

Redwood perked up his ears as she picked up the guitar and pulled the strap around her neck.

Her fingers hunted for the right notes.

She played softly and surely. The melody rippled, dabbling in light and darkness, touching pain then leaving it to play a moment in a field of rainbows and raspberries.

She tried to play away all the sad moments of the day. But inside her head strings of shotgun-thoughts ricocheted and her mind settled on teachers like Miss Blount, who she suspected believed in history more than they recognized the present.

And history, she knew, was sometimes changed by whoever was writing it down, the victories transposed and justified to suit the wishes of whoever was in power.

But the present, it stared you in the eye. Unblinking.

As unblinking and sometimes as ugly as somebody like Mr. Spellman.

She played on.

The Jehoshaphat cat watched a spider dangling from the ceiling, an eight-legged acrobat trampolining in time with the continuing guitar melody, one thread of sable sound.

The light from the crystal vibrated on the spider like neon.

When Meggie wove the last single plucked note, she heard the familiar jingle of her mother's keys.

Memory Alexander, tall as an Amazon, entered the house with a "Whew!"

She kicked off her schoolteacher shoes, flat and sensible Life Strides, and plopped down in the winged easy chair.

"What a day!"

Even though she was tired from the long soul-satisfying ordeal of the Panhellenic Council and the Sunday night return-home trip, she never missed a day of Monday-morning teaching. When she saw Meggie she perked up. An even row of teeth earned her what Meggie called a million-dollar smile.

"And how was teaching today?"

"A hard row to hoe. Like plowing clods out of pasture. Jewels in the rough. Seventh graders. I have been slaying ignorance all day. Talking, talking, talking," she said, not meanly.

"How about some tea and biscuits?" Meggie asked.

"That's just what my mouth needs, something soothing enough to put words to rest."

Soon the room filled with the aroma of buttermilk bread and broomwheat tea crushed from the dried stalks and lemon-yellow flowers of the wild bush that grows in the red hills of eastern Oklahoma.

"How was Berkeley High?" Memory Alexander asked after sipping the tea down to about half a cup. The broomwheat gently muted her words.

"Awful," said Meggie. "First, Miss Blount called me out of my name. *Nutmeg*. Then Mr. Spellman made Alton Gillespie mad and Alton hit him and got expelled from school. Now they say Mr. Spellman's going to resign."

"Good riddance to bad rubbage," said Memory, looking out the window across the street at the Rhinehart house where Spellman lived.

"Oh, the state this old world is in. The problems, the problems." Memory Alexander frowned, little dimples deepened at the corners of her molasses mouth. A serious pug nose. Africa rich and lush-colored lived in the deep lines wrinkling her face. She continued, "Kids can't be kids for some folks lingering overlong in childhood. Old gray-headed fools in competition with adolescents. Eternally infantile.

"Just keep remembering what I tell you, Meggie. Some of these modern-day Methuselahs don't have as much sense as God gave a goose. When it comes to relinquishing the things of youth to the young, they're like the dog sitting on top of the haystack—can't eat the hay and don't want the cow to get it.

"Everybody who picks up a book and stands in front of a class is not a teacher. Spellman's got a reputation among the teachers as being the kind of person who doesn't know how to look at young folks, just looked forward to collecting his check once a month. He looked at the check longer than he looked at his students; would look at a check long enough and could tell right away if a digit on his salary was off. But teenagers? Shoot. He looked right through teenagers, had already placed them on some low rung on the ladder in his mind. No, indeed, everybody standing in front of a class is not a teacher. And as far as that nickname, 'Nutmeg,' goes, it just means you've got spice. I always did have a preference for nutmeg, reminds me of your skin and your spirit. Spice-colored. Imagine rice pudding without nutmeg. Or sweet-potato pie missing nutmeg? Talk about bland!"

"Even so," Meggie answered in a troubled voice remembering Miss Blount's meanness, "that's not what Miss Blount meant when she called me Nutmeg."

Redwood at her feet, as though remembering the tone of Blount's words, put in his two-cents worth of agreement. He gave a short bark.

Memory Alexander sat her teacup down and looked carefully at her daughter, a lanky girl who reminded her of a sturdy sunflower stalk, her legs were so long.

"Meggie, you mustn't be so intense about things. You know how teachers talk to each other. Blount is having Technicolored conniptions. It's all over Berkeley Unified School District how you disturb the peace. When it comes to teachers you have to learn to take the helpful information they know and forget the rest. Daughter, drink the tea, leave the dregs."

Meggie was never good at apologizing. Didn't want to insult whatever bold spirit was causing her to be outspoken enough to uproot dumb contentment.

So she just gazed with affection at Memory Alexander, refreshed by the broomwheat brew. Her mother, who had her own relentless temper, often said, "Sorry is a sorry, sorry word."

That was the end of that lecture. Her mother was spreading butter and raspberry jam onto the fluffy biscuits and spreading a little more joy onto her life.

"I played my guitar today. Sometimes I wonder if I'm getting better or what."

"What did the music sound like?" asked her mother, going to the essence of the matter.

"Like a blue shawl of light," said Meggie.

"Well then, you're good, you are," her mother commented before yawning tiredly.

"Excuse me, Meg, but I must have my daily nap. These seventh graders have ripped the lining from my mind and only sleep will mend it."

Now Meggie, alone in the living room, replayed reggae words in her head while looking at the wavery light, fibrous as it slanted through the ribbed lampshade.

She remembered the lyrics:

Let's reach for tomorrow,
Today's not all we got.

The light shining down from the old-fashioned floor lamp re-created a spellbinding pattern—a fragile, crystal lace.

FOUR

Meggie jogged while the just-risen sun lay sleepy in the sky. A morning haze floated like white autumn smoke through a canopy of moss-covered Douglas fir.

Eucalyptus Forest, two miles away from her house and farther up in the hills, filled a brand-new world with towering spruce and western red cedar.

Meggie's legs pumped, stretching to meet the earth trail, again and again.

Here birds twittered, winging through the pine-studded canyons, flitting through the sycamore stands and swooping down on honey locusts.

Below on the forest floor rough-scaled lizards scurried, rustling through the dead leaves and dry twigs, scampering out of the way of her flying feet.

Disturbed, even the rocks moved.

A girl squirrel hugged an oak-tree branch then scrambled over to chatter on a limb as she watched Meggie race through the forest.

A spider scooted beneath a pinecone.

Mice skittered.

Meggie ran on, her lungs expanding, almost to a delicious bursting.

Sweat trickled down her brow and into her mouth. The saltiness fired her thirst.

Now she reached the young sequoia trees.

Passed the western hemlock.

Just fifteen minutes more of running. Almost time to turn around. Maybe when she reached the Sitka spruce by the curve she'd head for home and a tall cool glass of water before she died deliciously from dry throat and salt sweat in her mouth.

As she ran here in Eucalyptus Forest something began to clear up in her soul.

Something eased, undammed, sped with nimble speed to every needy nerve.

Something unlocked inside her head, shook off the biting chains, walked around freely in the upstairs of her mind.

Something rural, something rustic and untamed, flowed primal as Eden before her eyes.

Art.

A poem of timothy grass pastures.

A painting of spruce low in the sky.

A three-dimensional photograph of sloping pines.

The first art that ever arranged itself in green blades and uplifted branches still here green centuries and green centuries upon the earth.

At last she rounded the bend where the spruce waited. She started to slow her loping gallop before circling back when she saw the vague shadowed shape of an animal sprawled on the trail near the canopy of black spruce.

"Why's that deer lying out 'cross the trail like that?"

Why would it sleep in such a vulnerable place anyway, a public path where people run and walk when there are so many tall trees and lovely meadows beyond the thickets. . . . ?

"Maybe it's hurt," she decided.

As she jogged nearer she noticed the human legs, the back bent a little forward so she couldn't see the head.

"Oh it's not a deer at all. Somebody's tripped and fallen," she said to herself speeding up her gait, anxious to help.

As she shortened the distance between her and the accident victim, the haze thickened. Purple thistles stuck her in the scalp upsetting her newfound ease and crawling pinching down her back to her thighs.

When the stickers reached her knees she stopped before the reclining figure clad in a boy's blue jogging suit and red running sneakers.

She knelt.

"Hey!" she said.

He didn't answer. He wasn't moving. Probably passed out.

"Hey," she repeated, shaking him.

She pulled her hands back. The body was stiff. She stepped over him to look into the face.

But there was no face.

Only a hideous wound gaping open out of the neck.

No head.

She swallowed hard.

No head.

She struggled between two needs. Finally, she fought back her need to flee from Eucalyptus Forest and she gave in to her need to know.

Should have brought Redwood, one side of her brain commented common-sensibly. But you like to be completely alone sometimes, the other side of her mind answered matter-of-factly.

She searched the brush. Looking, looking, also alert, peering anxiously over her shoulder now and then aware that the killer might be near.

Something about the size of a head lay in shadow under a bush of bitter berries.

She tiptoed closer, stopped, and pushed aside the brush.

But it was just a large round rock. A sigh of relief. A sigh of anxiety.

Better go back home. Too far away from the path.

What if the killer. . . .

The trees whispered, "Look to the left."

Her body swiveled.

And there it was.

She stepped over to look at the clump of chestnut hair, then the ashen face. Shocked familiar cedar green eyes stared pleadingly, vacantly at her.

She sucked in her breath. And the rocks cried out the name.

Alton!

It's Alton Gillespie.

Alton, who'd stood up for her in class. Alton, who'd walloped Mr. Spellman.

Dead?

Hiccup.

Dead.

She picked herself up and flew off the hill down through Eucalyptus Forest, hiccuping. Her jogging now turned into a race punctuated with hiccuping hysteria.

She ran past Eucalyptus Lake, past the mesquite, past the scrubby shrubs, the white pine, the purple thistle-weeds, and the wild dandelion flowers. Still hiccuping. Scattering the crying rocks.

On out of the forest and through the waking hills she sped.

A driver, one hand on the wheel, sipped his first cup of coffee as his old sixties Volvo murmured and crept sluggishly through the morning. The driver watched half-surprised as Meggie outran his car, her chest heaving in hiccups. Meggie, Meggie, running, running down Euclid Avenue.

She did not stop until she reached Vine Street and her house, still hiccuping.

"Mama!" she screamed as she tumbled inside her door.

Her mother, startled from sleep, listened groggily to her daughter's raveled explanation. Meggie rambled, so upset about what she'd witnessed on the forest floor that Memory Alexander couldn't make head nor tails out of her words.

"Alton!" Meggie finally screamed so abruptly that the name loosed her throat, straightened out all the crooked words, and now she screamed that she had found Alton . . . between screaming hiccups . . . dead.

"Alton? Who's Alton?" her mother asked as she crawled out of bed to call the law.

"You don't mean the Alton Gillespie you told me about yesterday?"

Meggie nodded.

First Billy Watson. Now Alton Gillespie. Why?

Lightning zipped through Meggie's throbbing head.

A corncrake hollered.

FIVE

A slump in her voice to match her downcast mood, Meggie talked to her dog the way she often talked to herself.

"Well, if I can't ever be alone again I don't know any better companion than you, Redwood," Meggie said, thinking about how she treasured perfect solitude and how unsafe the world was becoming.

"Is God sleeping? Where is this Master of ocean and earth and sky Reverend Marvella's always talking about? Up there slumbering in the sky probably. Head pillowed on a cloud. Snoring!

"We are being harvested," Meggie decided as she patted Redwood.

"First Billy, now Alton."

Up in Eucalyptus Forest blue jays, wrens, and robins called warnings to each other in the temple of wind where evergreens watched.

Flicking their quick little wings, flying through arches of dust, hummingbirds looked over their shoulders even as they searched for nectar in the dry throats of fuchsia.

On a weather-worn bench shaped from experienced oak, Meggie and Redwood gazed out over the lake.

They watched the leaves floating on the water's surface,

eucalyptus leaves jumping like green, flat fish in movement that stirred and rippled the foliage.

A talking wind, dusty and dry, accented her sadness.

The trees bending over the water with the hair hanging down over their faces whined. And they were too tall to be the ghosts of Billy Watson or Alton Gillespie.

She shuddered.

But Redwood, scrunching down next to Meggie, thought he spied something delicious leaping at the edge of the lake.

While the dog was looking down, Meggie was looking up at the eucalyptus trees, through the green domes, imagining grandmother ghosts in gossamer gowns she could touch.

Suddenly Redwood sprang away from her as though a doggie bag of steak bones had suddenly appeared.

Watching Redwood darting between tall willows, Meggie soon realized that the steak and bones he chased was a wobbling toad hopping across the stones bordering the water.

Now Meggie followed the dog's progress, momentarily forgetting her sad concerns.

She was distracted by the hunter's look on Redwood's face as the toad bunched up its body, then bounced away to a lonely stone farther out in the lake just out of reach of his grasping paw.

When the toad took another leap, Redwood fell splashing into the water.

"Redwood!" Meggie called.

Redwood's unceremonious splash underscored the forest sounds of insects. A screech owl disturbed in his hollow trunk hooted.

Redwood swam back to the shore, climbed up on the bank, then shook the water off his fur and, with a disappointed look in his eye, came over and lay now wet at Meggie's feet.

"That's okay, Redwood, I don't think toads taste very nice."

Now other voices reached out to them. But this time it was not the wind talking.

"Nutmeg, Nutmeg, Nutmeg!" a trio of boys with tiny earrings embedded in their left lobes chanted from behind a nearby family of birch trees.

Looking like mockingbirds, the boys skirted the path around the lake, darting and hooting.

When she got a good look at them she recognized them as the carpenter's sons. Muscular, like they had been sawing wood for weeks, they were the color of planed dark oak. The tallest one often sat in Blount's history class staring at her.

"Leave us alone, you striped skunk," Meggie ranted, glaring at the tallest boy.

"You old low-backed gopher!" she called the second one.

"Long-tailed, egg-faced weasel," she laid out the third.

Meggie said to the wet dog, "Who invited them? Let's get out of here, Redwood. See what mean people make you do, take the names of skunks, gophers, and weasels in vain. I definitely prefer the company of skunks to these rascals."

But Redwood, taking a cue from Meggie's name-calling, snarled at the boys and started chasing them, barking.

"Here, boy," Meggie whistled in three short bursts that sent Redwood running to her.

"Nutmeg!" the three boys hollered again.

Meggie and Redwood started back down the hill for home.

"Nutmeg!"

The light in Meggie's midnight eyes ruffled the way light flashes on layered silk.

Then she stopped and without turning around gave the taunting boys a wiggle of her fingers in both holey pants pockets, eight fingers like spider legs abided perfect time with her swinging hips.

SIX

Two weeks had passed since Meggie had discovered Alton Gillespie's body up in Eucalyptus Forest.

Nobody seemed to know any more than she knew the day she found him. The coroner's report still had not come out.

And everybody wondered who or what killed Alton.

In spite of her mother's warning to stay away from the forest Meggie still came, drawn and pulled by the bright and dark green foliage of the woods. In respect for Memory Alexander's concern and because of the fright the corpse had given her, Redwood always accompanied her.

Today Meggie sat on a bench facing the west. The Golden Gate Bridge waited for the fall rain to wash it more gold. Yet the bay view of the bridge was wondrously striking even with the few autumn clouds that framed it falsely promising a rain she knew would not come.

While Redwood roamed the trails, she hummed and played her guitar, rocking back and forth as she strummed.

Softly, like the red sunset getting ready to fall under the Golden Gate into the bay water and roll over to the other side of the earth, she played.

Suddenly, between beats, she was aware of a presence behind

her. And it didn't feel like Redwood. No panting. No patter of paws.

The air so pungent with the undisguised aroma of dry sagebrush coming from the mound of serpentine rock to her left had a slight musky sweatiness on top of it.

"Who?" Meggie wondered.

From afar she saw Redwood exploring the canyon below her. Bounding in and out of the mesquite shrubbery, he hunted the small creatures hidden there.

Definitely not Redwood.

She turned around slowly, thinking what a shame it would be if she had to hit somebody with her precious guitar.

She tensed, her fingers stiffly wrapped around the guitar neck.

Behind her she saw the tallest boy of the earringed trio who taunted her the last time she was at Inspiration Point. He loomed close enough to grab her.

Sneaky.

Her skin crawled when she realized how far from her side she had let Redwood roam and the sun getting ready to go down and the ghost of the head of Alton Gillespie still a memory on the retina of her eye.

"What're you doing sneaking around like that?" asked Meggie, her voice rising, hoping someone would hear.

"I'm not sneaking. I heard the music. I just—"

"You just come to call me some more names?" she asked at the top of her lungs, scared but trying not to show it, so scared she forgot to give the three sharp whistles to her dog; but her loud voice did the job.

She saw Redwood had heard for he was racing toward them.

"Not today," said the tall boy.

"Oh, I see, you're by yourself. You're badder in numbers, that it?"

The staring boy was silent.

Redwood was on his way, running toward them; she talked louder.

"Thought you were the cat's meow. Come to find out you're the flea under his collar," Meggie ventured.

What if he's the murderer? What if he's the person who murdered Alton Gillespie?

"I'm not the cat, and I'm not his fleas either," said the tall boy. "My name's Matthew."

"And your co-hoppers?"

"I said we're not fleas. My co-hearts' names are Mark and Luke and they're my brothers."

Now Redwood raced on. Getting closer.

No, he didn't sound like a murderer. But murderers looked and acted like everybody else, often.

She remembered how terrible the boys' heckling had made her feel yesterday.

Fresh outrage stormed through her head strong enough to make her jaw crackle.

Redwood was almost there.

"Who do you think you're messing with?" she asked, her chest and chin stuck out.

She stood up, pushed the surprised boy back with a jab of her finger. "Can't you understand English? Didn't I tell you to leave me alone yesterday?"

When she thought about Billy Watson and Alton Gillespie, how the innocent get picked on by the bullies, her playing hand knotted into a fist and she jumped up and, feet flying, kicked Matthew two or three times in the soft ache of his belly.

Caught off guard by this physical attack, Matthew stumbled back.

Stunned, the air knocked out of him, he tripped, falling.

Then he found his equilibrium.

His face screwed up, he lashed out, forgetting Meggie was a girl.

Matthew swung hard the way a carpenter swings a sledge he uses to demolish a wall in an old building he's renovating.

Power in his punch, his fist flew past Meggie's ducking head so brutally she could feel the wind. She wasn't quick enough though; the follow-up blow landed on her shoulder.

It hurt so much, she couldn't see the trees.

"God, I didn't mean to hit a girl," said Matthew in a shamed voice as he knelt to help her back up from where she'd fallen.

Redwood roared up and pounced on Matthew, growling, and his bare teeth went to work on the boy who was trying to cover himself with his arms to keep the dog from biting him.

"Sic him, boy," Meggie urged.

Teeth gnashing, Redwood wrestled Matthew deeper into the earth, washing him in the leaf-strewn dirt.

Redwood chewed through Matthew's pants, slashing his legs. Fraying threads flew and whirled with the dust, a mixture of stirred-up dried leaves and parched autumn earth. Redwood ripped the shirt off Matthew's back and bit the arm above the elbow that the boy used as a shield to protect his face.

"Call him off!" said the wounded Matthew. Meggie sat nursing her shoulder. "Sic him, Redwood!"

"Call him off!" cried Matthew.

"Sic him!"

Then to the boy, "Don't you hurt my dog!"

"Hey, call him off!"

"Don't you touch a hair on his head," she warned the boy. "Kick his butt, Redwood."

"Call him off!"

The throbbing in her shoulder calmed a little.

"Redwood! Sit!" Meggie ordered when she was sure the boy was bested.

Redwood reluctantly sat, but he kept his eye on Matthew.

"He's fierce," Matthew hissed.

"Protective," said Meggie. "It's all right, boy," she said to the dog, while glaring at Matthew.

Redwood growled deep in his throat because while Meggie said one thing, the tone of her voice said she was still upset with this boy.

And Redwood had mayhem in his growl.

"Hush now."

Matthew stood up and moved toward Meggie. Redwood broke away from Meggie and leaped again.

For the throat.

Matthew dodged just in time.

"Redwood!" Meggie grabbed the leaping dog's collar and held him.

A swallow caroled and sound seemed to lose all dimensions. There was no top or bottom to the bird's call. And it flowed all the way to the bay and beyond that to the ocean without drowning.

The bird's pleading voice seemed to change the air around them.

"Listen, I'm not going to bother you," said Matthew. "I'm sorry about hitting you. You hit me first, and I was on automatic. A natural response."

Meggie grimaced, still stinging from Matthew's powerful left to her shoulder.

"I really didn't come out here to bother you. I just got a question for you, Nut . . . Meggie."

"I'm not the sphinx," said Meggie, on guard yet curious.

"Got some time?"

"That's all we've got," said Meggie. "Shoot."

"Meggie, why don't you like me?"

When Meggie looked at Matthew, she didn't know what she expected to see in his eyes. Under the thick lashes she saw a deep lake tinged with a despair she hadn't noticed before.

Spellbound by her gaze, he reached over and stroked Meggie's hand.

Redwood growled softly.

"It's all right," said Meggie softly to the dog. Redwood tensed, ready to rip open Matthew's throat, but he obeyed Meggie's voice, which now sounded easy and fear-free. Redwood leaned his head to the side looking at Matthew's hand stroking his mistress.

Meggie suspected that past the despairing eyes, down, down into the depths of this person, was an inquiring soul searching for his own blue quality of light.

She pulled her hand away finally and instead of hugging Matthew, which she was tempted to do, she plucked the guitar strings and stroked them into a haunting song of wondering that made Matthew think it was morning and bells were ringing in an empty church. And the song made Redwood settle into a mound at her feet and stay very still.

Meggie played remembering how Matthew always stared intently at her in history class. She saw that look again and what it meant hit her like a fragrant, cool breeze.

She blushed.

Her guitar strings became the loom she wove his question, "why don't you like me?" on.

She played until the answer echoed in the music. The sun spread its last fire and winked its orange-golden eye before it fell to sleep in the San Francisco Bay.

In the new darkness she put her guitar down, looked over at Matthew and said, "I think I do like you. It's just that I was trying so hard not to be anybody's victim that I didn't notice you."

Matthew walked with Meggie and Redwood down the hill to Vine Street.

At her door beneath the golden light from the evening lantern above the porch, Matthew gave her hand a good-bye squeeze.

Then he turned away and walked down the hill. Neither of them had noticed Rhinehart in the dark house across the street, peeking at them through his venetian blinds.

SEVEN

The three old men living in the Rhinehart house would remind any careful onlooker of the three monkeys that speak no evil, hear no evil, and see no evil.

One was croak-voiced and could not speak above a whisper.

One was almost deaf.

One was half-blind.

But all were evil.

The three of them represented something perhaps only a cautious realist knew. That the aged do not necessarily grow benevolent with the years.

A photographer taking their picture or an artist sketching their portrait might have mistakenly labeled them the good grandfather, the kindly old gentleman, and the wise elder.

In these three old men's eyes demons beat on strangely shaped drums, but one would have to have a particularly sensitive kind of metronome to feel the rampant rhythm of their evil.

The rhythm pulsated. *Tick. Tick. Tick.*

First off, they all rejected the signs of aging with pure unadulterated resentment. Another gray hair discovered after a fitful night of broken sleep could send Spellman, the retired teacher, whining into a whispering rage.

A slight figure, Spellman attacked his mirror. He held a strand of white hair in one hand and cursed out Father Time.

"Oh, you humpbacked, raggedy reaper!" he swore in a small, wounded voice.

Tick. Tick. Tick.

The need for a stronger set of eyeglasses would set off Boone, a retired photographer, fuming, "I curse the light!"

And Boone lifted his fat feet—so fat they laid over his shoes—and ground the eyeglasses into fragmented shards.

Tick. Tick. Tick.

The innocent gift of a hearing aid was an indignity that sent a stream of spite spewing from Rhinehart's mouth. A retired first-chair violinist of the San Francisco Opera's orchestra, he roared:

"I used to love the symphony. Now I can't even hear it. And I'm supposed to be content with the *memory* of the sound. Well, I'm not. I definitely the hell am not." And he looked like he could strangle any silly bird that opened its beak to sing.

Tick. Tick. Tick.

They all hated to take their store-bought teeth out of their mouths at night.

They had no grace.

And they all lived together.

"Why, I remember," complained the half-deaf Rhinehart, who had to always face the persons speaking so he could read their lips, "when I could hear carpenter ants chewing wood far away as Eucalyptus Forest my ears were so perfect." He folded his wrinkled lips over his false teeth. "I could hear an ant blink an eyelash! Could hear a rat piss on cotton!"

An ordinary person would never suspect the jealous venom Rhinehart harbored for the easy competence of young folk.

"Whoever said youth was wasted on the young never spoke a

greater truth," Spellman added, all murmury and muffle-voiced.

Because all three men lived together, they compounded their meanness.

Tick. Tick. Tick.

"I remember," said Blind Boone, purple veins protruding from his fat cheeks, giving a cartoon aspect to his great bulb of a nose, "better days."

Blind Boone continued, "I remember when I could see a flea hopping on a tourist down by Spenger's near the Berkeley pier all the way from my bay window high on Spruce Street."

"And I recall," said Spellman in that whispery voice, "when I addressed a crowd of students and parents in front of city hall after the great fire was busy burning down prizewinning buildings, I remember that the people could hear my advice all up in the hills. When I told them to hose down their houses to prevent the spread of flames, they did. Water everywhere. Articulate, that's what I was.

"And I think," he added (His sandpaper skin revealed so many red speckles from overshaving on his scrawny face and neck that he looked like an adolescent old man with a fresh crop of pimples.) "I think" (His two companions had to lean in to hear his next words.) "that this heart of mine's about to give out. It weakens the weakest part of the body when the heart's weak. My voice. Your eyes, Boone, and your ears, Rhinehart."

"Now that we've found the perfect solution, I'm worried about how much it'll end up costing."

"What's money without health?" mumbled Spellman.

Boone nodded vigorously in agreement but stiffened all of a sudden. Alert.

"I hear her," said blind man Boone.

Rhinehart rushed to the window. "I see her," said the near-deaf man after he inched two venetian blinds apart and witnessed

Meggie watering her yard and talking to Redwood and Jehoshaphat.

"I can almost smell the blood pumping from her heart to her veins," said Rhinehart. "And I want what's hers."

"Got to do more than want," whispered Spellman. "We know just how stingy you can be with your pennies. A hoarder. It's a well-advertised fact you're sitting on top of hundreds of thousands. Probably own Wells Fargo. Didn't you come out here with the horses?"

"Bank of America's where my money's at. Don't tell me what to do with my hard-earned cash, now!"

"Who's telling you? Hard-earned? You didn't work hard for it, somebody else did. All you did was invest it. No cause to get belligerent!"

"South Africa," Boone mocked.

"You can't stand powerless people either, so why're you worrying me about who suffers so I can be rich?" asked Rhinehart.

The men quieted then.

Finally Boone said, "When's he coming?"

"He'll be here directly," said Rhinehart.

"Patience then," said Boone.

"Time governs all," whispered Spellman.

"At least it used to," Rhinehart smirked.

"After this operation we can say we stole a march on old Father Time. Ha!"

In a dark nook under the ottoman trimmed in heavy silk, across from the couch where the impatient three men sat waiting, a spider watched. A black widow, shiny-oiled in her satin dress with a red hourglass just beneath her breast, was listening.

"Time governs all," one of them had said. Didn't she know it? the spider thought; she carried the time sign on her underbelly everywhere she went.

The spider, fascinated at the venom these men harbored, wondered where they mixed it. A venom more poisonous than even her bite. Maybe she could borrow a spoonful or two.

She folded her legs up under her, vowing patience. She wanted to see just how far they would go.

The doorbell jangled.

All three men jumped.

"I thought I heard somebody sneaking up," said the near-about blind one.

Rhinehart shuffled to the door and looked out the peephole.

"Well, well, well," he said, turning the knob.

The spider sprang up on her eight dark legs. She didn't mean to miss a thing.

There in the doorway just beneath the place where the spider's tarantula friend hung suspended stood a bifocaled man in casual attire, Hush Puppies on his feet, a medical bag jumping slightly in one hand, the other empty hand twitching, caught in a nervous movement that affects the sick and old. A patchy crop of gray hair straddled his head. When he operated, he had to take pills to keep his hands steady.

The gray-haired visitor sat down on the ottoman and proceeded to outline an amazing plan.

After a while the visitor left.

The black widow thought and thought about what she heard and saw; she couldn't believe her many eyes.

She wondered if the tarantula had been awake.

She had.

The tarantula hadn't missed a thing.

That night she sprang her scarred body up to the top bedroom, and after about an hour of listening to Rhinehart snoring, the tarantula, feeling a shift in the atmosphere, leaned forward to hear

Rhinehart's subconscious speaking through a dream.

"Charged your own mama interest. Then went on and ate a thousand black children's ears for dessert.

"I hope that money gives you nightmares.

"What do you think this is?

"Didn't you hear the drums in South Africa moaning and bleeding?

"Don't you know you can't dodge destruction?"

"No, how could I know that?"

"You know. Everybody knows that. You didn't care."

"I DID!"

"No you didn't. And you charged your own mama interest? A man like you, you're subject to do anything. You're gonna pay for that, oh, yes, you are. Africa, the mother of civilization, will not be damned. You're gonna pay!"

The light flashed on Rhinehart, a big bright illuminating arc of whiteness covered him like a sudden truth, and the sound was too clear, the meaning too insistent.

The spider saw Rhinehart jerk awake and let out a blood-curdling scream. The spider saw how he still heard the echo of his own damned voice, and how he kept brushing the sound from across his face.

The tarantula rolled her eight mad eyes up in her head; she couldn't believe her ears.

EIGHT

It was sunrise when the porch spider at Meggie's house oversaw the unfurling of the tiny American flag at the top of the staff and crossed her legs satisfied at the way it fluttered red and blue colors dramatically from the front window.

The porch spider sent the word down the line.

"Captain Alexander must be coming home. Memory has hoisted the Stars and Stripes!"

When the kitchen spider got the news she woke up immediately and started stirring around.

The kitchen spider liked to nest behind the warm corner pantry. Between the broom's straws she supervised the cooking of food, nodded her head when the concoction was right. She could tell the recipe cooks from the salt-pinching chefs, not by the aprons they wore but by the smells bubbling from their cast-iron skillets.

The kitchen spider was present when onions first got peeled and the vanilla tenders grated the vanilla beans and stirred the batter. When the coconut cake spoon got licked she was there.

The cheer in the house when Michael Alexander came home on leave from the army excited her. And she measured the pleasure of the welcome by the smile on Captain Alexander's face when he tasted his favorite meal: blackened catfish in Cajun sauce, string beans with red potatoes and red onions, and hush puppies dipped in cilantro butter, all washed down with ice-cold lemonade.

Sour cream pound cake with fresh-grated nutmeg was Meggie's own special contribution that never failed to get a blissful nod from her father.

On Captain Alexander's second day home, Meggie's friends increased the joy and noise in the house.

Matthew's brothers, Mark and Luke Davis, dated two sisters named April and May Spring. The Spring girls were known for their shiny black curly hair, one beauty more gorgeous than the other, with faces colored pineapple golden.

April and May lived in the flatlands about thirty blocks from Meggie in a plain and simple rented house.

These girls' mother was always hollering at them.

"With names like the ones I gave you, all light and springy, you'd think you'd be neater. But evidently you have an aversion to spring housecleaning!" said June Spring; she said this in spring, summer, winter, and autumn.

June Spring had it hard trying to raise two girls alone. Divorced since they were nine and ten. And the effort was wearing on her.

When Mrs. Spring couldn't find beauty in the architecture of the house, she tried to arrange for beauty's presence in the interior by overindulging in order. But no matter how organized the rooms, no matter how spotless the floors, beauty wouldn't come.

"Sometimes I wish your father was still here," she would moan.

April and May's mother would sweep the girls right on out into the street with her harping.

She had created beauty by giving birth to these two tropical brown girls, but she didn't know that or had forgotten.

It had been more than two weeks since Matthew had startled Meggie up at Inspiration Point and asked her why didn't she like him.

For as long as Matthew and his brothers, Mark and Luke, were old enough to hold a hammer and a nail in their hands safely they had helped their father repair and build houses on the weekend. They didn't have as much time to date as they wanted, what with baseball practice and homework and carpentering. Because their father was a widower, they longed for the company of women. When they couldn't see April and May on their free time, they would stop by to chat with Meggie.

They lolled on the sofa, watched television, raked leaves, murdered the Alexanders' groceries, but mainly they talked to each other. Over and under reggae music.

It was not long after that that April and May joined the group that gathered at Meggie's. These girls whose mother couldn't stand their messiness were the first to pick up the stray popcorn and crushed Pepsi cans from the family-sized kitchen's tiled floors.

Especially after they heard Michael Alexander say his second day home from overseas, "Meggie, where'd you find these live models of womanhood? We always did wish you had sisters."

All three girls rolled their eyes up in their heads as though they couldn't be more embarrassed, but they could not hide their pleased smiles.

Speaking of the carpenter's boys in a stage whisper, Michael Alexander said to Meggie, "I'm glad you've got such intelligent friends, Daughter."

The boys were so bowled over they commenced to acting charming and like they always displayed the good sense they displayed when they were nailing two-by-fours and carpentering cabinets.

Two weeks later, the three shiny skulls of the clean-headed boys started growing tiny whiskers that curled and shrunk the way black hair will.

"Buffalo cowboys," exclaimed Meggie, remembering that's what the Indians way back in another era called the black soldiers when they first looked at the Africanesque hair.

After a while the used-to-be clean-heads' profiles looked so acceptable that Miss Blount, Meggie's history teacher, and coincidentally Meggie's next-door neighbor, could look at them without turning her eyes away. In class she even called on the carpenter's boys, and what surprised her even more was that when they raised their hands they knew the answers.

The trio of young men could now walk down the street without attracting snide comments from Blount.

This did not last long, however, for soon the hair got past the "neat" stage, and when the three boys walked down the street with the girls, you couldn't tell the carpenter boys from Meggie, April, and May if you were walking behind them.

"It's a disgrace," Blount complained to Memory Alexander over the exhausted telephone wires. "And I know you parents can't do anything with them."

And her fear increased.

The clean-heads had become longhairs.

"Longhairs. And I don't mean Beethoven," Blount quipped.

Now the longhair friends, male and female, called Meggie just before visiting her house, asking, "Old Stumbling Block, where is she?" Blount fit Meggie's definition of Stumbling Block. The Stumbling Blocks were people that Meggie called road-blockers; one put snakes in the road, one poisoned the wells of the spirit, one flagged down anything that tried to fly.

"What?"

"Stumbling Block. Is she at her post?"

"Wait . . . I'll check. . . . Yes, she's there all locked up with arthritis, perched on her piano stool by the window."

"What'll we do? Sneak around her or go straight in front of the witch's watch?"

"Give her wide berth," said Meggie. "That arthritis affects the temper."

"We got it, Buddy," answered Matthew.

This was the same day that Memory Alexander helped Blount weed her yard.

No two could have been more alike in appearance.

Well, almost.

Tall, both. A little plump, but pleasingly so. Wonderful wrinkles lined both faces. Wonderful dimples bejeweled both smiles. Both had crowns of silver hair. Their major difference was as small or as large as one wanted to make it, for Blount was white and Memory was black.

In attitude, however, there was a ravine as wide as Strawberry Canyon running between them.

"Now Blount, you have the prettiest yard on the block, simply because you fuss so," said Memory all clad in gardening gloves and a straw hat to keep away the autumn sun.

"Well, somebody has to keep up standards," Blount remarked. She wore a smart Panamanian gardening hat with a little fuchsia-colored ribbon around the band.

Just then a Mohawk-haired student came bopping down the street.

Memory saw him first.

She rose up off her knees and, leaning on the fence, exclaimed, "Just look at all the Art!"

"What?" asked Blount, looking at this outrage marching down her sidewalk. "Wouldn't be a bit surprised if he didn't smoke dope and kill old people going around looking like that. A purple-headed rooster!"

"Oh," said Memory Alexander. "The hair, the hair, the uneven purple of the spike hair. The asymmetrical and symmetrical way it sticks up and lays down. The way it clumps the color. Art!"

"Art? You call that Art? Senility is creeping up on you. Woman, have you seen your doctor lately?" asked Blount.

Memory Alexander was still staring at the youth as though she hadn't heard a word Blount said.

"You're just as bad as these rotten kids," Blount decided indignantly.

Just then a stray dog raised his flea-bitten leg over her lilacs and relieved himself.

"Well!" huffed Blount, taking off her gloves, signaling the end of the neighborly weeding endeavor.

"Guess you call that Art too!" she said wrinkling her nose at the dog puddle.

She left Memory Alexander standing there gazing down Vine Street, looking after the Art walking around with purple hair.

Memory Alexander said that night at dinner when Meggie complained about how the neighbors treated black male adolescents, "In all fairness to Blount, she feels she has a reason to narrow her eyes. She gets hysterical when she reads the crime reports in the *Oakland Tribune*."

"Then she gets further riled up watching the eleven o'clock news," her father added.

"Soon after the news she goes to sleep and takes that mess into her nightmares. What she saw some adolescent do to some senior citizen on Channel 5 becomes her own boogeyman when she falls asleep.

"When I was young, the boogeyman was always older.

"These days not so for the older folks. Now the boogeyman's barely stepped out of short pants. Not only that. Some folks like little black boys but are scared of black male adolescents, the way some people like kittens but can't stand cats; the way some prefer little puppies but can't abide dogs."

Meggie too had seen the eyes of some of the teachers looking at black boys, change from kindness and warmth in kindergarten to mistrust and doubt in the ninth grade.

Anybody unfortunate enough to let those icicle eyes rake over him shivered and got chilled right down through the bones. Left you with a frostbitten spirit.

The smart boy in kindergarten was perceived a troublemaker in the seventh grade. Same boy. Same energy.

"That's a shame," Meggie said out loud. "Must do something, something to you not to feel safe in your own neighborhood, in the place you call home."

She was remembering Billy Watson, roughed up and shot and killed.

"I'm trying to understand it," said Meggie. "But it's hard. I'm on the side of the kids. Something ought to be done and I'm not talking about Police Review Boards."

"It's a downright dirty shame," said Memory Alexander.

"Being on the kids' side?"

"No. That there has to be a side. We all win or we all lose, why can't folks understand that?"

"Because it's not true," said Michael Alexander.

"In the real world, Meggie, somebody has to win, somebody has to lose."

She looked up at her father and a storm raged just behind his fiery eyes as he said, "Ugly people, may their tribe decrease. Ugly people will call you Nigger in front of your children while '*The Star-Spangled Banner*'s playing and the flag's draped over your coffin."

An uncomfortable silence fluttered, then settled an imaginary drop cloth over her father's face. Meggie held her breath. Memory Alexander started humming as she picked up a pile of students' papers to correct.

There it was, Meggie observed, just a glimpse of it. That tenseness in her father, that same tenseness she had seen in so many black men.

The next morning Meggie woke up listening to the usual choir of birds chirping joyously up, up in the fig tree waving leaves outside her bedroom window.

She heard them before she could see them. A choir of birds threw back their heads and opened their feathery throats.

"Sounds kind of thin this morning, must be somebody missing in the choir," whispered Meggie.

"I forgot. I forgot to feed the cat," she said sitting straight up in bed.

She pushed her way through morning and to her robe and slippers.

"Must have been cobwebs in my mind. How could I forget to feed the cat?"

Down through the kitchen and out the back door she padded. She saw the birds crooning their tune, huddled together like a skinny-legged quartet, and sure enough somebody was missing in the choir.

Below her, Jehoshaphat licked his lips. Choir feathers decorated the grass, such odd leaves.

"Meow!" sang Jehoshaphat, but he could not soprano like the puffed-up birds.

"I knew it. I knew it. Somebody's missing in the choir.

"I forgot to feed the cat," Meggie said over the breakfast table.

"That's funny. I thought you had," said her father. "He sure doesn't look hungry."

"That's because somebody's missing in the choir," said Meggie.

"What? What are you talking about?"

"Tell you later," said Meggie, a little disturbed. "School."

She thought as she made her way down Vine Street, why, in a world like this her father was right. The cat won. The bird lost.

NINE

While the singing birds welcomed morning, Redwood watched the grown spiders dancing in Meggie's October yard.

In the corner of the lawn near the lowest cedar branch a mama spider instructed her children in the fine art of parachuting.

Lined them up one by one.

Each tiny spider climbed up to the dizzy edge of a cedar branch, faced the blue aqua sky, and launched forth, looping the loop, looping the silk ribbons that the air played back and forth until the parachute took each and every baby spider on a balloon ride.

Each spider giggled when it looped the loop and flew away.

Redwood wanted Meggie to come out and play. He wanted to fly away, like a circus of spiders. He stood up on his hind legs and barked below her bedroom window.

"All right, all right," she said, sticking her uncombed head out of the window. Some mornings Redwood was better than a clock or her mother's voice or the choir of birds in the fig tree.

She pulled on her jeans and ran out to meet him.

Wagging his tail, he offered her his favorite stick from his mouth.

She took it and tossed.

He went dashing after, a streak of red wind, leaping across the red cedar bush and the jumping spiders. When he tired of chasing the stick and rolled on the grass under the Japanese bamboo, his eyes alert and his tail waving, his spirit reminded Meggie of the dawn of a red Sunday sunrise.

It was early.

Early enough to hear the "whack" of the morning *Chronicle* as it fell on the doorsteps and walkways of Vine Street.

Whack.

"Fetch it, Redwood," Meggie ordered.

And Redwood brought the paper into the house, bounding after Meggie as she opened the front door.

Michael Alexander found Meggie sitting at the kitchen table, her head bent at an intense angle, studying the front page of the newspaper.

The story said that a fifteen-year-old Berkeley High student named Donald Fuminori was found by the park rangers sprawled across the cow path up in Eucalyptus Forest in the area known as Inspiration Point.

The circumstances surrounding his death were mysterious.

Fuminori, according to the reporter, left for his usual hike up the hillside on Saturday evening, near sundown, saying he was going to walk as far as the four-mile mark.

Later, his body was found.

Meggie said, "Listen to this, Dad. 'Anyone having information leading to the discovery of his murderer or murderers, please contact the Berkeley Police Department. Anyone who noticed anything suspicious around that hour in Eucalyptus Forest, also, please contact the Berkeley Police Department.'

"They didn't say how he died," said Meggie. "That's because there's something unusual about the death," said Michael Alexander.

"What kind of unusual?"

"Sometimes there are ritualistic killings and the method has some strangeness about it."

"For instance?" Meggie prodded.

"Well, for instance," said Michael Alexander looking embarrassed—he hated talking about violence the way some parents hated discussing sex education with their children—"once someone was found murdered with her liver missing. Another time an eyeball was ripped from its socket and stuck in a victim's mouth."

"Awful!"

"Well, when those kinds of bizarre things happen the police keep the information secret, so when glory seekers show up claiming to have committed the murder, they can distinguish the kooks from the real slayer. Only the real murderer could have described where the eyeball went."

Meggie shivered. "So cold to be such a clear morning."

Michael Alexander looked sympathetically at Meggie. Violence affected her the way it affected him, and although he was a captain in the army, where injury and death of soldiers was expected, he never got used to encountering it.

The Alexanders' friends thought it odd that Meggie knew all about the birds and bees before she was seven. Sex was part of the cycle of life. Held an important place in the wheel.

Violence, though, led to death.

And that was another wheel altogether.

Meggie stared at the newspaper's picture of the scene of the crime.

There was a photograph of the gate, the gate off of Eucalyptus Forest, the one they all passed through to gain entry.

The light framing the picture looked eerie, as though the angel who kept day and night separated tripped and fell with the sands of time in her hands and thereby had gotten dusk and dawn all mixed up.

She looked closer. She had not noticed the tarweeds before, but there they were on the fringes of the picture, blooming too vigorously since summer had come and gone. What were these sticky, smelly flowers doing raising their stinking heads proudly so late in the year instead of drooping, as was their nature in October?

It was truly odd.

What then made Fuminori's death so different that the police kept the details to themselves?

Out loud Meggie asked, "I wonder what happened?"

"I'm sure, whatever it was, it's enough to give us nightmares," said Michael Alexander, who specialized in treating the nightmares of servicemen.

How could someone—in the middle of autumn, when the pungent mustards were dropping their yellow caps in the meadow—how could someone go out and murder somebody?

"Obviously it had to have been somebody who does not respect colors," Meggie said.

"Sounds like an interesting premise," said Memory Alexander, who had just joined them to survey the Sunday headlines.

"What would make a person disrespect colors?"

"Lots of confused people in the world," said Michael Alexander.

"Just last week one of the servicemen said his mother-in-law was the kind of woman who sat with her back to the ocean."

"Anyway," said Meggie, "who could go up to Eucalyptus Forest and look at the wind poppies and think about killing somebody? Now, just who would do a thing like that?"

For a moment they were quiet, thinking about the wind poppies, their ephemeral petals fluttering when disturbed by the slightest breeze, poppies like soft orange butterflies dotting the gentle hills of the forest.

"Well, everything deserves to live," decided Memory Alexander.

"Even spiders?" asked Michael Alexander, an amused smile lighting up his dark face.

Meggie looked up; her father's voice teased her mother.

"Even the spiders," said Memory Alexander.

"When I married your mama," said Michael Alexander, "she couldn't stand anything that crept and very few things that crawled. The woman is a million times bigger than a spider, but many were the nights I've stayed awake killing mosquitoes off the walls. Now a snake, a snake, will make her hurt herself."

"A snake used to, Dumpling, used to," said Memory.

"Remember that time you told your students they could bring their pets to school, you were having show-and-tell?"

"Yes, I remember," said Memory Alexander blushing. "Seven-year-old Zachary Taylor came to class, hugging a garden snake just like it was a kitten.

"I tried to be blasé about it, but my feet wouldn't obey my head. While the children were petting the snake I was up on my chair and couldn't get down. All I could screech was, 'Get the principal!'"

"What did the kids do then?"

"Took their time. Got the principal, finally; they knew they'd treed the teacher in a chair. They had a gay old time, taking their time.

"'Course my fear of snakes was the talk of the school."

"The snakes might have been the talk of the school, but spiders is the family secret," said Michael Alexander. "It was a spider sent your mama into labor."

"What?" asked Meggie.

"A spider. First a spider scared her and she went into a dead screaming panic. Then she doubled over. I thought it was still the spider she was gasping about. Come to find out it was serious labor. It was you, Meggie, ready for the world.

"Memory, my mama says you marked the child."

"Well, if my panicking over spiders marked Meggie, she was indeed marked," agreed Memory.

"It's the two-legged animals you have to watch out for," said Michael Alexander. "And don't I know it! I see the results in my office on the base every day.

"What parents do to their children emotionally and physically is enough to turn you into a recluse.

"One father in the dead of winter had the utilities shut off because he was mad at the mama.

"Even what sisters and brothers do to each other can be devastating. One sister cut her baby brother's eyelashes off with a pair of sewing scissors because everybody admired his eyes. And there she was a raving beauty herself. A classic case of sibling rivalry."

"Beyond sibling rivalry, which can be innocent enough, a lot of sickness in the world, and all of it's not in broken bones and diseases of the body," Memory Alexander agreed.

"Lots of parents haven't grown up, and a lot of sisters and brothers hate the sight of each other."

"And strangers?" asked Meggie.

"Well, we've taught you about talking to strangers," said Memory Alexander.

"Strangers may feel freer to be even meaner. Kind of think that's what's going on in this case," Michael Alexander said, referring to the newspaper.

"I take that back about everything deserves to live. Whoever's doing this doesn't," said Memory Alexander, a hacksaw in her voice. "Better to stay away from Eucalyptus Forest."

Having said that she stood up and announced, "Time for my morning bath."

Memory Alexander thought about the fearless snake-loving

students she had taught who'd gone on to high school as she soaked in the bubble bath, daydreaming.

But as she languished in the water, her thoughts turned from pleasant thoughts of American teenagers to dark visions of dank doorways and old men, toothless and mean, sitting before an early winter fire, trying to keep their bones warm and shooing old age away from the hearth.

Their rocking chairs parked in front of the fire had wheels. And the men kept putting sticks in the spokes.

"Now, why would they do something like that?" she asked as she turned the faucet dial to hot to take the chill off the water.

TEN

Curiosity seekers went up to the forest.

They crashed the gate, clumping down the elegant clarkia plants, trampling the thirsty lavender petals and their dry scarlet throats.

Instead of running from trouble, they ran toward it.

Gangs of people looked at the spot marked in chalk where the fifteen-year-old Fuminori had lain.

And every one of these calamity collectors had a theory.

"Probably drug-related," said one amateur sleuth.

"Somebody had it in for him, all the signs of a revenge killing," someone else surmised.

"Oh, he did it to himself, you know we've had a rash of teen suicides lately," said an athletic-looking man.

These tourists of pain were scavengers of disaster trying to fill up their empty lives with other people's hurt, as though their own wasn't agonizing enough.

Inside themselves they grinned at other folks' graves, smacked their lips at the suffering of strangers. Got high off of grief.

An undercover policeman mingled with the crowd, trying to pick out anybody who looked the least bit suspicious.

But what caught his sharp eye the most was a persistent hummingbird pollinating the ruby thistle.

And he didn't see anyone he wanted to take downtown in the wagon.

The carnival of fear left the people's voices and sat on the tree limbs that bent over Eucalyptus Lake.

But the spiders, now, the spiders were kinsfolk of fear, had seen its face so many times they were rarely surprised at anything humans did in the name of terror.

Some spiders up in the forest knew all about the murder.

They were astonished at the purpose behind it.

"Well, shut my mouth," said a tarantula.

When the spiders got to gossiping, one mother scorpion hid under a stump and kept her new babies busy so they couldn't overhear the horror.

The next week, seventeen-year-old Rita Gonzalez came up missing. The last time anybody had seen her she was heading up to the forest along about sunset.

Creepy and crawly notions burrowed under people's skin.

"It was just an unlucky coincidence," one reporter remarked on the nightly news, "that two teenagers met with bad fortune up in Eucalyptus Forest along about sunset."

Then the next week Regan Russell, the towheaded star of the football team, a Yellow Jacket halfback, went jogging up Inspiration Mountain in the forest. And he disappeared.

By now the panic reached full scale.

Parents forbade their teenagers to go up there at all.

And the notices were posted up all over Berkeley, on University Avenue and Sacramento Street and on over to Ashby Avenue. Missing teenagers. Has anybody seen Regan Russell, six feet three, one hundred eighty-four pounds, a muscleman, missing, blond, a scar on his left cheek?

And has anybody seen Rita Gonzalez, a brunette, petite, a

swimmer, able-bodied, but still a slight one-hundred-pound girl, perhaps unable to protect herself against someone using superior force?

But Regan; Regan Russell was nobody's pushover. Who would fool with him?

Rita Gonzalez and Regan Russell both last seen about sundown.

And up in Eucalyptus Forest the light wiggled and jumped from the bushes and crevices, up and down the trails it lit; it skipped over to the International Peace Grove and sat down on the monuments to Ralph Bunche, U Thant, and Pope Paul VI.

The light just couldn't be still.

Now it paused for breath.

Then it was off again running.

ELEVEN

Across the street in the Rhinehart yard, a steady stream trickled from a fountain and created a pond whose water was stained blue by the brightly colored rocks bedding the pond bottom.

On the ground in the shade of a weeping willow tree, whose sad limbs hung over the pond, bleeding hearts drooped among their fern leaves and bloomed odd flowers colored rose purple.

The window above the pond was vacant.

No old men waited at the venetian blinds and watched, spying on the young girl across the street. It was dinnertime.

Inside the house in the living room under the ottoman the spider traced a golden eardrop in her web and listened attentively.

The three men sat at the dining room table, having a sumptuous dinner of fried chicken, mashed potatoes, peas, white Langendorf's Bread, and Coors beer.

Boone, who had a love affair with food, looked with blurred dismay at Spellman, a finicky eater, picking at his peas, and chasing one around his plate with a fork, finally stabbing it as though it lived and he was killing it.

Today Spellman looked rather emaciated and as skinny as a road lizard. His black skin was rough as a reptile. A bumpy Adam's apple bobbed an extra bobble every time he swallowed.

Rhinehart, sporting a tweed hunter's hat, ate moderately.

Of medium height, he used his entire body to converse, nodding his crop of white, white hair, tweeking his mop-handle mustache, and arching his thick brows, which looked like white bushes protruding over a pair of deep set marble gray eyes.

When he wanted to accent a point, he stamped his feet.

Rhinehart manipulated the conversation and ordered the food around in its assorted bowls and platters.

Boone gobbled a chicken heart. He forked great chunks of meat and pushed them in his mouth, barely chewing the morsels before swallowing. He looked like Santa Claus without his friendly red suit on. Or a Buddha without a Buddha's benevolence.

Rhinehart leaned back in his chair, stamped one foot, and said in an extra-high voice, talking loud the way near-deaf people often do, "Well, we have a progress report from the doctor."

The two housemates opened their fish mouths in unison, like black-and-white twins of selfishness, greedy for what they didn't need and shouldn't have.

"What'd he say?"

"He said the first one didn't work because it was too long out of the body to do anything with. Had to get the timing down right."

"Well, did he?"

"Let me finish, would you? You'd think at your age you'd've learned some patience."

Boone stopped chewing for a moment, such was his vested interest in the answer. Very little came between him and his food.

Rhinehart washed a forkful of mashed potatoes down with a gulp of Coors beer.

He patted his mouth with an "R"-embroidered napkin. Then he took out his pipe and tapped the ashes out of its bowl before filling it with tobacco and lighting up.

Now he continued, the pipe hanging out of his mouth like a mouse tail. "Yes, he figured it out. The body's got to be kept alive until everything's ready. That's the best condition possible. No time between the body's parting and the parting of the heart."

"Sounds like a romance to me," said Boone, belching.

"The parting of the body and the parting of the heart."

"Except instead of being between a man and a woman or a boy and a girl, this romance's between the young and the old."

"A sharing of hearts!" Boone grinned just before wrapping his smacking lips back around a drumstick.

"How long, then, before we can share?" muttered Spellman.

"Doc said about a month."

"That long!" complained Boone.

"Is that long?" asked Rhinehart.

"It is when you're old and don't know if you'll wake up to see another day," whined Boone.

"Suppose you've got a point there," said Spellman whispering in that half-voice.

"What point? When you die, Boone, it won't be from old age; you're digging your grave with a fork!" Rhinehart shouted.

Boone leaned over the mound of greasy bones piled high on his plate and reached for his bottle of Coors. "Can't the doc hurry this thing along?"

Spellman pointed in silent mockery to the chicken skeletons on Boone's plate.

Boone, who could barely see, noticed the blur that was Spellman's bony finger pointing.

"Just because you've got ulcers and have to sip cream out of a saucer and pick at your peas like a bird is no reason to attack me for my healthy appetite, Spellman."

"I don't think Doc likes us calling him every day, says it

interferes with his train of thought," said Rhinehart, redirecting the focus back to their main concern.

"Anything that helps speed up the process is worth trying."

"Well, how long's it been since we took the money out of the bank? September. It was September. Could've been earning interest on that cash."

"Interest is based on time."

"Well?"

"If we don't make the heart exchange, you won't have much time anyway."

"And your money damn sure won't do you a nickel of good where you're going."

"They got plenty of rich men and bankers down there being barbecued in the everlasting fire," Boone cackled.

"And they'd pay a fortune for a cool drink of water."

"Or a six-pack of beer," said Boone, taking another large guzzle from the sweaty-cold Coors bottle.

"Water's cheaper. We're talking profit!"

"Package it right, you can sell anything," said Spellman, paraphrasing P.T. Barnum. "Just look at the folks nowadays paying a fortune for bottled water. Water's damn near free!"

"I still say there's where you might make a bundle, if you could go down there and get back."

"Where?"

"Hell."

"Stop cursing," said Rhinehart. "This is a respectable house."

"Right, right, don't dishonor the 'dead wife's memory.'"

"Speaking of her memory," said Boone, "why are you wearing that hat at the table?"

"My memory of it is she wouldn't let me wear it at the table. Now I can, every time I call up that memory," Rhinehart answered.

"That money ought to be working for us," Spellman mumbled low.

"Life's the best interest you can get," repeated Rhinehart.

"Call the doctor one more time; how could it hurt?" said Boone, wiping the grease from around his mouth with a napkin no doubt left over from the deceased Mrs. Rhinehart's linen treasure chest.

"Who's going to be the one?"

"I'll do it," rasped Spellman. "I've got most of my money tied up in this thing. Anyway, Boone, you're too busy picking your teeth. Rhinehart, you called last time."

After he got up from the table Spellman went into the nearby hallway and dialed the number.

His two companions moved forward in their chairs.

"Good afternoon. This is Mr. Spellman. May I speak to the—"

Spellman's own throat choked him, closing around his larynx.

Rhinehart and Boone jumped up at the same time, like twin jack-in-the-boxes.

"Hand me that phone, with your no-talking self!" Rhinehart demanded. "How the hell's anybody gonna understand you bumbling and stumbling over words?"

"Look who's talking," Spellman whispered, his throat unclogging, "I may lose my voice from time to time, but you can hardly hear. Talk about the pot trying to call the skillet black!"

Still complaining in a voice Rhinehart couldn't hear, Spellman handed Rhinehart the phone.

Rhinehart continued in a clear, loud voice.

"I know I've reached the doctor's secretary," said Rhinehart.

"Speak up, woman!" Rhinehart said, holding one hand over his unengaged ear and leaning into the phone. "I must speak to him. . . .

"Young lady, if you don't get the doctor to the phone I promise you I'll have your job.

"What?" said Rhinehart, his hearing fading.

Now Boone and Spellman were standing just behind Rhinehart, trying to understand every word said.

After what seemed like hours but was only a few minutes, the doctor came to the phone.

Rhinehart's tone changed and tried to take on its usual equanimity.

"It's been more than a month since we first met. What are you doing, my good man?" asked Rhinehart.

"What? Talk louder. . . . We know it takes time. . . .

"Right. It is the only commodity we've got. . . .

"Are you threatening us. . . ?

"What? Louder please.

"No, we haven't changed our minds; why would you even ask a question like that? What?

"All right. All right. We did promise to wait until the end of the week. . . . What?

"Stop yelling!

"What? No, we haven't forgotten to stay on alert. . . .

"We packed the freezer, got enough food to last a year. No reason to go out except to empty the garbage. . . .

"What've you decided about the candidate we mentioned. . . ?

"What?

"Well, nothing like using a product that's homegrown. Right in our own front yards.

"Talk. . . .

"I know you'd rather not. But we know what we're looking at and this model has eaten right, exercised right, and has a certain spirit that's rare.

"The heart of the matter, you understand, is this: she's one of the finest physical specimens this side of creation.

"We know you have to check her out.

"We know the plan calls for anonymity, but it's our money. And we want a say in the matter.

"No, we're not threatening you.

"We just want to live," Rhinehart said pitifully, his confidence evaporated just before hanging up.

"Wouldn't change his mind?" whispered Spellman.

"Nope," echoed Boone. "Nothing to do but wait a week."

TWELVE

The KPFA morning radio announced, right after Meggie's guitar playing, that the Berkeley police found the sixteen-year-old Regan Russell's body dumped on the roadside up in the forest.

The police were secretive again about the conditions surrounding the murder.

"I sure would like to be able to walk around in the world without fear. I'd like to take midnight walks if I want to," said Meggie to her parents, who joined her when she took a music break and popped Jiffy Pop popcorn in the big stainless steel kettle, then poured melted Berkeley Farm butter over the hot tender kernels.

"You've every right to be upset, but there's no way you're going to take a midnight walk out of this house and I know about it," said Michael Alexander, taking a handful of popcorn out of the heaping lacquered bowl.

"Over my dead sixty-three-year-old body," said Memory Alexander pouring three glasses of Welch's grape juice.

"A child rapist doesn't care one whit about your rights," Michael Alexander informed his daughter. "Neither does the crazy man going around mutilating people. That's probably what the police are keeping to themselves. This derelict has mutilated some part of the human body, and they're not saying which."

"Which part could it be?" wondered Meggie. The next day when she met with her friends at Berkeley High, Meggie repeated what her father had said, then added, "I don't like this curfew of terror."

"*You* don't? Imagine what it must be like in our house," said April. "If a plane passes over the house and casts its shadow, our mother screeches, 'Close the drapes, the madman's got wings!' At night it's hard to sleep, she's opening our bedroom door every thirty minutes to see if the Eucalyptus Murderer has snatched us away."

"Fall asleep finally, you dream about something terrible descending out of the sky and grabbing you. We're lucky to get to come to school in broad daylight," continued May.

"Well, I want to go back up to the forest. Up there where the air is free and the birds sing about it," said Meggie.

"What can we do about this madman?" asked April.

"Find this destroyer of the peace so we can get our forest back."

"But how?" asked May.

"Got to think like he thinks," Meggie decided.

"How would that be?" asked Matthew.

The six of them got quiet, trying to screw up their minds, trying to think like a madman, a rapist, a sadist, a person who enjoyed hurting somebody else, somebody who went around smiling when your house burned down, somebody who giggled when you broke your leg falling off a high limb.

Nothing came to mind.

"I don't know," said Meggie. "I kind of think we might be on the wrong path."

"What do you mean?" asked Matthew.

"Well, what if it's not a madman? I mean not a madman the way we think of a madman. When I think of a madman I think of somebody who acts without a motive. Something outside the person. What if this is somebody who's got a purpose?"

"What kind of purpose would that be?" Meggie started to shrug.

Before her shoulders could come back down, a clammy hand gripped them.

She shivered.

Then the unseen hand with frostbitten fingers touched the members of the group: Matthew next, then, one by one, the hailstone hands moved across all their shoulders 'til cold pellets rained down their backs.

April jumped and May hugged herself against the cold.

Matthew and the boys froze, still as statues. Meggie started to say did you feel that? but didn't. Each person thought that if they did not give voice to the chill palm of premonition, maybe it would disappear. So they just stood there, digging their toes in the earth, and saying nothing.

The bell rang. At the sound of its pealing, the chill dispersed, the silence broke.

"I think we'd better try to find out just what person is responsible," said Meggie. "Anybody want to do otherwise?"

They might have said yes, let's forget it, a minute before. But when the cold hand of fear hacked them to the shoulder blades and left icicles in their marrow, they knew they had no choice.

"Well, it happens up in Eucalyptus Forest, right around Inspiration Point. Why don't we go up there around sunset, all six of us, and see what we can see?"

"How're we going to do that without the folks finding out? We've got three families here."

Now they were walking back toward the school building entrance.

"And we're on curfew," said April. "Strictly forbidden to do anything but go to school and go straight home."

"Well, we'll have to arrange a meeting around sunset at . . . what time does your mother get home?" asked Meggie, turning to the Spring girls.

"About five on Monday through Thursday, but not until eight-thirty on Friday. That's the restaurant's busiest time."

"Why don't we meet at your place on Friday, and that's what the rest of us will tell our folks; then we'll hurry up to the forest and see what we can see."

"Hey, time to go, we'll be late for classes."

As they scattered, Meggie called out, "Anything's better than having a whole town of teenagers sitting like sitting ducks and scared to go to the places we want to go the most."

The six could hardly wait until Friday.

When Friday finally came, as agreed, Meggie dressed in army fatigues, khaki-colored in shades of green and brown.

"Why're you eating so fast, Meggie? Trying to get to the dessert in a hurry?" asked her mother.

"No, save the peach cobbler. Got a meeting at the Springs'."

"And how're you getting there? That's at least thirty blocks from here."

"Matthew," said Meggie, gulping her milk.

"We don't need to remind you, do we, about being careful?"

"Go ahead, join the crowd—the principal, the teachers, the police, other people's parents, the Springs' mother thinks the madman can fly through windows. Everybody reminds us that there's a hunting season for teenagers out there," Meggie answered angrily.

"I can see it's upsetting," said Michael Alexander.

"Multiply that ten times and you'll know how we feel."

"You don't have to be careful where you go!" said Meg.

"I wish it *was* just grown folk having to be careful," said Memory

Alexander. "I could handle that. I know ten ways to kill and others are hatching in my mind right now."

"Your mother was an Amazon in her other life," said Michael Alexander. "Hard to believe this is the same woman used to be scared of spiders."

Meggie's parents' concern made her choose and limit her next words most carefully.

They had some mysterious way of knowing when she was lying.

The doorbell rang.

"I think that's Matthew," Meggie said and sprang up from the table too quickly for them to analyze the words or the expression on her face.

She might not have bothered—they were too engrossed in their own terror for her, and so her lie slid her through the sticky web of parental fear and out the door into her front yard.

THIRTEEN

When Meggie thought about the parental web, she imagined a web so vast it stunted mountains, made them look like pebbles, made the oldest redwood trees as incredibly small as blades of grass. And the web, the web it covered the world.

Matthew waited for Meggie out in the front yard. There she walked into Matthew's embrace and closed her eyes. He hugged her so tight she could feel the tense power of his muscles right through his brown and green army fatigues.

Sighing deeply, she tilted her head up for a long, sweet kiss.

Then hand in hand they started out.

About an hour later all six of the fatigue-dressed, teen group crossed the gate and went into Eucalyptus Forest, winding their way up to Inspiration Point.

They huddled together, almost on each other's heels.

To the experienced eye they, in their camouflaged outfits, only looked a little like trees and bushes, mobile against the brown meadows and gentle green hills.

They spoke in hushes, already in their role as lookouts for lunatics.

"I think this spot's right," said Meggie, stopping near the path leading to the International Peace Grove.

Here, just off the hiking trail, the forest thickened with mesquite bushes and a copse of short pine.

"But the poison sumac?"

"Not so thick here if I remember correctly. But plenty of sow thistle."

It was five-thirty, one hour before sunset. The park was almost vacant. A few tenacious senior citizens out for their daily therapy walked the path, cane-free.

A little ahead of the older people, a teenager in a gray gym suit jogged along, looking behind him every few steps as though surely hearing again his parents' warnings about the dead teenagers up in Eucalyptus Forest.

He stumbled over little branches along the trail and finally he looked back so intently he slipped in a patch of cow chips.

May giggled.

The other five glared at her; they wanted to giggle too, but they dared not. Their eyes watered from the effort of holding in the laughter.

"What's that?" asked Meggie, listening intently.

"What?"

"Something. A roar."

"A mountain lion?" Matthew offered, trying to inject a little humor.

"No. Sounds like a motor."

"It's got a cough in it."

"No cars allowed up here."

"Look. It's a van. What have we here?"

They all leaned forward in the bushes. Six pairs of eyes.

Painstakingly and surely the yellow vehicle progressed.

The gears broke down and the van sounded as if it was going to stop.

"Oh," said Matthew in a dismissing tone, "it says 'Park Service.' For a minute there I thought something strange. . . ." And he poised one foot to step away from the bushes; it was time to go home anyway.

"Wait!" whispered Meggie, pulling him back into the cover of shrubbery. "Park Service isn't out here after five."

"That's right!" they whispered in unison.

"Why's that van here? It's not the plainclothes police; they wouldn't be in a van. They'd be mingling with the hikers and runners."

"Then who is it?"

"Maybe this is the clue we're looking for."

"You think so?"

"Can you see a face?"

Just as they all strained forward, the sun decided to take its swim in the Pacific Ocean. And it dived from out of sight, leaving a splash of darkness in its wake.

"No. Can't make out any features."

The van, swathed in darkness, stalked the awkward teenager who was determined to get his running in, Eucalyptus Monster or no.

But the teenager was wary. The cow chip accident had slowed his pace, eroded his confidence.

Over to the side of the trail he tried to scrape the mess off his sneakers.

When he looked over his shoulder and saw the ghostly truck in the new dark, he quickly joined the older people walking back down the path.

He fell in beside them, cow chip still glued to the soles of his shoes, and the van lost interest.

It turned its yellow self around and grumbled away from Eucalyptus Forest and down the hill toward civilized Berkeley.

"Wonder what that van was doing up here?"

"Up to no good," said Meggie. "This calls for another trip."

"Next Friday," said April.

"Now we'd better hurry," said May, looking at her watch.

"Takes an hour to get home. We've got to make time. Else Mama'll beat us home and park herself by our beds, and we'll never get any sleep, sure as my name's May."

"Let's jog," said Meggie.

And they started running, like the deer who lived in the forest; but the deer bending over Eucalyptus Lake looked at the teenagers out of the corners of their velvet eyes and wondered at the young folks looking a little like trees and shrubs moving so resolutely down the hill, going into the town the deer visited more and more to get away from the evil that the lake had warned them about.

FOURTEEN

Thursday appeared bringing a mixed California cast of weather.

From her window Meggie watched the dance of lightning on Inspiration Mountain.

A configuration of white sticks clashing.

Far off a rumble smothered a smokeless smoky sky.

A white leap of lightning overhead. White hot to the eyes.

A long-legged acrobat strutted, hissing between sky and earth.

How lightning danced.

The hide-and-seek show changed everything to shadow; lightning, jealous of the light, left the red-leafed trees looking like a negative on a photograph.

The dancing line would not be orderly. It stretched every which way multiplying into more white sticks.

Magnifying in numbers, it zipped from cloud to cloud and talked back like a woman with her hands on her hips.

The threatening storm backed off. Then suddenly in patches the sun was trying to shine. At the same time thunder roared, lightning drew her long legs back up into a white cloud. A violent but quick earthquake shook the bedroom, causing the crystals in Meggie's window to jump and chatter against the pane, spiritual bones talking.

"Is that old devil beating his wife again?" Memory Alexander asked at breakfast.

"No, I think God must be knocking the devil in the head," said Meggie. The thunder sounded like a boxing match, and she imagined Satan hitting the canvas again and again.

As soon as Meggie pronounced this possibility the sky cleared and the sun stayed out.

That evening Meggie, head down, walked home from school late thinking about one of the lines in Reverend Marvella's last sermon: "The devil's only doing his duty. And his duty is evil."

She was trying to entwine this line into the murders. So engrossed was she in thinking about the devil and evil and Eucalyptus Forest that she almost missed seeing the envelope stuck crooked, lopsided in the mailbox.

Wonder why Mama and Daddy didn't bring in the mail.

But when she took the envelope out of the box she noticed the letter had no stamp. Her name was typed in slate gray on its face, and there was no address under the inscription.

Who, Meggie wondered, her curiosity piqued, had personally delivered it?

A ghostly pair of frostbitten hands touched her shoulder.

She shivered.

Inside the house, she put down her books, opened the envelope and read the message from April.

Immediately she picked up the phone to call the Spring house, but nobody answered. Next she dialed Matthew's number.

"Matthew, can you stop over for a minute?"

She hung up the phone, her curious fingers turned the card this way and that way in her hand.

She jumped when the doorbell pierced her wondering thoughts.

"I'll get it!" Meggie hollered to her parents who were in the back of the house.

Matthew read the typed message out loud. "Female teenager and her guest needed for a moonlight hike in Eucalyptus Forest. All other openings are presently filled.

"Your name was selected to fill the only vacancy.

"The group will meet at Inspiration Point at the mile-and-a-half mark on Thursday at seven p.m. sharp."

At the bottom in the right corner was inscribed, "Police surveillance provided for your security."

"Thursday. That's today!"

"It's from April, with a little asterisk saying 'for girls only.'

"Females only, my eye!" said Matthew. "I'm going too. Always did want to be the only male around a bunch of women. Besides, a man might come in handy."

"It's comforting to see the police will be around; probably so many cops up there you can't move without falling over one of them," Meggie said matter-of-factly.

"It wouldn't hurt to give April a call anyway just to check," said Matthew.

"I tried. She's gone already."

She looked at the clock. "We've got to go if we want to make it there on time."

"Right."

"But wait," she hurried into her bedroom and shut up Redwood inside; they wouldn't need him for the group.

"Matthew and I are going to see the Springs!" she yelled to the back of the house.

"Fine, Meg," her father answered.

Meggie, taking Matthew's hand, was excited about the possibility of maybe discovering some more clues on this hiking adventure under the protection of the police and Matthew.

They started out. Here we go, just like undercover agents, Meggie thought to herself.

FIFTEEN

Up in Eucalyptus Forest at the mile-and-a-half mark, the full moon cast a crippled shadow over everything.

There was no April. No gang of hiking girls. And no police. A chill darted through Meggie's body.

The dense manzanita bushes nodded, urn-shaped blossoms bowed down in dust.

The crooked branches yielded brown fruit that sagged on the bush, almost dead from thirst.

The crash of the old oak tree on the lonely knoll a little distance from Meggie and Matthew sent a flock of sparrows chattering and fussing in flight from its toppling branches.

The thunderclap made Meggie and Matthew cover their ears.

Their nostrils flared at the reek of sulfur in the air.

Leaves, a blood-clotted hue in the autumn foliage of the white oak, trembled, still clinging to the tree's uprooted upside-down head.

Dizzy birds picked at the red berries of the fire thorns. The fruit from the pyracantha caused them to careen drunkenly until they heard a sound not too unlike the rumbling earthquake that troubled the oak tree.

The wind turned into thin black leather strips, whipped around, and almost knocked the birds from the branches.

Both Meggie and Matthew turned to run, but midstride they stopped in their tracks. Before they could see it, they heard the van.

And then it was there.

SIXTEEN

"What do you want?" trembled Meggie when she saw the two burly men in the van stick their heads out the windows, rabbit teeth jutting down over their bottom lips.

Out of the corner of her eye she saw the nightmare wings of two vultures.

The vampire birds dug their talons into the scabby skin of the eucalyptus trees and hovered hunchbacked above the spot where the van stopped.

What did the vultures know?

"What do you want?" echoed Matthew, knowing often men didn't pay any attention to a woman's words, at least this type of man, he thought, sizing them up. If these buzzards bit you, they'd give you rabies, he guessed.

Bloodsucking bats knocked blindly against the hood of the van.

The two brutes with tobacco-stained teeth did not answer.

Twins.

They leaned out of the van, hairy apelike elbows jutting out of the window. Massive bodies of monstrous proportions, jaws like hogs, Meggie saw that much. Hands, calloused and cracked. Just looking at them gave Meggie the gnawing urge to run and run and run and never stop.

The vapid faces in the van gave the boy and girl the once over, seeming to say these here are the ones we're looking for all right.

Their grimaces and grins suggested two horned devils who would grimace when most other people would grin and vice versa. Meggie imagined their looks mirrored the expressions you might see on folks who suffered from cankers festering on their inflamed brains.

One had a spasm in his face that twisted his grotesque features in such a way they shut the door on any thoughts of the man's humanity.

"What do you want?" repeated Meggie. Still they did not answer.

The other twin growled raucously, sizing up Meggie.

Matthew's muscles popped up, bulging his shirtsleeves out. He'd kill if he had to.

My mama said she knows ten ways to kill, thought Meggie; I should have asked her to show me a few.

The two men descended from the truck and advanced.

One swaggering twin swung a tree stump, back and forth, effortlessly.

The one with a twitching face brandished a needle and leaned back against the van, patient.

Matthew swung at the man who wielded the tree stump, knocking him off balance, but the massive monster bounced back up as though only a mosquito had startled him.

Next Matthew pulled his leg back and with all his force lashed out kicking. His foot connected with all the brutality the evil-grinning men brought out in him.

The tree-stump-swinging man spoke not a word. Then the tree stump swished up through the air and whacked down, almost pulverizing Matthew's flesh, in a language all its own, the articulate language of pain.

Meggie, barehanded, adrenaline pumping, tore into the attacker, her fist flying. She pummeled him, raining blows on his head, his neck, his back.

But he shrugged her off and she slammed to the ground.

Pain hiccuped.

Her ribs ached until she thought if she breathed she'd pass out. But the pain laid low—it was so frightened—and as she jumped back up, so did Matthew.

Matthew lunged first.

The ghastly pale assailant lifted the club again.

Then the club, with a resounding *whack*, knocked Matthew out cold at Meggie's feet.

Meggie grabbed a rock off the trail, still hiccuping.

It flew from her hand as deftly as David's stone hurled at Goliath.

It hit the popped-out eye of her assailant, and the man with the tree stump howled, clutching at the pain stabbing lightning from the socket to the back of his brain.

But the other twin, who had been standing back whistling, waiting his turn, suddenly sprinted into action. He grabbed Meggie. And it was like trying to hold on to lightning.

All legs and movement.

She was too busy to scream.

Finally he wrestled her to the ground.

The ugly hypodermic needle punctured her trembling brown skin powdered with dirt.

And the goon grinned.

The twins tossed Meggie and Matthew's unconscious bodies in the back of the van and covered them with tarpaulin.

"The silent treatment carries its own terror, don't it?" said the twin nursing his eye.

"At least this time you was careful. Last time you used that tree stump you knocked that other one's head plumb off before we could get him away. Good thing the doc didn't know about that."

"Don't you tell."

"I ain't tellin'."

Next thing Meggie knew she was waking up surrounded by colorless white—cold white walls, stiff white sheets covering her body. She looked down at herself still clothed but wrapped in an antiseptic white hospital gown.

"We've been rescued," she said to herself. "The police finally got there. We're safe in a hospital."

Out loud she said, "But where?"

Nobody answered.

Wait a minute. There was no cord to call the nurse with. And why would she still have her clothes on?

Something was funny here.

All she could hear was the ticking of the clock.

She couldn't think.

Be calm.

How?

She imagined a blue shawl of warmth and the sound of her mahogany guitar. Braiding strands of invisible light she picked the bronze string, playing the air guitar in her head.

The music tingled. Soft. Softer.

The clouds in her head started disappearing. The blue shawl of light.

In a subdued voice the chords whispered.

She knew it was first light by the way the pale strands of sun reached through the window. By the way the sun's small fire played in the sky, it had to be just daybreak.

"Daybreak!" Her folks wouldn't even have missed her. They'd think she'd come in late and was still asleep.

She heard a low groan.

She moved her head painfully in the direction of the sound. Her head ached so piercingly it felt as though a rifleman was shooting, using her brain for target practice, reloading and backing up and starting all over again.

Matthew! That was Matthew in the bed across from her. He must have a headache too.

Now everything was becoming clearer. Of course he had a headache.

Those men, those men up in Eucalyptus Forest, those men up by Inspiration Point in the yellow van had slammed Matthew with a tree stump, picked up the weapon as though it were a toothpick and slammed Matthew on the side of the head.

She studied him. Matthew's head looked like a thousand yellow jackets had stung him. One of his eyes was closed and he groaned in pain even down in the false sleep the needle must have given him.

She jerked, trying to jump up and go to him.

Then she discovered she couldn't move.

She was buckled to the bed.

This was no ordinary hospital.

She opened her mouth to scream and then realized the advantage of being still and quiet, of pretending to be under the spell of the drug from the needle that had robbed her of consciousness yesterday evening.

She was glad she had locked Redwood in his room.

He would have ripped those rough men's throats open or died trying. If Redwood had mangled the men, she and Matthew would have missed this "hospital" connection to the murders. If the men had silenced Redwood she would have lost her faithful dog.

And they planned to kill her and Matthew, she realized. Like they killed the boy the police had found and wouldn't say what happened to him. Wouldn't reveal which part of his body was missing.

She gasped; she knew then what had happened to Alton; the one with the tree stump had knocked his head clean off.

Matthew was out of it. Too much pain, she could tell from the texture of the groans.

Her brain started working, slowly, like a machine that had rusted from nonuse.

I'm in a room, she thought, I'm in a bed in a room, I'm imprisoned in a bed in a room, I'm chained and imprisoned in a bed in a room. What to do beyond waiting to be killed?

"Meggie," Matthew groaned. "Oh, Meggie."

"I'm here," she said, turning her aching head with effort. The headache was blinding. The hospital buzzing fluorescent light turned the pain a sickly green.

But Matthew's groans came from his deep false sleep. He didn't even hear her answer.

"Meggie," Matthew groaned. Matthew hadn't been kidding her then when he told her he dreamed about her every night.

Voices floated to her.

Not Matthew's this time; other voices. Not the horrid men's either.

As the voices drew nearer, she realized they were coming to this room. She shut her eyes tight, too tight, then made herself relax the lids so they looked more natural. Like natural sleep. But this sleep had been most unnatural, she remembered.

The two voices floated over her bed.

"Turns out the old men were right. Fine physical specimens we have here. That girl with the mark in the middle of her forehead is a real find. We'll make the change quickly."

"At what time?" the other voice asked.

"Well, we've got to get the old men over here. Prepped and ready."

"Can have them here inside an hour or so; they're home on alert waiting, they don't go any place."

The other person must have nodded. He said, "Two girls and one boy for three old men. Interesting combination. But these young organs, we've got to get them pumping, pounding at their height. Two ways to do that: exercise and fright. We'll use fright. That one over there with the bump on his head won't be exercising before it's time if we don't help him back to consciousness. Give him a shot, he ought to come around; then the fright testing can begin. Scare the heebie-jeebies out of them. Got to be careful though; too much for that last boy, he died of fright and his body part wasn't any good."

"That organ fairly stuttered. Couldn't use it after the donor died of fright. It wouldn't work right."

"You make me sick. Always repeating the words I've said. I'm the one with the master plan. I'm the one checking blood types and organ sizes by rifling the hospital records of these kids to match the old men's needs."

Meggie could almost hear the other one shrug.

SEVENTEEN

Finally the doctor and his assistant left. And Meggie unglued her eyes and looked out the window. Judging from the strength of the sunbeams now, it was about six thirty in the morning.

"Matthew!" Meggie whispered.

She heard him stir. The shot they gave him was bringing him around.

"Meggie?" This time the voice was more clear, as though he was just groggy.

"Matthew, they've got us in a room. We're being held here for some kind of organ exchange for old people. They're going to frighten us almost to death and do it."

"Do what?" Matthew asked in a muddled tone.

"Matthew, get a grip on your mind!" she whispered fiercely.

"What, Meggie?"

"Matthew, we're in a . . ." how could she describe where they were? ". . . in a hospital-prison, we were captured by two rough men last night, drugged with a shot, and brought here so this doctor could take one of our organs."

"Which organ?" said Matthew coming to life, and thinking of the organ that all sixteen-year-old boys were shyly conscious of.

"Not that one," said Meggie quietly. "They want something I've got too. And I don't have one of those."

She wanted to giggle, but her fright scared the giggle away.

"Then what. . . ?" She could see Matthew try to pull himself up on one elbow and find out it was impossible.

"What the dickens?"

"Yeah," said Meggie in sympathy.

She wanted to tell him about the knot the size of a goose egg on his head but decided that wouldn't help matters.

"Meggie, I'll protect you," said Matthew in a stronger voice.

"We'll protect each other," she repeated as staunchly as she could.

Then she stiffened.

Voices outside the door.

"Here they come," she said.

EIGHTEEN

The two rough-moving twins wheeled Matthew and Meggie, still strapped to their hospital beds, down a long winding corridor that seemed to continue forever through a series of swinging doors.

The farther they went the lower the temperature kept dipping. With clumsy precision the twins bumped their beds into the walls that tunneled them through the labyrinth.

Finally they came to the last white room. Meggie's teeth chattered when the twins parked the bed.

The room here, chillier than the corridors, was as cold as January.

"Wanna bet on what scares these?" the twitchy-faced twin said to his brother.

The brother got all up in Matthew's and Meggie's faces. "Gonna be hard to predict just what these little niggers will git upset about. Never know about a nigger."

"Dunno, maybe the snakes. Worked on that other gal." Twitchy jerked his head toward the corner.

In the corner strapped in a bed just like Matthew's and Meggie's, a girl who fit the description of the missing Rita Gonzalez moaned. Terror had made a home in her dark eyes.

"I dunno. I dunno 'bout these here new pimple-faced patients."

"Let's see what happens with this little carpenter boy."

"I seen him before. That's right. Always helpin' his daddy so nice?"

"That's him."

They turned Matthew's head toward a screen. Images of snakes did not move him. Pictures of the tigers and wasps didn't take his breath away either. It was something totally commonplace and ordinary. Bees.

"Ayuh. We have it. It's bees. Who woulda thought? A Berkeley High Yellow Jacket scared of bees!"

"That'll be easy," said the doctor, entering. "Now for the girl."

They showed the same writhing snakes, the angry bees, and the threatening tigers. She watched, fascinated. When they showed her a family of crawling spiders, her face showed a higher degree of agitation and her pulse increased.

"I think we got it. Spiders," said one twin.

"Spiders."

"It figures. Girls don't like spiders. How do that nursery rhyme go? 'Little Miss Muffet sat on her tuffet eatin' her curds and whey, 'long came a spider and sat down beside her and frightened Miss Muffet away.'"

"Now that we got the instruments of terror, Miss Muffet, we be ready."

"Only a few hours before surgery," the doctor decided. "Go get the trio of recipients," he directed the twins.

"Oh, Miss Muffet," said the one on the left, "I wish we could be here to see you on your tuffet, all frightened."

"Come on, quit looking at her like that. She done *zung* you in the eye once. I'm scared a her."

"She tied up, ain't you Miss Muffet?"

"Didn't I tell you to go get the recipients?" said the doctor. "Now scat!"

After the twin faces of evil left, the doctor stood writing in his chart.

Meggie thought she'd ask what the plan was.

"Why have you brought us here?" she asked.

"Curious?"

"Just thought I'd ask."

"Seems you're going to be part of a little experiment."

"What experiment?"

"Heart transplants."

"Heart?"

She could hear Matthew let out a sigh of relief, even though they both knew that without a heart the rest of the body parts you kept wouldn't matter.

"Why not do it the regular way, in a regular hospital, waiting for a donor to die?" asked Matthew.

"Oh, I've done that, but this is more experimental. You see, I have a theory. It has three parts to it. First of all, I believe a young heart at its prime is better than an older one that's been used too long or a younger one that's not quite developed. And so I chose to experiment with teenagers.

"Secondly, I think the time between death of the donor and the removal of the heart has to be minimized. In other words, the patient dies one minute and the heart is removed the next.

"Thirdly, I think the heart ought to be thoroughly exercised, primed, if you will, near the moment of death. It should be beating its strongest. Therefore we will instill fear in you until the heart is pumping quite rapidly."

"Oh, I see," said Meggie weakly as the doctor moved with his chart over to Matthew's bed.

Finally finished he turned and left the room. "They tried with Regan Russell," said the girl still gripped in her vices of terror, her voice strained.

"Are you Rita Gonzalez?" asked Matthew.

"Yes."

"They're looking for you all over Berkeley."

She cried, "They'll never find me!"

Soon Rita's cry turned into a scream. The scream into a waking nightmare.

NINETEEN

"I had this dream, this nightmare, rather," said Memory Alexander. A fragile glass shard of held-back hysteria chipped at her voice.

What Michael Alexander heard was this hysteria.

Also, it was not Memory's words he was listening to so much as what she didn't say.

Dressed in his plaid pajamas, Michael Alexander hopped out of bed, pulled on his velvet red robe, then checked Meggie's room.

She wasn't there.

Because frequently she did not make her bed, he couldn't tell if it had been slept in or not, but Redwood whining on the floor tugging at the crazy-patch quilt with only Jehoshaphat under it did not make him feel more at ease.

If she had gone walking or running this morning she would have taken Redwood with her.

Then a cold certainty struck him.

This had something to do with the murdered teenagers. He rushed to the kitchen; last night's dinner had not been put away and Meggie's lemon-and-raspberry chiffon pie sat where Memory had left it on the table, untouched in its saucer from last evening.

Memory, scarlet-robed and wearing green high-heeled slippers, looked, fixed in one spot, out the living room window. She said,

"The nightmare started with the yellow wildflowers growing in the Rhinehart yard. And then I saw this image of Meggie, but she wasn't there. 'Course Meggie's fine," said Memory, refusing to even look in Meggie's bedroom.

Redwood came into the living room and complained in that canine something's-wrong whine.

Memory peered across the street at the Rhinehart house.

Uh-oh, thought Michael Alexander, she's out there on a limb of hysteria and sounding perfectly calm. And wearing those high-heeled slippers. A gift from one of her women friends. Something she would never ordinarily do, having once said, "A woman should only wear high-heeled shoes as weapons."

"Why, it just can't be!" Memory exclaimed.

"What?" asked Michael Alexander.

"Those flowers over in the Rhinehart yard. Those flowers only bloom on rocky terrain, I tell you. Chaparral land."

"What's that? What flowers?" asked Michael Alexander.

"Thought I saw something shine on some golden eardrops across the street at the men's house."

Michael Alexander followed his wife's gaze. "Something light over there all right."

When Michael Alexander looked at Memory he realized that subconsciously she knew that something was wrong with Meggie. She was trying to push it to another place in her mind where she could effectively deal with it.

And so she focused on the strange flowers in the Rhinehart yard.

"Golden eardrops definitely aren't supposed to have that silvery light. I'd better investigate," she said.

Memory walked across Vine Street, still in her robe, another thing she would never think about doing when her mind was clear, to get a closer look at the golden eardrops and to see what was making them shine so.

"Why," said Memory in the Rhinehart garden, "it's golden eardrops all right. So rare in these parts. And the silver is the silver of a spiderweb. What delicate tracery!"

Inside the Rhinehart house Spellman stood at the window looking out.

The telephone rang.

"What!? Yes, we're ready," said Rhinehart. "Five minutes!"

"Uh-oh," whispered Spellman when he discovered the silver-haired Mrs. Alexander under the window. "We have company. We've been found out," he said in a squeaky half-voice etched with heightened alarm.

His whisper was so low and the excitement before them so fruitful nobody paid attention to Spellman. Boone and Rhinehart busied themselves putting on jackets, laughing at the prospect of stealing a march on time.

"Well, Boone, I think that plaid jacket suits you well, old boy," Rhinehart offered, generous in his hypocritical complimenting of "Balloon Boone," the nickname he called the plump man in private.

At the window Spellman whispered, frozen in time.

While Mrs. Alexander stood in front of the Rhinehart house staring at the flowers, Michael Alexander took the opportunity to make some phone calls. First he called the Spring family and discovered from April that they all had gone up to Eucalyptus Forest last week in search of the killers and kidnappers of the teenagers.

"Wait," April said, frightened, "let me remember everything. We were supposed to go back tomorrow."

She listened to what Michael Alexander asked her, then answered.

"The only strange thing we saw last Friday was a yellow van.

"No, sir. It was inside of Inspiration Point where no motor vehicles are allowed.

"The strangest thing about it is this: it was after five. The Park Service wouldn't send a van up there then. And it seemed to be following this kid in a gray gym suit until he panicked and joined some older people taking their daily exercise."

Across the street Memory Alexander said, "I'd like to ask them how they got these golden eardrops to grow like this."

She rang the old men's doorbell.

Rhinehart said to the door, not seeing who was on the other side, "We're coming! We're coming! The van's here," he hollered to Spellman and Boone. "Going to get our hearts!"

Memory Alexander jumped at the rush in the old man's voice. So early in the morning—

Then she heard a roar behind her.

She saw a yellow flash.

"What's the Park Service van doing down here?" she asked the air.

Back across the street Michael Alexander looked out the window and his heart pounded. The van, that's the van April mentioned.

He called across the street to his wife.

"Memory, darling, we have a phone call!" And he succeeded in keeping the panic out of his own voice.

"Well, now," said Memory turning like a sleepwalker away from the door, "who can it be?"

When she got on their side of the street, Michael Alexander ordered, "Get in the car!"

Redwood dashed into the Volkswagen hatchback too.

"Why, Michael, the phone!" said Memory.

"The kids, the yellow van has taken them someplace, and we're going to follow them. Meggie's not here. She's been taken someplace by these people."

Stealthily the Alexander Volkswagen backed out of the driveway and followed the van.

The three old men bounced in the yellow van's backseat, tipsy and light-headed with expectation. They continued their joking in the speeding van for the duration of the short ride.

Spellman thought, I'm so happy, I'm hallucinating.

When Rhinehart opened the front door, he thought, it was only the driver of the yellow van standing there waiting to whisk us away. And the Alexander woman he thought he had seen—and that he feared had come to point her finger at them and keep them from their youth—was nowhere to be seen.

All in my mind, he thought.

TWENTY

"All in my mind," Meggie whispered. "This can't be happening."

Rita Gonzalez screamed.

She screamed until she didn't have much voice left.

Three glass cubicles took up most of the space in the entire hospital-prison room, except for an aisle at the end of all the cubicles and a small walkway between each cubicle.

Each of the three captives—Rita, Matthew, and Meggie—lay strapped to their beds in each cubicle. Rita was screaming third in the row. Matthew was listening to a low hum second in the row and Meggie was hiccuping first in the row.

The snake, evidently, had been hiding under Rita's bed. Now it unwrapped itself from the iron bedpost.

Matthew and Meggie wanted to cover their horrified ears while Rita Gonzalez screamed weakly, but they couldn't. Just as they couldn't turn their eyes away from the terror.

The snake now slithered coldly over Rita's neck, then sat coiled atop her head.

And Rita screamed hoarsely.

Overhead in Matthew's cubicle a collection of bumblebees buzzed madly in a round straw basket. The basket, hoisted high above his head, had a pulley of two strings hanging down from it.

Above Meggie another similar basket was hoisted, but no sound emanated from her straw hamper.

Meggie whispered, "It's hard to think, Matthew."

"I know, but we've got to do something."

They saw the back of a nurse's head; she stood outside the door, listening before entering.

"Nurse! Nurse!" called Meggie.

The nurse, her cap peaked like a Ku Klux Klan woman's white dunce cap, looked in the window cut into the door. Her red eyes aglare, as though she'd just come off a three-day drunk.

"Nurse, I've got to use the bathroom something horrible," Meggie hollered.

"Who cares?" said the nurse entering. "At seven thirty you get the spiders. You're next, Sweetheart. I can't wait to hear you scream."

Meggie and Matthew both looked at the clock on the wall. It glowed 7:15.

"I'll make you a bet," said Meggie.

"A bet?" said the nurse.

Matthew groaned with dismay when the nurse turned sideways and he saw the pistol in the holster strapped around the waist of her uniform.

The nurse continued, "You're in no position to bargain, my pet."

"Still," Meggie tried, "how about it? If I don't scream, will you let me up to use the bathroom?"

The nurse's eyes smoked over, shifted, then she thought, what the hell? When they forgot to let the patients use the bathroom beforehand she was the one who had to clean them up before surgery so the doctor wouldn't smell the mess they made. Might as well save herself the trouble, but not screaming she knew was impossible; when she let the spiders down on this one, this one would scream as loud as the girl with the snake and she'd have plenty to clean up, if she hadn't already gone to the toilet.

Way she figured it, she didn't have anything to lose.

If the girl didn't scream, the nurse wouldn't have to clean her up.

If the girl did scream, which she would, nothing changed from the way it would have been if the girl didn't ask.

"Sure, why not? But I know you'll scream. You haven't seen spiders like the spiders we've got for you."

And the nurse, looking at the glint in Meggie's eyes, thought of terror.

The nurse laughed raucously as she looked at the clock and teased the girl, getting ready to release the crawling spiders.

"What have we here?" asked the nurse, jiggling the string holding the basket of spiders hoisted over Meggie's head.

"But first you have to unbuckle me," said Meggie.

"If I don't scream, you're not going to come in here with these spiders and unbuckle me, are you?"

"Got that right, kid. I'm not coming into anybody's spider cage. Okay? I'm coming in there to unbuckle you now, but don't try anything smart. I got a pistol right here. And I know how to use it. Already used it, in fact, on that first black boy we got for one of the three old men—he got too violent. Had to kill him before the doctor was ready. Messed up the timing. Doctor couldn't use him."

"Billy Watson," Meggie gasped.

The nurse, paying what Meggie said no mind, went into the glass cage and carefully unbuckled the girl.

True to her promise Meggie did not move. "That's a good girl," said the nurse, backing out of the glass room.

"Here we go," said the nurse.

Grabbing the string that she controlled outside the cage, the nurse slowly lowered the basket of three hundred tarantulas down from the ceiling.

The basket now sat on Meggie's belly.

"Now!" proclaimed the nurse.

She yanked another string and the straw hamper opened.

Three hundred tarantulas creeped out across the white sheets, crawled in and under the folds of white linen and onto Meggie.

"Ugly!" shivered the nurse as she watched the writhing mass, her face all screwed up, corners of her mouth turned down.

But the spiders smelled no fear. Meggie started giggling.

"This one's gone mad," said the nurse, taking a Camel out of her pocket.

She tapped the cigarette with one long, red-speckled fingernail, lit it, then drew deeply on it as she watched the show.

The spiders swarmed all over the bed, touched Meggie, then explored the floor, the glass walls.

Soon Meggie stopped giggling when the spiders stopped tickling her.

And she called to the nurse.

"I'm coming out to go to the bathroom now."

The nurse almost swallowed her cigarette she was so amazed to watch the girl stand up. By now the spiders had left this donor alone.

Meggie walked to the glass door, opened it, and started to the bathroom.

The nurse took out her gun. "This one must be queer in the head," she said out loud, talking to the ceiling. But it wasn't the girl's head they needed, and they needed the girl alive.

When Meggie passed the nurse she gave Matthew a conspiratorial look.

On cue Matthew started talking to the nurse, who held her gun pointed toward the bathroom.

"Do you like spiders, Nurse?"

"Can't stand them," she said in a perplexed voice, thinking about Meggie's reaction to the critters. "Why'd they leave her alone? Why didn't she scream?"

"Well, I'll tell you a secret," said Matthew.

"What's that?" said the nurse, all jumpy.

He started telling her about the spiders up in Eucalyptus Forest who had a People contest. The prize, said the king spider, would go to the person judged most scared stupid of spiders.

"When you're scared stupid you can't even scream," said Matthew.

This relaxed the nurse some and she turned around to face Matthew and to hear the rest of the story.

"Meggie turned out the winner," he said.

"How?" asked the nurse.

His story was so elaborate Rita Gonzalez almost forgot about the snake, but she couldn't; she screamed in a chilly, raspy, almost inaudible voice. She went on screaming even when she saw Meggie creep out of the bathroom brandishing a heavy metal pole taken off an IV apparatus.

Meggie lifted the metal weapon and came down hard, whacking the nurse soundly upside the head, and the nurse slumped over and crumpled to the floor with her mouth open, her drooling spit sputtering out the ember of the Camel cigarette.

"Meggie, Meggie, you've done it!" said Matthew. Rita wanted to cheer, but she managed to say, between screams, "I hear somebody coming!"

Meggie unbuckled Matthew and the two of them dragged the nurse under the bed.

Then Meggie and Matthew ran back into their glass cages and lay the buckles so they would appear locked.

Meggie screamed. She screamed as loud as she could.

The two-ton twins looked through the little glass window. "Yeah, it's working. One's screamed herself out, another one's screaming, Little Miss Muffet, and one screamer left to go. We're going to put bees down your pants, boy! Ha, ha, ha! Thirteen more minutes."

Then they were gone again.

Meggie and Matthew hopped out of their beds and released Rita, careful of the snake that had now slid back onto the bed railing and lay entwined there like the snake symbol of the medical profession.

Meggie took the nurse's weapon and she and Matthew put the nurse in the spider bed and buckled her down good.

Meggie and Matthew opened the window, then each took hold of Rita.

When they dropped to the ground the nurse came to and continued the sound of screaming.

She screeched in an ear-piercing voice, shriller and higher than Meggie's feigned hollering.

The spiders smelled fear this time. And they bit the nurse in her scalp, in her eyes, on her legs; got under her white uniform and bit her stomach, her hips, and one sat nibbling on her ear.

TWENTY-ONE

The nurse's loud squalls still ringing in their ears, Meggie, Matthew, and Rita slid down the outside wall.

One of the first things they noticed was the yellow van parked under a warped-limbed elm.

There were so many crouching trees secluding the place that it was hard to tell just where they were.

The three crept low beneath the stiff-leaved loquat trees, smelling the white flowers of the tree, too sweet, the decay breath of death.

"Where are we?" asked Meggie.

"I don't know," said Matthew.

"Anything look familiar to you?" Meggie asked Rita.

"No," said Rita in her whisper.

"Did the snake . . . ?"

"It didn't bite me. It didn't bite me. All the time I was expecting it to, but it didn't."

"When we were taking you out of there I got a good look at it. It looked different. Come to think of it, I don't think it could've bitten you," said Meggie.

"Defanged," Matthew decided. "It couldn't bite."

"I already spent myself as though it could," said Rita.

"We know what you mean. It's all right," answered Meggie as she gave Rita a pat on the shoulder.

Their surroundings looked familiar, yet unfamiliar. And the ride from Eucalyptus Forest had not been but a few minutes. Ten minutes at the most. Five miles from Eucalyptus maybe.

Meggie's and Matthew's muscles were so well toned, they could run ten miles. But what about Rita? She wasn't up to much.

"Where the heck are we?" asked Meggie again.

"We'd better hurry up. Just go, no matter what direction. First we'll climb the fence," she decided.

A high wrought-iron black rusty fence peaked in sharp angry stakes. In places they could see a thin wire twining its way around the metal barrier.

"Uh-oh," said Matthew. "Electrical wires."

"We'd be fried to a frizzle from here to Fresno if we even touched that fence."

Rita sagged as though she couldn't take another step. All spent up.

"Don't worry, don't panic," said Meggie, trying to think.

A sharp alarm disturbed the air.

Any moment the crew would be upon them. The alarm sent them scurrying for cover between several scratchy, spiked yucca plants.

The whine escalated, then another sound joined it: fierce barking, the staccato language of a dog.

"Redwood!" said Meggie.

"Let's go!" said Matthew.

But Rita wouldn't budge. "I can't move," she said.

"Stay here. We'll come back," said Meggie, and they left the nurse's gun with Rita so she might protect herself.

Meggie and Matthew headed back to the center of their fear, back to the hospital-prison they'd just escaped.

Meggie stood on Matthew's shoulders and jacked up the window. She shimmied in first and he climbed after.

The nurse lay still sprawled in the bed, and no one had rescued her from the spiders. She looked dead.

Cautiously they opened the door to the hallway. Looked both ways, couldn't remember at first which way the twins had wheeled them in.

They started running toward the sound of Redwood's barking.

Running into dead ends where the barks echoed too faintly.

Turning, then running the other way.

Finally they heard voices and a more vocal Redwood.

"Why, whatever do you mean?" the doctor was saying.

"We think you have our children here," said Michael Alexander.

"Children? This is a geriatrics hospital!"

In the sitting room older people sat, the arthritic, the lame, the senile. Some with canes, others in wheelchairs.

"Why's that alarm ringing?" asked Memory Alexander, dangerous anger that she had pent up inside getting ready to cut loose.

"What's going on here?" she demanded.

Michael Alexander gave the room the army stare, fixing everything in its place, aware of everything that moved. He spotted Spellman. Rhinehart, ahead of him, was trying to sneak out the door, leading Spellman and Boone away.

"Spellman!" Michael Alexander commanded. Redwood whined and scratched at the door leading from the sitting room.

Memory Alexander followed the dog, Michael Alexander followed his wife, letting the two men go in favor of protecting his very own.

"Don't open that door!" shouted the doctor.

"I think I'd better," said Memory huffily.

And she slammed the door open so hard the knob knocked the doctor down.

She brought her high-heeled slipper down on his hand as she rushed to meet Meggie and Matthew flying down the corridor.

"Call the law. They're killing kids in here," shouted Meggie.

"They're stealing hearts!" exclaimed Matthew.

"Whoever heard of anything so ridiculous?" said the doctor, nursing his hand.

"They've been murdering teenagers in here!" said Meggie.

Relieved to see Meggie and Matthew safe, already Michael Alexander had picked up the phone and dialed 911.

"People've been murdered. . . . I don't know where we are, this place doesn't seem to have an address. But I'm keeping the line open until you get here. Just follow the telephone signal."

Now the two strong-arm twins appeared, flexing their muscles.

"Those are the men who kidnapped us and hurt us, Daddy," Meggie accused with a pointing finger.

Captain Michael Alexander moved quiet and deadly.

He grabbed one twin and bumped his thick head against the wall, knocking him cold.

Meggie and her mother tripped the doctor midstride as he ran toward the door.

"That'll teach you to mess with people's children!" said Memory as she kicked the doctor in the groin with those high-heeled slippers.

Matthew punched the second twin and drew back to wallop him again just as the goon snatched Meggie back, eliminating the chance of Matthew getting in another hit.

The goon said, "Hold it, Mack, I got your girl. I'll bash her brains open."

At the same time the doctor jumped up and grabbed Memory just as the captain came to help his wife.

Memory's heart raced as the doctor pressed a scalpel to her throat telling Michael Alexander, "Come any closer and I'll use it."

Matthew and Michael were as helpless as babes when they realized the danger that Meggie and Memory faced. They had no control over what would happen next.

Then suddenly out of the tense silence, the scream of ten police cars whining around the corner unnerved the doctor and the goon, and they decided to get away before the police arrived. The cowards didn't get through the door before Matthew and Michael collared them.

Tension released, Meggie breathed easier when the officers walked through the entrance.

And even Memory, whose heart had been racing faster and faster, managed to breathe a sigh of relief.

Meggie and Matthew led two officers around the side of the building to rescue Rita, the missing teenager, crouched between the yucca plants, clutching the gun.

"Rita, it's us. Rita."

Rita told her story, then fainted.

"Call for an ambulance," one officer told the other. Next the police saw the room of glass cubicles, the dead nurse, the snake, the spiders, and the swarming basket of bees.

"Whew!" said the officer in charge. "They weren't playing at all."

When Meggie began to explain who the hearts were for, the officer said, "Well, it will all come under investigation. Of course we can't accuse the patients of any wrongdoings, but the doctor and his staff will be arrested right this minute."

The ambulance finally came for Rita. It took her to Herrick, a real hospital, for treatment and observation.

Meggie and Matthew climbed into the backseat of the Volkswagen, with Redwood between them.

When they pulled up to the Alexander house, a welcoming committee of April, May, Mark, and Luke greeted them from the front steps.

"We got our forest back. We got back the Eucalyptus Forest," Meggie announced triumphantly, giving the victory sign with Matthew.

Too worn out to celebrate, Meggie announced, "Let's meet tomorrow. I'm going straight to bed."

EPILOGUE

Meggie went straight to bed and dreamed she walked around unencumbered up in the forest, that she played her guitar 'til the spiders crawled from under their stumps, unstrung their calligraphy webs hanging between the bushes, and crept out of their tangled tracery under the pine trees.

When they were all assembled they swayed in six-eight rhythm, rolling six of their eight eyes and stomping their eight feet, until she set the guitar aside.

Then she stood between two pine trees.

Between one dedicated to U Thant and the other to Ralph Bunche. The spiders gathered in a circle around her.

"Confronted with so much evil in that hospital I didn't think I'd ever be warm again," she said to the congregation of spiders.

Glaciers in her breath. She shivered.

Noon.

"Keep a light in your heart," Reverend Marvella had repeated in a recent sermon.

Noon. High light.

When Meggie thought of what God's forest meant to her, she thought of cedar, for cedar means the promise of life.

She placed cedar twigs around the circle.

Meggie braided cedar into her thick-locked hair.

Then, taking her sharp-bladed ax, she began to chop wood from the cedar.

She raised the ax and it fell on the wood, scoring it with a whack. *She broke the doctor of evil's neck. Sliced it in two.*

The sun warmed her and brought out the good sweat.

She raised the talking ax again. Armpits soaked with salt water. Sweat and splinters flew.

Spellman's wood flew out of the bark from the tree branch, looking like a neck with broken vocal cords.

She lifted the ax high and crashed it down again and again. *A wood-knot looking like a cold Boone eye mocked her. She shattered it and sent a thousand broken eyes skipping along the forest floor.*

Rhinehart. Rhinehart, she cracked open ears, split them like eardrums with the loudest whacks she could manage.

The promise of life. A sprig of cedar.

Joy like the sap of cedar leaped up in her limbs. She could see the noon light skipping through the trees.

The light in her heart. *Keep a light in your heart.*

Let not your heart be troubled; Meggie played the words in her head on an air guitar.

The noon sun helped her sweat away all the anger. When her spirit was quenched she turned her face toward the sun and chased away the shadows.

As the guitar song played in her head, Meggie made a covenant with herself.

She knelt down and, bowing her head, prayed to God.

The blue shawl of light waited.

On the translucent cloth, seven crystals sparkled. "Look closely at what the spindle spoke," a voice said.

She peered at the shawl. From every facet light winked.

And the joy made her eyes water.

"Put your hand on the crystal thread," the guitar melody called.

She touched a ray, a blue purple iris stood up inside her.

The hate and the hurt fell away like scales.

The guitar sang every song it promised it would.

And the crowd of spiders looked on and waited. Now she picked up the guitar, carefully placed the strap around her neck.

As she played the guitar the spiders responded. They moved with her down the hill, thousands and thousands of spiders following the sound of a mahogany guitar just blessed in the ceremony of cedar.

Without digressing she led them straight to the Rhinehart house and the guitar spoke its orders in rhapsody.

Meggie woke up hearing strange chord combinations juxtaposed on top and through each other. Eerie notes that together produced an unjangled sound.

A disturbed trouble made straight in the resolution of the melody.

She had slept 'til noon. She quickly dressed and reached for her guitar to re-create the sounds.

Cedar green sprigs. Cedar on the guitar.

The smell of cedar filled her room as she played, easily echoing the astonishing notes of her forest dream.

When she had the music just right, she looked up to see the familiar figure of Dennis Bell looking into the Rhinehart house and talking to himself. Loudly enough to hear him, but not loud enough to distinguish one word from the other.

She opened the door and heard him say, "There they are. There they are. The ones that done it. . . . The ones that killed Billy Watson. Uh-huh. Said they wanted a black heart. There they are. There they are. The ones that done it. . . ." Over and over again.

She crossed the street, wanting to know more.

When she stood by Dennis and looked in the window she saw the three men sprawled out on the living room floor.

At first she thought they were drunk, but seeing not even a snore stir the mustache on Rhinehart's face, she ran home and called the station.

The police called the pest-control man, and sure enough when he came to write his estimate he said that never in his life had he seen so many and so varied of the creatures under one roof. A web greeted him at the door, one brown scarred tarantula stood out from the rest.

Later on the pest-control man, stopped by Meggie's to say that when the police got there they found a hoard of spiders had inundated the Rhinehart house.

"That's what happens in a house when a woman's not around," one commented.

The pest-control man said that surrounding the mother tarantula were many spider babies.

He found spiders nestled in the coves and corners of the ceilings. Black widows clung to the undersides of mattresses and under the ottoman and couches and chairs.

He had given a handsome estimate for the job he expected to do.

"Such tiny, tiny things. How could they have killed three men?" asked Meggie as she hugged the dog, patted the cat.

"The coroner said," boasted the pest-control man, glad to be the, one spreading the news, "it looked like baby tarantulas and eggs were found inside the old fellows' brains, as though the spiders were looking for something soft. As though spiders had nested there and drove all three men insane just before they died from brain fever brought on by the infestation."

"Well," said Meggie, looking for a long minute at Redwood, "I don't believe a word of it. A spider wouldn't hurt a fly."

Redwood did not bark his usual "Amen."

He had been present sitting on a stump the noon of Meggie's dream.

Through the window Meggie watched the pest-control man drive off without accomplishing his mission because between the time he first saw them and when he returned to the Rhinehart house to spray his poisons he couldn't find spider one.

At last the first rain of the season started to fall.

Meggie watched a few drops of water turn to magenta rain, an illusion caused by a red light in the corner of the window.

In that corner of the glass panel a small baby tarantula with a lightning mark across her back tracked across Meggie's line of vision, then stopped and started weaving. Meggie leaned forward to get a closer look at it spreading a silver trail, remembering the last words she had heard in the green, green forest of her dream, a calligraphy made audible: "*When the people you ought to trust betray you, turn on the light in your heart. Nobody, nothing can keep you from it.*

"If the unanointed preacher, the jackleg politician, the careless teacher, the abusive parent, if any or all of these should try to turn you from the light, tell them No.

"Pull the shawl warm 'round your shoulder. Keep your hand on the crystal thread. Tend long the steady, flickering light.

"Shimmer."

Bright Shadow

1. Who are the central characters?
2. What is the advantage of reading Thomas's debut novel, *Marked by Fire,* first, before reading *Bright Shadow,* the second novel in Abyssinia Jackson's family saga? Do you think each of the novels stands alone?
3. Do the two novels' titles relate to each other?
4. Abyssinia falls in love for the first time in *Bright Shadow.* Do you think she is mature enough to understand her feelings?
5. Does maturity have anything to do with matters of the heart, like falling in love? Should it? Describe a situation in which you needed a tremendous amount of maturity to handle it.
6. How do Abyssinia's parents respond to her attraction to Carl Lee? What is the difference between Abby's father's reaction and her mother's reaction to the couple?
7. How does each parent act out his or her deep emotions in coming to grips with their daughter's first romance? How have your own parents reacted to relationships that you have been in?
8. What are examples of unhealthy couples' relationships in Abyssinia's community? Who are some of the healthy couples? What behavior makes these healthy or unhealthy?
9. What are some indications from the story that all may not

be as peaceful as it seems in Abyssinia's town. Describe a situation that you've been in in which you learned that what seemed perfection on the surface was not really good underneath.

10. In *Bright Shadow,* what's an "old maid"? What's a "young maid"? Are either of these expressions fair or unfair?

11. When asked why she planted weeds in her garden, what is Abby's reaction? What two losses in her life make her feel this way?

12. What explanation does Abyssinia give for why the weeds are returning?

Water Girl

1. Who are the central characters in *Water Girl*?

2. How would you describe Amber's parents? What are their positive character traits? Which of their traits do you think could be improved upon?

3. How would you describe Amber's character? In what ways is Amber adventurous? Describe ways in which you are adventurous.

4. Where does the story take place? Name at least three locations.

5. Who is Amber's best friend? What role does she serve in Amber's life?

6. What was the high point of the story for you? Why was that particular event a high point, and what is its significance to the novel?

7. Why do you think the book is called *Water Girl*? If you could give the book your own title, what would it be?

8. Would you call Amber's boyfriend a hero? Why or why not?

9. Describe Amber's passion for music. What are her other passions? What are your own passions, and how do you fulfill them?

10. How do the men in Amber's life—her brother, boyfriend, and so on—respond to her being "different" and to her tomboy ways?

11. When Amber hears stories about the mistreatment and persecution of people of other cultures—Latinos, Native Americans, Jews, African Americans, and Japanese Americans—she gets depressed. What issues in society do you feel are important, and which do you feel most sensitive about?

The Golden Pasture

1. What is the significance of Carl Lee's grandfather's riding into town to see his grandchild? Describe a situation in which your parent or grandparent returned to your life after being absent.

2. Why is the book called *The Golden Pasture*?

3. What are the physical descriptions of three of the main male characters in this novel? Describe their personality characteristics.

4. What are the names of some of the famous horses, recited by Gray Jefferson? Do the names match the horses' personalities and history? If so, how?

5. What are Carl Lee's and his friends' stances on crying? Why do you agree or disagree with their take on crying?
6. Compare and contrast Carl Lee's grandfather with his close friends' grandfathers.
7. How does Carl Lee discover the mystery horse? What name does he give the horse? Why is that name significant?
8. What significant event happens at the rodeo?
9. Would you call Carl Lee a hero? Why or why not? What heroes have you known in your own life?
10. How does passion come into play in *The Golden Pasture*?
11. Which episode or dramatic action was the most significant for you? Why?
12. What other novels that you have read or want to read feature African American boys as heroes?

Journey

1. Who are the central characters in *Journey*? Describe their personalities.
2. Under what circumstances does Meggie first discover her spider?
3. Describe Meggie's parents. What are their strengths and weaknesses as parents?
4. Which of Meggie's personality traits do you most admire? Which of your own do you most admire?
5. Describe the book's setting. Name at least three locations.

6. What is Meggie's dog's name? How did she come across the name that she called him, and what is its significance?
7. What was the high point of the story for you? Why does that part have so much significance for you?
8. How do each of Meggie's parents display their emotions in dealing with Meggie's independence?
9. Some people seem to be a lightning rod for problems. Do you think Meggie is one of them? Why or why not?
10. Why do you think the book is called *Journey*?
11. Would you call Meggie's boyfriend a hero? Why or why not?
12. In *Journey*, spiders are the "good guys." Who are the "bad guys" in the novel?
13. We humans live in the world with all kinds of creatures and critters. Describe other creatures—in addition to spiders—that are important, and discuss the role they play in the earth's ecology.

Fun Fact:

Joyce Carol Thomas used to be frightened of spiders! When she was a child, a family of poisonous black widows made a home under her bed. Although they never bit her, Joyce would fall asleep thinking about the spiders. She even dreamed about them.

Finally, Joyce decided to try not to be afraid of them—even to make friends with them. Her peace offering included the writing of *Journey*.